SKIN DEEP

THE DARKWORLD SKINWALKER SERIES

Skin Deep

Lost Soul

Last Chance

Blood Promise

Scorched Fury

Fate's Edge

Grave Debt

Oath Bound

THE DARKWORLD SOULTRACKER SERIES

Blood Magic

Demon Kin

Blood Curse

Demon Soul

Blood Moon

Demon Bones

Blood Born

THE DARKWORLD IRIN CHRONICLES SERIES

Retribution

Requiem

Resonance

Revelation

Adult Sci-Fi

HANDS ASSASSIN

Death Dealer

Death Mark

Death Strike

Hand's Assassins Series

∼

NEW ADULT CONTEMPORARY THRILLER W/A TONI VALLAN

Beautiful Collision

Beautiful Conviction

∼

PSYCHOLOGICAL HORROR W/A TONI VALLAN

Dark Shadows

Splinter

Skin Deep

A SkinWalker Novel #1

Copyright © 2013 by T.G. Ayer

All rights reserved.

This is a work of fiction. Names, characters, places or incidents are either the product of the author's imagination or are used fictitiously, and any resemblance to actual persons living or dead, business establishments, events or locales is entirely coincidental.

Cover art by Eduardo Priego

Editor: J.C. Hart

ISBN-13: 978-0-473-42925-6

SKIN DEEP

USA TODAY BESTSELLING AUTHOR

T.G. AYER

Dedication

For Dharshini- daughter & assistant.
Rumpelstiltskin once asked me for my first born, and in return he said
he'd make my dream come true. I said no thanks – my first born is my
dream come true.
Isn't he a fool?

CHAPTER 1

There was a razor-fine line between protector and vigilante, and right now I knew I was skating it blind.

Funny thing was, I didn't give a damn.

Tangled nerves sparked liquid fire within my veins. Muscles tightened, knees locked in a solid crouch. I slid the tiny vial into the chamber at the top of the arrow and readied the crossbow, taking care to keep my fingers clear of the poisoned tip.

The diminutive arrow was designed to sink into the creature's flesh, eliminating the possibility of it being removed. The longer the poison remained, the quicker the death.

With the weapon prepared, I lifted it into position, and settled in to wait and watch from my perch across the street from my target's destination. The rooftop view of Chicago's night sky was glorious. Faint strains of a string quartet wafted from the restaurant below, adding to the romance of the night. But romance was not the reason I crouched here, merging with the shadows, supporting the steel crossbow with strong, steady hands. While its weight was solid, it was also a comfort. So strange when its purpose was to end a life.

But my mark had not yet arrived.

I sat—a mere shadow, invisible in my dark turtleneck and black leather pants—on the rooftop of a four-storied apartment building across the street from *Adriano's*. A five-star restaurant that catered to the rich and the privileged few, the waitlist for a table for two was nothing less than two months.

Unless you knew whose palms to grease.

"Come on, you bastard. Don't make me wait any longer," I muttered beneath my breath.

Larson Keyes: Politician, adulterer, wife-beater. King of vices. But none of it mattered—Senator Keyes was already dead. Contained within the flesh-and-bone shell of the man was certainly *not* a man. Inside the polished exterior, something insidious and gut-wrenchingly evil now lived, had taken slow and deliberate control. Neither the senator, nor his family, would ever know he'd been killed by a Wraith; a possessor of bodies, devourer of souls.

I forced my jaws to unclench—my teeth hurt.

A sudden wind gusted around me, tugging at my hair, pulling slim strands free from the thick braid which hung to my waist. Loosened strands whipped around and stung my cheeks with tiny slaps.

The glittering night was subdued now. Even the chatter of traffic was a whisper on the air. Then, a powerful engine throbbed below, turning the corner and drawing closer. An old Bentley pulled up to the curb and poured its passengers onto the sidewalk. Two young women—rail thin to the point of skeletal— were draped over their distinguished host, doe-eyed and adoring. I restrained the bitter urge to vomit.

Silver hair, arrogant lines. My target had arrived.

"Game on."

The girls tittered, and the night air drew the sound to me, crisp and clear. If I'd accessed my panther hearing, I'd have heard the words he'd uttered to them. But I wasn't interested in anything he had to say.

Enjoy it while you can, you piece of scum. Tonight, I will send your sorry hide back to the Darkness where you belong.

Muscles bunched, tensed. I steadied the weapon, balancing it on my knee. Then, I inhaled slowly, took aim and fired a single silent shot.

Below me, the Wraith clutched his chest. His breath clattered in his throat, Adam's apple bouncing in tempo. His eyes bulged, face caught in a horrible grimace, pulled taut in a gross parody of shock and agony. Screams echoed around him as the large man crumpled to the unforgiving concrete.

The sight of Keyes' now-lifeless body spurred both horrified girls to run in terror. They did not see the dark wispy shadows spewing from his mouth, did not see those shadows writhe and curl and twist away from the body, smoky gray fingers reaching for the tiny rips in the Veil, seeking to escape to the questionable safety what lay beyond.

They should be grateful to be blessed with such blindness. I certainly would have been.

The body of the host now lay discarded, a dried husk of a man who'd been smiling and preening mere minutes before. Desiccated skin lay sunken on bones, papery thin and fluttering in the breeze.

Under the cover of darkness, I rose and stretched my cramped limbs. I would have plenty of time to contemplate the blood on my hands.

Impossible to avoid the body count. After all, I was a killer. A Wraith-Hunter.

But even though it's the Wraiths I track and sever from this World, it's the body of the Host I have to terminate. The same Host who dies soon after the Wraith takes up residence, smothered by an evil blackness which sucks the life from him until what's left is a living shell without a soul. The Host was a lifeless puppet, and it didn't matter. My heart still shattered a little, ached a little each time I lined my target up within the crosshairs of my scope—every time I watched a Host die by my hand.

And, after the deed, I was still a killer.

As the daughter of an Alpha SkinWalker—and an Alpha by birthright—killing wasn't an alien concept to me. The only problem was, I'd cast off that mantle of responsibility two years ago and fled from the family compound, hiding out with my Grandma, Ivy Odel. Grams had been happy to take me in and had even helped to get me into the local high school to finish my final year.

I'd run from a lifetime of loneliness, and I'd found something to hold onto when I'd moved to Chicago. But it really didn't have anything to do with being away from my dad or my Alpha responsibilities.

I'd discovered a power.

Away from family and responsibility, I'd stumbled on the ability to track these demonic creatures by the residue they left behind. And I'd felt useful for the first time. I was helping people —even if just indirectly helping those whose lives were affected by the wraiths who'd been slowly penetrating the Veil and entering the human world.

I couldn't lie that it wasn't satisfying; the ability to kill the wraiths and to help others at the same time—even if they were humans. A different power.

For a panther shifter, power wasn't an unusual thing. Power comes to a walker when the first shift comes on. With that transition from human to animal, a walker gains strength and an expansion of the five senses, but an alpha's powers and abilities are ten times more powerful.

Turning into a powerful panther should have been an attractive concept to a lonely teen, looking for validation, for attention. But I'd never wanted it. Perhaps because it had everything to do with who my father was, and nothing to do with me.

Perhaps it had everything to do with a girl who'd been abandoned by her mother.

So, I'd turned my back on it all.

And even now I avoided shifting as much as possible.

The problem was, my wraith-hunting brought on the blood lust. Spilling blood brought the lust on and it took everything in me to hold the shift back.

Moisture filmed my palms as the panther clawed for freedom. And sometimes, even my heart missed a beat or two. Slick palms and a dubious pulse were understandable as the blood lust began to take a hold of me.

Heat simmered in the whorls of my ears as the blood of the feline surged through my veins. A phenomenon for which Grandma Ivy had an interesting theory—hot ears meant somewhere, someone spoke your name.

Not in a good way either.

If Grams were right—something I did not doubt—and my ears were some sort of psychic thought-detector; then I'd bet my twisted Panther DNA it meant some mean-assed Wraith was groaning for my head on a bloody spike. A fair number of those Shades lost in the Ether would have me to thank for their current address. But, as yet, none had dropped by to voice their dissatisfaction.

I stuffed the small crossbow into my backpack and left the rooftop, turning my back on the sirens. As they sang in the distance, I slid down the fire escape, forgoing the use of the rungs. I dared not tempt Fate. It would be difficult to save anyone else from the black clutches of another Wraith if I were stuck in a prison cell. I didn't believe the humans would understand my actions, nor believe my claims. Even more importantly, I couldn't risk my revealing the existence of the supernatural world.

My body zinged with pride as I jogged away. Then I came crashing down from my temporary high.

I was probably the only one proud of me. Would my father

care? Only enough to admonish me. And maybe warn me not to ruin his precious reputation.

Would my mother care? Who knew? We hadn't seen or heard from her in twelve years, not since the day she'd walked out on us without so much as a fare thee well. She'd left behind a husband, a son and two daughters, but she'd left more than an abandoned family in her wake. She'd left pain, anger, desperation, and loneliness behind, and as far as I knew, she'd never looked back.

And I wasn't sure that I'd want her to.

Heading back to the Rehab Center, I sent a prayer of gratitude to the Lady Ailuros. Some knew her as Bastet, but to the panther SkinWalkers across the American States she was Ailuros, the guardian goddess. To the Alphas she signified the core power of the feline.

To me, Ailuros was the light in my darkness, the faith I held onto even when I'd cast off the unwanted mantle of Alpha—as much as I could anyway, considering it was more than a physical thing to just throw away.

Now, as a supernatural creature walking the streets alongside humans who were entirely unaware of our existence, the goddess gave me the strength to keep going.

It wasn't easy to lie to my friends and coworkers, but I lied every day. My job as a trainee drug counselor gave me access to a patient information network which acted as a grapevine for the abused. One of the ways to sniff out a Wraith.

Along with countless other addicts, Senator Keyes' daughter Katie had sought secret refuge from his beatings within the euphoria of drugs. Her young, innocent face had been etched with the strain of living with a father who was no longer the man she'd grown up with, but rather a demon from another plane.

And I'd only known it because Wraiths left a residue on their victims.

The strange power I possessed gave me the ability to see the residue a wraith leaves in its wake. A substance in their breath, in their touch, the residue clings to those the wraith comes into close contact with—and those they tortured and abused.

A substance only I could see.

Katie had worn the pale peach tendrils around her in a misty shroud. An almost coral sign akin to a neon arrow.

Wraith marks the spot.

And I wasn't about to complain. That very residue allowed me to track them, hunt them.

And kill them.

CHAPTER 2

The door stood open and my supervisor walked back and forth, already arranging the chairs in a cozy circle. Clancy grinned as I entered. "Hello, Miss Tardy," she teased. I stuck my tongue out at her and stashed my backpack behind the desk.

I always arrived at least thirty minutes early, something she teased me for often enough. Today, despite still being wired from the hunt last night, I was only fifteen minutes early, so technically, she was right and I was late.

I'd headed to the group therapy session in spite of the dull headache pounding my skull with the feverish tenacity of a jackhammer. Post-assassination stress headache. I blinked the thoughts away and focused.

While these sessions weren't compulsory for the clients, my attendance was mandatory as far as I was concerned. I'd never missed a session since I started working for the Sandhurst Center for Rehabilitation—also known as the Rehab Center.

"You okay?" Clancy's voice cut through my thoughts and I realized I still stood at the table, stock still.

I nodded. "I'm fine, just a headache." I squeezed my forehead, trying to massage the throbbing away. The pain had crept up on me, so unbearable now I couldn't swallow without feeling it pulse in my throat and in my skull.

Clancy tucked her long, dark hair behind her ear and walked over to me, her green eyes narrowing on my face. "Look, take off if you're not feeling up to it, okay? Go home and sleep it off."

I shook my head and regretted it immediately as a sudden throb gripped my head in an agonizing vice. Swallowing a groan, I said, "No, really, I'll manage."

"Alright. But you look like crap. What will our kids think?"

A giggle escaped my lips. "Yes, Ms. McBride. I'll put on a happy face for the kids," I answered, my voice still dry but filled with laughter.

Clancy grinned and rummaged through the desk, rearranging paperwork, her hair hiding her features. Our coloring—hair, eyes, even skin tone—was so similar many people assumed we were related. I took it as a compliment. Despite being Human, Clancy embodied everything I wanted in a friend and mentor. And she always had my back.

But she didn't know I wasn't Human. And I had no intention of finding out how she would react to my true identity. What would she think if she knew her bright young counselor was a Panther ShapeShifter? Humans weren't known for their acceptance of the unknown and I wanted our relationship to remain just the way it was.

A hum in the corridor announced the first arrivals, who usually waited for company before they entered. Clancy and I fiddled with paperwork until the group settled. Still officially in training, a qualified counselor often joined me for assessments. And each class proved an educational experience for me.

The stragglers trickled in and the group began to settle.

I hovered, tucking my hair in place, ensuring my collar hid the back of my neck. From hairline to lower spine, the skin of my back was imprinted with the tapered, irregular pattern of a Panther's pelt. Very few Walkers have such a Mark.

A blessing and a curse, it meant I was special—the same special I'd run from. I'd never asked to be an Alpha Panther, to be responsible for the lives of all the members of our clan. Maybe running had been the coward's way out, but it had been my only option. Chair legs scraped the floor and around me the hum of voices rose and fell. I forced my mind to focus on the gathered group, and my attention fell on one particular boy.

Todd Denfield, one of our regulars, sat back in his chair, almost melting into the metal backrest. A picture of enforced, bored non-attention. When Todd's rough voice broke the usual beginning-session silence, nobody in the room was more surprised than myself.

"How do you become gay?" Heads turned as the fourteen-year-old boy voiced the question, eyes downcast.

Silence smothered the group, palpable and thick. My jaw stuck, unsure how to respond. But even as Clancy and I shared a quick glance to decide who would respond, one of the other patients answered the question.

"There's nothin' wrong with bein' gay, Todd," Sam answered. He was one of the older, already-rehabilitated kids, who often returned to attend the open forum. He admitted it reminded him of what he had to lose, of how hard he'd worked to pick himself up from where he'd fallen. "Maybe tell us why you're askin'?"

Todd gave him an impatient glare and shook his head. Eye-watering bright fluorescent light glazed his dark hair, gelled and spiked to stand straight up in places, while curtaining his eyes in oily fronds. "So—how does it happen? I mean, how do you know you're...gay?"

"You just do, like knowin' you're straight." Sam looked around the room. He received a chorus of nods. It seemed the simplest answer, and the best one.

"And can you stop?" Todd asked. "Like today you're gay and tomorrow you're straight."

"There are people who are bisexual, which means they find both sexes attractive. But I don't think a person's sexual orientation can change overnight." Sam sat back, satisfied with his explanation.

Todd stared at the older boy, dark eyes thickly lined in black. He'd failed to hide the purple crescents hugging each dull orb, betraying nights of sleeplessness. Todd's upper lip curled. A thankful smile made slightly grotesque by two tiny silver piercings that clung to the soft flesh of his lower lip. As I watched him, the telltale signs beneath the pasty-pale goth foundation became clearer. Faint coral smudges stained the skin at his neck, almost hidden by a thick, studded-leather collar. His clothing looked unnatural, uncomfortable. A staged, gothic treatment, which I'd always taken as an outward indication of his inner emotional turmoil. I'd been presumptuous. So blind.

Good thing Clancy knew I felt a bit under the weather. At least now, she wouldn't realize I sat there almost paralyzed with shock.

How did you miss the signs, Odel? You're slipping big time.

They'd been right there in front of me all along and I'd missed them. The peach residue which clung around Todd's neck screamed of a Wraith's touch, something I saw every day— because it's my job to hunt the god-damned soul-sucking freaks.

I let out a tiny breath of relief. Todd wasn't the one possessed. Perhaps his father? But, the many traces of pale peach and coral located around Todd's neck and arms proved the Wraith definitely abused the boy. I may be too late to help him. My stomach twisted. This lack of observation and awareness could mean the death of an innocent boy.

Aching head temporarily forgotten, I contemplated my next move as the session disbanded and the kids trailed out of the room and down the hall.

I sighed as Clancy waved a quick goodbye, shaking a finger at me – a warning to go home and rest. I began stacking chairs to move them to the storeroom, still chock-full of guilt for being so blind to the presence of a Wraith around Todd. No matter how much I convinced myself the make-up Todd had slathered on hid the signs too well, spotting Wraiths was my job.

The vicious throb returned with a vengeance once silence descended on the room. I tried to ignore it while it ate further into my brain, further into my neck and shoulders. I sat heavily on my seat and rolled my head from side to side, hoping the movement might relax the muscles, while I pressed desperate fingers into lumps the size of peach pits pebbling the muscles in my neck.

A Wraith-hunt now was inconvenient to say the least. But, headache be damned. I had to make time for a bit of recon at Todd's house later in the day.

A boy's life hung in the balance.

CHAPTER 3

My head still throbbing, I dragged my body from my office, to make a stop at my friend Tara's shop. Tara was a MetalSinger, an Ethereal Fae with the ability to manipulate any solid substance with only the power of her mind and the blood that sang in her veins. Though Tara's gift lay in working metals, her real power was the strength of her heart.

When I'd arrived in Chicago to stay with Grandma Ivy, I'd needed a weapon for protection. Grams' friend Storm had generously provided Tara's name as a legitimate weapons forger and I'd had a crash course in direct contact with an Elemental Fae. I'd never trusted anyone easily but she was one of the most caring people I knew. Somehow it had been easy to trust her. Deep down I hoped I'd never regret it.

I set off, jogging the three blocks to Tara's shop, worried because I hadn't been able to get her on the phone. Though eager to see the modifications she'd made to my old bow, I was more interested in the ammo she'd been developing. Tara was a weapons manufacturer, but for me she often went above and beyond. She knew about my Hunting and she and her mother Gracie had been searching for just the right substance to fill the cartridges for my jazzed-up bow. Just the right substance to kill a Wraith on contact.

When I reached the shop, a closed sign hung in the window, and peeking in through the front window confirmed the place was draped in shadows. I had more luck at the rear entrance. A broken exhaust pipe propped the back door open. An iron security gate still shut me out though. Tara's vague, gray shape moved about inside the dingy back room.

I peered into the room. Ebony tendrils escaped a haphazard topknot and clung to Tara's neck and shoulders, slick with sweat. Her pale skin, like most Elementals, bore the swirled markings of the Elemental Fae Court she came from. The glamored patterns remained unseen by Humans unless they had the Sight.

Through the bars, I watched her smooth the curved blade of a scimitar with the tips of her fingers. The metal glowed red against her fingertips as they slid along the blade, shaving fine slivers off until the edge became so sharp it disappeared. Tara honed bladed weapons capable of slicing through bone like butter.

I swallowed back the bite of metal as the warmth from the room bathed my skin. Although Tara worked with metal, she never needed a furnace to heat the material to a red-hot, pliable substance. She did pretty well with just her fingers.

She ceased her work and laid the blade on the worktable. Rising, she dusted her hands on the seat of her pants. I hadn't dared to disturb while she worked, only rapping my knuckles against the door now as she stretched.

"Hey, look what the cat dragged in," Tara said, grinning at the pun. Feline jokes were a favorite of hers, and she managed to throw a different one at me every so often.

Corny, but cute.

She shut the gate behind me, leaving the door open for fresh air. Besides a fear of overheating the room, she possessed a second elemental trait—claustrophobia. Adaptation to the

Human way of life took longer than a few decades, but most elementals managed to a certain extent.

"Sorry, I called, but..."

"Yeah, I've been busy back here. A couple of orders keeping me frantic." She shrugged an apology and moved to the table where the scimitar blade sat. Even without a handle, it was still a vicious enough instrument. "What do you need?"

"Just running by to pick up the bow. Is it ready?"

"Oh, sure." Tara led me into the silent shop, where the odor of metal permeated the air and the dust motes danced in the dull afternoon light.

"Where's Gracie?" I asked.

"Mom was called back to Court. Something's going on and they needed her right away." Tara frowned for a moment then disappeared behind the counter. Something must be up in the Fae courts if Tara was worried. I hoped her mother was going to be okay. They both lived on the edges of the Court's rule, probably breaking a few laws with their weapons manufacturing, never mind their specific, made-to-order ammunitions.

Tara popped back up seconds later with an object wrapped in black felt. She laid the package on the counter and flipped the edges open to reveal my crossbow. I'd missed it. Small enough to carry around in my backpack, shiny black steel; it was as lethal as it looked.

"I've made a few special modifications for you." Tara reached into a drawer beneath the counter and handed me a small box. Inside sat a row of tiny vials.

Tara picked out a single tiny bottle, popped the chamber open on the bow and slid it into the slot. Then she readied the weapon. "This vial is packed tight with microscopic needles. Each needle is filled with a lethal poison. You have to take careful aim because the glass splits on impact and the needles enter the body in a fine spray. It's so fine it's undetectable. And untraceable." Tara smirked, very proud of her efforts.

"Thanks, this is just amazing. How do you always know what's perfect for me?" I shook my head as I asked the question, and as expected, she shrugged.

Minutes later, bow tucked discreetly in my backpack, I headed home.

I ENTERED my apartment the usual way, taking the steel stairs of the rattling old fire escape, two risers at a time. The fire escape's rusted bolting threatened to dislodge in too many places. At times it swayed, rebelling against my weight. Light on my feet, I was in no danger of plunging seven stories to the broken side-walk. I wouldn't be so bold as to assume the nine-lives theory applied to Walkers. And I wasn't itching to put it to the test, either.

I filed away another mental note to get the rusted bolts replaced. My guests used the other entrance to my home—an ancient cage-like contraption, which only worked because my Walker friend Anjelo worked wonders with mechanical what-nots. His smarts were busy impressing the teachers at Crawdon. The last I'd heard he was up for a scholarship or something. I snorted. Guess he'd better be super careful not to let it slip that he wasn't even Human. It would blast his scholarship to smithereens.

Only once had I used that abomination of an elevator. Despite my confidence in Anjelo's nimble fingers and equally agile brain, I became a total wuss when confronted by The Cage itself. Images of the rickety box plummeting to the basement had me fleeing for my trusted fire escape. Somehow, the fire-escape's tenuous hold on the outside wall didn't bother me, nor did any other equally obvious dangers my preferred entrance posed.

Grandma Ivy's apartment building sat a few blocks away from the Rehab Center in a part of the city that avoided being seen or heard. It straddled the last street of the residential blocks and the first streets of the mostly abandoned industrial quarter. The location was ideal—skirting the city and yet close enough for easy access to uptown, downtown and the abandoned sector.

Wind buffeted my body and tugged at my clothes with grim ferocity as I reached the topmost landing of the fire escape. A quick jimmy opened the window, which yawned into the living room. The top floor of the old building, loft-like in size and stature, provided the space and freedom I adored.

It was kind on Grandma's bank balance too, though I didn't ask too many questions about that. Before I left home, accounts and money were the last things on my mind. My father and brother dealt with mundane things like bills. My father's voice simmered in my ear now. Reminders of choices and decisions and living with the bed I made.

Independence had many prices. Not that I complained. I preferred my current bed, thanks. Although I had a part-time job, my work at the center paid well enough for my needs. What I earned, I happily spread evenly over clothing, my bow and the ammunition for my jobs. I was a Wraith-hunter, not a mercenary, and when one of my marks ate it, no money ever changed hands. The release of their victims was sufficient payment for me. Grandma, in her intermittent visits, took care of groceries and rent payments.

One day soon she'd have to tell me where in Ailuros' name it was she disappeared to so often. She never stayed gone for very long, maybe a couple weeks at a time, and she always came back satisfied and happy, if a little drained. She never poked her nose into my business, but made sure I attended college and kept my grades up. She knew my studies were important to me because she knew I loved my job at the center.

But despite her support, I never worked up the nerve to tell her about my Wraith-hunting. I was terrified she'd demand I stop because of the danger I put myself in. I'd been hunting for so long that danger no longer bothered me, but I knew my family would kick up a fuss about it. Good thing they never knew Wraith-hunting had been all about on-the-job-training and a few near-death experiences before I got the hang of it.

Still, sometimes I envied the Human kids at the local college. Such simple, painless lives. I made headway with many of my patients, but I could never take away the reasons they sought refuge in drugs. I saw so much agony and suffering that sometimes, just sometimes, I longed for release. And the power of the Hunt was such a release. A way to make a solid, tangible difference instead of talk, talk, talk.

But lately, something was really wrong. The frequency of Wraith possessions had increased. In the last month, I'd eliminated twice as many as the previous three months combined. Something made them bolder. Stronger. More violent. And the Veil between the Earth-World and the Wraith-world had seemed strange too. Flimsy, tattered in places. And there was no-one I could go to about it.

With one leg inside the loft, I paused astride the sill, cocked my Panther ears, and flared my nostrils. I listened. Scented the room for intruders. Somewhere, a trucker gunned his engine. It spluttered and spat before roaring into life.

All was safe and I swung the other leg into the room and forced the protesting window shut. Having lost its protection against the elements decades ago, the wooden frame stuck, now swollen from the rain. Still, I preferred it that way—harder for intruders to get in and out fast.

I tugged the band from my loosened braid and ran my fingers through the thick mess, rubbing the sore spots on my scalp. When I was younger, I found it hard to understand why my hair differed from the rest of my singularly blond family. Greer's hair was white-blonde to pure white, and Iain's was a warmer shade of my sister's pale. Guess my mother bequeathed only one child with her lustrous locks. For a long time, it had been just one more thing setting me apart from my family. Too late to avoid the chip from settling securely on my shoulder.

Cat, our cat, entwined herself between my feet, almost tripping me up. She purred her welcome, then stalked off to find a dust bunny to play with. Well, at least she'd cared enough to say hi. Grandma Ivy's precious pet was a bit of a diva, but she was the only company I had. A glance at Grandma's bedroom door confirmed it was ajar. A sure sign Grams was not home. I hadn't expected her this week, anyway. But it was okay with me. For now, with my head still pounding, I desperately needed a bed.

LATER THAT AFTERNOON, after a couple of hours of fitful dozing that miraculously relieved my headache, I sat staring off into space. My fingers filled more of the tiny cartridges with serum, while my mind remained on Todd and the Wraith I had to eliminate to save the boy. It never hurt to have extra ammo. And it never hurt to be prepared for the kill.

I kept myself busy.

Busy cursing myself.

Stupid.

At last, I had half a dozen extra vials filled, ready to be loaded into my bow's special housing. I packed and prepared to leave. Recon topped my to-do list. Since I'd had no knowledge of it until today, I had a bit of work to do. Work that needed to be done in spite of the danger it always posed to my identity. I had to risk it though.

As the only Wraith-Hunter around I owed it to Todd and to his undead father to do my job.

CHAPTER 4

I stood in the shadows of a huge elm on the corner of a nondescript street in a very suburban part of town. In the daylight, I would expect to see little girls skipping and little boys riding around on bright red trikes. But the night hid the niceness, making everything look the same, gray and dark and haunted. I watched from the time Todd came home until the Wraith returned as well.

Tonight was for observation. Wraiths were strongest at night. Weakest at dusk and dawn, not to say they became helpless during the day. I just preferred to fight them when they were less strong. Why make things harder for myself?

I relaxed and borrowed night sight from my feline self.

A sharper, more focused vision.

I'd poached my Panther's ears long before I arrived. And now I listened to the sounds the two occupants of the house made as they prepared for dinner. One, young, innocent and troubled. The other, ancient, evil and filled with glee.

It still amazed me how blind I'd been to the torment of Todd. I stared now at the front porch virtually glowing with peachy tendrils. I'd seen enough. They were settling down for the night.

Maybe the Wraith felt satisfied with his efforts of being a good father for the evening.

As I turned to leave, a sound within the house caught my feline ear. Something crashed. Could the Wraith have decided the charade had stretched on long enough? I crossed the road, ducking behind a bush of rhododendrons, their heavy scent no longer sweet. I crawled to the nearest window, staying low.

Inside, an angry, raised voice filtered through the curtained window. I peered through a slit in the drapes, where the two halves had failed to meet.

Mayhem greeted me.

A side table lay overturned, an old lamp shattered, the solid base crushed to dust. An armchair sat on its side. Then I saw the Wraith and his captive. It held Todd by the throat, suspended in midair by only the power of the undead. Todd's eyes bulged—pain, fear and shock warring. At his temples, blood vessels enlarged slowly as he grappled with the hand at his throat. He kicked as he struggled desperately for air.

Todd's arms flopped limply as he began to lose consciousness. It was now or never. I sprinted around the house, readying my bow. Made a mental check on the two vials already in the chamber as I ran. At the back door, I gripped the handle and paused when it opened smoothly. The Wraith feared no one and his arrogance allowed me to slip in for the kill.

I followed the sound down the hall to the front room where Todd was now a frightening shade of blue. He no longer gasped for breath, no longer kicked helplessly.

Almost no time left.

The Wraith, his back to me, still had no knowledge of my presence. In their true form, Wraiths have no substance, but yet possess strong Magyk. When contained within the body of a mortal Human, they have limited access to their powers, although they still remained powerful enough. I preferred my kills at a distance, usually eliminated them in sniper mode. I'd tried hand to hand combat a long time ago but the creatures were unpredictable and sometimes too strong. But this Wraith didn't afford me the luxury of distance.

And though the Wraith lacked super hearing power, he did possess an acceptable level of hearing. When I stepped into the room, he turned. His lack of attention to Todd changed nothing of the boy's circumstance. Todd remained midair, dying a slow and painful death.

Had I been wrong about the limitations of their power when in Human bodies? Had something changed? They'd increased in numbers, and increased in strength. Plus the Veil was more fragile than ever. What was going on?

The Wraith speared me with a venomous glare. I was so focused on the foul creature that I barely heard the sound of Todd's body as it landed on the ground in a crumpled heap.

In that brief moment, my arrogance betrayed me. He sneered, his eyes a smoky black. I lifted my bow and aimed at the creature's chest. It mattered where I hit him, because it was the mortal shell which had to be killed a second time. I'd thought I had enough time...

He covered the distance between us with lightning speed and hit me—a full body slam. I went down, still holding the bow across my chest, stunned and confused by this new and unusual show of speed. My weapon, about a foot in length, could double as a club if needed. Unfortunately, the Wraith's body crushed it against mine.

His foul breath enveloped me; coral wisps encircled my head. His thrall – with which he would've ensnared his human host before he'd taken possession – failed to work on me, but I gave him points for trying. All I wanted was him off me. Desperation and hysteria fueled my strength, and I shoved hard. I managed to move him enough to tilt the head of my arrow toward his head.

He smiled through crooked, yellow teeth. The smell of death rolled off his body in waves, and my stomach churned bitter bile.

Most people couldn't smell these vile creatures. My ability to sniff them out helped a great deal. Not so much when I was stuck nose to nose with one. I struggled in his putrid embrace, and he laughed again. He was so sure of himself. And while I stared into the black, swirling depths of his eyes, I fiddled for the trigger on the bow, my finger bent awkwardly against the soft flesh of his chest.

His fingers crept to my neck as he began to close the distance between his mouth and mine. My time was very limited. The Wraith's kiss—the worst possible death. My heart thundered as he inched closer. Once his mouth locked onto mine, he would suck the breath and life out of my body. Before long, he would absorb every bit of moisture from my flesh until I became a dried-out husk. The process was excruciatingly slow and agonizing. I'd rather dispense with French-kissing soul-sucking monsters. I had better things to do with my time.

At last, I felt the lever click and counted the milliseconds as the cylinder retracted and the spring coiled tight. In the next moment the barbed arrow exploded from the chamber and smashed into the wall behind the Wraith. A shower of tiny splinters spewed onto the floor.

Damn it. Slick. Real slick.

There went my only option. My weapon was crushed against my ribcage, pressed uselessly between our bodies, and I lay cheek to cheek with death, helpless.

No. Not if I can help it.

I still had my feline strength. I wriggled my hands upward from where they'd grasped the bow and its trigger. The black metal dug deeper into my ribs. Good. Pain proved I still lived. I snaked my hands around the Wraith's neck and squeezed. I tried to concentrate and pull some latent feline power from within me, but nothing feline came to my aid.

It was something stranger than all the anomalies of my life so far. My hands glowed as I squeezed the demon's neck. Glimmered the palest gold. The elegance of the color looked misplaced on the body of the Wraith. What other powers did these creatures possess that I was not aware of? My hands still glowed, growing warmer. Warm and bearable. Was it the Wraith emanating this golden glow or was it me?

The Wraith struggled within my choke hold, gasping. Bent on freeing himself, he let go with one hand and I could've tossed him off me and ran. But I stayed. Had to finish it.

I watched the swirling blackness as it began to fade from the creature's human eyes. The Wraith screamed and my skin crawled with the sound as it rippled across the fine hair on my body. I still held him in my golden death grip.

The Wraith exerted all his final energy in digging his thumb in my throat. The lights dimmed and as the Wraith died I slipped into a gray unconsciousness.

I wasn't sure how long I'd been out, but a rapid, semi-violent shaking brought me swiftly back. Todd, in his desperation to awaken me, entirely missed the fact he'd succeeded. He continued to shake my arm, saying my name over and over again, a desperate mantra. My turn to shake him. He stopped speaking and stared at me, the dark eyeliner smudged in streaks on his eyelids and cheeks, his hair mussed and no longer neatly spiked.

"Thought you were a goner for sure," he whispered, as if he were afraid someone bad would hear his words and seek him out.

"Are you okay?" My eyes raked his skinny frame, checking for obvious injuries. He could have undetectable internal injuries. "What did he do to you?"

"Tried to throttle me." As he spoke, bitterness flooded his eyes. "Bastard."

How to proceed? I'd never had to discuss the business of Wraiths with a victim before. Never had my fights with those soul-sucking leeches been witnessed before. My worried gaze flicked to the remains of the Wraith, but it seemed Todd, in spite of his youth, understood my dilemma.

"Don't stress. He wasn't my Dad. Not for a very long time, anyway."

"When did you realize?" Taken aback at his calm, I was curious.

"When Sam told me you didn't unmake the gayness inside you. That's when I knew something was way wrong with my dad. He'd been acting funny this last couple of months. Weird and mean and real nasty. Knocked me out a couple of times too."

I waited for him to continue. These were the most words the boy had strung together since we met.

"He...he became something else." Todd looked at the remains of the Wraith and shook his head. "*That* is not my father."

"So what do you figure he became?" I tread carefully.

"Dunno. Maybe he went a little crazy? Multiple personalities or something like that?" He didn't believe those words. Not for a minute. Mere psychological justifications for what he knew to be something far stranger. His face darkened. "To be honest it was more like he was possessed by something. Something evil. And strong."

He brushed his hair away from his face. I caught sight of a huge purple bruise on his forearm. Grabbing his arm in a light hold, I looked straight at him, eye to eye. "Did he do this to you?"

"Yeah. He hurt me all the time. Broke my hands and legs all the time." He stopped talking and sat there, watching me, mulling over something. His arms were streaked a violent purple with yellow highlights. He'd admitted to having had his limbs broken recently. But no physical signs indicated he was hurt apart from the shocking bruise.

"You heal?" My matter-of-fact acceptance of the ability to heal gave the poor fellow some confidence to own up.

He nodded and the look of relief flooding his eyes brought tears to my own. I understood what he felt. "What's wrong with me?"

I shook my head. "There's nothing wrong with you, Todd. You're just a special kid." I ruffled his hair and he didn't resist.

"But why am I this way?" I understood his need to know. At least I came from a family of Walkers. No matter how dysfunctional, I'd at least known what made me different from the start.

"I don't know." I kept an eye on the body. On the door. We had to get moving.

"You can see them, can't you?" Todd seemed to accept the possibility that something evil had possessed his father's body.

I struggled with a response to his question.

"It's a little more complicated than that. I can see their residue. They leave it on whatever they touch. I saw it on you."

Todd rose to his feet and approached the corpse that was once his father.

"What happens when they take you, like they took my dad?"

"They're a parasitic entity. They kill their host, slowly enough for them to fill the place left by the soul of the mortal. You father would've died a few days after being possessed by the Wraith. And it's why we can't detect them on their host. I can only track them through the people they hurt along the way."

Todd nodded in silent understanding. "This thing was walking around in my father's dead flesh. Nobody would ever have been able to give my dad the peace he deserved. Thank you." He looked at me, an earnest honesty on his face. "My father was a good man. Not a great man. But a good man—in his heart." The boy tapped his chest.

"Do you have somewhere to go? Somewhere safe?"

"I can stay here." He refused to meet my eyes, clearly not wanting me to see his need.

"It's better you don't. In case his friends come looking for him."

"Do they have like...social networks or something?" Todd scrunched up his forehead in distaste, obviously disliking the thought the soul-sucking killers who had taken his father from him would dare to be social creatures with friends and families like normal people.

"I don't really know. I've only ever seen one of them at a time. And I never stopped to chat about the sociology of Wraiths." I failed to educate him on the fact my association with Wraiths was wholly based on the method of dispatch. "I think it would be safer for you to be far away from this place for a while."

"Wraiths?" Todd let the word tumble over his tongue, testing it as he would the taste of a chocolate. "What are they?"

"They are the darker branch of the Ethereals." My response was automatic, as if it was expected he'd know what an Ethereal was. In a split second, I realized how vastly different our worlds were. But at this moment, those two worlds collided and now, however indirectly, I had the blood of his father on my hands. And I had to be the one to break it to him that the world he lived in was a second reality, and he'd just had about the worst introduction into this world.

I had to give the kid some credit, though, he was no mouse. The strength of the man he would someday be flashed through his eyes. "Ethereals?" His eyebrows rose, curiosity peaked.

"Creatures with the power to control the air and atmosphere. The Wraiths are Dark Ethereals. Beings who live in the blackness and the shadows, and feed off the evil energies they collect. They used to never need to come out into the open before."

"So what changed?" He stared at me with eyes as black as the Wraiths, only they sparkled with life and courage. At the moment, they swam with bitterness as he spoke. "What made them take my dad? He never did anything to anyone."

"Look, Todd, I can't answer that question right now without speculating. And the last thing I want to do is give you the wrong answer. You deserve more than a half-baked guess."

I rose, skirted the body and tiptoed to the window.

"Grab some things and let's get going. I have a place I can take you. You'll be safe there." I looked over my shoulder at the boy standing forlornly at the bottom of the stairs, one hand on the banister and gratitude on his face. The only person I knew who could help was Storm. He'd already taken a whole group of Walkers and Humans under his wing—a multi-species clan he called City Deep. I was pretty confident he'd know how to help Todd.

I shooed him away, tapping my watch to remind him to be quick. Turning back to the window, I opened the drapes a tad, keeping an eye out in case the Wraith had been expecting company.

Soon we made a hasty departure from the dark and lonely house on that dark and lonely street.

And my heart ached for Todd and his initiation into adulthood.

CHAPTER 5

With Todd safe at Storm's place, I headed back to the Rehab Center.

Blood had always stirred the Panther, who lived beneath my skin, inside the very flesh and bones of my body. My Wraith kills, though, had never affected me this way before. Perhaps it's because I got so close. Perhaps my Panther knew I'd killed with my bare hands.

And the fact that it was dark didn't make it any better.

Unlike the Wolf-Walkers, who remained at the complete and utter mercy of the full moon, feline Walkers were night-called; the darkness a tempting place to break free of the fetters of the human body.

Most of the time the burning need to Change was easily tamped. But when the call of darkness was combined with the call of blood, things became a little harder to control.

And now the Change was coming. Any minute now. The adrenaline of the kill pulled my Panther to the surface with a strength that shocked me to the core. Pushed for time, I moved into Walker speed and sped through the streets while white heat sluiced through my bones, the muscles of my arms, and the flesh of my back. My spine and thighs rippled, shifted. Changing.

Damn. Too fast.

I spared a rueful glance at my new leather pants. And ran faster.

Had to make it to the Center. Only a few blocks away. I ran, my speed super-human, my need super-charged, covering ground fast enough to make it to safety before my Panther took over.

I took the corner of the street behind the Center at breakneck speed, intending to head for the nearest of the gaping holes pock-marking the rusted fence.

The wind changed before I stepped off the curb. My ears perked and I skidded to a halt, panting slightly, my backpack thumping against my side. The scream of tires on blacktop echoed on the night air, shattering the silence as it grew ever louder.

Closer.

Followed in tandem by the whining wail of sirens. A battered sedan scorched down the street, suspended by only two wheels on the turn. The angry whip of charred rubber spiked the air. Horizontal again, the car jumped the curb and skidded sideways, avoiding a collision with the fence by mere inches.

I shrank into the shadows at my back, expelling a long, stale breath. My Panther—still reined-in within my body—bucked and jerked, craving release.

I let her surface.

A little.

For now, super-sight would be welcome. Adrenaline surged, different again from the calm fervor of my wraith hunts. I blinked. Heat nipped at my corneas as I released my Panther sight.

Sight, which sliced deep into the black nothing hugging the sidewalk, transformed my eyes into a solid Panther emerald. For the moment, plain old Kailin Odel was back to being Kailin of the Clan Panthera.

My cat sight adjusted, focused. The blackness surrounding the darkened vehicle changed depth and color, became lighter, clearer.

Someone shoved the rear door open, and I cringed as it creaked and complained. The occupants remained shrouded in the shadows of the vehicle's interior. Something large, long and heavy hit the ground with a dull thunk. Then the sedan revved as unseen sirens drew closer, louder. The vehicle spun around and skidded off the curb.

The battered car roared away, a police cruiser close on its tail with sirens screaming blue murder. It didn't take a genius to figure out the parcel had to be awfully incriminating for them to chuck it into the garden in such a flaming hurry.

My nostrils twitched at the stench of exhaust smoke, and my heart thumped as I waited to cross the street. I flicked a furtive glance at the dull red glow of taillights disappearing into the darkness. A breeze skimmed the sidewalk, ruffling my hair, and I hurried across the street as the sounds of sirens faded in the distance. I paused a few feet from the bundle, released my Panther's nose and sniffed. Whatever I'd expected to scent on the air, it wasn't the tang of copper drifting toward me—strong, rich and intoxicating.

Blood. Fresh blood. A luscious odor, laced with tendrils of the familiar.

I moved closer, my mind warring with my emotions. This was no bundle of rags, or some stolen junk those thugs had thrown away, but a living being. The blood surely meant the person now lying on the sidewalk needed medical attention.

I stood over the bundle, the odor of the blood so cloying, filling my nostrils until I felt the urge to gag. And in a moment of doubt and fear, I hesitated.

Now or never.

I took a deep breath and crouched beside the silent form. My hand quivered as I reached out and touched the scratchy, ragged fabric covering the shoulder of the silent figure. At first it resisted my tug, stiff against my touch, but one more gentle urging turned him toward me.

I gasped, my throat closing on the sound. My heel caught as I pulled away, and I staggered backward as hot horror burned through my veins. The face glistened, bloody and mangled. Raw muscles and ligaments lay exposed, bare. A low moan of horror echoed around me. Chills streaked up my spine when I realized the stricken sound had originated from my own throat. The familiar richness of him clouded my mind, clogging my throat and drugging my senses.

A Walker.

A feline from the scent of him. A Cougar to be specific.

My throat spasmed, silencing a shriek as he stared at me. His breath whispered—shallow, irregular, the sound ragged as he labored in his final moments. He gripped with desperation to the disappearing threads which held him to this mortal earth.

His face held my gaze, and somewhere behind ribs of ice my heart clenched, threatening to implode. My own face stared back at me, reflected from within eyes as blue as oceans. Eyes filled with excruciating pain and desperate fear. He didn't speak, just studied me for a few moments with those glorious eyes.

Recognition. Gratitude. Relief.

Then...release.

Life flickered and sputtered out of his beautiful eyes—eyes unable to close even after his soul departed his mortal body. Eyes stark and ghastly within a face flayed of every inch of skin.

Mere seconds had passed, although I would've sworn it had been hours. Screeching tires again interrupted my horror, and the sedan skidded beside me before I could do much more than scramble away from the body. The killers had managed to lose the cops, and now they'd returned to retrieve the body.

They hadn't bargained on having a witness.

The cold-cocking of guns set my body on fire.

It also did something worse. With mortal fear gripping me, my imminent Change refused to take second place anymore. My body churned the fear and my Panther grasped at the visceral power of the adrenaline in my veins.

I ran.

A gunshot echoed around the garden, the sound ping-ponging off the aging brick walls of the surrounding apartment buildings.

I gasped as a blast of searing pain slammed into me, as a bullet buried itself deep within my shoulder.

CHAPTER 6

I crashed through the lot, leaving countless well-loved plants and flowers smashed in my wake. The Rehab Center backed onto a communal garden, through which I now ran headlong, desperate to get to the safety of my office.

I flinched as a bullet whizzed by, so close to my ear I could smell the heat of the spinning metal, could feel the scorched air move against my skin as it missed its mark. A second slug plummeted into a bed of chives inches behind me. Dashing through a line of wilting delphiniums, I dove for the safety of the shadows. The back wall of the Center simmered in pitch darkness, sufficient cover as I stumbled inelegantly up the short flight of stairs to the rear entrance.

No time or courage to look back.

When I reached into my hip pocket for the keys, pain coursed through my shoulder. *Damn.* I curled my right hand around my abdomen, struggling a little before I managed to fish my keys out without dropping them, a miracle in itself considering my shaking fingers.

Another bullet buried itself into the wall next to me, spewing a cloud of fine dust onto the stairs. I ducked too late, and grimaced. An inch to the right and I would've been pleading my case to the good Lady Ailuros, hoping for her kindest mercy.

My hands trembled from the spiking agony in my shoulder. Thick night plastered the building, hiding me from the shooters. As I bent to jiggle the key into the rusty lock I felt blood warm my back, thick and slick.

I wasn't scared.

Of course not. I'd just witnessed the death of a Walker, seen the result of his horrible torture. I'd also just been shot in the back by a couple of morons who couldn't shoot straight.

My fingers shook so much the key wouldn't slide into the damned lock.

Nope, not scared at all.

Visions of meeting an undignified end, splattered across the back door of the Center, teased the edges of my mind. I was way too young to die like this, not to mention way too smart to have gotten into a situation like this in the first place. Sure, I hunted the ruthless wraiths, and killed them too. But what use were my poisoned arrows and fighting fists against the blaze of bullets?

I gasped as another murderous metal missile struck a foot from the door. No use counting rounds—two shooters, and no idea how much firepower or ammo they packed.

Just move.

I groaned in relief when the door swung open. Slipping inside, I pulled it shut behind me, waited until the lock clicked, then raced up the dark stairwell at breakneck speed. My boots echoed on the concrete steps, disorienting and slightly discon-certing. Down the hall I fled, pain and my Panther fighting for priority.

My jelly knees quivered, and I made it only as far as the end of the hallway. I bent over, holding onto the wall, waiting for my legs to behave, trying to catch my thunderous breath. The wall felt cool beneath my fingers, a stark reminder that my body burned, on fire with need. Agony spiked my wounds, fed my urge to change, fired my Panther's desire for release.

This wasn't the usual way my hunts ended. My conscience flicked me an admonition as my mind's eye drew an image of my dad, his scowl shadowed by his graying eyebrows. He wouldn't approve of my hunts any more than he approved of my leaving the colony. I'd passed from his guardianship to my grandmother's, still deemed a traitorous child in his eyes. He'd never spoken the words aloud, but the hardness in his eyes had been condemnation enough. No progeny of the Alpha should, or would, desert the sanctity of their Alpha family, especially not to live among the Humans.

But I'd kicked wraith-butt night after night, without the help of my judgmental father. I refused to allow him to affect my concentration, not when my life depended on my own reflexes.

I scanned the silent hall. My frantic gasps seemed loud enough to rouse the dead, but it wasn't the dead I feared. Clem, the super, would be just down the hall, and I'd prefer not to disturb the man. He was creepy enough in the *day*time. Besides, how would I explain my bullet wound to the cantankerous codger, or what I was doing here so late at night?

I flipped my wrist and checked my watch: just after eleven. A siren wailed in the distance. A car door thunked in response, an engine revved viciously, and tires screeched as the sedan sped away.

In spite of my grip on the wall, the world around me—hall, walls and all—spun drunkenly. Was I passing out from the pain, from lack of blood? Or was my Panther emerging while my body flailed about in agony, unable to fend her off?

It didn't matter.

I'd rested plenty, and had not much farther to go—only one flight of stairs. Take one riser at a time. And don't forget to breathe.

Each step up made my head lighter. At the landing, I hung a

left and shoved a key into a lock for the second time in a handful of minutes. The state of my hands and my heartbeat remained unchanged. So did the cold bite of the bullet wedged in my shoulder. Thank Ailuros it was steel and not silver. Though silver wouldn't kill me, the metal had the power to hamper a Walker's healing process.

Something to be said for small mercies, then.

I was strong, and hard. Had to be. Nobody would come charging to my rescue. My father?

Keep dreaming, Odel.

My brother, Iain, had submerged his head so deep in Clan work only my blood-drenched corpse would warrant his attention. Given my current condition, I could be seeing Iain soon enough. And Grandma Ivy? Well, she was off on some jaunt in the Sahara or some African desert region. Very mysterious stuff. She'd made me promise not to tell my father she was more of an absent guardian than he'd ever been. Seemed even his mother would rather avoid confrontation with him, so who was I to complain?

I crashed into the office and shut the door, sending a prayer to Ailuros to hold Clem in slumber a little longer. I leaned against the clouded glass window, taking a few deep breaths before maneuvering the gauntlet of chairs set up for the next morning's group session.

I stumbled to the closet a few feet to the right of the desk. These last few minutes had felt like days of agony and fear. My breath still came in hysterical hiccups. Where had the cool, calm wraith hunter gone?

Things changed when hunter became prey.

My fingers closed over the knob of the closet door as another wave of dizziness hit. This time it laced my throat with bitter bile. Hidden in the closet, in a hidey-hole behind a wall of shelves filled with detergents and stationery, were my weapons and ammunition, spare clothing, first aid stuff, anything I may need after my hunts. I'd constructed it and hidden it so well. Thankfully neither Clancy nor even the cleaners had noticed it.

The shelves loomed around me, as I pushed my way into the secret space behind them and collapsed on the floor, nearly comatose with pain. Even sitting down with my back to the wall, the world still tilted and turned. I swallowed hard. It felt as if I'd swallowed my tongue.

Just one more thing I had to do before I gave in to uncon-scious bliss.

I felt around in the bottom of my backpack for my mobile phone, not daring to remove my head from against the wall. Clutching the phone, I whispered Anjelo's name into the device. The darned thing promptly advised me to speak more clearly, its tone annoyingly authoritative, seeming to laugh at me.

Damned machine.

Clearing my throat, I spoke his name again, this time restraining the urge to shout at the piece-of-crap phone.

Dial tone. Thank Ailuros.

"Kailin? What time is it?" Anjelo grumbled, his voice thick with sleep, grumpy and perplexed. He loved sleep, even more than his widely known love affair with Italian pasta. Nothing the school cafeteria supplied would ever tempt his taste buds. Anjelo had gourmet taste.

All he would've heard was my grunt of pain as I slid further to the floor, the phone suddenly too heavy to hold to my ear.

"Kailin, you okay?" His voice gurgled as if I were underwater —hollow, strange.

I took a deep breath and gripped the phone, pulling on every last dreg of energy, and said, "Sure. Shot. Bleeding. But okay."

My voice cracked on each syllable, and I barely heard his urgent request for my location. I scowled at the phone, again so heavy it began to pull my hand to the floor, inch by inch.

Why was he shouting at me? I could hear him perfectly.

I spoke with a false calm. "I'm at the Center." Then I let the phone fall, unable to bear its incredible weight.

Sounds filtered to me through the phone. Scrambling. The low thudding of someone bumping into things in the dark. Muffled oaths, and then a slamming door.

Good. Anjelo's coming.

Anjelo Alvarez was my closest Walker friend. When it came to my Wraith-hunting secret, he'd been determined to stay out of it —typical Walker, raised on the old diet of prejudice against Humans. He'd turned sixteen a few months ago, and even though Walkers lived longer lives and aged slower than Humans, I refused to endanger him. Besides, he was no Alpha, didn't have the super-strength that came naturally for me. So I was happy to keep him as far away from the Wraith's as possible.

But calling Anjelo wasn't going to endanger him in any way. At least I hoped not. And I had nobody else to call. I sighed and the world spun.

Anjelo was coming. I just had to hold on.

The bullet deep within the muscle of my back moved slowly, one hairs-breadth at a time. Crushed bone within my shoulder began to knit together. Tiny shattered bone fragments disintegrated, absorbing back into my shoulder blade.

All Walkers could regenerate when injured. But Alphas, with their genetic advantage, were better at it. Those genes were awful nice despite their mutation. Now I hoped my mutated genes would make themselves useful and heal the wound, which burned through my shoulder with all the fury of a newborn volcano.

A half-moan, half-sob spilled from my lips as I leaned heavily against the cool comfort of the closet wall, my shoulder healing and expelling the bullet in a slow and excruciating process.

Darkness took over as I bled profusely onto my beautiful new leather pants.

CHAPTER 7

$\mathcal{A}$ voice called my name, the sound hollow and tinny, as if the speaker yelled at me from the other end of a dank and darkened tunnel.

I summoned the energy to crack open my eyes.

Twin images blurred then merged slowly to form Anjelo's face hovering inches above mine. Concern contorted his brow, spoiling the softness of his gentle baby face. His furiously gelled blond spikes gave me comfort.

Thank Ailuros he'd come. I was as grateful as a girl could be, what with being shot and losing so much blood and all. Anjelo's face blurred again, then cleared up. My relief that he'd come was somewhat tempered by the knowledge that Lily, Anjelo's over-possessive girlfriend, would have a thing or two to say about him helping me in such a nefarious situation. Maybe, just maybe, Lily wouldn't need to know about it.

I sighed, glancing at Anjelo. The stark worry on his face amplified my own fear before my mind raced off on another tangent. Odd time to register it, but I found his tweed peak cap, now scrunched between his fingers, a total contrast to his character—far too Mr. Watson. I would've said it aloud, given the chance.

I squinted at him as his mouth moved. Sounds blended into an unintelligible bleating, as he stood there shaking a finger at me. Imagine that: an I-told-you-so while I sat on the floor, blood pouring from my wound, in the throes of icy agony. Had I known I'd get a telling-off, I may have called someone else to help. Or preferred to die in peace.

A sobering thought; I had nobody besides an eager Skin-Walker teen to help me put my pieces back together when I fell apart. Still, the images came, and my body grew colder for them.

"What the hell were you thinking?" Anjelo's voice broke through my morbid self-pity. His eyes darted over my body, searching for the wound. He crouched beside me and grabbed my arm, not as gently as one should handle a newly shot person.

A sharp hiss escaped my thinned lips, both shoulder and honor suffering equal levels of agony. I bent over, away from the wall, so he could better gauge the damage.

He leaned forward. "How deep?" Funny how I gathered from the wary set of his shoulders that he wasn't offering to fish out the bullet. Wuss.

"To the bone," I replied.

"Has it started?"

He meant the healing. I nodded, feeling my head swim.

If the bullet had lodged too deep, any healing would be halted until we removed the offending metal. Thank Ailuros, he didn't need to perform that type of extraction tonight. He wouldn't have, anyway, given what a sissy he was. I grunted.

"What have you gotten yourself into this time?"

"Wasn't my fault." Hard to bristle with indignation while I lay sprawled and bleeding at the feet of my scolder. I'd be wasting my breath. We'd argue again later, as I was way too tired to make the effort now.

"When is it ever? Always said one day you'll get yourself hurt.

And wasn't I right?" He waved his hands at both my torn body and shredded clothes, sighing as if *he* were the one shot and bleeding out pints.

Oh, the drama.

Somewhere deep inside me, a warmth grew as I faced his care and concern for my well-being. He hated my Wraith-hunting. Perhaps it was my freakish ability to track the creatures that put him on edge, or the fact he was ill equipped to help me in any way. He was the foreseer of my doom—or damage, in this case.

Anjelo shook his head. "You might as well tell me what happened."

Had I just heard resignation in his voice? And, he placed his hands on his hips for Ailuros' sake.

"Thanks." I grunted. "Um, there's a body in the garden. We need to get it out of here."

"What? You killed someone and left the body where any idiot could find it? Sloppy, Kailin, real sloppy." Good thing space in the closet was minimal or he'd be pacing.

I let him have his say. It required far too much energy to put him in his place. We usually avoided discussing my Wraith-hunting activities. Anjelo also disapproved of the risks I took to save "mere" Humans. Typical Walker macho bullshit.

Besides, the dead body had nothing to do with my wraith-hunting. When he ceased his nagging, I continued, "Someone dumped a body in the garden as I was returning from...well, as I was coming here. They saw me, took a few shots, hit me in the shoulder. I made it into the building just in time. I think the sirens scared them away."

He rounded the shelf and looked out the tiny window, which overlooked the back of the building. The window had a good view of the garden from where he stood, but the question was whether he could see the body at all.

"We have to get the body out of there," I said, trying to keep from going hysterical. "Those sirens may not mean the police are on their way here. But we can't take any chances."

"Why would we need to get the body?" He looked back at me for a brief moment, his eyes an equal blend of suspicion and accusation.

"He's a Walker," I said a little too loudly, my hackles rising in defense. I couldn't help it. I hated ill-based accusations of any kind. Anjelo's eyes grew large—I had his attention now. "We can't have the coroner examining the body of a Walker. Too many reasons why it would be a very, *very* bad idea."

He turned back to the window without a response. Anjelo with nothing to say was akin to a waterfall without the water. He kept his eyes on the garden below, and his body suddenly stiffened.

The scream of an ambulance provided cold confirmation. We'd lost our chance to get the body away from prying eyes. He'd taken too long to get to me. And I'd passed out when I should've been doing something better with my time.

Anjelo returned to me when the scene outside no longer held any interest. He looked at the puddle, cooled and congealed, behind me. "You've lost a lot of blood." His face darkened with fear, but of the self-preserving kind which told me exactly what he was thinking. What would Iain say when he found out? But, then again, how would he find out? I lived my own life; I hoped he'd remember that.

"Really? What makes you say that?" I couldn't help it. I'd lost my blood, not my sense of humor.

"Stop being a smart-mouth. How do you feel?" He sat beside me and tipped me forward with gentle, quivering hands. This time he ripped the shirt off my back to get a better look. "At least it's stopped bleeding."

"And the bullet?" I'd tracked it as it made its way through my flesh, and could now feel the pressure of its presence somewhere near the epidermal layer. It stung like the blazes. Being a Skin-

Walker had its advantages, but this kind of pain I could so do without. I didn't complain though, glad to be alive and still thankful for Ailuros' mercy.

"Almost to the surface. Should be out soon." He pressed the area around the bullet, still gentle and cautious. "I can see the point."

"Can you get it out?" I looked at him over my shoulder.

His face paled, as if he'd been drained of the good red stuff himself.

"The wound will close up faster if you get it out now. Then I'd be able to move around, at least." Watching him fight his inner war should've been more amusing. "Come on. What good are you as a Walker if you can't deal with a tiny bit of blood?"

"Blood I can handle. Digging bullets out of girls...not so much." He rubbed his forehead.

"You'll have to learn sometime. Better get on with it."

"How? With what?" He raised his eyebrows and shoulders in unison—stalling tactics.

With my foot, I nudged a small black case, the size of a cigar box, toward him. He bent and opened it. The sound he uttered was far too similar to choking. Why did my only savior have to be such a wimp?

"Come on then."

"Where did you get...? Never mind. Forget I asked." He shrugged, resigned to his lot. "Which one?" He eyed the row of gleaming, surgical steel operating tools in the box.

"The one that looks like a tweezer. Slide it around the bullet. It has grooves, so as long as you keep a good grip, it should come out easily."

"Will it hurt?"

"Not really. Nothing I can't handle. Everything hurts so it won't be much different." I wasn't about to tell him it would damn near kill me.

"Okay, here goes." He held the instrument before him as if it were a spitting viper, shooting little tremors through his fingers, but he steadied his hand and I leaned over.

"It's going to gush. You'll need this." I ripped the rest of my shirt off, rolled it up and handed it to him. It left me in only a sports bra, but the time for modesty had long since fled.

He touched the tip of the tweezer to the edge of the wound, and I dug my fingers into my arms. The movement of the cool metal against my flesh sent waves of blazing agony through my shoulder. I'd have to hold on until it was over. I breathed through the next shift of those iron teeth and then relaxed, feeling nothing while he pressed the teeth around the edge of the bullet.

"Right. Here goes. You ready?"

I dared not speak, managing a quick nod.

He tugged at the bullet and it shot out, slipping from his grip. Blood surged like water from a burst dam. White-hot pain exploded in my arm, worse than when Anjelo had first introduced the tweezer into the wound. My throat clenched and I dry-heaved, almost passing out in hot misery.

He held the shirt against the wound. Thankfully, he couldn't see my reaction, or his hands wouldn't have been so steady and sure.

"Don't press it. You need to let all the blood leak out."

"I attended all those same mandatory Walker Physiology and First Aid classes you did. I do remember the lessons." His tone swam with annoyance, and I wasn't surprised when he added a tiny bit of pressure to the wound.

"Anjelo."

At the hiss of his name, he grunted and lessened the pressure, then lightly swabbed until the blood subsided from a flow to a trickle, then to a slight ooze. I tamped down my frustration.

"Thought you said it wouldn't hurt so much." I heard the smile in his voice.

"I lied."

He snorted.

I panted through each wave of pain. "Like I was gonna tell you it would be worse than being shot in the first place. You'd have run back home before I finished the sentence."

He remained silent, but failed to smother an angry breath. He swabbed the gory hole in my back and bandaged it over. All done, he bent to pick up the bullet, which had rolled along the floor and come to rest near my knee. He twirled it between his fingers, now unfazed by the blood and bits of dark red goop still stuck to its warped body.

"We'll have to find somewhere to hide it," he said. He was right. It was evidence.

"I know the best place for it." I smiled. I couldn't wait to get home and flush this particular piece of evidence down the toilet.

CHAPTER 8

*L*ogan Westin leaned against a filing cabinet. It was safer. He knew, if he sat in that comfy-looking armchair, he'd fall asleep as soon as the police chief started talking. Not a good impression to make, so he preferred standing.

Murdoch was headed in—Logan could see through the office glass the chief's well-endowed stomach leading the way as he maneuvered his massive frame through the warren of desks. Chief Murdoch was a force to be reckoned with. He also happened to work for Omega, feeding information to the paranormal information network, which policed the non-Human community.

The door opened and Murdoch's physical presence engulfed the glassed-in office. "Westin, you look haggard. Understand you're straight off a mission?"

Logan nodded, his glance skittering to his new supervising partner Jess, who sat silently in the twin to the armchair Logan refused to enjoy. Sleep deprivation only seemed to affect mere mortals like Logan and his team—never the enigmatic Jess. Plus, she minded her own business, guided him through most of his cases, and left him alone most of the time. That's what he liked about his new partner.

Logan blinked as Murdoch drew him out of his silent introspection.

"Sorry to do this, Westin, but we needed the *special*, special ops on this one." He didn't look the least bit sorry as he sat heavily in his chair, although worry weaved his dense eyebrows together into a fat, hairy caterpillar.

"What do you have?" The webs of fatigue, which had enveloped him minutes ago, retreated, ripped apart by Logan's innate curiosity. Curiosity and determination. He was Omega's youngest agent, a fire-mage who'd gotten there only because he'd been so busy trying to make up for his past, he'd forgotten to have a life, to enjoy his youth before it passed him by.

He'd turned nineteen three months ago, and spent it like any other day—working. His birthday seemed like a long time ago, but back then, he had no supervising officer to reprimand him for insufficient R & R. That was before Jess walked into Omega—quiet, officious, seemingly intent on sorting Logan's act out.

"A John Doe—found in downtown Chicago." Murdoch tossed a few stills to Logan. "These were just uploaded from the scene. The techs are still there. What do you make of it?"

Logan scanned the pictures and passed them to Jess. She spent all of five seconds looking through the half-dozen images before dropping them on Murdoch's desk.

Logan didn't need to look at the images again. They were etched into his memory for a lifetime of nightmares. The victim's body lay bare, every inch of skin flayed, including the eyelids.

"Notice anything strange?" Murdoch's voice was low, emitting an undercurrent of concern.

Logan clamped his jaws on the word "strange." The last few years had been nothing but strange. Things needed to be pretty whacked to appear strange to him, as numbed as he was to the weird and unexplainable.

"The claws, you mean?" He reached out and touched the shots of the corpse's unusual hands—human fingers ending in garish animal claws.

Feline claws.

"What do you make of it?" Murdoch watched Logan, intent on gauging his reaction.

Murdoch was all too familiar with the paranormal. He wasn't a mage, but his wife, Chloe, who possessed a special ability to calm the traumatized and unstable, definitely qualified as paranormal—a regular walking sedative. But she had chosen to work outside Omega's investigative squad as a social worker of sorts, helping families deal with raising kids born with or manifesting paranormal abilities.

Logan turned to Jess, having almost forgotten about her. She had a weird way of disappearing, despite her physical presence.

"SkinWalker," she said, her voice soft and musical, her eyes too calm for such a revelation. "Cougar Walker to be specific."

"Thought they were a darned reclusive bunch?" Murdoch grumbled, his eyebrows waggling. "What would they be doing smack bang in the middle of my neighborhood?" He frowned and leaned forward to grab the stills, his stomach smashing into the table. He studied them for a few seconds, then met Logan's eyes, his face a few shades darker with worry. "Answers, Westin. Get me some answers."

Logan nodded, the movement sharp and brisk. He opened the door and waited while Jess moved past, listening as Murdoch called for a squad car to take Logan and Jess to the scene. They remained silent, deep in their own thoughts, each probably thinking about human fingers and feline claws.

They passed through the police station, exiting the building swiftly and silently. A cruiser waited outside, its flashing lights making the back of Logan's eyes ache.

DARK SHADOWS clung to the streets when Logan and Jess arrived at the scene. Logan glanced at the sky as he left the car, grateful for the veil of darkness. The light of day would only throw this whole mess into a starker, more glaring reality. He paused at the yellow tape cordoning off the area, and studied the surrounding scene.

Buildings stood on two sides, hemming in the planted garden and wire-mesh fencing barely doing its job. Too many police officers milled around; perhaps movement gave them purpose. Murder was common enough on these rough streets, but this particular victim would've touched a nerve for many of the city's finest. This kind of debasement delved into unfamiliar territory.

Logan understood their discomfort better than they would ever know.

Ruby lights spun and flashed coarse red hues from the roof of a nearby ambulance, a gurney waiting before the vehicle's open doors, like an offering to the maw of death. Logan and Jess ducked beneath the cordon and made their way toward the gurney.

A strange silence hung over the scene, broken by hushed murmurs. Murdoch's men were familiar enough with Omega, but it didn't mean they welcomed Logan or his fellow officers with open arms.

Omega's officers outranked the city's lawmen, notably a sore point, but Logan Westin's youth had started more tongues wagging and set more tempers aflame than anything else. Hard-working, long-serving officers simply didn't respect rookie officers who outranked them.

Logan registered the glares and curious stares, but merely nodded and greeted those whose eyes met his, hostile or not. Beside him, Jess appeared oblivious to the flagrant hostility.

They reached the gurney seconds after the paramedic enclosed the body in thick, black plastic. Logan glanced inside the bright interior of the ambulance. All those life-saving vials, machines and tubes were useless for tonight's passenger.

Even with Jess there, Logan hesitated. Being a mage didn't mean he automatically had an iron gut. He took a breath and unzipped the body bag. Black plastic crackled and the metal zipper grated aloud, slowly revealing the face of the victim.

As he stared, the ghastly face stirred another dark memory free from his mind. His first mission, in a warren of hidden caves in Jerusalem, proved similarly macabre.... Thirteen dead women had been strung from the roof of the spooky cave. The sliced-open corpses, no segment of their skin spared by the blade, had spilled their precious blood into thirteen golden bowls beneath them. The half-congealed blood had still been warm when Logan arrived at the horrific scene. Those earth-mages had been bled to death for their powerful essence.

Yet as gruesome as those murders had been, the body of this cougar Walker, flayed of its skin, seemed even worse. Garish somehow. Must be the way the lack of skin turned a person into a slab of meat.

"Go on, we need to inspect the corpse," Jess urged.

Logan slid the zipper down further, exposing most of the upper body and the hands.

The fingers.

He wanted to examine them firsthand. Logan's chest constricted and Jess tensed beside him, as neither of them breathed. All ten digits ended in curved black claws etched with blood. And seeing them in the flesh, so to speak, was all the more evocative. His first case with a Walker and it had to be a dead one.

CHAPTER 9

*P*olice officers had cordoned off the area but made way for Logan and Jess to reach the scene. The soil was a mess. A tomato plant lay squashed, its ripe red fruit pulverized.

The aroma of mint flooded Logan's nostrils—trampled plants broadcasting their disapproval. Footprints littered the garden, a tangle of tracks almost impossible to identify. He hunkered down over the shallow depression left by the body. He checked the soil, the plants, and the broken fence, which ran along the plot. Anywhere that could provide a clue. Nearby, a crime scene tech dusted the curbside, and another photographed a hole in the fence. Logan suspected they needn't bother. Any prints left out there, or on the holes in the fence, would be distorted by a thousand others.

He called one of them over, a young woman, all blonde hair and serious poker face, and instructed her to vacuum the site. He'd have Omega's lab review the contents of the vacuum bags later. Something was sure to show up. In the meantime, they'd need a DeathTalker for the corpse.

Jess walked in the wake of the destruction left by the footprints, her own blonde head down, eyes probing. Her hair, tied low on her head, flipped over her shoulder as she bent to inspect the soil. Logan watched her silently. There were so many things he didn't know about his new supervising officer. He really disliked this business of not being in the know, but he was still the kid in the outfit. Although the team gave him the utmost respect, he still happened to be Omega's youngest operative. Ever.

He returned his attention to the forensic tech's progress. She'd gridded, marked, and photographed the area, then attached a sterile plastic bag to the specialized vacuum and sucked up the dust and debris for each quadrant, then labeled the bags for Omega testing.

Logan approached the officer in charge, who threw him a glance, part suspicion and part relief.

"So what's the situation here, Officer Romano?" Logan snagged a glance at the older man's badge, also noting olive skin, which appeared paler than seemed possible, even in the strong floodlights.

Romano kept his eyes on his notes the whole time he spoke and stiffened his fingers to hide the intermittent tremors. "Young male, about six foot. Cause of death looks to be trauma from the...er...from being skinned. No blood on the sidewalk, not much on the blanket he was wrapped in. No other visible wounds." He clapped his book shut and seemed relieved when he could stop talking.

Logan scowled, staring off into the distance. The flaying would've taken place somewhere else, after which the body was dumped here. A dumb place to dump a body in this condition, he thought. "Time of death?" he asked.

"Coroner called it...time of death 11pm," Romano said.

Logan nodded and made a mental note to have Omega double check the TOD. Couldn't hurt to be sure.

"Witnesses?"

"No." He shook his head sadly. "Just a bunch of residents who heard the shots."

"How many?" Logan asked absently as he stared out across the lot.

Romano frowned at Logan, perplexed.

"Shots? How many shots?" He looked back at Romano, curbing the impatience in his voice.

"Er...seven. Ten, maybe. From what those guys told us, nobody can agree." He scanned the mixed crowd of residents straining at the police barriers and wondered how reliable they were.

"And shells?"

"Four so far." Romano looked over at a tech scanning the area with a material detector, the screen revealing what lay within and below the soil of the now-mutilated garden.

"Have you checked for patterns?" Logan asked, already knowing the answer. The Chicago PD was efficient. Murdoch made sure of that.

"Yeah." Romano hailed another tech walking by, borrowed a tablet and tapped at it, his forehead twisting in concentration. He placed the screen in Logan's hand. A map of the area glowed on the face. Little pinpricks of red lights flashed next to the outline of the body. Logan and Jess studied the screen. She pointed at the pattern, which placed the first shell a few feet away from the body and each one farther away, moving across the left quadrant of the garden.

They both looked up simultaneously and stared straight ahead at the three-story building next to the garden plot.

"What's that?" asked Logan.

"Downtown drug rehab," Romano said, tucking his thumbs into his belt.

"Have you inspected the alleyway yet?" Logan kept his eyes on the squat building. He saw the outline of a door at the top of a short flight of stairs. If there was a light bulb above the door, it wasn't working now.

"Tell the techs to look there." He pointed at the door, as Jess hurried toward them, then added, "Check the walls for bullet holes."

"What are you thinking?" Jess asked.

"Don't you already know?" he quipped.

"It is not as if I hear your thoughts clearly, as if what you are thinking comes to me in neat little sentences. I receive images and feelings and words. And sometimes they aren't easy to unscramble. I can still sense your emotions, though, even when your walls are up." She spoke the words so matter-of-factly, as if she knew he'd believe her just because she said so. She looked at him with clear, hazel eyes set in a porcelain face. She was a beautiful woman any guy would love to work with, but he wasn't any guy. Besides, he wasn't into older women. Although Jess looked about Logan's age, he got the feeling she knew a lot more than she could possibly have learned in such a short life.

"You are having one of those 'feelings' again?" She tilted her head at the question.

"Yeah, someone took shots from over there. They ran in the direction of that door, and I wouldn't be at all surprised if they got inside. See that light?" He pointed out the light blazing from the second floor. "That same someone may be inside the building. Could be the shooter, could be a witness."

Romano sent his techs to search the alley, and Logan turned his attention to the scene. Romano hadn't mentioned the claws yet. Seemed he was keeping that particular piece of information under wraps. Or maybe he just didn't want to know. The police would probably concoct some run-of-the-mill, gang-related cover-up to keep further questions at bay. Good thing Logan had never been the kind of person to blindly accept what someone else told him, even those in authority.

"I will call HQ. We need a DeathTalker." She made the call

while Logan spoke to the police officers, then combed the scene a second time in case he'd missed anything. Logan liked to be thorough.

He listened as Jess requested a DeathTalker. They gave him the heebie-jeebies, with their pale corpse-like faces and glazed eyes. Those white eyes, the irises so milky they were barely discernible from the whites of the eyes themselves. Logan had no idea if DeathTalkers were born with those scary eyes or if they were the result of the trauma experienced in each session. He'd never dared to ask. He respected them, of course. On more than one occasion, he'd seen the toll communication with a spirit took on a DeathTalker.

He'd felt sorry for them, bound to those almost malevolent rituals by the powers they'd been born with. Logan shivered. He'd be witness to another Death-talk soon enough.

"They will send her soon," Jess said, as she walked up to him.

"Soon" for the Walkers meant any second. The *Human* soon meant any time in the next few hours. Logan still appreciated those differences, being one of many mages who'd come into their powers in their early teens, old enough to remember life as a normal human.

"She will know where to find him," she stated to put Logan at ease, as if Jess knew he'd wondered how the DeathTalker would appear at this particular scene without creating mayhem herself. "She will go directly to him."

Logan glanced at the ambulance, where a DeathTalker would soon materialize right beside the corpse, drawn to it by her affinity for death.

Seconds ticked by.

Jess touched his shoulder and walked toward the ambulance. One door stood open. The other hid the gurney and its grisly passenger. The lights had dimmed somewhat. Shadows clung to the corners and provided enough cover for the woman who sat so solemn, like a grieving widow, beside the corpse.

She beckoned them in with a slight tilt of her head, which remained hidden within tumultuous folds of drab gray silk. As usual, she was dressed in the same dull color as all her sisters.

Logan had learned Demons saw color better than grays. Gray —a non-color—was safe for a DeathTalker to wear. It hid them from the creatures living in the Ether—or the land of In-between. From what he knew, the DeathTalkers were naturally attractive to the evils in the land of the dead, so it was a wise precaution.

Jess leaned over and spoke low in his ear. "Pipe down and stop thinking so much. We do not want to disturb her while she works."

Logan waited, mildly annoyed by her freakish ability to read his mind, until she crawled into the tiny space. He never complained when she used her power on a suspect or a snitch, but it didn't feel right to be on the receiving end of a mental probe. Guess he needed to be more conscious of putting up his walls. He followed and pulled the door shut behind him. He wanted no chance of anyone peeking at a DeathTalker in action. Especially when they weren't even supposed to exist.

She wasted no time, waiting only until he shut the door to begin. She lowered her hands to the chest of the corpse, heedless of her fingers sitting on raw flesh or of the congealed blood clinging to her pale digits. Her eyes closed as she murmured words in a language dead for thousands of years.

Then she leaned over him and closed the distance between her mouth and the opening in the face of the dead man; an opening that had once been, when it had lips and skin, his mouth. Then she stopped, her lips almost touching his mangled skin in a macabre caress and drew in the deepest of breaths—deep, to the bottom of her diaphragm. The movement caused the silken shroud to billow from her shoulders, and she injected the air into the mouth of the corpse. She shuddered as the last of her breath left her. Then she paused and sat up to take another lungful.

Minutes ticked by, and though Logan knew what would happen next, he almost wondered if the Calling had failed. Soon, a gray mist began to rise from the dead man's mouth. The snaking coil of dirty-white smoke billowed from him, twisting and turning, seeking.

It found her. The smoke floated to the DeathTalker and she cracked open her mouth. The vapor filtered through the smallest of openings, into her body and her spirit.

She was possessed by the spirit of the dead man.

Jess leaned forward and whispered, "Can you speak awhile?"

The gray-shrouded form nodded and lifted her face to the light. The marbled white of her skin gleamed, cold and luminescent. Blue veins raced across her skin. Gray strands of hair traced her cheek and shoulders.

"Do you remember what happened to you?" Jess's voice lilted, a soft lullaby.

The DeathTalker would soon speak with the voice of the dead man. Logan regretted he would be unable to ask the victim for his name. The dead did not utter their names when they walked the Ether. One's name could bind you to a Demon. Forever. Only after their fates were sealed was it safe to speak the name of the dead.

In the Ether, they only knew their death, the time and place and circumstances, and they were doomed to experience the moment they perished over and over until their time in the In-between had passed.

"Can you speak of it?" A nod. "Tell us. How you come to die this way?"

"Dancing. I remember dancing. Music. Lights. And then nothing," she said, the tone deeper, voice of the dead Walker more gravelly than her normal musical cadence.

"Then what happened?" Jess asked.

"I don't know. I woke up and the man was there."

"Do you know who this man is? What was his name?"

"Don't know his name. Old man. Crazy." The DeathTalker tilted her head, but it was the spirit who controlled her movements. "Something else. Spooky. Evil creature."

"What did he do to you?" asked Jess.

"So much pain. He cut. I watched." No emotion tainted his voice. The spirit of the dead Walker revealed only snatches of emotion.

"You were awake while he did this to you?"

"He gave me a drug. I was awake while...while he cut the skin off my body...wanted him to stop. I couldn't move.... I couldn't.... I felt it all. Asked him so many times. Begged. He didn't care.... Said he wanted my skin in perfect condition." The head tilted again. "Have you seen my skin?"

The dead were childlike, unfocused, and tended to lose their concentration often. They needed guidance to get back on track.

"Did he say why he wanted your skin?" Jess prompted him.

"No. Just that he had no choice." The DeathTalker shook her head, her gray strands shimmying like a colorless waterfall.

"Where did he take you?" Jess kept her questions short, knowing every minute the man's spirit remained within the DeathTalkers body was a potentially deadly minute.

"Hospital," he replied, his voice shaking, yet no fear threaded within the timbre.

"Were there any other people there?"

"I don't remember." The DeathTalkers face crumpled with sorrow. Tears pooled in her white eyes. "I don't remember."

"Did you see anyone else?"

"Just the pretty girl. She was my friend. She stayed with me until the light came."

"Where did you see this girl?" Both Logan and Jess leaned forward.

"By the roses. Such pretty roses..." His voice trailed away into nothing.

Then it was over.

The DeathTalker's face remained still, as if all life had left her body too. Then she began to shake as the spirit she held within fought for release. Her head fell back and her mouth opened, releasing the sinuous cloud of gray. It twirled and twisted, seeking its home back in the mouth of the dead man. He was at peace again. The DeathTalker sat up straighter, an air of fragility around her as if a soft breeze would be enough to knock her over.

"I apologize. He has been through much. When a person is traumatized in such a fashion, they are not long for this realm. Their soul cannot take the memory of their death. It seeks release from the torment and if we force him, his soul may be torn apart before he is ready to move on." Her voice undulated, musical, like soft reedy chimes floating softly on the air. So unlike her deathly pale façade.

Then she shimmered away, dissolving before their eyes until the seat lay bare, and Jess and Logan sat alone with the corpse.

CHAPTER 10

While police, paramedics and onlookers milled around outside, I remained sprawled on the floor of my stuffy storage closet. I propped my heavy head against the wall, dozing. Pain ate at my shoulder. Vicious, gouging, merciless teeth. Gratitude for my body's ability to regenerate was exceeded only by the accursed agony I endured as damaged nerves and torn flesh reattached deep within the canyon of the wound. As excruciating as the pain of regeneration was, the process of removing the bullet had caused the deepest agony.

I eyed my friend as he moved restlessly around the small space. The scent of my blood was cloying. Anjelo glanced furtively at me, checking if I'd seen his discomfort. A deep hunger glimmered within his eyes and his throat convulsed. The room was too small with no window to release the seductive perfume, which hovered thick and strong in the air. Our eyes met. Mine wary, Anjelo's apologetic.

The stuffy, coppery scent of my blood would act like a drug to Anjelo's latent beast. His skin rippled, and his jaw fought to transform. But his own instinct dampened his Change. He was within snuggling distance of a powerful, injured Alpha Panther female. He wouldn't dare engage in a losing battle. Anjelo's jaw clenched as he turned his head away from me, trying to keep his hunger in check. The wait for me to recover some semblance of strength might prove to be his undoing.

Red light peppered the wall behind me, mottled my cheek. The wild spinning inside my skull faded, replaced by an intense awareness of our proximity to the cops combing the garden. An awareness which gathered my energy and forced me to make an effort to extract both Anjelo and myself from this mess. I dared not linger, dared not endanger my ally. Guilt doused some of my adrenaline. This young Panther followed in my footsteps, whether I liked it or not. I should be setting an example. Perhaps it was a good thing he was my conscience.

Would I manage without his reluctant help?

Fat chance.

"We have to get out of here." The words scraped out of my throat in a husky sob.

"*You* have to get out of those clothes." Anjelo scanned my blood-soaked garments with a raised eyebrow. "We don't need that kind of attention."

Strength ebbed slowly into my flaccid limbs and I soon regained enough to stand. At the best of times, I hated being helpless. This was by no means a good time. While I sat on the floor, my wound had continued to bleed slow and steady. The wound had leaked blood down my arm, onto my fingers and dripped unnoticed to the floor, collecting beneath me. I'd been sitting in a pool of the stuff, oblivious even when it soaked into my pants.

Before I'd gotten myself shot, I'd intended to return to my office and change out of my black camo. I usually wore high-necked tops anyway to hide my panther birthmark, which marked my spine and neck. All Alpha's bore the deep, dark tattoo-like mark of the nature of their animal, but most were fortunate enough to have them in places easy to hide.

I only needed Anjelo to help me remove the wet, sticky clothes. *Poor guy.* He left me with a wad of wet towels to clean up, each square about the size of my palm. Anjelo paced while I cleaned.

I helped him clean blood off the door handle to the storeroom after achieving a fairly blood-free state with a blanket of forcibly induced calm thrown in for good measure. Thankfully, the rest of the room looked clean. It dawned on me then, more like a lightning bolt straight into my brain, my office lights were on. Voicing my concern to Anjelo made it worse.

"If we switch it off, someone might notice and get suspicious." Anjelo was right. "But if we leave it on, some smart-ass is bound to investigate."

"Well, that's that. They'll check the building soon enough."

"We have to get out of here," Anjelo said, his pacing a dead giveaway to his tension. He was incapable of lying to the law and we both knew it. I, on the other hand, was a master at subterfuge.

"Check the hall and the ground floor. Quick recon. Give me the all-clear and we can make a run for it." When he started to protest, I held my hand up. "Wasting time, Anjelo."

He turned on his heel. I didn't miss the hurt expression in his eyes and immediately regretted the snark, but it got him moving. Only a few minutes had ticked by when he came barreling into the room, shutting the door as quietly as he could.

"Someone's coming."

We were too late. Dawdled for too long. I shoved him into the closet.

"Stay there and be quiet."

The pained, caught-in-the-headlights expression on his face may have been comical had I not been in a murderous rush to reach the desk. *Mental note—have a good giggle when we're in the clear.* Even laughing at my friend's expense seemed like a luxury at this moment.

I switched the closet light off and shut the door, hoping to

Ailuros that Anjelo wouldn't go berserk in the now dark and tiny space.

Hurrying to the desk, I stuffed my ear buds in and turned up the volume. My eardrums vibrated. Laptop switched on—check. All wires and bits plugged in—check.

I was ready.

Ready to handle whoever walked through that door.

No one would be coming to help me, not when the mess was my own creation. Even though I hadn't asked to be shot, I could imagine my father's face if he saw me now. Those cold, gray eyes would spare me the briefest of accusing glances, if he bothered to look at me at all. Corin Odel remained devoid of every emotion except for anger. And, in my case, disappointment.

I pretended to work. The more I waited, the more stressed I became.

And stress was dangerous.

Stress summoned my Panther. And so far, I'd managed to keep my feline form subdued. The effort to tamp my animal down zapped more from me than I expected, and I wiped off the beads of perspiration coating my upper lip.

My body ached, my shoulder ached more.

Fatigue dulled my senses.

I blasted Beethoven at full volume as I hunched over my computer. And almost missed the knock when it finally came.

CHAPTER 11

The door opened a few feet in front of my desk. I scented my visitor as he entered the room, but kept my head down. I smelled sweat and adrenaline and ozone. Strange. He smelled electric. Or electrified. Weird. But nice. Sort of gooey, tingle-in-the-stomach nice. I still hadn't laid eyes on him. Knowing my luck, he'd be an ogre.

A pair of booted feet entered my line of vision and left me no choice but to address him. I looked up, intending to feign surprise with a touch of fear. I had no trouble with surprise. His youth, not his presence, elicited the emotion. He didn't look much older than me—no more than eighteen. Humans aged faster than Walkers did, and their age showed. My eighteenth year loomed like a death knell, but I did look a lot younger. It posed a problem when Grandma Ivy had insisted I attend the local high school if I wanted to stay with her. The headmaster at Crawdon High had demanded proof of my age before admission. A good thing I was only in school six months before graduation.

My visitor's dark hair stuck up in boyish spikes, as if he'd just run his fingers through it in frustration. My neck hurt with craning it to take in his full height. He cracked a smile. Clearly, he didn't smile much or had forgotten the art long ago. His mouth turned up at the corners, but his eyes remained cool, calculating and contemplative, as if he recognized me from somewhere.

My fear was real too. The effect he had on me scared me so badly; enough for me to wish I were very far away from him. But at the same time, he enthralled me. Ugh. This is what got girls into trouble, all this hormonal bullshit.

I pulled the buds from my ears, dropped them on the desk and rose to my feet. His height made me insecure enough to stand, and then it was too late to sit down again without looking totally idiotic. Hot pain stabbed my shoulder from the movement. It took considerable effort not to wince and I concentrated on his chin. Firm and stubbled, it screamed determined and stubborn. I decided I liked his chin. Very much.

Get a grip, you idiot. He's a bloody cop.

"Hello. Sorry if we startled you. I'm Agent Westin with the Chicago PD." He didn't look the least bit sorry. He waved a hand at the other agent who still stood by the door. Blonde, beautiful and silent. "That's Agent Carnarvon. We're the ones making the racket outside."

He nodded at the large windows behind me. From my position, the red emergency lights flashing outside never reached me. The light reflected against the white sills of the windows and threw a haze of pink on the wall to my right, but not enough to draw my attention.

"Sorry, I didn't hear." I indicated the buds and the music drive lying on the desk, its little green light blinked on pause.

"Ah." A light bulb expression lit his face, now I'd proved to be musically inclined instead of deaf. "What're you listening to?"

Was he trying to make conversation? My shoulder ached and I was in no mood for a chat.

He's way too good-looking to get me on a bad day. Life ain't fair—so get used to it, Kailin.

"Beethoven," I answered flatly.

"Oh, I don't have the patience for classical. Jazz is more my style."

I blinked and waited. He wanted to discuss music while my poor friend suffocated inside the closet. The blood-filled closet. Panic surged through me. Anjelo sat among my bloodstained clothes and towels. It was a danger to his Panther as much as the Hunt was to mine.

Dear Ailuros, please look after the poor guy.

"We're checking the building out. There's been a bit of commotion outside." Westin cut right to the chase.

I kept my face blank. Not going to fall into the trap, thanks.

"What's going on?" I turned on my heel and hurried to the window, peering in the direction of the lights. "What happened?"

"Someone dumped a body in the community garden."

High shock value required. I hoped my expression of horror did it justice. Part of me registered the presence of Westin's beautiful partner. Her disinterested glance flitted over me. I ignored it.

"When?" I faced him, hoping for a sign. *Had my little act convinced him yet?* I needed to tone it down, though or I'd get found out. The last thing I wanted was to ingrain in his mind that I was a total wook.

"Not long ago, about an hour or so." His obsidian eyes focused sharply on my face, watching for the slightest tell. "What are you doing here so late, Miss...?"

"Odel. Kailin Odel. I work for the rehab center. Teen rehab counselor."

His eyebrows raised in disbelief. I could almost hear the sound of tumblers and springs clicking and clacking away as he tried to guess my age.

"A bit young for a counselor."

"Counselor in training," I said, stressing the word 'training' with a raised eyebrow of my own.

"Is this a night job?"

My brow twisted in confusion. Blood loss began to tire me out.

"School?" Agent Carnarvon, by the door, scowled.

"Oh. I'm at U of C, Detective. But it's okay. I look young for my age so I get that a lot." I waved a hand at the files. "As you can tell, I have tons of paperwork to clear for my supervisor. It tends to pile up while we aren't looking. Clancy's got a group session at noon tomorrow and I thought I'd better give her a hand and get a head start writing up some reports."

"Planning on going home at all?"

"I won't be much longer," I replied.

"It's a dangerous neighborhood, Miss Odel." His eyes assessed me. I'd have given anything to peek into his busy little mind. A part of me didn't mind the assessment, especially when those dark eyes lost their glacial pall for a few seconds. I imagined a more intense, dreamy look in his eyes.

Get a grip, Odel. Fantasizing about the cop won't keep your ass out of jail.

"I don't live far away. Just a short walk around the block. Besides, everyone knows me pretty well. I can take care of myself."

"If you don't mind me saying.... You're very young to make a career decision, especially one as intense as a counselor."

"I'm a youth and drug counselor, Agent Westin. My background allows me to empathize with them. I understand the patients. It's why I can make real progress with them. Besides, I'm still a trainee counselor on the staff. I'm supervised, though not as much as before." His needling annoyed me. I hated questions about my age. So I was young. He didn't know Walkers aged slower than Humans. I should've cut him some slack, but he'd already pushed my buttons. Add to the fact I was beginning to like his company far too much—that broad expanse of chest—it became a recipe for cataclysmic disaster.

I took a long, assessing look of my own, noting his lack of

gray or wrinkles. Talk about the pot calling the kettle black. "You look pretty young yourself. For a detective...."

Agent Carnarvon smiled behind him, though she didn't meet my eyes.

"Touché, Miss Odel. I guess I deserved that." He flushed a little. "Just a few more questions and we'll be out of your way. Did you hear any gunshots?"

I shook my head, not trusting my voice.

"We believe someone witnessed the drop and the killers shot at this person. From the pattern of the damage in the garden, we traced him to the rear entrance of this building. We've checked the building, but all we've found were empty offices."

"Have you asked Clem?" Redirection always helped. If I nudged him toward Clem, maybe he'd leave me alone. This was taking far too long for poor Anjelo to survive the cramped closet.

"Clem?" he asked.

"The super. Lives in the basement," I snipped. He should know this. He was the detective, not me.

"Okay, we'll check with him. What time did you get here tonight?" His eyes traveled the room as he spoke.

"Around eight." Not many people hung around at eight, so there'd be no one to confirm or deny it.

"So you didn't hear anyone enter the building in the last hour or so?"

I picked up my ear-buds and he fell silent as they swung from my hand.

"Mind if I look around a bit?" He raised his hands in apology. I figured he was a by-the-book kind of guy and declining such a request would raise further, possibly damning, questions.

"Sure, go ahead." I had no choice. He'd check anyway or get a subpoena and be right back. Poor Anjelo.

My heart clenched when he walked to the closet and opened the door. His fingers searched inside for the lights and flipped the switch. The light flickered a few times, as it strained to connect the electrical points to illuminate the bulb. It succeeded and stayed on. It brightened the closet and haphazard contents in stark detail.

He peered out the window on his left, which sat on the same wall as the windows in my office, and looked down on the garden below. He scanned the shelves and the walls for far too long. Did he sense something in there? I leaned forward, tense. Waiting. Forgetting the silent Agent Carnarvon who waited by the door.

Then, my chest clenched with shock. Anjelo had missed a spot. Right there on the threshold, an inch to the left of Agent Westin's shiny right boot, sat an equally shiny ruby puddle Waiting for him to see it or step in it. I dared not imagine which would've been worse. Thankfully, his feet blocked his partner's view of the evidence.

He completed his scan of the closet interior, after paying special attention to the fake wall sealing off my special storage area. I was sure he'd hear my heart thundering all the way in the closet. If not mine, then probably Anjelo's.

Satisfied, he switched off the light and closed the door, his boot heel missing the traitorous red spot by a breath and a heartbeat.

"Thanks for your time, Miss Odel." He'd seen enough. I couldn't be rid of him fast enough. "You really should be leaving the office earlier, when it's safer. The city is far more dangerous than you may realize."

He held out a card and I reached out for it. At the same moment, Westin moved forward as if he knew I'd have to reach to grasp it. I expected the sharp stab of pain in my shoulder as I stretched, testing muscles that preferred to be left alone. I didn't expect the sudden blaze of heat sparked by the meeting of our fingers. Warmth pulsed from the point of contact all the way up my arm to my chest, constricting my lungs so I couldn't breathe and speeding up a heartbeat already hammering double time with nerves. I grabbed my hand back, glancing up and hoping I covered my defensiveness.

Our eyes met and I knew from his expression he felt something similar. He looked startled and a bit disturbed. As if whatever he felt made him uncomfortable. My pulse raced, this time with anger. He obviously wasn't too thrilled. I sat back down, deciding on silence rather than blurting out my thoughts. Westin cleared his throat and gave his head the tiniest shake, as if he was trying to dislodge the wooly threads of slumber.

"Are you willing to sign a statement? Even if you haven't seen anything. It's part of the investigation." He frowned as he spoke. Clearly, his mind was elsewhere and the words he spoke formed automatically.

"Sure." Model citizen.

"And we'd need your supervisor's details to corroborate your employment." I fished around in Clancy's drawer and passed Westin a business card. This time, we both took care to ensure we avoided contact.

I leaned against the backrest of my chair and crossed my legs to wait while he studied it. I flicked my foot back and forth, as he spoke.

"Are you sure you haven't been in the garden this evening?" My forehead creased. He stared pointedly at my booted feet. "You've got soil stuck in your soles."

"Yeah, I've been in the garden. I'm there every now and then. I have a little patch of flowers I take care of. Or try to." I nodded at the vase of Delphiniums sitting precariously on the edge of the overflowing desk, slightly wilted but still a glorious deep blue.

Again, I'd stymied him, but he seemed satisfied with my answers so far. I could tell something still bugged him though. Throughout our conversation, he kept looking at my hair.

Glorious ebony tresses was the way Grandma Ivy described it. Said it reminded her of my mother. I always found it strange my father's mother didn't hate her daughter-in-law for abandoning her family. She had the most annoying habit of stroking my head as if I were the cat, though I never dared to demand she stop. When it came to Grandma Ivy, submitting was the easiest option.

"Do you use the back entrance often?" There went my heart again, faster than a freight train.

"Of course, Detective. It's the route I take to tend my flowers. I'm not lazy, but I certainly won't walk all the way around the building to get the garden. I use the back door all the time. During the day, of course. The light outside hasn't worked for ages. I've complained but the super never does anything about it."

"Probably why we found strands of hair the exact shade of yours on the step outside the back door."

I nodded, the offending dark strands stirring back and forth. The plait had held, but barely, and dozens of tendrils had escaped during my evening's activities.

"We've bothered you enough." He hesitated. "Thank you for your help." He retreated from the room after holding the door open for Agent Carnarvon, then shut the door behind him. The tap-tap of their footsteps receded down the hall.

I stretched my arm, stiffened from controlling the shivers of pain, which ran through my shoulder. Relief flooded me while adrenaline ebbed from my limbs. That damned spot of blood had almost given me a stroke. Not to mention my body's traitorous reaction to his touch.

Disgusted with myself, I shut the computer down and gathered my stuff. My shoulder ached like crazy, but I had to clean up the spot. Grabbing a fistful of tissues, I opened the closet door and swiped at the offensive blood spot. I rubbed until not a trace remained.

It was a good thing Walker blood differed from Human in one vital construct—it lacked those properties which allowed Human blood to be picked up by UV light.

As I rose, my shirt stuck to my back, sticky and moist. Good thing I'd changed it before he arrived. If I'd had my back to him as he left, he'd have seen the wound on my shoulder, fresh blood seeping through the clean shirt. As I rose, I heard a sound from the closet.

Anjelo. Damn, I'd almost forgotten him.

Okay, did forget him with the minor issue of one darned drop of blood.

Pushing into the hidden space, I let the light shine into the small area. Anjelo sat on the floor, eyes half transformed to exotic panther as he controlled his blood urges, playing a game on his mobile phone. And I'd wasted my time worrying about him.

We left the center, careful to keep to the shadows. Anjelo insisted on walking me home—as if I were just a cub. My hero. As grateful as I was to Anjelo for his help, my mind fixated on a pair of obsidian eyes, one gently stubbled, very sexy chin and the warm glow on my skin where our fingertips had touched so briefly.

CHAPTER 12

Stumbling into my apartment, I hobbled to my room and undressed. One-handed, the simple task took longer than expected and it wore me out. I sank onto the edge of the bed to catch my breath, sparing the tiniest of peeks at the photo frame sitting face down on the nightstand. The cheerful faces of a once-happy family lay hidden between the glass and cheap wood of the table. I didn't need a physical reminder of my fractured family unit. Not today. Not when the gaping hole in my shoulder spat agonizing streaks into my flesh and all I wanted was someone to make it all better.

At last, I dragged myself to the shower, hoping the hot water would help soothe my muscles and encourage sleep. Later, I collapsed on the bed and closed my eyes, yearning for the release of slumber. Easier said than done.

Sleep refused to come, as images of the skinless man and his eyes, unable to close, staring off into eternity, danced behind my eyelids. My shoulder ached, reminding me I'd come close to meeting the great Ailuros. I knew I needed rest, but how was I supposed to sleep when the odor of Death's fetid breath still hung on me?

Why did the murder affect me so deeply? I'd seen and done far too much to get squeamish at the sight of a dead body. But he'd been a Walker. Perhaps it was the skin, or the lack of it, that bothered me so much. Who'd do such an awful thing? To a Walker? What if there were others out there, at this very moment, at the mercy of the murderer? If Walkers in the city had gone missing, Anjelo or Storm would've said something. I needed to tell the clan.

City Deep.

It was what they called themselves. Ourselves, rather. My clan. Honorary member. In return, I was a watchman of sorts. Kept an eye out and passed information to Storm on the Wraiths and their numbers, and he helped me, like giving me Tara's number for the weapons I needed. At least Storm understood and never gave me the look of condemnation I often found on Anjelo's face. Storm was Grandma Ivy's enigmatic friend. He was a benefactor to many of the Walkers in the city, especially to the kids. He ran a shelter of sorts for the Walker kids, provided guardianship for them so they could attend Crawdon, and gave them guidance and leadership too.

I remembered the lumbering city when I'd first arrived, filled with steel buildings and concrete highways—and Humans. So many Humans. I'd lived in the city for a year, fulfilling my promise to Grandma Ivy and attending school, pretending to be nothing more than Human. Most of them kept themselves too busy in their own lives, making ends meet, trying to get ahead. Never any time left in their day to mull over the possible existence of mythical creatures forgotten by time.

None of the Humans I knew could imagine a whole other world out there, that every time they spoke to me, they spoke to a living, breathing creature from the Old World.

They had forgotten the Old People. What had trickled down through the ages to the modern world were hazy pieces of the puzzle, like snatches of a conversation overheard by an erstwhile eavesdropper. Only parts of the real truth. Somehow, the legends of the Werewolves had remained in the annals of history while those of the Cat Walkers disappeared. We weren't complaining, though. Non-existence had its merits.

And those Humans fortunate enough to be aware of our existence had no concept of the intensity of hatred Walkers harbored for their pitiful kind.

When I looked back at the naïve innocent I'd been, I realized I'd been no different to the Humans, cloistered in their little worlds living their tiny little lives, thinking they were the beginning and end of their existence, where nothing mattered besides them. And there I'd been on the flip side, believing I was the only Walker in the city. How stupid. Just because I hadn't encountered Walkers when I arrived in Chicago, hadn't met any in Crawdon, didn't mean they weren't there. And I remained in my wonderland. Until the day Anjelo arrived on my doorstep.

owntown Chicago—1 year ago

THE USUAL HUSHED tenor of the Center's reception room was transformed into a country fish market when the main doors were flung open. An unconscious boy was half dragged, half carried into the room. Two boys supporting their burden yelled for help.

"He's been shot."

Even as those words were uttered, a ruby stain bled through his tattered gray shirt. There was a rush to get to him and I found myself the first to reach the boy, not more than fourteen, at the center of this mayhem. One of my first group sessions with my new supervisor Clancy McBride, had ended minutes before.

The city had been my home only a few weeks when Grandma Ivy had demanded two things—school and a job. Knowing her generosity would not survive any disobedience on my part; I enrolled at the local high school, Crawdon, even though it would only be for half a year, and looked around for a job.

Lucky for me the Drug Rehab Center had been looking for what they called Teen Service Liaisons. Sailing through the preliminary tests and promising to complete a raft of courses, I became the youngest ever recruit of the Rehab Center. Now, six months later, I often went home satisfied with the successes I achieved. Even more satisfying were my courses at the University of Chicago. Cognitive and developmental psychology, behavior, social interaction; it all fell into place when I walked into the Rehab Center and talked to the people who attended the sessions.

Today I'd been looking forward to going home to relax after a particularly difficult session. Not much chance of that now.

By this time his friends had laid him on the floor, his color had begun to fade. He was young, but not too young for the streets. I yelled for a camp bed used in the overnight stay rooms and guided him securely onto it. I scanned the room for an adult face, eager to transfer this huge responsibility to someone older, more capable. All I saw were patients and one teen volunteer at reception staring at the boy, shocked.

Even so, something tickled my senses. A slight odor of familiarity. I thought it was just my imagination. Since being in the city I'd had a few instances of passing people in the street and picking up on a tell-tale odor that could just be another Walker. And it had always just been my imagination.

With a sigh, I pointed them to a door off the entrance room. The room served as a group session room and was light and airy —as good a place as any to keep him until the ambulance arrived. His blood loss was severe and I was pretty scared he wouldn't survive without surgery.

Once he was settled, I took his vitals—to make sure he wasn't going to die on my hands. I received a nasty shock.

His dramatic entrance had dulled my perception a little. My concentration had been focused on the wound and not the victim. One touch told me what he was.

A SkinWalker.

A Panther Walker like me.

A mutual shock by the startled look in eyes heavily lidded with pain, and etched with recognition. Touch was very important to my people, and our sense of smell was especially keen. That, and the ability to hear and feel vibrations beyond Human hearing.

With this ability, I recognized the boy for what he was by the rhythm and vibrations of his heartbeat and the flow of the blood through his veins, not to mention the spicy aroma of his blood. Shock slowed my reactions and I hesitated. The boy's friends and other curious onlookers had filtered into the room. I dared not tend to him with all these people around me. The strength I required to deal with him when I removed the bullets would certainly be questioned by the many anxious onlookers. In spite of being well built, I was small in stature. A show of extreme strength would garner far too much curiosity.

And I'd need my strength. Walkers were extremely strong even in their Human form. While under great stress, they were known to shift to their animal forms to control the pain. And the boy's transformation with a Human audience was very much not an option.

Another man entered the room, nudging the boy's companions aside. Reaching his side, the man grasped the boy's hand. The boy was clearly on the same wavelength as I was.

"Storm. Please, I need them out of here." The boy rasped into his friend's ear, waving a hand at the crowd. He managed a weak smile. "Please, this will be difficult enough. I don't want the whole gang hearing me scream like a girl when the doctor here takes the bullets out." He spoke a little louder so the gathering crowd would hear him.

My head popped up at the mention of Storm's name. I'd only ever spoken to my Grams' friend Storm over the phone. Could he be one and the same?

But for now, I had to pay attention. I bit my tongue. I was no doctor. What I knew had been learned patching up hundreds of injuries for my brother during my young life. SkinWalkers healed super-fast, but it was by no means a clean process. We bled much like any other living creature.

I carefully cut away the shirt and dabbed at the clotted blood at the wound's entrance.

I looked up from my ministrations only when the room had emptied and the boy was alone with the Storm fellow and me. I met the boy's eyes with an unspoken question, flicking my gaze in the direction of his companion.

"It's okay.... Storm is safe—he knows...." The young man's breath hissed out and I feared he might have a perforated lung in addition to his extensive blood loss. He opened his eyes briefly to meet mine, and then he sighed weakly. It took seconds to realize he'd slipped into unconsciousness; probably caused by blood loss.

I hesitated. The boy trusted Storm. But despite my suspicion that it was looking more likely that Storm was Grams' friend and someone I knew and could trust, I hesitated, not sure I was happy with Storm being there, and watching. Part of me wanted to get him to leave.

"Don't bother trying to get me to leave." His voice was musical, edged with a dry humor. Creepy. He'd echoed my thoughts, and I did not like it one bit. "I know you are like him."

My puzzled expression extracted a chuckle.

"I know what he is. What you are too." His eyes flashed golden and entrancing.

Shock silenced me.

"I am able to sense the reality of things. I know the evil in people, the good too. I can feel the otherness in people as well. And you are...Other." He spoke with a slightly infectious calm. Did he have some Magyk he was using to spellbind me in some way? I knew enough about Magyk to know those who held the power could control their subjects—make them do whatever they wanted. Even SkinWalker clans had their fair share of Mages.

I spared him a brief glance, tall and dark, olive complexioned, his black hair framed his face in a tumble of feminine curls and yet he exuded masculinity, apparent to anyone with an X-chromosome. So he was easy on the eyes—Grams hadn't told me that.

"Oookay...we don't have time to discuss the weather while this poor kid lies here, bleeding all over the floor. Rain-check?" I arched an eyebrow.

I had to work fast. This late at night, most of the other counselors were home with their families. As a result, I got more than my share of night shifts. But Clancy was one of the more dedicated social workers at the Center, usually on call twenty-four-seven. I couldn't risk either her or another counselor popping in to witness what I was up to.

Whilst removing the bullets I was grateful for Storm's presence as he held the boy down while I worked, just in case he came to and struggled. Human medication didn't work so well on Walkers. So the surgery was done with the boy unsedated.

When I'd finally removed the bullet and cleaned the wound, I allowed myself to utter a long pent-up sigh. With the bullet out of his flesh, his body would begin its rejuvenation, healing itself from the inside. Exhaustion weighed down my muscles while relief gave me enough energy to stay on my feet. And a hint of something unexpected tingled in my brain as I savored the knowledge there were others like me in the city. I'd expected to feel crowded or annoyed that my secret was now in jeopardy, but I also knew the boy was able to trust Storm the way Grams did. Sucker that I was, I believed his assurance I could trust him too.

Thankfully, my patient didn't take long to reawaken, even after the trauma of my poor excuse for surgery.

"How are you feeling?" I asked, tucking the blankets gently around his neck.

"Better...." he rasped.

The kid had courage. And I was curious.

"You from around here?"

His eyes revealed his hesitation. Some inner battle was waged beneath the frown. To tell me more would be to make himself vulnerable, to trust me. Perhaps he had the same issues I did with that.

Moments later, he reached a decision and when he spoke I was surprised.

"Kai, it's me, Anjelo Alvarez."

Shock spasmed through me as I searched his face, studied the lines and remembered the little boy I had once known. Funny, in spite of being so near him for so long I hadn't recognized his face. Older, weathered from his time on the streets, and a little bit tired. A face belonging to one of the many kids who'd taken to following me around the colony, trying to emulate me. I'd been reluctantly popular.

And this nitwit had taken emulation one step too far.

"Anjelo." I wanted to shake him. "What in Ailuros' name were you thinking?"

"We saw you leave....Gave us the courage to try a new life as well."

"Did you not stop and think how dangerous this could be for you?" Blood thundered to my brain.

"You did it and you're a g..." he said. A poor defense.

"You dolt. I may be a girl but I am strong, trained. Alpha trained." I stressed the last two words. A bit unfair, but not everyone was born to Alpha status.

"Everyone knew you were fine, so we thought it'd be okay if we did what we wanted too." He looked at me hopefully.

I was livid. Not with Anjelo. With myself. I'd never intended to influence anyone. And now, my act of defiance had resulted in my young pack-mate being hurt. Indirect or not, I bore the weight of responsibility squarely on my own stupid, stubborn shoulders.

I met Storm's eyes over Anjelo's prone body, and thankfully saw no judgment in his expression.

"This is Storm." I hid a smile at the belated introduction. Anjelo continued. "He's given me a place to stay, and he's bossed me into going to school here...some place called Crawdon High." Anjelo blew out a breath.

"Great. Well, then, you'd better work hard. And I guess I'll be seeing more of you." Anjelo's eyes, dulled with pain, suddenly brightened at the prospect of seeing me more often. I still could not understand what he saw in me, but I wasn't about to disappoint the child.

He grunted, a poor imitation of a laugh, and lay back, clearly happy with himself. And somewhere inside me, a little part of me was happy too.

CHAPTER 14

*L*ogan laid his heavy head in his hands, grateful to have the weight off it. He continued to gnaw at the new evidence, turning it over in his mind, getting at it from every angle. Jess had gone back to HQ to file a report. Now she stood before him, studying his frustration with an annoyingly calm expression.

Guess it wouldn't help to kill the messenger.

"All the tests are complete?" He looked at Jess for a response.

She nodded.

The blood would've been put through every test Omega had, double and triple checked. The result was the same. The DNA of the SkinWalker was clear enough. A perfect amalgamation of Human and Cougar DNA. Natural mutation. The lab certified this was not a genetically engineered creature, and not a clone either. Logan had ensured that piece of paper went missing from the file sent to the coroner. And the one sent to the Police Chief, of course.

"We knew the corpse belonged to a SkinWalker, so no surprises there."

Logan continued reading.

"Sample is positive for SkinWalker—specific to Genus Cougar. Comparison with sample batches all positive. Traces of Neurotoxins found: awaiting results."

It was the last bit of information that alarmed him. His head swam. Lack of sleep, lack of food. Everything would catch up with him soon and he'd be dead on his feet.

Literally.

THE NEXT MORNING, after a much needed sleep in, I headed for the Rehab Center. Something always needed to be done and I needed to get my mind off dead Walkers and unusually powerful Wraiths.

I'd barely gotten the computer running and was about to start entering the notes from our last session when the door clicked open and Dr. Heide glided in. No knocking required for her in her facility. Hair as dark as mine hung from a center part, framing a petite, oval face. Beneath the sharp glare and her unsmiling Arctic expression lay the remnants of a beautiful woman. She wore her shield of ice as well as she wore her anti-quated Donna Karan suit. Her eyes revealed an emotional vacuum and although laugh-lines wrinkled their corners, I couldn't imagine her capable of such a warmly Human act.

She regarded me with those beady black eyes—so like a crow with its glassy, predatory stare. Even the set of her shoulders implied she'd arrived ready to fire at the bull's-eye seemingly marking my forehead.

"A right mess you've gotten yourself into, Miz Odel." She slapped a piece of paper emblazoned with the Chicago PD insignia onto my desk.

Taken aback by the verbal attack, I fumbled for a decent response. Clearly not the best reaction, as it seemed to confirm my guilt in her mind.

"While this investigation is under way, you're on paid leave.

Consider this a token of my appreciation for you as a member of this staff, however junior." She flung the words over her shoulder as she turned to leave.

Guilty—and suspended—until proven innocent.

"Don't make me regret this."

I was about to ask how being suspended was an indication of her appreciation when she stopped at the doorway and said, "You need to understand the severity of this situation. If you give me any further trouble, I'll see to it you're permanently suspended." Her gaze drilled frosty holes into me and she razed me with one last stare.

The words wafted back at me so cold I could almost see the ice crystals forming on them as they floated toward me. She left me cold and perplexed, listening to the clacking of her heels on the tiled corridor.

The police. They probably dropped by and told her which of her staff had been questioned the previous night. Staff who were now a liability. The mere hint police investigated the facility would be cause for concern, especially with the number of ex-convicts treated within the rehab programs.

Losing registered patients meant losing revenue and Heide was no doubt concerned she may lose the subsidies the center received for each patient who attended a formal session. Heaven forbid such a thing should happen under her watch. It occurred to me it was quite the miracle I was still around.

I grabbed my backpack; the solid presence of the bow beneath the rough fabric comforted me as I locked up and headed out of the building. Teeth gritted, I tried to banish the vision of Heide's face floating in my memory. She'd made it clear on numerous occasions I was too young for such serious work. But Clancy either had a lot of clout or knew which of Heide's buttons to push to get her way.

I needed to prove I was not a threat to the center.

For myself.

And for Clancy.

MY RUN-IN WITH DR. HEIDE, more like Dr. Jekyll actually, left me fuming. I bit my cheeks, administering another expletive a crushing death.

I scanned my visitor head to toe, unable to decide if his visit pleased or annoyed me. In the end, the tripping of my heart confirmed him as a welcome sight. I was grateful he hadn't been any earlier. Then he would've walked into my oh-so-demeaning run-in with Heide.

"Hello." An awkward silence followed, as if words failed him. Or he had forgotten what he came to say.

I silently filed away mental notes and ran through the sequence of the previous night's events—the version I'd discussed with Westin, of course.

"More questions, Agent Westin?" I skipped my greetings and flushed guiltily. I met his eyes nonetheless. I was raised to be polite, and it seemed social etiquette held importance to him too. He scowled in rebuke. "No Agent Carnarvon today?"

"Yes and no." Granite eyes pierced mine as he answered both questions. "Just routine. And I need your signature to confirm your statement." He patted the folder tucked under his arm. He wore a dulled black leather jacket—the one he'd worn last night. Seems we made the same fashion choices. "And Jess had some other investigations to do."

A bullet slammed into the brick façade of the building behind me, sending tiny shards of brick and mortar flying like lethal rain. Westin shoved me to the ground, scanning for the origin of the shot. The shooter either sucked or meant the shot as a warning. Heart thundering in my throat, I lifted my head, needing to get a bead on the creep. The heavy metal of my bow poked uselessly into my back.

"Stay down." He emphasized his words with a second shove to

my left shoulder. The same shoulder still aching from last night's bullet wound. Stars spun at the edge of my vision and I bit down on a feral growl of pain. Glad the wound had sealed overnight, I lay horizontal on the concrete, lacking both the energy and inclination to do anything else but will the discomfort away. It hurt like the blazes. The agony was curiously edged with a second palpitation of my heart. Within the melee, and beneath my misery, my mind and body registered the impact of Logan's body against mine. I tried to hold on to some of the blazing heat for as long as I could.

Westin pulled his gun from the holster inside his coat, jumped to his feet and ran for the vehicle the shot had been fired from. Another shot issued and shards of brick sprayed onto my head, this time close enough to convince me they shot to kill. My heart jumped, fear filling me as images of Logan lying face-down in a puddle of blood swarmed through my mind. Gears squealed and the sedan sped off. Too fast for a bipedal chase. Something Westin seemed to concede to as he slowed his chase, pausing in the middle of the street, gun drawn and aimed at the getaway vehicle.

I marveled at his grace and athletic power. His youth did not detract from his obvious skill. While lying on the concrete, pain still making my head spin, I gawked like a schoolgirl drooling over her first crush.

CHAPTER 15

*L*ogan aimed his pistol at the fleeing sedan and pulled the trigger. He simultaneously focused a stream of heated energy at the rear left tire; any resulting explosion would be attributed to his shot. The tire hugging the wheel glowed a faint orange as molten air built up within the rubber tube.

The car hung a left at the corner and the tire exploded with a flat blast, sending shreds of rubber onto the street like black confetti at a goth wedding. Some still ablaze as they landed. Pumpkin colored flames spurted, then faded to smoky wisps, leaving tiny piles of melted rubber littered across the street. Though he'd shot at the car, he carried nothing but blanks. He caused far more damage with his mind than with mere bullets.

It wasn't enough though. The gunmen, intent on getting away, sped down the street, mangling the back tire rim. It clanged on the blacktop and sent showers of cobalt and orange sparks spewing in its wake.

Frustrated, Logan shoved the Glock into his halter. The gun was standard issue for all Omega operatives, and in his case, provided a cover should he need to use his power. He'd only tried a controlled stream of Magyk, wanting to avoid blowing up the entire car and hoping to slow them down long enough for him to get closer. Anything bigger and people could've gotten hurt.

The image of a blackened restaurant marred his vision.

Unbidden.

Unwanted.

Charred bodies seated at wrinkled and melted Formica tables, no longer their original bright blooming red. A patch of melted checkered-tiled floor around a pair of sneakered feet. Black scorch marks blossomed from the sneakers. Even the ceiling above bore burn marks in a circular pattern. As if something had exploded where he stood. An explosion large enough to incinerate everything within a twenty-foot radius in the beat of a hummingbird's wing.

Sirens sounded in the distance and the vision dissolved, replaced by the now empty street and the babbling crowd drawn by the gunshots. He turned back to Kailin to find her surrounded by a group of concerned citizens.

Shouldering the onlookers aside, he made his way to her. He crouched down next to her where she sat, holding her head in her hand. He searched his memory. Did he shove her hard enough to injure her? He tried to move her hand away to get a better look at the wound. She resisted, glaring at him, then glancing pointedly at their interested audience.

"Okay, people. Give the lady some air." He rose, waving the onlookers away with a flick of his badge. "Just a small bump on the head, nothing serious. Thank you for your concern."

He heard and understood their concerns. What was their neighborhood coming to? A murdered man dumped in their communal garden, now a young woman shot at in broad daylight. People were concerned for their safety.

The crowd heaved and pulsed like a sardine shoal, then dispersed as quickly as they had appeared.

Logan helped Kailin to her feet, confident she suffered no head wound, and bent at the knees to grab her backpack. Beneath his hand he felt the defined muscles of her biceps tighten. A quick glance at her bloodless face confirmed her tension. Her pack weighed heavy in his hand and he held onto it, not sure she was able to carry it; he still wasn't convinced she totally escaped injury. Her eyes fixated on her bag, jaw clenched.

A police car pulled up, lights flashing, sirens ripping eardrums. The officer came over to them, recognizing Logan immediately.

"What do we have here?"

"Drive by. Three or four shots fired. You should find the slugs in the wall over there." Logan nodded at the wall, where the fractured stone clearly marked the entry points of at least three bullets. "Bag them and get them to O-Lab A-SAP."

The officer nodded and dipped a hand into his vehicle, retrieving a roll of neon yellow cordon tape.

"O-Lab?" asked Kailin as the officer walked toward the wall.

"I work for an organization called Omega. We have a separate lab to perform tests on all evidence in conjunction with the local police department. Sort of arm-in-arm, but we can be sure no evidence gets tampered with. Besides, we have access to some pretty high-tech methods of analysis."

"Oh?" She nodded. The action caused one dark curl to fall to her cheek, reflecting the midday-light. Today a low ponytail hung to her waist. The same style his mother had favored. Right now Logan would rather steer clear of memories of his mother. Especially when the attractive Miss Odel was around.

"I'll give you a ride home." Logan clenched his jaw, bracing for resistance. He unnerved her, that much was clear. But she did pretty much the same to him.

Hesitation clouded her eyes, suspicion muddying the clear green. Whatever inner battle occurred, the ride home won because she nodded and eyed her pack again.

Logan slung it over his shoulder and something he was sure would've killed him had the bag landed any harder promptly stabbed his shoulder blade. His gasp was a blend of surprise and pain.

In the next instant, Kailin grabbed the strap.

"I'm sorry. I'll carry it." Concern flooded her eyes, along with an emotion he could've sworn was fear. Which made no sense at all. He had no intention of harming her. Hadn't given her that impression, either.

"I'm not afraid of a bunch of deadly books, okay?" He scowled. "I can manage. Just as long as your books don't bite as well as they stab."

Her smile was warmth and sunshine. Hesitant, and clouded by worry, but warm nonetheless.

"Where did you park?" Her soft words drifted by as she scanned the now-empty street.

"Around the block."

She raised her eyebrows as they turned the corner to find his unmarked loan car littered with tire fragments. He turned the wipers on a few times to clear the windshield.

"Did you shoot the tire out?"

Logan looked at her, surprised. "You didn't see the fireworks?"

"Sorry. Eyes closed and kissing sidewalk."

"Oh." Relieved, he considered a white lie "No. I didn't shoot it out. It...exploded."

Kailin leaned forward and gazed up at the sky. Then she smiled.

"Divine intervention rocks," Logan concluded.

She remained silent on the drive to her place. She didn't seem in the mood for talk. That he could deal with.

Now, adrenaline free, the reality of the attempt on her life sank in—dead weight. She was a target. But why? Last night she'd denied any knowledge of the body dump and the shooting. And he'd believed her. She was either really unlucky or one fabulous liar.

Logan insisted on seeing Kailin to her door, wanted to be sure she made it safely home. It had nothing to do with the fire she sparked within him. Nothing at all.

They rode up in a rickety birdcage of an elevator, probably a hundred and fifty years old if it was a day. A nerve bulged at her temple and the whites of her knuckles matched her fingernails eerily well. She had a right to be tense and nervous.

"I think I should give the place a once-over before you lock up for the night."

She looked at him, eyes wide with surprise. Her youth so clear in her face and expression.

"No, really. It's fine."

"You can't really be so sure, Miss Odel. Do you have an alarm system?"

"No." As if anybody had them these days. "And you can call me Kailin. Miss Odel seems a bit formal considering I owe you my life."

"Well, then there's no way you can tell the apartment's safe from standing outside here." He didn't intend on backing down.

On the next breath he expected an argument, but she relinquished her keys and stood back to wait until he completed his inspection. He left her at the door the signing of her statement all but forgotten.

All done, he handed back her keys. A spark of something on her skin fled through his veins. Pure heat. He'd leave her be until he could figure out what the strange rush of electricity was all about.

Tomorrow was another day.

I felt the surge of heat sparked by the meeting of our flesh. Again. The keys felt warm from his skin, but I didn't think it would've caused the spark. He turned to leave. Somehow, his departure seemed wrong. He'd saved my life and here I allowed him to drop me off at my door as if we'd merely been out for a walk.

"Agent Westin?"

He turned at the top of the stairs. "You'll have to call me Logan, you know. Or I'll stick with Miss Odel."

I nodded. He waited.

"Would you like to come in? I'm pretty sure a hot cup of something is in order."

He still hesitated.

He came toward me and laid a hand on my arm. "You should be okay, Kailin. If you're concerned about being alone, I'll put a car outside. Just say the word."

I was disappointed. Why, I wasn't sure. Still, I hoped he'd come in. I shook my head. The great Wraith-hunter incapable of holding a simple conversation. Ridiculous.

CHAPTER 16

The doorbell rang later that evening and I opened up, expecting to see Logan. He'd forgotten to get me to sign the statement. Instead, I got a smiling Jess. A Jess who'd been overshadowed by Logan. I'd barely registered the other woman before and got the distinct impression it had been Jess's choice, and not my weak attention span for people in the immediate vicinity of the delectable Logan Westin.

"Hi. Is Logan with you?" I glanced down the hall, still expecting the brute to follow his partner into the apartment.

"No. No, I thought we'd better have a...discussion." Jess walked in and made for the sofa. She seated herself before I could suggest it, but I took no offense at all. Her beauty would knock anyone off their feet. And I was certainly knocked.

Strange she would want to talk to me in private. I scanned her face. No telltale signs. Nothing. At all. How was it possible for a person not to register any emotion in their face? Then I picked up a strange scent. I'd followed her to the living room but remained standing with one sofa between us.

Sweetness filled my mind, seeping into my skin, intoxicating. Divine.

I snapped open drowsy eyes that had drifted slowly to a close.

A Titan. I'd heard of the effect they had on Humans. Clearly, they had a similar if milder effect on Walkers.

"Don't be alarmed, please." The voice was soft, gentle. "There is something you should know."

"What do you want with me?" I was a little scared. Titans were massively important in the scheme of things. I was a puny nobody next to a Titan, and having one stand in the middle of my living room was not conducive to my personal calm and serenity.

"I am here to watch over you, however indirect it may seem." Another enigmatic answer, with a matching smile.

"Why would a Titan take the time to watch over a mere Walker like me?" As agitated as I was, I still found myself inexplicably calm. Something she was doing to me perhaps? Titans had unknown powers, beyond anything mortals could understand. How far would I get trying to bully a Titan into telling me what I wanted to know? At any rate I needed an answer.

"You are more important than you realize."

"So you knew about me then? The first time we met?" She nodded serenely, not commenting on the subject change. "And didn't tell anyone I was a Walker? Why?"

"It is not my place to become involved with the workings of your life. I am here to guide you when I am required to, to ensure you remain on the right path."

It took a while to absorb what she was saying. The fact I was speaking to a living breathing Titan was enough to have me breathless, but knowing she was deliberately placed into my life was worse.

"I came to tell you that you can trust Logan. You can trust him to help you. It is what he is meant to do. It is his purpose."

"Me? His purpose is to help me? Sounds a bit melodramatic."

"Kailin, I know you are the Hunter. Ni'amh – it is what we call you."

"You have a name for me?" I was befuddled and slightly impressed. "What do you mean 'The' Hunter?"

"Yes. Ni'amh is a Hunter well known in our prophecies." Jess nodded and even the simple action looked wise. "You are the one foretold, who will help defeat the New Army of Wrythiin."

I frowned. She stopped making sense with the word 'foretold'. I shook my head.

"Please, hear me out."

For some reason I couldn't explain, I was filled with foreboding. As if I knew what she was about to tell me and I knew it wasn't going to be good. When I remained silent she continued.

"The prophecies say when the veil begins to shred, the creatures of Wrythiin shall slowly regain their strength. The Cat shall lead the fight and cut them to the quick, but without the help of the Mages and all earthbound Ethereals, her fight will be for naught."

I was puzzled by everything but her mention of the shredded Veil.

"Are you talking about the Veil between the worlds?" Jess's nod was sharp. "It has changed recently. When they—when the Wraiths died, they used to swirl up to the atmosphere like they were looking for a way out. Now the shadows just circle around and disappear into nothing, almost like they're escaping through tiny holes."

Jess nodded, as if she had expected such strange news.

"I trust that you will call me should you need me?" She handed me her card, so similar to Logan's. With a slight nod, she walked to the door, leaving me wondering if she realized she'd left me more confused than ever.

STARK WHITE LIGHT shivered above me. Bare fluorescent tubes ran in neat lines along the high ceiling above the platform. Anjelo had a way with wires and brought life to the abandoned darkness of the disused train tunnels. The power was most likely redirected from a few surrounding buildings. Steel turnstiles squeaked as stragglers joined the growing crowd milling around the platform.

I'd been here many times since the Clan had drawn me in. Often enough to be oblivious to the tattered movie posters dangling from walls, shuddering on intermittent rushes of air from the stairwell. Or the barren, rusted vending machines lining the graffiti-covered walls pilfered like tombs for their treasure and left as a stark reminder that nothing lasts forever.

The station, unused for decades, abandoned by the city council, became the perfect hideout for City Deep's growing membership. Away from prying eyes, it contained a rabbit warren of old train tunnels lurking beneath the city. From here, we moved around the city with ease. This subway beneath Chicago's streets had once formed part of the historic Chicago Loop.

People, silent and expectant, filled the platform. Anjelo and Storm sat at my side in the eye of this tornado. Lily stood a foot behind Anjelo as though on guard. City Deep was a motley crew of Walkers and Humans, and others whose powers seemed, even now, so unreal to me. Storm's work with these people had saved them from the streets, given them a better life. He sometimes seemed larger than life to me. Now, I sensed those entrancing eyes could see right into my soul.

Unnerving.

Made me fear he could see the blood on my hands. I steeled myself against the urge to wipe them on the front of my jeans as we waited for the last few people to arrive.

I began to wonder if revealing the information to the gang was a mistake, when Arthur, a Walker who had been with the gang for over a year, raised his hand awkwardly, directing his question at me.

"Who was he?" Seemed some of City Deep's population had gotten wind of the killing already.

"We don't know. Yet," Storm responded, his voice calm, invoking calm.

Everyone began to speak at once, their voices echoing along the bare platform and disappearing down the pair of gaping holes at the end of the track. Storm stood, hands outstretched, urging the group to quiet down. Many here knew nothing of what we were talking about and were getting impatient.

"Thanks for coming, everyone. We're very sorry about calling you here so suddenly, but it *is* an emergency." He didn't wait too long before giving the gathering a rundown of the body dump in the garden and his possible genetic identity. The revelation sent the group into a buzz and I stopped Anjelo as he inhaled to cut into their voiced concerns.

They needed to feel the community spirit. This was not a pack, but they had a pack spirit. Storm let his words sink in before saying, "The first thing we need is a head count."

"You mean like a census?" a voice piped.

"Yes. Exactly like a census." Storm nodded. "Then we will know if anyone is missing and who they are." Storm scanned the room. "If there is anyone you have not seen in a few days, contact them, make sure they are fine, and let me know either way."

The group conferred in tiny bunches and came up with a handful of names, agreeing to check them all out immediately.

Storm spoke again. "There is danger out there. Danger we still have to identify. So far it is a danger to the Walkers only because this victim is a Walker. We don't know anything else. But we need to be careful. The Deep may be more at risk, just because we have this... integrated clan. Because we all live so close together, and if the killer is targeting Walkers, there is a chance he could make a mistake. On the other hand, if the killer isn't targeting Walkers specifically then everyone is in danger. Either way we all need to be very careful." Storm's concern hung heavy in the crowd. The last thing he needed was to instill a fear for the Walkers within the population. There were factions that would use this as the opportunity to split the clan. But, I could see he had no choice. They had to be aware of the danger.

"What's the police doing about it?" a woman called from the center of the throng, black eyes flashing with suspicion.

"So far, they're following the normal procedures—forensic investigation, questioning the community, things like that," I answered taking my cue when Storm nodded at me.

"Can they tell? That the dead guy is a SkinWalker?" The question had hung in the air, and even though I didn't want to admit it to myself, I knew the answer and couldn't lie to them.

"We'll know more once the autopsy is done, but they'll figure out something's different. We have the animal inside us. It'll be in our genes. They'll do the blood tests, find the anomalies and then—"

"Then they'll search the city, ripping it wide open until they find every one of you people." He'd remained silent until now. Samuel Collins leaned against a wall at the back of the crowd, one foot against the wall. He casually cleaned his fingernails with the blade of a small knife, head down, face hidden by a fall of oily black hair. If I hadn't recognized the voice, it would've seemed like he hadn't spoken.

"They don't know anything yet. We may be able to avoid it by being careful. And by looking out for each other." Anjelo's last words held a hard edge, a message to Samuel—his opinion was not the only one that counted.

"I've always said something like this would happen. These abominations will be our ruin." Samuel's rant began to take on an evangelical quality as he faced the crowd and spewed his thoughts. His position at the rear of the crowd had been deliberate. The whole group had turned to him when he spoke. The entire gathering now focused on him instead of Anjelo.

Samuel, one of the more abrasive clan members, often vocalized his distrust of paranormals, including the Walkers. Scarier yet was the fact he had scored a few followers. They stood at the front of the group, amen-ing his claims as he spoke, staring at his face twisted with an enraged fervor, which seemed to incite any underlying prejudices the listeners may have. Samuel had been one of the oldest homeless people taken in by Storm and despite his dislike of paranormals, had remained with City Deep, probably for the comfort and security Storm provided. He liked to stir trouble when the opportunity presented itself.

Usually Storm quelled his rages. I looked at him on the other side of Anjelo.

He eyed Samuel beneath a fringe of thick lashes, as if contemplating the heated words, yet allowed the man to pour out the venom. My fear was Collins would infect other susceptible members, but Storm seemed unconcerned. In fact, most of the crowd now seemed not to react much to Samuel's voice or his words, as if they barely heard the words at all.

I watched Storm and my skin tingled as a premonitory feeling filled me. I was about to witness something strange and amazing. Storm turned to me when Samuel's voice came to a sudden stop, as if he ran out of breath and things to say all at once. Storm smiled a knowing expression. I wanted to ask him what he'd done, but it wasn't the time or the place.

Anjelo began fielding questions from the chattering group, while I succumbed to my thoughts. Samuel's words rang in my head. From blood tests and the unique gene capable of identifying the Walkers and whatever hematological studies those blood samples would undergo, to the frightening possibility of what may lie in store for Walkers should the news of our existence become public knowledge.

My heart knocked against my chest, the sound vibrating through my ribs. My blood would also be among those samples sent to the labs.

They'd soon figure out the identity of the second person who'd been shot on the scene and Agent Westin would be knocking on my door. I wondered how I'd feel about seeing him again. The twist in my heart confirmed the hurt was still raw.

I wondered if his team would figure it out. Come straight for me. I feared their treatment of me. Humans were not known for their compassion for things they didn't understand. They'd been afraid of Magyk—so afraid they burned people they feared possessed such abominable power. What would they do if they knew Walkers existed? I refused to think about it and focused on the room and the people clamoring for answers to their questions.

THE CROWD DISPERSED QUICKLY and soon only Anjelo, Lily and myself remained. I stayed on the aluminum seat, giving the couple some privacy as they stood near the platform's edge, expecting them to leave with the rest.

"I hope you're happy now." Lily's sharp words jarred my reverie. I'd been thinking about obsidian eyes and electric touches.

"What?"

"All you think about is yourself. Did you even stop to think you may be endangering Anjelo?" Lily closed the distance between us and jabbed her finger at my chest. She was dangerously close to getting herself knocked on her ass. One look at Anjelo confirmed he knew exactly what would happen if she didn't get out of my face. Soon. He gripped her arm and tugged her back.

"Lily. Shut up before you say something that gets you in trouble."

"Do you seriously think I'm afraid of your goody-two-shoes Alpha princess?" She threw his arm off and déjà vu struck. I'd done the very same to Logan last night. Lily turned on me again. "Just because you're an Alpha doesn't give you the right to traipse around, endangering other people. Who do you think you are?"

"Lily, get a hold of yourself. You're beginning to sound crazy. Who does Kailin think she is? You really want to know?" He rounded on her, not bothering to wait for her to respond. "Kailin is *my* Alpha."

Lily's face paled. But only for a few seconds.

"So what? You aren't in your clan anymore. She has no right to endanger you like this. Just because she always gets her pampered way doesn't mean you need to be at her beck and call." Garish splotches of color dotted her pale face.

Usually an attractive blonde, Lily's stress showed. Sure, Anjelo had been in a tiny bit of danger while helping me, but I'd called him after and he sounded fine. My heart still tap-danced in my throat, and I recognized the familiar stab of disappointment beneath my layers of emotional armor. I wasn't easily liked. I didn't make friends quickly, either.

Grow up. Not everyone has to like you.

Still, no sense in denying my disappointment. Involving Anjelo in my mess could jeopardize his relationship. Regardless of Lily hating my guts, I wouldn't dare cause Anjelo any pain.

I turned and left. Confrontation usually got me in terrific trouble. I'd had the pleasure of providing a couple of bullying schoolmates with well-deserved bloody noses. Now, the platform behind me lay silent. At least Lily's venom ran its course for the moment. I understood her fear well enough. She was protecting someone she cared for, and for a scary second, I envied Anjelo.

I gritted my teeth as emotion burned in my throat. Going home alone again. Guess it was Fate.

CHAPTER 17

Logan sighed as he finished reading the lab reports. The dining table of Omega's Chicago apartment was littered with reports and photographs.

Jess said, "Yes, I believe I felt a similar frustration to you when I read the report."

"It's strange. Why would the bullets match? This means the shooters who left the body in the garden are the same ones who shot at Kailin. Are they trying to kill her or frighten her off?" Logan rubbed his forehead and scraped his fingers through his hair.

"Do you think Miss Odel was the target all along and perhaps she is lying to you about not being in the garden when the body was dumped?" Jess's face gave away nothing of her own opinion.

"It's very likely." Logan nodded. "What if she witnessed the body being left in the garden and the killers saw her and tried to get rid of her? She'd hardly be inclined to share that information with us, would she?"

"And the second shooting would no doubt mean she knows she is a target and-"

"And that means she's even less likely to share information

with me." Logan groaned. Interacting with the enigmatic Kailin Odel wasn't all fun and games. She was a decidedly frustrating woman. And she was hiding something from him. Whatever it was he meant to find out.

Logan leaned forward and scanned the paperwork. The initial tests had found a drug in the victim's blood, that much they knew already. The toxicology report had finally arrived. Results confirmed. Neurotoxins capable of affecting brain function in a Walker regardless of species.

A drug in the system of the dead SkinWalker meant a substance on the streets that could drug a Walker. Something their background checks had claimed was not possible. No known drug had ever been able to knock out a Walker of any clan. Now they had proof such a drug existed and was infiltrating the streets. The papers Logan held in his hand were quite clear— the drug was instantaneously addictive.

Logan rubbed his eyes. "But I thought there were no drugs on the market capable of affecting a Walker."

"Apparently not. We have this." Jess held out another file. "Murdoch has pulled some files for us. Word on the street is there is a drug invading the clubs."

Logan flipped through the file. "Well, we can't know if the victim used the drug for pleasure or if the killer used it to subdue the victim. Whatever the drug is, it wasn't in the victim's blood for very long. So either it's something the killer gave him to knock him out. Or the victim had taken the drug and been abducted very soon after." He sighed again, frustrated. Then he spoke almost to himself. "A drug that's addictive to a Walker... That's huge."

"So far it has just been a rumor, but it seems to fit."

Logan nodded. "Yeah, not likely for a Walker to go to the police and complain about drugs that suddenly have the power to waste them. But if it's already known there is a drug in supply, then this tox report may link the drug to the killer." Then he went silent for a moment. "What we need is an undercover Walker."

"Someone to infiltrate the clubs?" asked Jess.

"Yeah, someone to flush out the dealers." Logan felt adrenaline surge through his veins. This was something they could actually do, as opposed to just reviewing lab reports and banking on rumors "Do we even have Walkers in Omega? I haven't met any yet."

"We do." Jess nodded. "But not many. They don't trust humans easily. So they like to keep their interaction to the minimum. I will see if we can bring one in." Jess was already pulling her phone out to make the call.

Logan rose and grabbed his jacket from the stand behind the door. "I'm going to pay our target a little visit."

LOGAN POKED AT THE DOORBELL. It barely rang before the door opened.

Kailin gave him a cool smile. "Agent Westin. What can I do for you today?"

He raised an eyebrow at the formality, but then recalled his abrupt departure from his last visit. "I never did get that signature."

"Must have been the exploding tires and flying bullets that distracted you," Kailin said as she opened the door wider and waved him in. For a moment Logan stood inside the door, unsure of how much he should say. "Please come in and have a seat. Maybe you can have that something hot you declined the other day?"

"I'd love that." Logan saw a flash of something in her eyes as he spoke. Had she been disappointed he hadn't stayed last time? His stomach clenched with the memory of that night. He'd wanted to stay. Really wanted to. But she was possibly witness to a crime. The last thing he needed was to blur the lines between work and emotion.

He grabbed a stool at the kitchen counter and waited while she pottered about making coffee.

"So where do I sign?" Kailin asked as she set his steaming mug on the table in front of him.

Logan drew a rolled-up file from his jacket pocket and removed a sheet of paper. He slid it across to her and fished inside his pocket again for a pen. "Take your time and read it again if you like."

When Kailin picked up the pen and leaned forward to sign the statement Logan said, "Are you sure there's nothing in there that you want to change?"

Kailin's head shot up and her shoulders went stiff. Her eyes narrowed, tension fairly radiated off her. "What do you mean? I told you everything I knew."

"I just want to be sure. New evidence has come to light that makes me consider you a possible target. You may be in danger."

"What do you mean 'new evidence'?"

"We've had the bullet test results back. We also compared the bullets from the garden to the ones from the day you were shot at." Logan swallowed, keeping his eyes on Kailin's face as the blood drained from it. He'd give anything to know what she was thinking. "The bullets match. We can confirm that at least one of the shooters from both nights is the same person. Is there anything you need to tell me?"

She hesitated, fear tightening her features. "No. No, I told you everything I know."

"Kailin, we have proof that the people who tried to kill you are the same as from the night of the body dump." Logan leaned forward and asked softly, "Were they shooting at you?"

"No, of course not." She threw her shoulders back, an air of confidence slipped over her face, controlled and calm. She looked down at the statement and scribbled her signature without the slightest hesitation. Logan had to give her credit for getting herself back under control.

"Well if you do want to make any changes to the statement you can always call me." He laid a card on the table. He'd given her one already but he knew people rarely hung on to them unless they were already of the mind to contact him.

She picked it up and frowned. "So what exactly is this 'Omega'? Sounds a bit ominous, like FBI or CIA but stranger."

Logan wanted to smile. She was pretty astute. Although the card didn't use the word 'paranormal' the very name lent itself to the unusual. "You're close. You could say we're like the FBI for the strange."

"For strange what?" She scowled as she asked the question.

"Strange, unusual happenings. Weird things that go bump in the night."

Kailin laughed but she couldn't hide the strident pitch of the sound that said he'd touched a nerve. She knew more than she was telling and her reaction made him fairly certain she wasn't one of the totally blind humans who had no idea Paranormals even existed.

"Strange, unusual and weird. Doesn't seem like that's much of a job," she said, looking down at the card again. Then she placed it beside the telephone on the counter.

"You'd be surprised. Just today we received confirmation of a strange drug that's infiltrating the Chicago streets."

"Aren't there always drugs on the street?"

"Yeah, but remember I deal with the strange and unusual and this drug affects a group of people who throughout history have been known to be unaffected by either drugs or alcohol."

Kailin's eyes widened. He'd hit a nerve. "I guess you're right then. Those would be pretty strange people. Isn't everyone affected by drugs and alcohol? And even caffeine?" She lifted her mug and took a sip.

Logan figured he wasn't going to get anything further from

her. "In any case, I will make sure you are safe. Call me if you need to go out and I'll send an officer with you."

She shook her head and came around the counter to stand beside him. She looked about ready to throw him out the door. "That's very generous of you, but I can take care of myself."

Logan rose to his feet, and was suddenly nearer to her than he'd expected. He hadn't realized she stood so close, but he certainly wasn't complaining.

His proximity charged the air between us; my body tensed in response. Energy simmered in the slim space between our bodies. Heat and electricity swirled. Time turned on itself or stood still. I wasn't sure.

He didn't back away. Why wasn't he backing away? And for that matter, why wasn't I backing away? I hadn't realized how close I'd stood to him. At the time I'd just wanted to get him out of my apartment, my head spinning with matching bullets and strange drugs and my name on someone's hit list.

I swallowed hard and would've taken a step back, but he curled his hand around my neck. Any resistance I had crumbled into nothing. He lowered his head, incapable as I was of resisting the pull.

Our lips touched, a brief meeting of the softest flesh and the most heated of breaths. I melted against him. Fire raced through my veins when he deepened the kiss. Our bodies drew closer, fitting so well nothing could get between us. My heart pounded in my chest and I ignored my Panther as it clawed for release.

Both wanting more, we drew closer. Too close to the edge not to jump. Hot breath mingled and heartbeats thundered between us. And, just as suddenly, white-hot energy surged from his mouth, through my veins, searing me alive. It filled my body, a delicate burn, strong, powerful but gentle as it surged through my veins.

Then I was pushed back, away from him, repelled by some invisible energy rush. I frowned. What a strange thing. Like an electric shock but duller and more powerful.

I should've welcomed the abrupt end to our interlude. I didn't need this complication in my life. But what was with the weird heat? My nerves still tingled with the remnants of it.

He stared at me, his face filled with remorse and regret.

And fear.

Great, all I had to do was kiss a guy and he ran for the hills. Nice going, Odel.

I backed against the wall, hoping I'd reached the door and be able to retain some composure.

"I'm sorry. That shouldn't have happened." Logan reached for my arm.

I jerked his hand off me, shaking my head. "No need to be sorry. I'm pretty exhausted after all this excitement. Think I'll get some z's." I injected a little bit of light-and-breezy into my voice hoping he'd assume this incident was nothing I'd get all upset about.

"I'm not sure what just happened. Did I hurt you?" His face twisted with concern. But I didn't care. It wasn't often I got close to someone, especially in an intimate way. And I'd just been rebuffed. Wonderful. I wanted to crawl into a dark place and lick my wounds. All my wounds. Including the newest one traced across my heart courtesy of Agent Westin.

Suck it up. It was a mistake. Move on.

"I'm fine, Logan. And thank you. You saved my life, I won't forget." Chin up, voice clear. I sounded pretty convincing.

Logan scowled; maybe he still worried about the flare of energy blasting both our bodies seconds before. I'd rather forget the incident. There wouldn't be a repeat of said activity. Lesson learned.

My searching fingers found the doorknob and I almost flung

it open. "Thank you for coming." He was still standing beside the counter. "Oh, and don't forget your statement."

He grabbed the paper and shoved it into the file. Then he walked toward me, rolling it up and stuffing it back into his pocket, all the while looking a little uncomfortable, a little lost, and a little afraid. What did he need to be afraid for?

He paused at the doorway. "Lock up tight. Be careful and don't go anywhere alone." Back to being the professional.

With that he turned and walked out of the apartment.

Yeah, I'd learned my lesson all right.

CHAPTER 18

I answered Storm's summons, eager to have a possible face and name for the unknown, nameless skinless Walker.

I headed off to Giorgio's, everyone's favorite Italian restaurant, entering the softly lit eatery and walking into a tangible blanket of smells that made my mouth water.

Smiling at the dutiful maître-d, I thanked him and held onto my jacket and bag when he tried to take them away. I slid into the empty chair in front of Anjelo and Storm, stashing my backpack, still loaded with drug-filled vials and steel bow, at my feet. I was much more comfortable knowing it sat a toenail away.

"Right, what gives?" I raised an eyebrow at Storm, hoping he had some solid information for me.

"All the chapters have called in their counts. Anjelo did some legwork for me. We have a couple of names, and only one possible." The table remained silent as a waiter appeared at my elbow and filled a glass with ice water. I waited for him to leave then sipped the cool liquid, wishing Storm would hurry up and spill. Better drinking than biting my nails.

Storm nodded at Anjelo to continue. My young friend was

turning into Storm's little protégé and I had to admit I liked it. With Anjelo in his last year at school I needed to know he was going to move on to a good career. Storm had helped me get into university and I knew he meant to look after Anjelo's studies too. "We have four missing persons in total, over the whole Chicago basin." Given the incredibly high rates of crime within the downtown Chicago area alone, that number was pretty tiny. City Deep must be doing something right to keep its members safe. "Two Humans. A drifter, Frank somebody. Been AWOL a whole week. The second Human is female, a drug patient, may even be one of yours."

He slipped a photograph, crumpled and greasy, across the table. "No, not one of my clients."

"That leaves only two Walkers, Jeremy Ryan and Sal Odenzi. Ryan's a Cougar. Odenzi's a Wolf."

"Right, that leaves us with Ryan then," I replied, looking at Storm. "Forgive me for stating the obvious, but this seems far too easy." How well organized was Storm's clan, that he could obtain this kind of information within one night?

"Why would you want such a thing to be difficult? I have been overseeing City Deep for a long, long time. Anjelo and his team were efficient to say the least. And with such a danger looming we met with little resistance to our census," said Storm, his voice its usual musical baritone, managing to be both sexy and annoying at the same time.

"Sorry, I guess I expected it to be a little more difficult to identify him."

Storm watched me with enigmatic eyes. I wriggled in my seat and I wished he would direct those gorgeous baby-blues elsewhere. Thankfully, Anjelo cut through my discomfort.

"He was last seen by his friends going to a popular club. Well, maybe 'friends' is too strong a word. He's only been around a couple of months."

So the dead Walker was a newcomer to town. Did he step on the wrong toes? Or just in the wrong place at the right time?

"Well, any ideas on where he came from?" Both Anjelo and Storm shook their heads in unison. Guess that's the part Storm's clan census had missed.

"The nearest Cougar Clan is not far. I believe they are up near Geneva Lake?" If Storm thought he was being helpful, he certainly didn't know Justin, Alpha of said clan, very well.

"No. No bloody way." I held my hands up, ready to rise and wash them of everything.

"You're the only one who would be able to get a quick audience." Anjelo's voice rumbled low, while he watched me for a reaction. He looked about ready to run from the table if I so much as coughed in his direction.

"Oh? And why's that?" Let him spell it out for me, the cheeky sod.

"You're an Alpha, Kailin. You want to be difficult, don't you? He'll allow you an immediate audience. He has to afford you the respect."

I sat back and chewed my lip. Anjelo was right. Alphas traded a certain level of respect amongst each other. For once, my status would make things easier for me to speak to Justin about the murdered Walker. But I was not about to go there alone. "Well, if I have to go, then so do you, my friend."

"Kailin, I'll be eaten alive." Anjelo paled. I'd probably cause him more trouble with Lily. Likely cause myself an equal amount of hassle with her as well.

"Oh. Stop being such a drama queen. I'll protect you, as long as you behave."

I caught what looked suspiciously like a smile curving Storm's mouth. *Well. What do you know. The guy has a sense of humor.* Even though he'd helped me over the years and knew my Grams, I didn't get too many opportunities to come face to face with

Storm. Thrown into proximity with him recently, I seemed to be learning something new about him every day.

For one moment I considered telling them what Logan had revealed—that I was a target. Then I stopped. We had enough going on right now, didn't need to start breaking out Operation Protect Kailin. Besides, I could take care of myself.

I glanced at Anjelo. "Come on then."

"Can't I at least finish my spaghetti?" He cast a forlorn eye over his plate.

"Fine, eat your din-dins and let's get out of here fast. I have things to do."

JUSTIN LAKE HAD a reputation for being tough—a real guy's guy. Iain had other more eloquent and less ladylike words for him. Alphas weren't easy to deal with; this I knew from a lifetime of experience with my father and brother.

And Alphas, in turn, afforded each other a special respect. I was in no position to go in with guns blazing.

I stopped and looked around. This was Cougar territory and here we were, the trespassers, a pair of Black Panthers blatantly trespassing. Most of the feline packs considered us freaks. Not surprising considering we were the most powerful feline clan around.

The gene anomaly that gave our pelts their blackened hue resembled the abnormality in the albino cats. They too were considered outcasts, but more readily accepted due to their mostly non-violent natures.

Justin would have a perimeter guard out. Iain had always spoken of his military precision with a certain admiration. I borrowed my Panther ears, allowed them to soften and lengthen. I caught a slight rustling as guards moved in the trees around me. Over Anjelo's annoyingly loud breathing, that is. He kept a few paces back, but his panting could've woken the dead.

The guards' breathing hummed, low and soft—trained to blend into the foliage. But I could scent them as well as they could scent us. And they never hid their presence, allowing us to locate them. I wasn't intimidated. I glanced at my bumbling, reluctant companion, certain if Anjelo became aware we were being watched, he'd give off sloughing waves of fear that would entice them to us, inviting them in for the kill.

Four guards emerged before I got to the edge of the grounds, emanating waves of pure animosity. The rigid set of their shoulders meant they could smell the Alpha in me. Probably the only reason I still stood in one piece.

They approached me two on each side. Tough guys. I'd brought my bow along for the ride, my backpack nestling it close to my body. Even unarmed, I was not afraid. I could take them, and from the wary glances they exchanged, I knew they knew it too.

They slowed their approach, their steps cautious.

Anjelo came crashing through the brush, complicating the serious nature of the meeting. I sidestepped off the path, hoping he wouldn't crash into me. I could hardly be intimidating while lying at their feet.

One of them, tall, bulky with a shock of red gold hair, stepped in front of me, eye to eye, paying no heed as Anjelo came to a skidding halt beside me.

"Who are you, and what do you want? This is Lake's land." His jaw clenched… relaxed. Clenched again.

"I am Kailin Odel, Panther Clan. I need to speak to Justin—it's urgent." A copper eyebrow rose. Indifferent. I squelched a sigh. I was in for a hard time.

"Follow me." He turned on his heel and stalked toward a large house flanked by a dozen modest homes on either side. It had the feel of a modern housing development. Pretty place Lake had carved out for himself here. Their protectiveness made sense.

They waved me into a small front room, a reception area of

sorts, while Anjelo remained on the porch, guarded by Red. There I sat for a full ten minutes without any further attention. I'd expected someone to come back—at least to say how long Justin would be.

I hated waiting. Unless I was hunting. Then I savored the anticipation. Now I fidgeted until I finally gave up and left the room. I crossed the hall and walked straight into a large sitting room, empty except for one rather large male Cougar.

"I wondered how long you'd be." He smiled, a hint of white teeth glittered and I wondered what his canines would look like fully formed.

"Well, I didn't want to offend you by barging in." I retorted, hardly ready to apologize for the intrusion. And happily taking in the sight of the blond Walker, all broad shoulders and toned muscle.

"You just did." He gave me a wry smile.

"I have other stops to make. If I stay here any longer, I'll be late getting back home."

"So, Kailin of the Panther clan, what's this matter of urgency you need to speak of?"

He watched and listened as I recounted my discovery of the body and its condition.

"So what's it to me?" Justin leaned back, the chair squeaking its protest.

"The victim was a Cougar. I scented his pack in his blood." A vision of the flayed face hovered before me and I squeezed my eyes shut. No weakness. Not now.

Justin leaned forward in his chair. I could smell his awareness.

"And you waited this long to let us know?" His eyes glittered.

"I found out who he was in the last couple of hours. And you happen to be my first stop. I wanted to tell you face-to-face. Not some impersonal phone call telling you one of your pack mates has just been murdered." I leaned in, hands on the table. We faced each other, mere inches apart.

"When did you find this body?"

"The night before last. Around eleven."

"And it took this long to find out who he was?"

"Listen, Justin. The body was skinned, not an inch of flesh was left. We had no way of identifying him until a count was done and someone figured out they hadn't seen him for a few days." I found it so difficult to say his name—Jeremy. It was easier for me to continue thinking of the body as just a body, and not a person.

Coward.

"Who's next on your list?"

"Byron, then Iain."

"Left your brother for last?" He punctuated the question with a curve of his eyebrow.

"Yes. Is that not acceptable to you?" I barely checked my attitude at his snippy tone.

Why did he care what order I was visiting the packs? I refused to participate in some male pissing contest.

"Anyone missing in the last few days?"

"This is a free society. I don't control the movements of everyone in the colony." Justin avoided my eyes. He knew something and wasn't ready to share.

"Did you send someone down to the city? Jeremy Ryan?"

Justin stilled, taking his time to answer.

"We aren't obligated to you just because you gave us the information."

"No, you're not obligated, but head counts are being done across all the packs. The first victim may have been a Cougar, but there may be others we don't know about yet. We can't take any chances. He may not be from around here at all. He may be from the Deep. Who knows? We need to be more vigilant until this scumbag is caught."

"Fine. I'll get a count done and call you." He hesitated. "Okay, Kailin, I owe you this at least." Justin shoved his chair back, as if suddenly uncomfortable. "Jeremy was one of ours. We haven't heard from him in a while. We'd assumed he'd 'defected.'" A wry laugh.

"What was he doing? Infiltrating our Clan?" I was bristling with anger. The nerve of them.

"It's wrong. Clans are of one people. Not a mishmash of every pack around, thrown in with Mages and Humans. It's not right." Justin turned, raking me with a glare so icy I knew he believed every prejudiced word that fell from his lips.

"We *are* one people. We have a common need—community. There are those who are not happy with this integration, and they have the right to voice their opinion. The Deep is a combination of all the people within the city who need help and need a society where their own has failed them."

"A bunch of misfits then?"

"Yep, and proud of it." I smiled. "Oh and there's something else. I've been told there's a drug on the streets that may be addictive to Walkers. Know anything about that?"

Justin stared at me, his face tight. "What? You know that's not possible, Kai."

"Yeah but I had to ask. There's no solid proof as yet. Just rumor. But if you hear anything please let me know." He nodded.

I turned to leave and threw a glance back at him again.

"Why do you still hate each other?" I asked.

He remained silent at first, cogs turning in his head. "You should ask him." Justin shook his head. "Just leave it, Kai. It was a long time ago, and hate leaves canyons of pain in its wake."

"Is it worth it?" I wanted to know, simply because I'd seen the same loss and longing in my brother's eyes when he spoke of Justin. "Wouldn't Sonia want you two to be happy?"

He rose and came to stand before me. Should I be afraid of this large Walker?

"It's complicated."

"So is life." I looked up at his strong, yet gentle face. "You were friends for so long."

"The best of friends," he whispered, his words soft, reminiscent. I wished so badly they would at least try to rekindle that friendship. Shattered by the death of a sister and a wife, I didn't believe it should stay that way. Sonia would've wanted them to be there for each other.

Justin read it all in my eyes, and I was glad when he opened the door and let me out without a word.

After my run-in with Justin, all I wanted was to go back home. Knowing Justin for the better part of my life had certainly not given me any prior understanding of the man. I hated the bad blood that simmered between Iain and Justin. Sonia's ghost still shimmered between them. Iain's wife; Justin's sister. And Justin blamed my brother for Sonia's death. Or maybe for not being the one to die instead of Sonia.

DONE WITH JUSTIN, I headed off to meet Byron Teague. Wolf Alpha, and danger personified. His pack happened to be the largest wolf pack in the state of Illinois, which pretty much made him the big cheese of Wolf Alphas for miles around. As much as my instinct told me to turn and run, I owed it to him to clue him in. Especially after what happened to Jeremy. If the killer was after a SkinWalker, all Walkers were in danger.

I looked over at Anjelo as we stepped out of Cougar territory onto a safer, uncontrolled portion of the mountainside. Emotions spun in his eyes, a carousel of relief, gratitude and waning fear. I felt like a total heel to have to put an end to his happy smile.

"We have to speak to Byron." I hadn't mentioned a visit to the Wolf Prime, knowing it would elicit a bad reaction. SkinWalker packs tended to be just as prejudiced as Humans, and the canine-feline divide was often more insurmountable.

The smile faded slowly from his lips, followed quickly enough by his eyes.

"You know, I always knew you were a bit...strange." He tapped the side of his head and glared at me. "But I never thought I would see the confirmation that you were crazy. You have any idea how dangerous that will be? It won't matter that you're an Alpha. You're a damned feline Alpha, and that makes you prey. You are friggin' insane."

It always paid to allow Anjelo's ravings to run its course, so I let him continue with his tirade, uninterrupted. After a while, he ran out of points to consider, ran out of fingers to tick off with reasons why this was a very bad idea.

"If you go to Byron, I won't go with you."

"Who said you were invited?" My question caught him in a twist of comical surprise.

"Fine, I'm going home." He brushed past me, the air around him reeking of damaged ego.

"Home?" I squelched my giggle. He did look amusing, pursing his lips in annoyance.

"Yes. I'm going to see my mother." He rounded on me, as if to continue the line of thought with a well-placed insult and stopped. And I loved him all the more for it.

It would've been so easy, caught up in anger and annoyance, to jab me on the lack of my mother's presence. But Anjelo had stopped. Even in the heat of anger, my feelings came first, and I felt a rush of love toward my friend and ally.

"I'll meet you there. After I see Byron."

Anjelo had no choice but to walk away. Fear and ego were not happy bedfellows.

Unlike Angelo, I had nothing to fear from the Wolf Pack. Byron would see me out of respect to my brother and father, if not out of respect to me as an Alpha.

CHAPTER 19

The Wolf-Walker colony nestled in the foothills of the valley, over the next ridge. One might consider the proximity of the feline and canine colonies an invitation to danger, but both colonies were policed well enough to ensure neither group sought each other out. Anjelo was wrong to be so concerned for my safety. Or perhaps it was his own chicken-skin he was afraid of losing. Either way, we would've traveled relatively unharmed, straight to Byron's lair.

And although I'd expected Byron would be less than helpful, his lack of interest in our predicament bordered on insult. Unlike the Cougars, these guys wasted no time in bringing me to their Master. I was marched right up to the edge of Byron's desk, where I waited, flanked by two of his most muscle-bound guards. I gritted my teeth at the invasion of my personal space, at their uncouth treatment, but thought it wisest to bite my tongue.

"Give me one good reason why I should give a hoot? It's a Cougar problem, not a Wolf one." He spoke the words, clear he considered Cougars and other Walkers of a similar ilk, to be nothing higher than a cockroach on his version of the food chain.

"The killer may not only be targeting feline Walkers, Byron. He hasn't established a pattern yet." Déjà vu anyone.

No response there.

"We'll get involved if and when we are convinced it's necessary."

"So will you at least do a head count?"

I was beginning to feel a little dizzy. What was it with these damned Alphas? It seemed to be a sore point when they were asked to count the members of their colonies. Or perhaps they didn't take kindly to a female giving them orders.

"Every pack in the Chicago basin is, at this moment, processing their colonies, ensuring they know where everyone is. Are you telling me some stupid racial prejudice means you won't do the responsible thing because the cats are doing it?"

I was so disgusted with his childish behavior I barely registered the words as they left my mouth. Barely registered Byron as he flashed toward me, claws drawn on huge hairy paws, each easily the size of my head. Then the room tilted. I was falling. I'd expected my head to crash in the polished redwood, and when the crunch of my skull on the wood did not come, I found myself flat on my back, Byron lying beside me, one paw cushioning my head while the other was splayed at my neck, claws bared.

His body, transformed, he lay next to me in an almost-cuddle, but this little rendezvous was about as far from making out as the North Pole was from the simmering plumes of Yellowstone. I was deathly afraid. Not of what Byron might do to me, but more of what might happen if he accidentally touched me with one of those scalpel sharp claws he was waving in front of my face.

I knew this was an attempt to show me who was boss. And I was thoroughly enlightened. This power play was getting tiresome.

"Put a lid on it Byron. There are too many lives at stake to be playing games. I don't have the time to waste on your territorial dominance games while the killer is out there ready to make his next kill." I kept an eye on his claws as I spoke.

The surprise in his eyes mirrored Anjelo's, and he transformed slowly, back into the version of himself far more easy on the eye than the hairy, growling canine. Byron lifted himself off the ground in an easy glide, and lent me his hand. I ignored it, my pride still burning from my undignified visit with the floor.

"You're lucky you are an Alpha, Kailin. Or you'd be dead just for your smart mouth."

And I would've believed him had it not been for the tiny curl of amusement on his lips.

I'd PUT my visit to Iain last on my agenda, mostly because I wanted to find some excuse to avoid it. But, here I was, entering the colony grounds, and heading straight for Iain's home. The sun hung low, and the sky darkened to an inky hue. A beautiful night awaited us. I pressed my thumb on the keypad, very glad I was still logged with the security company.

Since I'd left, two years ago, I'd returned only twice. Both times to see Iain. The only person in my family still on chatting terms with me. My father's coldness seeped into my bones—I'd seen him only once since I'd left. Greer had visited my apartment a few times, bringing with her the cool, hauteur of the snooty elder sister, come to make sure Grams was taking good care of me. Had she come bearing a care package, I may well have tossed her out on her patootie.

But she'd come to gloat. Something about a job in Seattle. Some newspaper gossip column where she could hide her identity well enough, and still get far away from Father. Seems I wasn't the only one running from the winter of our father's heart.

I hadn't seen her since, and that was over a year ago.

"Iain?" I called, loud enough to echo through the house. Better to warn him than to get mauled to death by my very own brother.

"Kai?" He rounded the corner, coming into the hall from the kitchen, dusting crumbs from his shirt as he drew close for a bear-hug. I loved those huge crumpling hugs. One of those squeezes could last me for days; these days they had to last me for months. "What are you doing here, kid?"

"I actually have some troubling news to discuss."

"Come on in, then. You might as well make some coffee while you talk." He smiled in anticipation and I sighed and followed him into the huge kitchen.

Shaking my head, I walked around the island to the countertop where the huge stainless-steel coffee machine still sat. It was an ancient contraption and I hated it with a passion. Hated it because by some stroke of awful luck I happened to be the only member of my family who could actually make a drinkable cup of coffee with it.

I set to work, my hands busy while my mouth rattled on. I filled a silent Iain in on the whole goings-on including my visits to Justin and Byron. He wasn't happy.

I handed him his cup of freshly brewed coffee, and he inhaled the aroma.

"You should've come to me first." His tone was thorough Alpha male.

"So you could go tell them yourself? So when would you have done it? Before or after all the chest pounding and name-calling?"

"Shut up, Kai."

"Well, it's done. I'm still alive, and they are both duly informed. No harm done." I looked at my cup, mixing it studiously.

"Still, you should've left it to me. Dealing with Alphas is a dangerous business."

I clamped my jaw shut before I could recount Byron's attack. Wouldn't want to start a Panther-Wolf war. It took fourteen years for the last feud to end, and peace has always been the preferred status quo. And, I wouldn't dare tell him I'd interrogated the Cougar Alpha. Those two were already on the verge of ripping each other's throats out, no need to give him a reason to start all over again.

"Where's Father?" I asked in-between savoring my drink.

"Off-colony. There's something he needs to sort out." Now it was Iain whose drink was far more interesting.

"Have you heard from Greer lately?" I asked. Iain's eyes narrowed. "What's wrong?"

"Nothing."

"Don't give me that, Iain. Is something wrong with Greer?"

"No, she should be fine."

"Have you or father heard from her?"

"No. Have you?"

"Not since she came to say goodbye, and that was a year ago. Must be living the Seattle high-life." Iain's brow knitted in confusion.

"Seattle?"

"Yes, dear brother. Greer told me about her job at the newspaper in Seattle." I spoke slowly, as if to a child.

"Oh. Yes. I get it." He nodded. Then fell silent.

Everything he said should've sounded perfectly fine and believable. But something was bothering him, and it had to do with Greer. Bullying Iain into telling me more was a waste of time and my breath. I'd get royally pissed off and he'd just walk off calm as you please.

I told myself I'd done my duty, given all the Alphas the information they needed to keep their clans safe. But my visit to Iain left me unbalanced. There was so much he hadn't told me, evading all those questions about Greer, and where father was and what he was doing. Something heavy settled in the pit of my stomach. I hoped Greer was safe. Hoped she was not in trouble. Heavier still the feeling that I was still outside the loop. Still kept at arms-length from anything important. Why hadn't they told me the minute Greer had gone? The minute they knew anything, shouldn't I have also been told? But maybe I made my bed by leaving.

No time for self-pity. I'd have to check back with Iain in a couple of days to make sure she was okay. But for the moment, I had other pressing matters on my mind.

I SAT ON MY BED, toweling my hair, trying not to think about the various spots of pain dotting my body.

My mobile phone was yelling at me to answer the incoming call. I hated the thing, but could never do without it. Usually I had a blue-tooth earpiece, so I didn't need to put up with its persistent ring, but showers and technology weren't pretty play-mates. I'm pretty sure the result would be electrocution. I'd rather not find out first hand.

A new number blinked on the screen. Before the murderer had begun to troll our neighborhood, I'd have answered the call with a flick of a button. But today I hesitated. It was silly.

Stop being stupid Odel. Answer it.

Later I wished I hadn't.

"Kailin, it's Byron." His voice was sharp, raw.

"Hello Byron. Done your head-count yet?" I'd had enough of stubborn superiority from the clan leaders to last me a lifetime.

"Yes. It's why I'm ringing. We were short six until half an hour ago." His voice held a tremor which served to chill my marrow with foreboding. I knew I wasn't going to like what he had to say.

"All but one of them returned this morning. Bunch of stupid kids...too scared to let us know, they left it the whole day. Went out on the town. Boozing, clubs, you know how it is?" Wolf-Walkers, much like any of the other Walker clans, had no problems with alcohol. Most alcohol had no intoxicating effect, thankfully. Unfortunately, it had a different addictive result. Alcohol was like candy to Walkers. "They all came home this morning, except for Evan. Faith was too afraid to tell me. Now we may be too late."

It hit me like a medicine ball to the head. Evan and Faith were Byron's twins. This was now a very big problem. "How's Faith?"

"She's in shock..." Byron's voice shivered a little. "I'll be out as soon as I get things sorted here—"

"No. Stay with Faith and the pack. We'll look for him." I was afraid Byron would scare away any witnesses. Wolf Alphas didn't have the most subtle interrogating skills. They ran more along the lines of talk-or-I'll-rip-you-to-pieces. Those types of life threatening scare tactics were not so effective.

It was best Byron stayed home. It may hurt his ego to have a girl to do his dirty work—the girl being a Panther would make it harder to swallow—but I was all he had.

"I'll get things calmed down here, and then I'll be straight out."

I was not going to go head to head with an Alpha. I'd fight him though, if he pulled any strong-arm tactics, but I left it for now. "Byron, which club did they go to?"

"It was Club Wylde." Byron paused, and I heard the soft mumble of voices. "Spencer will finish questioning them soon, and he'll have the report emailed to you in the next half hour."

In Spencer's case, a half hour meant exactly a half hour. Spencer Caulfield was very thorough. Undercover at a local police precinct after training at the Chicago Police Training Facility, his aim had been to police the pack with better organization skills. Spencer was particular. I sighed. At least the report would be detailed. Detailed or not, Spencer's investigative reach was limited. Probably why Byron sought me out instead of instructing his guard-dog to go fetch. My territory perhaps? Or too many cats for Spencer's tender faculties.

"And Kailin? Evan's only just seen his first Change. He'll be volatile, dangerous. Whoever has him.... They'll be in danger." I'd forgotten about the effects of a Wolf-Walkers' Change time. Unpredictable. Extremely dangerous. Now he was captured and threatened, he'd be more of a danger to everyone, including himself.

"Alright. Oh and Byron, one more thing," I said.

"Yes." he prompted.

"Can you tell me if there were drugs available or in any way involved with the kids?"

"Drugs? Kailin you know we are immune to the—"

"I know that. But word is there's a drug out there right now that is addictive to Walkers. So I'm just checking."

"Okay hold on." I heard the soft drone of his voice. "Faith says they were offered something but she didn't take it. She thought it was a joke. But she can't be sure that Evan refused it."

"Okay, thanks. And Byron...I'm sorry. Evan's smart, I'm sure he'll be fine." What I actually meant was I hoped he'd be fine. At this point I couldn't even hope to guess the outcome.

"I wish I could be so sure." His voice was a father's heart grieving for a son. Sometimes people get 'feelings'. A sense of loss when someone close dies. I hoped Byron's feelings weren't coming from some deeper father's instinct. I wanted to help get Evan home to his family, not track down another skinned corpse.

He cut the call, and I was glad I didn't need to say goodbye. My throat was far too tight to manage words. I dried my hair and twisted it away from my face with a clip dangerous enough to be a weapon itself. There goes my evening, then.

I speed-dialed Anjelo.

"Hey, how you feeling today? No more holes I hope?" Cheeky, but not far from the reality of my life these days.

"Byron's kid Evan is missing," I said, my voice flat, devoid of the shock I was in.

"When? Where?" He wasn't counting the holes in my body anymore.

"Last they saw him was Club Wylde, last night. I'll have the statements of his friends in an hour. In the meantime, round up a couple of people to join us. We're going clubbing. I'll meet you at the Deep."

"I'll sort out the tickets. We'll have to wait until opening time."

"Which is?" I'd never been to Club Wylde. My evenings were often filled with other pursuits—like killing Wraiths. Besides, I liked my personal space. The thought of gyrating on a darkened dance floor, hip to hip with scores of unknown bodies...ugh. Not my thing.

"Ten-pee-em, Kailin." Uttered with such patience.

"Sorry, I'm not a club-crawler okay. That's your thing."

"Probably the touch-me-not Alpha in you." He obviously thought it was a joke. But he was right. "I can go without you. Have a look around and give you a full report."

"Not happening. I want to speak to the manager of the club. Best place to get the information is from the guy in charge."

"Fine. If you want to tangle with Sully you can come."

"Sully?"

"Yeah the club owner. Name's Sullivan, but goes by Sully."

"He's a Walker?"

"Must be to own a club like Wylde."

"So you don't know his species?"

"Sorry Kai. I go to dance, not to fraternize with management." Anjelo snorted.

I ended the call and gathered my things. I usually don't carry my bow unless on a hunt, only the knife in my boot. But today I wanted my weapons with me. This killer had kicked the heat up a notch and I was beginning to get uncomfortable.

What pissed me off was the killer's audacity to poach a young kid at a nightclub. And worse yet, kids were now a target as well. Most clubs overflowed with both Humans and Walkers, bumping and grinding the night away. He'd need to have a Walker detector to know who was who.

He'd need to have a Walker on his side. We had a traitor in our midst.

CHAPTER 20

*E*van twitched a finger. Sensations tingled into his body as the world came back to him a little at a time. He lay supine on a surface unexpectedly and tolerably comfortable. The thought caught him by surprise. Why would it be unusual? He was a bit fuzzy on the details.

The only thing he was certain of was his last memory. The club.

He backtracked, struggling with a hazy memory of the events of the day. Then he remembered leaving Club Wylde with Anita. Yes pretty Anita with the generous boobs and the pouty red lips. Being away from home was wild. Club Wylde was way wilder. But he didn't feel so wild right now. His body ached, and his arms no better than limp pasta. His eyes….

He opened them, blinking away the gritty dry coating. The neon-red club lenses stuck tight to his eyeballs, made him blink automatically as his eyes tried to generate some moisture. Lifting his hand to shove the thing around his eye to work up some wetness, he found said hand firmly attached to the metal rails on the right side of the bed. The other hand had met with equally ignominious fate.

He surveyed the small room, enough space on either side of the bed for his Aunt Zelda to fit her generous hips. But that was it. A teensy window high up on one wall, way too high to jump to. Even if he changed. And maybe that wasn't a good idea either.

He lay on the bed, listening for movement, any sound that told him someone was around. The thought he might be all alone was scarier than wondering who had tied him to the bed and what they wanted with him, and he strained to hear the slightest noise. He allowed the change to condense his eardrums, lifted his ears a bit—borrowing some of his wolfish hearing might do the trick.

EVAN DIDN'T NEED his wolf senses. He didn't need to fear he was all alone. His captor was just down the hall. He'd be visiting Evan soon enough. Something the boy was better off not knowing.

CLUB WYLDE WAS an enormous abandoned factory. We entered onto a balcony, immediately bombarded with a full view of the gyrating dance floor. A living, breathing sea of dance. The crowd heaved and pulsed with the grinding rhythm. Music crushed my lungs, hammered my eardrums. Bass throbbed through my veins, reaching greedy fingers for my heart. I blinked, drunk with sound.

We descended the wide staircase and plunged into the melee. Bodies crushed me, swayed me to their seductive rhythm. Hands and hips gyrating, hypnotized by the beat. Colored lights flashed. On. Off. Swirling, turning, dizzying. Faces, smiles. Here. Gone.

Before I'd entered, I'd worried I was a bit under-dressed. So wrong. All black knee-high boots, black leather mini, sequined racer back tee. Compared to the girls with tiny shorts and pearlized bras, I was the overdressed one.

Lily jabbed Anjelo in the ribs, giving him a dirty look. He'd paid the price for ogling a girl while his beloved was standing right next to him.

Only Anjelo.

He strode up to a nearby bouncer and spoke a few words to him. The guy's face remained expressionless as he nodded and headed for the stairs to tell his boss he had guests.

Only moments later, the guard returned and signaled for another nearby bouncer, all beefy muscles and emotionless eyes.

A strong hand closed over my right arm, digging cruelly into the soft flesh. I shrugged the hand off a little and the grip loosened. These bouncer types were not the most hospitable guys around. While my first instinct was to resist, spin around and knock each of them flat on their sorry asses, I paused. I needed to get Sully on our side, and as much as I would take pleasure in turning these two turkeys into stuffing, I went quietly.

I followed Anjelo as they led us up a second metal staircase on the furthest end of the heaving dance floor. Meanwhile, hips swirled and booties undulated in a mess of suggestive sensuality, to the pounding bass blasting from a hundred speakers.

Lily followed a few paces behind us, a salivating gleam in her eye as she stared into the crowd. I assumed the dance-floor called but she gave it a regretful glance and fell into step beside me, curiously unhindered.

I scanned the club, ascending the stairs, counting the exits. Four in total—each flanked by a pair of guards, burly, surly fellows who surely pumped iron all day and ate little kittens for breakfast.

The double doors opened onto a large room extending the whole back end of the building, with picture windows providing a view of the dance floor. Done in dark tones of black and navy with a touch of white, the room was elegant and ominous at the same time.

"Greetings, my friends."

I searched for a voice. The single occupant of the room was draped over an ice-white leather sofa, lazily swirling a bright green liquid in a highball. A black beanie covered his head stopping short of his generous eyebrows, black silk trousers matched a black silk shirt, out of place in this room and in the club filled with preening, predatory males flaunting their goods. Relaxed in his icy throne, he had the air of a feline, seconds before it pounced. Leopard Walker. I shared a glance with Anjelo, whose look of recognition confirmed he now knew Sully's species.

The air was spicy with fear, and I registered the scents rolling off the bouncers in great waves. Even his own men were terrified of him.

Great way to keep 'em in line, Boss.

"Sully, I take it?" Take this bull by his horns.

"And who do I have the pleasure of addressing, my sweet?" His voice was oily, so dark, and I swallowed the slime suddenly coating my mouth.

His eyes glittered. Black coals stripped me bare, cutting right through me, and I would've choked had I not been feeding the nexus of vengeance lying beneath my heart. Now more than ever I wanted to catch this killer. This murderer preying on Walkers. And I needed to be strong to deal with the likes of Sully.

"Kailin Odel." He rose, his drink now forgotten while this pretty new gem caught his attention. He sniffed. "Alpha Kailin Odel."

When he stopped before me, taking my chin in his steel fingers, I knew with utter certainty he was capable of snapping my neck with a twist of those brutal paws. And as I stood so close to him, I breathed in his cloying cologne and his Leopard Walker fragrance with it. My Panther clawed to get out.

His reaction was so sudden, so strong I was left standing immobilized with shock.

A loud growl ripped the air, softened only by the thunderous bass of the music still pounding in my ears and quivering my heart with every beat. We stood there, face to face, a handsbreadth apart, his canines bared, the corded muscles in his neck bunching.

I sensed his anger, and this only spurred on my own rage. But I tamped the Panther down first. Now we both knew who we were dealing with.

"Look, we don't have time for a territorial pissing contest. I'm not interested."

My directness elicited a reaction both unexpected and surprising.

He laughed. Full and hearty.

I blinked.

"You're one tough chick you know that."

"Been through enough shit in the last few days. I don't have time to play games while Walkers are dying out on those streets." I hadn't meant to be so vehement, but rage reared its vengeful head and snapped in Sully's face.

That caught his attention. His double-take was as painful to watch as his expression was comical.

"Dying?"

"Obviously you're not as well informed as you thought you were." I shot the burly guard next to me a satisfied look as his neck bloomed a pretty rose. Someone was in for it. "There's a killer out there who's been preying on Walkers. We were hoping you would be able to help us."

"I'm not really sure how I can help you. What is it you need?" Sully sat back, crossed his legs and stared at me, one foot swinging back and forth like a pendulum, ticking off my time.

"We're looking for a boy. From what we know, he was last seen here in this club." My gaze didn't waiver.

"Lots of boys come to this club. In fact, hundreds of boys

come to this club." The foot swung and his eyes remained on mine. "I don't see how I can be of any help."

His cold, hard expression convinced me we weren't going to get much out of him.

I plucked my phone from my pocket and brought up the image of Evan that Byron had sent over. "We're looking for him."

Sully peered at the phone, pursed his lips and shook his head. "Nope, never seen him before."

"Could we at least have a look around? Talk to the bouncers, maybe?" I asked, my tone lowering a few degrees. I wasn't in the mood for niceties.

"Feel free as long as you don't disturb my guests." He grinned, a cheery, pleasant smile that was completely false.

We circulated the club, walking through each of the three floors trying to pretend we belonged. No surprise when we came up with nothing. No surprise when none of the bouncers recognized Evan. I sighed. What were we looking for? We had no idea. We certainly weren't going to find the missing boy in the middle of the dance floor.

But we were Walkers to begin with. Walkers with incredible tracking skills. I dug into my little purse for my phone and made a quick call to Byron. Thankfully he was still occupied with his distraught daughter and agreed to send Spencer with some of Evan's garments.

We didn't have to wait long; we met Spencer outside the club a mere half hour later. He drew alongside the curb, and rolled the window down. His steely gray eyes regarded me with curiosity and a large dose of scorn. Of course, I didn't expect anything less.

Without a word, he handed over a jacket, and drove off before I could even say thank you.

"What's his deal?" asked Anjelo staring off into the darkness at the disappearing taillights.

"Wolves."

"Right," he answered with a delicate shudder.

I studied the brown leather jacket that belonged to the missing boy, then raised an eyebrow at Anjelo. "You want to go sniff?"

Behind him, Lily's face darkened, her anger blooming her cheeks, but all Anjelo did was laugh. "Sure, not often I get to exercise the old muscles." And in a breath and a blink, Anjelo's nostrils flared and widened.

He reached for the garment and held it close to his nose, breathing the scent of the boy in, noting each nuance of odor in the fibers. Then he nodded and stepped back.

Wolves would no doubt be better at this than us, and I wondered why Spencer hadn't offered his services. Maybe Byron needed him.

Anjelo backtracked to the entrance to Club Wylde, then stiffened and took a deep breath. He was onto something but I daren't ask him anything, very afraid he may lose the boy's scent. I hadn't planned on letting Anjelo do the job alone anyway, so I allowed my nose to transform and took a deep breath of the garment myself.

I followed Anjelo, followed the scent too. As faded as it was, the wolfiness of the odor still wafted strongly on the sidewalk, on the door he must have held on to. We followed the scent one step at a time taking the corner and moving only two car lengths down the road.

And there we lost the trail.

"What happened?" Anjelo asked, frowning.

"If we assume someone is after Walkers, then we can easily assume that he may have been tossed into a car or something." I glanced up and down the street, the lack of lighting making it difficult to see much more than shadowed shapes. "Would've been easy. We can barely see anything ourselves, even with our cat-vision."

Anjelo clicked his tongue, just as annoyed as I was.

Our investigations hadn't gone as planned. One, Sully was not going to be of much assistance. And two, we needed help.

I knew just the person for the job. Even if I had to battle my inner demons.

Or desires.

CHAPTER 21

Back home after our club visit, my mind was in turmoil as I punched in a text message to Logan. I'd been ready to dial when my clock dinged—after two in the morning. The little card Logan had given me was a crumpled, unrecognizable blob of red. I'd asked nicely if he could come over when he got the chance. Then had to constantly convince myself it was the right decision.

But now, fear, worry and helplessness warred. I worried it was wrong to ask for Logan's help, especially when he had no idea what world he would be entering. But then again what exactly was it that he worked in? Strange and unusual?

The knocking at my door broke into my thoughts. Who would be popping over at this hour? Dread iced my veins over. Not another missing Walker.

I opened the door to reveal a rumpled and sleepy-looking Logan Westin. My heart thudded against my ribs. Rumpled and adorable.

I barely heard his greeting above the thundering in my head. Great. My timing had so sucked. I should've thought before texting him. Should've known he'd think it was urgent and run right over. I'd pulled him from slumber at two am in the morning. I had good reason – Evan—but it felt wrong. Wrong to expect his help when he had no idea what we were. No idea he was stepping into seriously dangerous territory. Wrong to lie to him. Wrong to even think of revealing to a Human. And, my strange attraction to him helped not at all.

Although my heart told me otherwise, the last thing I needed was any kind of serious involvement with Logan, but it was important he was included in our search for Evan. Logan and Omega had resources and contacts which I could only dream of.

I gave Logan the short, Walker-free version. Guilt festered, eternal damnation to my soul.

"So is there anything unusual about the boy?" Logan asked, his eyes wide awake and boring straight into mine.

"What do you mean?" I hesitated.

"I work with strange and unusual all the time, Kai. You didn't call me because this kid is perfectly normal. Talk to me." I was distracted by him calling me Kai. What a fool. But I concentrated on Evan, wanting to tell Logan what he was but so afraid of bringing trouble to our species. What if Omega was an organization that eliminated our kind? I shuddered.

"Kai?" I looked up and met Logan's eyes. He had a strange look on his face. Worried yet determined. "Okay, look. I'm going to tell you something and I figure your reaction will tell me what I need to know."

"Okay," I answered carefully.

"Omega investigates the strange and unusual of the paranormal kind." When I raised my eyebrows he continued, "We were called into the body dump in the garden because the victim was not normal. Not human. You understand what I mean?"

"Yeah, not normal. Not human. So what was he?" I asked, treading carefully, not wanting to give anything away. What if he was on a totally different track and I blurted out the truth? *No, slow and careful, Odel.*

"You've heard of werewolves, right?" he asked. And the blood drained from my body. Could he really know the truth? I blinked and nodded and he spoke again. "Well wolves aren't the only creatures that can transform into humans. There are cats that transform t—Kailin is there something you want to tell me?"

"What do you mean?" I tried to feign nonchalance.

"Your face tells me you know something. You look like a vampire just drained you."

I couldn't take it anymore. He knew so much already. I'd have to cross my fingers and hope he'd be able to help us find Evan. Cross my fingers and hope I was doing the right thing. "Okay. Fine." I sighed and sank into the nearest sofa, running my hands through my hair. I hadn't realized how exhausted I was until now. "Evan is a Walker. He's a wolf."

"Do you know him?"

"Not directly. I know his father, Byron Teague. He's the clan Alpha."

"So Evan is an Alpha too."

I nodded. "A recently changed Alpha."

"Which makes him more dangerous."

"You know a lot about Walkers," I said.

"Like I said, I investigate the paranormal." He smiled. "So how do you know these Walkers?"

"I've been in the city for a while. You hear things. Meet people." I shrugged, hoping he wouldn't dig deeper. I stood up, felt a lot like pacing, but didn't. "So your agents...are they experienced with this type of thing?"

"Yes, don't worry about it. Omega will try and find out more. And Chief Murdoch will help as well."

"The police chief works for Omega? And he knows about Paranormals?"

"Murdoch's helped out a lot in the past. So yes, he knows." Logan paused, his brows furrowed as he played with the buttons on his phone. "How long has he been gone?"

"Since last night. At Club Wylde." I ran through the details of Evan's disappearance and our visit to Sully's club.

"Okay," Logan looked up and gave me an encouraging smile. "Thanks for being honest with me. I'll get the team rounded up. We'll help you find Evan. We'll put the word out on the street, get Omega on the case."

"Thank you." I spoke but it was almost a whisper. Logan looked up and met my gaze. My eyes burned with a mix of gratitude and regret.

He reached out and gave my arm a little squeeze. Whether it was just a gesture of comfort didn't matter because it became more in an instant. That's all it took for me to give in. Just the touch of his warm hands on my skin killed all resistance. He came to me, standing so close the heat of our bodies intertwined in the sliver of space between us. He held my arms gently, staring into my eyes, he frowned as if fighting himself the way I should be fighting myself against this madness. The air shimmered thick and heated between us and my breath came in short, sharp bursts.

Memories of our recent close encounter of the passionate kind flitted through my mind and also somewhere low in my stomach. My throat was dry and swallowing did nothing to help. I was never good at romance, rebuffing any and all advances from the guys at school who had thought me half-way attractive. Dating was something I had no experience with. Dating, along with any other lovey-dovey stuff.

He came closer and I leaned my head against his chest, listening as his heart thudded against my ear, as it began to increase its steady pace. He sighed and the sound made me pull away. Suddenly I needed the distance. Getting carried away now was a bad idea. His rejection still burned. His eyes may have been regretful, but he hadn't apologized.

I stepped away from his reach and shook my head. The tiniest of apologies. I turned from him, wishing he would leave and make things easy for me.

"Kailin?" I turned, my heartbeat increasing to a fever pitch.

He was right there behind me. Perfect. Like the heat and tenderness of his kiss was perfect. He warmed my heart, and all I wanted was to get closer. Rumpled hair was more rumpled, the world fell away and all that was left was Logan and me, and this amazing, fiery passion enveloping us.

Heat simmered where we touched. Lips. Hands. Bodies. But this time I wasn't afraid. And this time he didn't pull away. He tamed the fire before it burned too bright. And when, at last, we came up for air, and he smiled at me, it was the fiery passion that burned in his eyes which held my attention and took my breath away.

But I said nothing. Just smiled shyly at his flushed face.

He touched my cheek and smiled. "The way you make me feel...it's like nothing I've felt before. I don't understand it and yet I do. Do you know what I mean?"

I nodded, understanding exactly what he was trying to say.

"I shouldn't let my emotions mix with work." I nodded but inside I was smiling. "I'll see what I can find out and get back to you soon."

"Thanks, Logan. I guess we—Evan needs all the help he can get."

Logan nodded and headed for the door.

No more words.

I believed him too. Believed he would do whatever it took to protect me. And more important than this intense heat we had between us, was the trust. This crazy kid, who had somehow become a paranormal lawman, who'd weaseled his way into my stupid affections, had just forced me to trust him.

Things were getting too complicated.

$\mathcal{N}$iko bent over the boy's arm, tapping the vein with an expression bordering on tender. He was often enthralled by the bodies of his fellow Walkers, brought to his knees by the sheer beauty of the physical and biological make-up of his species. During his self-imposed exile he studied both, formally and informally, everything he could to understand the physiology and biology of a SkinWalker.

Niko grabbed the hand of the unconscious boy, gripping the wrist with a strength he drew from his untapped rage.

Flesh pressed against bone and bone began to bend to the pressure. Then he withdrew his hand. Perhaps it was fear he may destroy the vial of precious adapted strain, or perhaps some minute part of his human side bade him pause before he caused permanent damage to the boy. In a few hours the boy's arm would show a purpled bruise and swollen flesh and muscle from Niko's ministrations. Even if the bruises took longer, the four gashes in the tender skin of his arm, where four broken claws had sliced open skin and drawn blood, would be a silent, if not painful reminder.

The copper spice of blood rode the air, and Niko had a second overpowering wave of need douse him. This time it was the rage of hunger and not envy. The Blood Call was infinitely stronger to Walkers like him—the ones who were not.... normal.

Niko strove to check his blood desire. The task at hand was to test the drug and pray it worked.

He pressed the needle against the young skin until it slid through into the vein, butter smooth. A bead of red slipped out the edge of the wound and Niko was transfixed. But only for a moment. He pressed the plunger down until the entire content of the vial was emptied.

Now he had to wait the requisite time before he administered the inciters. Niko's own blood had contributed to developing the drug; had been the very reason he'd begun to work on the drug in the first place. He studied the digits of his right hand, each one ending in a sharply curved claw; ignoring his left hand which held the mangled, damaged claws.

It was far as he was able to get the transformation to go, for him or any of the other Unchanged. If this drug worked he might be able to use the results to develop his special blend a little further.

For now he waited.

Niko checked the boy's vitals. Evan was the name of the youth. A Wolf-Walker. It didn't matter too much the species he used. He'd discovered years ago that the fundamentals in the DNA strands were the same. The blends with the Human genes were the same too, irrespective of the animal a SkinWalker housed within him. He knew by now the drug had filtered deep into the boy's bloodstream, dulling synapses, axons and dendrites. Administering a sedative-like hold onto the hormones linked directly to the inherent process of the Change.

The room was stark and lifeless despite its two very alive occupants. The bright fluorescent light cast an unflattering glare on the ugly peeling walls, the faded green sheets and blankets, turned steel handles and bars into shiny glowing metal. Stark.

He watched the bars on the monitor as each one lit a bright green, rising slowly like a growing tower until the machine beeped a triple warning. Ready for use again.

Niko held the paddles of the Defibrillator in his hands, watching until each bar lit one after the other, until the indicator light glowed green and the machine was ready. Without hesitation, he held the paddles to the center of the youth's bared chest and watched as the supine form was electrified into life. Evan's body jerked off the bed in a perfect curve, feet and shoulders still touching the mattress.

EVAN JERKED INTO FULL CONSCIOUSNESS, pain slicing through his skull. And then the pure warmth of the Change slinked through his veins, taking hold of his body and mind. The wolf within him pushed for control. It was a living thing, almost a parasite owning a part of his body and mind. A permanent roommate who sometimes wanted his own way with things. The change was a primal need and he was unable to deny himself the ecstasy of the invitation.

His muscles burned, a simmering fire stretching and twisting while Human bones and tissue warred with the conquering wolf. Fingers sprouted claws, shortened, thickened, furred. Evan's back curved and realigned until the restrained became painfully uncomfortable. The wolf struggled in his ungainly position, forelegs bent and tied at each side, bent to almost breaking point.

NIKO GROWLED his rage and slammed his fist into the tray on the trolley at his side. It flipped in mid-air, tossing its contents across the floor. Shiny silver scalpels and scissors and syringes spattered the white linoleum floor, landing with high plinking notes, so musical and so out of place. He growled again, the pure sounds of an enraged feline. At times like this, when his rage controlled him, he could feel the Panther inside, desperate to be released from its prison. As desperate as he was to release the cat. He tasted the ecstasy in the partial release he achieved with his claws and ears. But it teased and tantalized him.

Some Pariah were luckier than Niko. Like Brand, his Synthe distributor. He knew the streets, peddled Niko's special strain of his drug to the Walkers in the city. He even brought Niko a satisfactory subject or two. Brands goons, though, were more than a tad inefficient. Look at what they did with the last skinned corpse he'd worked on. Dumped in a garden of all places. And now they had a bunch of Walkers sniffing around. And one of them was an Alpha. Not that he couldn't handle an Alpha – he was one himself of course – but he could've done without the distraction.

Niko studied the vials of the drug. It promised release, much like Brand had promised release. But Brand's methods of release were unsavory to say the least—Niko knew he'd never be able to partake of a Human meal the way Brand and his followers did. Maybe he'd left his clan, and maybe he was Pariah but that didn't mean he was no longer a Walker. And the Walkers lived by certain tenets. Without those rules who knew what would happen?

At least the drug had given him strength. If only temporary. But the benefits outweighed the discomforts. It made his body stronger. Stronger so he could find the perfect way to transform himself fully to his Panther form and back again.

For the Wolf-boy, the trauma had brought on a full change. Niko needed to force him to change back. He had to get this right. The throbbing at his temples slowly receded as he calmed himself. Calmed his beast.

He went to the Defibrillator and waited for it to recharge.

He slapped the paddles on the now fur-lined chest of the wolf. Electricity coursed through the animal lifting it up and almost off the bed, only to fall back once Niko removed the paddles. The wolf's body began to shiver, small tremors ran through his body from head to toe. The power still sped through Evan's body, until he howled in agony. Agony at the impending Change perhaps, at having to return to the prison of its Human form.

The transformation happened again, this time in reverse. Like switching a movie onto rewind, taking the form of the wolf and forcing it back into the shape of the man. He allowed Evan a short respite. The boy needed to recover his energy. Because the next try, if successful, would rob him of every bit of strength he had left.

Niko filled two syringes with the drug and laid them aside, they would keep until the boy had rested.

CHAPTER 23

*L*ily closed the door of the toilet stall and hung her bag over the rusty hook. For such a popular club, Wylde certainly had the ickiest restrooms. Her hands shook, and her blood burned for the ecstasy awaiting her in the package hidden in her bag.

Anjelo had assumed she'd go home with him, and on any other day she may have acquiesced, but tonight the lure of the Synthe was unbearable. She just couldn't bear to wait a moment longer. She'd barely been able to control herself, the need for her next hit so overwhelming that she'd taken her frustration out on him. A small part of her brain, probably the practical Lynx within her, rebelled and reminded her every so often that the drug was not so good for her.

She knew her addiction was getting worse. But she couldn't care less.

What a relief when Kailin had left the Club. At the moment, Kailin was not one of her most favorite people. All that black hair, and curves exactly where they should be. Drove Lily insane. Thankfully Anjelo only had eyes for Lily. The problem was every time Kailin beckoned, Anjelo ran. It wasn't as if he had to, but for some reason he was compelled. Lily still smarted from her recent altercation with Kailin. She'd gotten no reaction from Miss Know-it-All. Nothing. The snoot had turned and left. And Anjelo hadn't been too happy she'd opened her mouth in the first place.

She pulled out half a dozen strips of toilet paper, laying them carefully side by side so the entire toilet lid was covered. Drawing the package of glittering powder and a tiny mirror out of her bag, Lily sat on the toilet with a moue of distaste. She balanced the mirror on one knee and dealt a small amount of delicate white dust onto the mirror. A little powder, a little sniff, and a lot of bliss awaited.

As she leaned over to breathe in the beautiful poison she caught a glimpse of her distorted reflection. For the smallest moment, she was shocked by the image of a girl whose eyes simmered with such desperate need that it pulled her face into a grimace of hunger. But the need gripped hold of her far too tightly and she caved.

Now she waited, all tense muscles and expectant breath, until the drunken bliss dissolved her muscles, and erased the ache living within her. She ached to Change, and hated herself and her body and everything wrong within her. Growing up, Lily, like all her friends and siblings, had looked forward to the time of Change with scared anticipation.

She'd had no fear for intense pain nor for the shock to her bones and muscles caused by a first-time Change. Like her friends, she couldn't wait. The Change was the door to adulthood and Lily craved her maturity with a passion. But when her time came and went without the tiniest twinge to mark the onset of her Change, she grew worried. Everyone worried, and waited with her, but the years went by one at a time. Three years of doctors and tests and waiting and still Lily was unable to let her Lynx out. It was there, she knew it, felt it all the time and it shared her agony and desire for release.

Then she was an outcast. Disappointment to her family,

decreed ineligible for a mate by Walker law. Something about deformed cubs resulting from such a wrong union. So she was shunned. Never mind whatever was wrong with her body was not of her doing. So she left the city of her childhood and ended up here. With Anjelo.

Even with his understanding and his care, the pain still lingered within her body and the memories still filled her mind. He couldn't make her whole, and now she was sure nobody could.

But, everything was so much better after a shot of Synthe. The music more rocking, and life so much more beautiful. All her senses shifted into overdrive and she loved it. Because she forgot the Lynx breathing within her, wanting out. Forgot her pain, at least for a short time.

Anjelo would throw a fit if he found out about her habit. Yeah, he'd be mad, and so disappointed in her. So far Lily had managed to keep her Synthe-dependence a secret. She'd been so careful to stay away when she was high. Brand had told her the drug couldn't be detected even by the smell sense of another Walker. Although she believed this she was always nervous to be around Anjelo when she was high. Probably her guilt.

For so long she'd dealt with her pain without the help of Anjelo. And how happy she'd been when Hiro introduced her to Synthe. Hiro, with his exotic eyes and cute accented charm, had taken her aside a few weeks back. He was a Fox-Walker, and she was in no danger from another Walker. Until he showed her the drug. She'd refused at first but Hiro was a talker, had used words to tug at her heart. And he'd seemed so kind. Even his boss, Brand had encouraged her to at least try it. She was glad she had.

In all her life she'd never heard of any drug, Human or otherwise, which worked on a Walker. And she'd thought she was an extremely fortunate girl to have found such a thing of wonder right here at Club Wylde. Right place, right time. Not that she was the type to indulge. Was there even such a thing as a potential drug user type? If there were, she wouldn't have identified with it. Not until now, when the pain filled her bones and her mind, and the voice in her head sounded like all the meanest kids at home. The voice taunting her night and day.

A few trips to Club Wylde and she'd been able to get her fix each time. But it got so much worse. Each high was more intense, more beautiful than the one before, and each downer was so peaceful. No pain, no anger, no sorrow. Pure bliss. Worse too was her income from her part-time job at the Deli was feeding her habit, and she had to rely on Anjelo to help her out with money for school. He thought she was sending money home to her family in Arkansas. Another rotten lie. But the wait for the next fix had become unbearable. The constant need buzzed inside her, an insidious bee, stinging her, stabbing her, demanding the next taste of euphoria.

When she left the ladies-room, she was deep within the arms of the Synthe. She walked right past the two men leaning against the wall outside the toilet. Didn't see the mean glint in their eyes, the air of expectancy about them. Didn't notice the look of recognition passing between them when they saw her. Nor was she aware when they followed her, as she weaved through the throng of prancing dancers and onto the center of the dance floor.

When they bumped into her and she fell forward, sprawled on her stomach like a stranded starfish, she didn't feel the slight prick of a needle in her neck as the two men helped get back to her feet. Only saw their faces swimming before her eyes until she slipped into a haze darker and more vile than the Synthe.

CHAPTER 24

The clanging racket of the birdcage as it rose from the ground floor announced my visitor, but it was my nose that told me Anjelo was on his way up.

The smile on my lips died at the state he was in. Disheveled, tired with what was closer to a beard than a five-o'clock shadow. My heart twinged with worry. I remained silent. My sense of smell was at its peak, with all the craziness of the last few days. Another scent came off him in waves. Fear—pure and unadulterated fear. From the tense ridge of his jaw, it was something bad. Real bad.

"It's Lily." His voice simmered with pain. "She's missing."

Rigid fingers scraped furrows through his pale hair.

The answer left me reeling. "Wasn't she with you when I left the club last night?"

I'd headed straight home—weighing the pros and cons of getting Logan and his team on board. The very last thing I'd expected was for a Walker this close to us to be in danger. Our arrogance had been flung sharply back in our faces. It was tearing Anjelo apart.

"Yeah, we had a look around and Lily wanted to stay. She

seemed...preoccupied...on edge," Anjelo's eyes darkened with guilt. "We had a fight. She insisted on staying at the club, I insisted she come home, and she walked off, so I left. She's a big girl. I thought she'd be fine." His words were more an effort to convince himself he'd done the right thing, but it didn't work.

"Anjelo, come on. You weren't to know this would happen." Grief deafened him and he heard nothing.

He sat on the sofa, hopeless. I lurked, helpless. Even Cat, who officially hated him, sensed he needed comfort and jumped into his lap for a cuddle.

I perched on the arm of the sofa and addressed the back of his blond head. "Did anyone else stay behind?"

"Just Gia, but she bailed not long after us. Said she hadn't seen Lily since I left anyway, so she couldn't help." Anjelo rested his head in his hands, as if his fear weighed him down so he was unable to support it. He kept his head turned away, didn't look at me, and I guessed he hid his tears. Such unmanly things, tears.

"Have you looked for her?"

Anjelo nodded. "I went back to the club. Tried to track her." Anjelo gave a shuddering breath then shook his head with regret and frustration. "I lost the trail on the dance floor. I followed the trail from where I left her last, at the staircase leading to the entrance. She'd gone to the ladies' room, then back to the dance floor and then...poof into thin air."

My heart ached for Anjelo.

He drew in a breath. "I asked around, bartenders, security guys, and nothing. Nobody saw anything. The place was filled, probably a full-on fire hazard. I guess nobody would've seen anything even if they'd been looking right at her. Or else they're just lying to cover their asses."

"That's good. I've spoken to Agent Westin already about getting his unit involved with our search for Evan. Maybe he can help us with finding Lily."

"That's crazy, Kai. The police? If they find out what we are, we're all dead. They're Human, you know?" If anything my revelation had given Anjelo something else to be upset about. I was happy. Sort of. At least it gave him a brief respite from his personal agony, even if he was busy lampooning my bright idea.

I sent Anjelo home with strict instructions to shower and eat, and I placed a call to Logan to come over. It wasn't long before I opened the door for him.

Now he stood, uncomfortably flipping his phone over and over in his hand. I stared at him.

"Hey Kai." His eyebrows were raised to match the question. "You had something important to ask me?

"I need your help."

"What is it?" His voice changed as he became aware that I was upset. I hadn't realized how much Lily's disappearance had affected me. There was no love lost between Lily and myself, but I adored Anjelo and seeing him hurting was hard to handle.

"Someone else has gone missing. Another Walker. And this time it's someone I know. She's my friend Anjelo's girlfriend."

"When?" The look of helpless frustration on Logan's face was worrying.

"He hasn't seen her since last night. At Club Wylde."

Logan sucked in a breath. "Okay, give me the details. Where exactly she was last seen, what she was wearing. Everything."

I gave Logan the run-through, brought him up to speed on Anjelo's search too. Finally, the story all told, I sighed, weariness pulling me down.

"I'm guessing Anjelo is a Walker too?" Logan asked, his eyes unfathomable.

I nodded. It wasn't worth running circles around him trying to evade the truth. "So what do you think happened to her?" I asked softly even though I knew what the answer would be. Sucker for punishment.

"Abducted, probably. From the way Anjelo lost track of her so abruptly, it seems to be the only conclusion."

I had a sudden thought that perked me up a bit. "The cameras." Club Wylde didn't look like the type of place able to run without a smart security system, which no-doubt also included state-of-the-art video. "Club Wylde must have cameras set up around the dance floor, for security. We'll just ask him if we could have a look at the tapes."

"And I suppose you think 'pretty please' will work on him?" Logan asked "Do you know him?"

"Yeah, we met when we went to the club to look for information on Evans disappearance. I think I can to get him to help. He seemed...honorable. Maybe not legal, but he lives by a code and I think it's a pretty strict one. As long as we don't endanger his territory, we'll be okay."

"Well, just to be on the safe side I'll get us a warrant," he said. Then he paused, "and Kai?"

"Yes?"

"Don't go in without me."

"Okay." And I actually meant it. That search warrant would be helpful if Sully put up a fuss.

I hoped.

LILY OPENED HER EYES. Fear muffled the cry in her throat, a strange weight pulled on her body. Although her eyes stared wide open, only pitch darkness surrounded her. She was stiff with fright. Blind. She was blind. A terrified gasp left her throat. The sound bounced off the invisible walls encapsulating her. The eerie echo chilled her to the bone.

She remained on the cusp of consciousness, registering only small glimpses of the room in which she was being held, her body too heavy to move more than her eyelids.

She blinked repeatedly, desperate to get the woolly haze out of her eyes, and tried to make sense of her surroundings. Her eyesight adjusted to the pitch-dark room, and she could at last make out the outlines of the bed she lay on. A table beside her, and a large door ahead.

She struggled to turn her head, lift it off the pillow, straining to see more of the room. The action was far too much for her drug weakened body and she slipped back into the safety of darkness.

It was hours later when she resurfaced from her drugged bliss. It was still dark around her, but knowing what to expect, she was not as alarmed as before. She lay on the bed, her breathing short and erratic. Memories flickered through her mind. Shattered pieces of her evening softened by the gentle haze of the Synthe. Two men, holding her on the dance floor. A prick of pain on her neck.

When she tried to touch the still tender spot she found she was bound and buckled to the bed. She struggled, pulling frantically at the soft, warm leather straps buckling her to the iron rails circling low around the bed. The large, thick straps only made Lily want to struggle to get free. She sensed the action futile. She was no match for the strength of the leather, and the buckles clanked loudly against the iron railings.

She froze again, fear gripping her muscles. The metallic notes of her struggle echoed around the room. Her first instinct was to create a thunderous racket, but then realized it meant she would be confronted by her captors far too soon. The echoes petered out into the darkness and all was quiet again.

The silence was as frightening as the dark, and far more terrifying was the noise she had made. She strained to listen for movement, and sound to confirm she was not alone.

Lily's mind filled with questions. Who were the two men, and what would anyone want with her? Anjelo had warned the whole clan to be aware of any suspicious people. To keep an eye out. So far one SkinWalker was killed and another was missing. She dreaded the thought she may be the third person abducted by the killer.

Hot tears filled her eyes and overflowed at the side of her face, falling into the hair by her ears. Now she wished she had listened to Anjelo. Her body still craved the drug, but she was now in control of all her faculties. The cold light of post-Synthe clarity was filled with pain and regret.

"WAKE UP, BEAUTIFUL." Niko nudged Lily in the arm, impatient to get some answers from the girl. She had been under far too long and he wasn't prepared to wait any longer.

While she slept he'd taken the liberty of drawing a few vials of blood and running a batch of tests on the samples. Niko had immediately stopped cursing the two fools who'd brought her to him.

Her blood had been swimming with those freakish alleles. And it certainly did not hurt to have another Pariah to experiment on. Besides, she could provide two important things: information which was vital to him and a living, breathing source of fresh blood supply for his serum.

"Yoo-hoo, pretty girl." Niko coaxed her out of her haze.

Lily blinked and tears filled her eyes. Her eyelids fluttered and she seemed barely able to open them. Niko glanced at the bright lights blazing down on her. The darkness would've been replaced with light so bright it no doubt sent shards of stabbing pain into her eyes. A thought Niko enjoyed.

She squinted against the glare and turned, searching for the voice that had been calling her.

And stared up at Niko.

The girl trembled, swallowing uncontrollably.

Niko could smell her fear with his inner Panther. Bah. Who needed the ability to smell things like fear and desire in another Walker when the ability to Change was non-existent?

"Who...who are you?" Her voice cracked on the words, her throat probably parched from Niko's drug.

"Now, my dear girl, don't worry your pretty little head about that." Niko smiled down at her, baring his yellowed teeth.

The girl's eyes widened, her gaze moving to Niko's mouth and he watched as a shiver of disgust rippled through her. His benevolent smile dulled, barely reaching his cold, flat black eyes.

"Why are you keeping me here? What do you want with me?"

"Information, my dear girl. Start by telling me who you are." He aimed to sound fatherly, so kind. And for a short moment she looked tempted to confide the information. But then she fell silent.

Niko lost patience with her. It was time to show her he meant business. He started by grabbing her forefinger and jabbing the scalpel under her fingernail.

She gasped and tugged against the grip. She'd be regretting that, Niko thought as he shoved the scalpel deeper. The girl gasped and sobbed.

"Lily...Lily Marks," she whispered the words, each syllable thickened with agony, and peppered with harsh sobs.

"Are you a SkinWalker?" Niko applied the tiniest bit of pressure on the scalpel. He had the grace to feel a shiver of guilt pass through his body. Of course he knew what she was but it always helped to lay down the ground rules.

Niko watched a moment of defiance flit across her expression. She would refuse to rat on her friends and give him any more information that would endanger not only herself but the entire city clan. She was a smart girl. Admitting to her species was a dangerous thing.

"What? I don't know what that is?"

Niko edged the scalpel further under her fingernail with a slow, precise movement and soon blood dripped from the wound. Bright red droplets on the pale sheet.

"Okay. Stop. Please stop." He was breaking her down. Shame

bloomed red in her cheeks as tears fell from her eyes. Niko knew shame. It would be burning deep inside and she'd hate herself for her lack of courage. Yes, Niko knew shame very well.

"Are you a SkinWalker?" he asked again, more firmly.

"Yes." She turned and looked up at the bare ceiling. Her face tight, her expression resigned and angry.

"Species and clan?"

"Lynx. I'm not from around here." She said, the words tripped off her tongue automatically. She struggled to remain unemotional about her betrayal, and Niko felt a tiny bit sorry for her

"So who do you hang out with then? Who's your Alpha?"

"I don't have an Alpha. I'm my own woman, thanks." Still she didn't look at him, even though she knew he'd react to her moment of defiance.

He jabbed the scalpel further and with a sharp tug, yanked her nail off her finger. The flesh was red, raw and dripped blood. The nail landed on the concrete floor without a sound.

WAVES OF AGONY wracked through Lily's finger, shooting up her hand with vicious speed. She screamed with the pain, breathing hard as the agony hit her, over and over again.

"We'll have none of your smart talk my dear. Answer the question, please or we start with the next fingernail."

Lily was deathly afraid she'd begin to cry and would be incapable of speaking through the sobs. If it happened she'd be in worse trouble than she was now. Who knew what this sadist was capable of?

"Anjelo, he's not really an Alpha, though. But I answer to him."

"Are there a lot of you? How many?"

"What business is it of yours, creep?" Lily knew she was delaying the inevitable by denying him the knowledge he desired. But the voice inside her—her Lynx or her conscience, she wasn't sure which—screamed not to reveal anything to him. It spelled danger.

He inserted the scalpel under the nail of her second finger and waited.

"About twenty...please stop."

"Tell me about this Anjelo. What is he?"

"He's a Panther."

"A Panther you say? Then he is perfect." He rubbed his hands together.

"What do you want with him?" Despite the pain, fear for Anjelo's safety waged war with fear for herself.

"Never you mind, my dear. I have my reasons. He's potentially quite important to me."

Lily was stiff with fright. She wondered what this crazed man wanted with Anjelo because he was a Panther-Walker. On an impulse and in an instinctive effort to protect Anjelo she said, "He isn't the only Panther in the city. There are more. Why don't you leave Anjelo alone and take one of them?"

"There are others?"

"One I know of, and she's an Alpha." Lily spoke gasping with pain.

The man seemed happy with her answers and looked at her with narrow, contemplative eyes.

A Panther Alpha in the city.

How helpful.

The door soughed open and Brand strode in. Niko wrinkled his nose. Brand reeked of blood and Death. The least he could do was consider his personal hygiene. He remained silent as Brand walked to the gurney. The girl stared at Brand with eyes filled with horror.

Brand was in partial transformation. Something Niko hated

simply because Brand and his gang were able to gain it and then turn it back. They were not Pariah like Niko.

Niko watched as Brand softened his features and returned to his fully human form. The girl sobbed, more horrified now she recognized the Walker standing over her.

"It's you," the girl stammered, her eyes round with horror. Few people knew how strategically placed Brand was.

"This one is mine, Niko." He glanced over his shoulder. "Make sure you take good care of her. She is mine when you are done with your little experiments."

With that he left, in a hurry. Niko suspected he had to get to his base of operations. Synthe dealing was a lucrative business. And Walkers like Lily depended on Brand's generosity.

Her blood test had detected residual particles of Synthe. Amazing how his pet project had developed into such a lucrative little side business. Since she liked the drugs, Niko decided she may as well have more. It had been a while since he had a Walker to test his new adaptations on.

He'd keep her. Brand could find another plaything; he always did. This girl would stay with Niko.

Hopefully she wouldn't crumble under his ministrations. Hopefully she would provide a little more information on these 'other' Panther-Walkers in the city.

CHAPTER 25

*S*ully did a double take when Logan, Kailin and Anjelo walked into his office. They caught him unawares as the morning sun streamed through the windows set into one long brick wall.

Logan had wondered if Kailin would wait for him, and was surprised to find she did. He hoped it meant she'd open up a bit more. More. What was it really that he wanted more of he wondered. Was it the heat and passion that sizzled between them each time they were alone together? He clenched his jaw.

"I seem to have won a popularity contest." Sully smiled, though his attempt at pleasantry was stiff and cold at the corners of his mouth. Murdoch had been forthcoming with a file on Sully. But the man before him seemed different to the images it held. Lighter, perhaps from the sunlight highlighting strong cheekbones and a stubborn chin. Friendly, yet preoccupied.

"Mr. Sullivan. I'm Agent Logan Westin." Logan tacked on a smile. "We're actually here to ask you for a favor."

"Sure. What can I do for you?" Sully's smile gleamed, bland and unpromising.

"We're looking for someone. A young girl named Lily Marks.

I believe she frequents your club." Logan walked to the glass opposite him and surveyed the now empty dance-floor. A lone bartender was sweeping the wooden surface of the lower dance floor, ultra-careful. Probably painfully aware the boss watched from above. Something glittered in the pile of dust and dirt he was about to sweep up, and he watched as the bartender bent over and picked up the object.

He examined it slowly, and threw a quick look up at the window. Had he not seen Logan watching he would undoubtedly have slipped it into his pocket, for his hand stopped in mid-air and he straightened with a jerk.

He left his pile of dirt, probably decided he was better off bringing it up now. He had no idea who Logan was, but friends of anyone's boss could endanger a guy's job, or his life, and Logan had a feeling the latter provided stronger incentive. Sully had a deadly air about him that wasn't just a threat.

The bartender bounded up the stairs and knocked softly at the door. He entered as Sully turned to the door. The young man drew close and whispered to Sully, slipping the object into his employer's palm. He left soon after, beads of perspiration dotting his shaven head.

Sully twisted the little silver charm within his fingers as he waited for Logan to continue. The interruption had been untimely for him, but important to Anjelo who said, "Can I see that?" Recognition flared in his eyes.

Sully, regarded him for a moment, then tossed it to Anjelo who caught it with shaky hands.

"It's Lily's. I got it for her birthday." Anjelo's palm shook as he tipped his hand toward Logan and Kailin so they could see the tiny silver charm fashioned into a little dancing girl.

"This, at least, confirms Lily was on that dance-floor at some point after Anjelo left, the catch is broken. It may have come off in a struggle." Logan pinned Sully with a glare. "Do you have cameras focusing on the dance floor?"

Sully nodded

"Could we have a look at your tapes from last night?"

"Happy to help, but I'd need to know, what for? All this talk of charms is confusing. And who is Lily?" he asked as he walked to a small closet at the back of the room.

"The young girl who was with us yesterday. She's missing. Never came home last night. And she was last seen here in the club." said Kailin avoiding eye-contact with Anjelo.

"Are you trying to imply something?" Sully's shoulders were rigid, his face flushed.

"No, not at all." Logan shook his head reassuring the Club Don they had no such intention. "We want to find out what happened to her, just following every lead possible. And your tapes might be crucial in our search."

"I should insist on a search warrant you know." Sully mumbled. "But I'm a nice guy."

"It's good that you are assisting us, Mr. Sullivan." Logan smiled. "I do have a warrant if you would like to see it."

Sully's jaw tightened and he waved Logan off, then proceeded to replay the tapes from the previous night. Sully's muscles tightened, tendons straining, no doubt he forced himself to maintain a friendly face. Logan stood aside, making space for Kailin and Anjelo to view the bank of monitors replaying the tapes from the various cameras around the club. There. One screen held the moving images of Lily and Anjelo, displaying their argument for all to see. Logan didn't need sound to tell him the nature of the argument was volatile. He followed Lily's movements through the club after Anjelo left. She stood at the edge of the dance floor, fists clenched, anger and disappointment gleaming on her face. Then she turned and elbowed dancers aside as she disappeared into the restrooms.

While she'd had her little tantrum, she'd been observed by two men. Scruffy types with baseball caps shoved tight onto their heads, who took up position outside the toilets after she entered.

When she left it was clear they'd been waiting for her. The positioning of the camera and their caps had hidden their faces as they stalked her, until they followed her onto the dance-floor.

Logan glanced at Anjelo who remained deadly silent while they watched the blurry black and white replay. Even when Kailin flinched as the two goons grabbed Lily in the middle of the roiling ocean of dancers, Anjelo had continued to watch, unblinking.

They half carried, half dragged the now unconscious girl to the door. The bouncer at the exit nodded to them and opened the door before they could request it. As if he knew them. As if he had expected them to be dragging an unconscious woman out the club door. Logan wished he could've gotten a look at Sully's face, but the Club boss faced away from him, staring at the monitors, a large vein throbbing at his temple. This video implicated his employee in Lily's disappearance. It wouldn't be a great leap of imagination to assume Sully was in some way involved. But they still needed his help.

At Kailin's direction Sully stopped the tape there and rewound it until the minutes after they left Club Wylde, isolating the camera focused on the Japanese bouncer. The goons spoke to him before heading to the restrooms.

"What his name?" Logan asked

Sully remained silent.

"Sully?" Kailin prodded.

"Hiro Mishima." The name scraped cold through gritted teeth. "He's been with me about two months. Just great. I need to find out who he's working for. Will you excuse me? I need to make a few calls."

A ferocious scowl contorted Sully's face as he turned to Logan while Kailin and Anjelo continued to scan the tapes. Logan looked at him, and in the instant their eyes met he saw a violent, angry nature within their depths. His expression sent shivers up Logan's spine.

He'd allowed them to look at his tapes, but clearly he didn't like it at all—there were things going on in his club he seemingly had no idea about. Or maybe he did know and wasn't thrilled with being investigated. Now he retreated to a shadowed corner, speaking on his cell phone in low tones while keeping one eye on the cameras as Kailin and Anjelo studied them for clues.

Logan remained unsure why Sully would bother to help them at all, especially with the glares he sent their way. But the tapes were exacting proof of how slack he was in keeping his staff in line. A woman had been abducted right out from under his nose and he'd gone about his business totally ignorant. If word got out, his Club, his livelihood would be in serious jeopardy. If he cared at all about his reputation. Logan had the niggling feeling he didn't give a damn that he could have blood on his hands.

HIRO WASN'T hard to track. I mean, a gang of Walkers was like having a team of sniffer dogs on hand 24/7.

Anjelo had surreptitiously sniffed the area where Hiro had stood at the exit. "Fox-Walker. I have his scent. This one's strong around the club. I'm sure we can follow it."

I glanced at Logan. He'd never be able to keep up with us at Walker top speed. My mind whirled to come up with an excuse and I opened my mouth, then closed it as Logan's phone buzzed. He stepped away, returning a few moments later with a scowl on his face. "I've got to go. You think Anjelo will be fine talking to Hiro?"

I nodded.

Logan hesitated then nodded and walked off, already on his mobile as he disappeared around the block.

Anjelo and I followed the scent for a few blocks. At last we came to a drab apartment house. The scents of other Walkers mingled and confused the trail. We followed it up a darkened flight of stairs. The spike of stale urine and rotting garbage assaulted us, worse with our Panther noses on full blast. Up to the third floor, we turned left and tracked the pungent aroma of fox to the third door on our left. He was home.

Anjelo knocked. I couldn't have held him back, even if I wanted to. If Lily had meant as much to me as she did to Anjelo I would be in the same permanent state of hysterical fear and fury.

He knocked again and the door cracked open. Anjelo shoved the door onto Hiro and pushed into the room. Hiro turned, stark fear swam in his glossy eyes. He tried to make a run for it. Too late. Anjelo swiped him hard across the side of his head and the Fox-Walker went down. Three lines of blood marked the fox's cheek—Anjelo had transformed his hands to claw-tipped paws.

Hiro, taking the swipe as a challenge, transformed part way too, his vicious black claws glinted in the bright light streaming into the window. Anjelo's growl brought me back to the fight before me. Claws and teeth went flying, growls and high-pitched yips blended into a cacophony of rage.

Hiro's teeth sank deep into Anjelo's forearm. Anjelo growled and plunged his claws into the fox's back. He would've transformed the entire way had I not stopped him. A fight between a fox and a Panther was not a fair one at all. We needed the fox alive, at least until he gave us the information we needed.

Anjelo finally regained some sense and calmed down sufficiently to tie Hiro up. His muscles bulged with the effort to restrain himself from wringing the fox's neck. I transformed a single claw and held the lethal tip to the side of Hiro's face.

"Not so brave now are we, chum?"

He remained silent until I prodded his cheek, drawing blood.

"What do you want?" He faced me but his eyes watched my claw as it hovered an inch from his face.

"Tell me about the two goons you let abduct an innocent girl from the club."

"What? I did nothing." My claw touched his cheek again and I found it was quite sufficient to encourage him to spill. "No...wait...it was Brand's guys."

"Who's Brand? Is he the dealer?"

"Yeah, he's the Boss. What the Boss wants, the Boss gets." Hiro shivered with double layered fear. Brand's retribution, and my shiny claw.

"What did he want with the girl?"

"I don't know...please." Hiro cringed as Anjelo growled and shoved his face a hot breath away from Hiro's own bleeding one.

"I think he's telling the truth." I backed off slightly, hoping the bouncer would take it as a show of faith. "Where can I find your boss?"

Fear tightened the Japanese man's features, pulling his almond shaped eyes into thinner slits. "It's too dangerous, he'll kill you." He kept shaking his head over and over again.

"I'm a big girl. I can take care of myself, Hiro. So tell me where I can find Brand and I will leave your pretty face in one piece."

"The old abandoned warehouse at the edge of the Dead Zone." The Dead Zone was an expanse of abandoned buildings, once a thriving commercial center. There had been whispers the Mayor intended to raze the area, but it was potentially an expensive and time consuming project. No work had been done over the last four years since the plan had been announced. In the meantime it became a hunting and feeding ground for the cities underworld. Hiro laughed, the sound flat and emotionless. "But don't say I didn't warn you. He's one sick bastard."

"What do you mean?" I asked taking a step closer to him.

"Brand likes his meals alive and kicking. And human." Hiro smirked. We would never have seen that coming.

CHAPTER 26

*I*t was late in the evening and I was deep in thought, running the happenings of the last few days over in my mind, hoping some clue would pop straight into my head.

The high quiver of hysterical screams filled the street outside my window. The tenement across the street was filled with people, some squatters but most legally occupying the apartments. There were times when life or sanity proved difficult to control and people killed each other in those apartments. It had taken me a while to understand this part of Humanity.

The sick, messed up side, when anger lifted the hand of a father to beat to death his precious child. When a lover spilled the blood of his soul-mate in a drunken rage. That never happened in Walker communities. SkinWalkers place a high value on the lives of their children, the reason why my brother fought me tooth and nail when I decided to leave the colony.

But worse, to me, were those Humans who hurt for the sake of it, for the pure enjoyment of the act, for the sensuality of being the one in control of life. I rebelled against our way of living because we were forced into a hidden existence, but being among Humans had opened my eyes to the beauty of our society.

It wasn't unusual for people to scream and yell in my neighborhood. But the screams I heard now stabbed my stomach and pierced my skin. Although premonitions and psychic perception skills were not unheard of among SkinWalkers, it wasn't common, and certainly didn't run in my family line. Yet I felt chilled, as if my own spirit had walked across my chest.

I didn't waste time peeking out the window overlooking the street. Didn't bother to shut the window behind me as I flew down the fire-escape on winged feet. I skidded into the street, to find a crowd of people milling around. Seemed the scream had affected a number of residents. A woman in a faded nightgown all ruffles and frills, a man in his boxers, a pistol in his hand and his generous beer belly sagging low. No time to be grossed out.

I elbowed my way through the throng which got tighter the closer I came to the hysterical woman. They were people as concerned as I was. Concerned or plain curious. The tone of those screams held more than fear, it was the note of unadulterated horror which sent shivers through my soul, and made my Panther snarl to come out and fight.

On the street I pushed my way toward the source of the wails, afraid of what I would see. My first thought was 'Please not another skinned Walker'.

Anjelo and Logan and everyone who was working on this case were on tenterhooks. I wasn't surprised this was my first thought.

I paused, sniffed and smelled blood. Memories swirled in my mind—of muscles bare and bloody. Mental shake, I got hold of my thoughts and focused on the scent. It was tainted with other smells lingering on the air. Bodies and food and alcohol coalesced in a miasma of rank odor.

But one scent sang a soprano. Human blood. Not a Skin-Walker. But something was not right. This scent was familiar. I questioned it. It was natural. When I'd seen the first corpse, flayed and bloody, I recognized the odor of familiarity on him.

This was the same but vastly different and my heart knocked painfully against my breastbone.

The crowd parted before me as I reached the hysterical woman. She stood over a body, of which all I could see were a hand and two feet.

Ailuros help me, I know this scent.

Feet shod in familiar boots.

Dear Ailuros. Not another friend.

I moved closer. The woman turned, still sobbing, to be comforted by another bystander. She moved away and my view was unobstructed.

Shock and grief robbed the air from my lungs, the blood from my head. Blood pooled beneath the supine form and I fell to my knees, heedless as it soaked into my jeans and stained my hands, still warm as it bled into the ground. I reached for the lifeless, blood-drenched body of Clancy, my supervisor and friend.

My body ached, my heart felt hard and cold, a heavy rock had replaced the beating thing that once lived there.

I reached out and touched Clancy's face, not sure if I should. Her skin was icy beneath my fingers. The front of her clothes were ripped to shreds and pieces of her blood-soaked clothing clung to the open wounds. Even the hoodie she wore was blood-ied. My hoodie, the one I'd last seen hanging on a hook in her office. She must have grabbed it because of the rain.

My Panther raged, hurting me physically as it craved release. A sudden fullness in my fingers...my claws began to push at the tips, begging release. All around me words and whispers melded together in an agonizing hum.

I didn't want to see her this way. Didn't want to see those long gouges striding her abdomen and upper thighs. Didn't want to accept those wounds as real. My Panther clawed me, a female craving vengeance. I recognized those wounds. They were inflicted by a large, strong feline. A deadly feline.

Hands held me. Someone spoke to comfort me. I shook them

off. Who would do such a thing? A rogue SkinWalker? What in Ailuros' name was going on?

Someone was killing my people, and now it seemed one of my people had just killed my innocent friend.

There was more to this than I could assimilate and I welcomed the sound of the sirens as they drew closer. Sirens meant Logan was coming. Coming to help me.

But too late for Clancy.

WHEN LOGAN KNOCKED on my door I was tempted to not answer. I didn't want company. Didn't want to see anyone. But I opened it anyway.

Logan's eyes were liquid with sympathy and empathy, and a touch of grief. He'd run through what had been found on Clancy's body. "I thought you should know."

Slivers of metal.

My mind reeled—even the coffee I swallowed had none of its usual comfort. The horrific wounds on Clancy's body were made, not by the claws of a Panther, but by claws fashioned out of metal. But for what damned reason? I rolled the facts around my head and only reached one conclusion.

We had the same coloring, similar height, similar preference in clothing. Clancy's murder was the work of the sadist, of a killer who still stalked the Walkers of the city. Perhaps they'd mistaken Clancy for me. The killer wouldn't know I'd been dismissed. Since I'd discovered their wretched leavings, they'd tried their best to kill me. I'd been smart and strong and evaded them so far. Probably got Clancy killed with my tenacity.

Logan hovered.

I hated hoverers.

Now I knew why he'd been treating me like a piece of cut glass. Why his watchful eyes flitted over me time and again.

Swallowing tears that squeezed my throat with silent cruel fingers, I stared out the huge windows at the scenery of darkened buildings, my arms twisted close around me.

Logan shifted behind me. The air at my back warmed as he wrapped his arms around me, holding me so close, drawing away the chill from my veins. My need was instinctive as I sighed and turned, seeking the comfort of his embrace. He held me so close I no longer felt adrift on the sea of my grief.

Logan's comfort strengthened the temptation to give in, but though tears singed my eyes I blinked them away. I had no time to break down into a bawling mess. Metal slivers meant I knew one person who could give me some answers.

I pushed him gently away, offering him a small smile. "Thanks. I think I needed that," I said, my voice soft and gritty.

"Is there anything you need? Anything I can do for you?" Logan asked. Though I'd moved away his hand had remained at the back of my neck. Now he shifted his palm to cup my cheek, the tender move drawing tears to my eyes again.

I cleared my throat and shook my head again. "I'm fine. I should be going anyway. I've some errands to run."

"Okay." Logan relented. "But you'd better ring me if you need anything, okay?"

"Yes, sir." I answered, giving him a two-fingered salute.

Not only had I lost Clancy, but my usual side-kick was also AWOL. I'd heard nothing from him since we'd shaken up the Fox-Walker. I knew where he was though. Somewhere out on the streets, looking for Lily. Until today, I hadn't accepted the depth of his love for the girl. Lily had made her dislike of me painfully clear. But, so busy was I in my own personal mayhem, I'd never taken the time to find out why. Too late now.

The city slept. Ignorant of my loss and my guilt. Taking a shattered breath as silently as possible, I channeled a Zen calm. Or tried to.

Clancy was gone. Ripped to pieces and left on my doorstep. A freaking message? Or a fatal mistake. Well, the bastard would pay. He had no idea who he was dealing with. My gaze drifted to my backpack by the door and the reassuring jut of my bow on one side. I planned to keep my weapons close. Insurance. Just in case.

But this time I need the help of someone living, not an inanimate weapon.

As soon as Logan left, I locked up and headed for Tara's. I pulled up my jacket sleeve, jogging the three blocks to Tara's shop, worried because I hadn't been able to get her on the phone, and because my desperation was becoming a fearful, tangible thing.

Everywhere I turned I was losing the people I cared for, and I couldn't help but feel the lead weight of fear line my gut.

I dug my hand into my pocket and brought out the tiny plastic packet to lay it carefully on the table. I refrained from dropping it into her palm, preferring not to ask for trouble.

She pulled the bag toward her. The metal slivers glinted as they moved within the plastic. It took only a few seconds more for Tara to recognize them.

"Where did you find this?" The words were harsh, a low growl.

She hadn't yet touched the metal, but her eyes glowed at the sight of it. I didn't fully understand the way a MetalSinger worked but I knew Tara long enough to know she recognized any metal she had honed.

When she dropped the metal shards into her palm, her shoulders tightened, her whole body one tense muscle. Cold dread seeped into me. More than recognition simmered in her dark eyes as she looked up at me. Horror filled them too. Followed by a film of tears.

MetalSingers not only honed metal, but were so attuned to the substance they could read the memories contained within them. A sense strengthened when the metal was one which they themselves had honed.

Tara's knew this metal intimately.

Tears streaked her grubby cheeks as she choked on the words, "I never meant for that to happen."

Her words hit me, hammered at me so hard I gasped for breath.

"What are you saying?" But I knew the answer. The weapon that killed Clancy had been created by Tara's hands. I backed away until the edge of a table dug into my hips, all the while keeping my eyes trained on Tara.

Her pale face was paler still, the blue veins in her temple throbbed. I could smell her grief.

"They...what they did to her...." Tara hid her eyes in her hands although I suspected the action did nothing to relieve her agony.

"What do you see?"

"It's...disjointed." Her words came in small pants, as if she were jogging and holding a conversation at the same time. "The memories are jumbled."

She slid to the dust laden floor and propped her elbows on her knees. Her head tilted back against an old washing machine. The walls of the room were lined with old, broken down machinery which Tara used to salvage metal for her weapons. She was good at the outdated concept of recycling.

In her fingers, the shards of metal glowed, absorbing Tara's energy into itself in exchange for its own memories.

She struggled with the visions those pieces of metal brought her. I wanted to comfort my friend. I wanted to scream at her, but in spite of my grief-driven rage I gritted my teeth. I had so few friends left, what good would it do to be angry at Tara. I'd lose one more friend.

So I stayed where I was and waited.

At last the steel slivers lost their glow, and she sighed. A heavy, sad sound which made me want to sob.

Tara got to her feet, and waited for me at the door leading into the house.

"Come. We both need a drink."

CHAPTER 27

What Tara needed was a good dose of vodka. Walkers were immune to alcohol, even Moonshine had the same effect as a glass of water. Tara, on the other hand, was a lush. She'd get drunk on the fumes from a glass. But she needed more than a glass of water to calm her frazzled nerves, so I set about making a pot of coffee. She sat, silent while I puttered around. It looked like she needed comforting more than anything, but she wouldn't allow anyone to see her weak and fragile.

We sat at the kitchen table, steaming pot between us on brown Formica pretending to be oak. It was dark outside and a lonely bulb cast dim light onto the table, sending grotesque shadows across the dulled surface. Tara stared into her now empty cup, smudges of blue underlining her haunted eyes. I clamped my teeth shut on the dozens of questions which wanted out. This was difficult for her in ways I wouldn't be able to understand.

We were both experiencing different angles of this particular grief, and I wasn't about to question the validity of her personal conflict. Although, for a selfish moment I wondered how she would be going through anything worse than my loss of a beloved friend and mentor. I let the thought go, though, and waited for Tara to speak.

Tides rose and fell, suns died, while I waited, but only minutes passed. We had to start somewhere, couldn't sit here all night waiting for the other to talk. Just breathing hurt. Especially when I remembered Clancy would never take a breath again.

"What was it?"

Tara looked at me, confusion darkening her eyes.

"I mean what kind of weapon did the splinters come from?" I kept the harshness out of my voice, speaking soft and slow.

"A set of steel claws, skeletal in construction. Each claw was made to slip onto a finger, and function like the real thing."

"Was it someone you knew? The person who commissioned it?" I had to force myself to pace my inquiry, to curb the rush of fervent questions I needed answers to.

"A Walker by the name of Brand came in a few days ago, explained how he wanted to give his friend a gift. He said his friend had lost his claws in an accident." The words were barely audible, I had to strain to catch them.

"What kind of accident would do that?" I asked, more to myself than in expectation of an answer.

"I wondered, but I didn't ask. I had no reason to suspect anything. Besides, I don't ask my customers intrusive questions." She stared at the empty cup and I automatically refilled it.

Silence claimed the room again, a heavy and oppressive thing, entwined with guilt, grief and self-recrimination.

She met my eyes; hers were glassy windows to an inner turmoil I could understand. "I thought I was doing something good, but it looks like all I did was put a weapon in the hands of evil."

"So he seemed legit?" I steered clear of further morbid thoughts, sticking to the facts.

"Yeah, he seemed...concerned for his friend. Pretty good act. He had me convinced." A scowl of self-disgust.

"You can't blame yourself. You weren't to know." I found I actually believed those words. Found it comforted me as well. I was relieved. I didn't blame her or hate her. We were both caught up in something I had yet to understand.

"He gave me a sketch of what he wanted. Any metal and I would've picked something up. But it was a piece of paper."

"Do you still have the sketch?"

"Yeah, I'll get it for you—"

"Leave it for now, relax a bit, tell me...what would be the reason for the splinters to break off?" I was curious about those tiny pieces. Shiny little clues left behind, crumbs for us to follow.

"Well, I'd made the claws for ornamental reasons, not as a weapon so I didn't finish the edges as I would have for a blade meant for combat." So simple.

"It was still sharp enough..." I refrained from completing the sentence. Now my skin iced over, hair stood on end.

I placed the packet on the polished wood on the table. It lay between us like an island. Somewhere where danger waited in silent glee, and one step onto it brought with it a mortal price. Tara stared at the glinting metal shards, as if they were alive and would jump out at her any second. She met my eyes, as if hoping I would change my mind, and knowing at the same time I wouldn't, and neither would she.

"Could you? Please? Just to see if you can sense anything else. Get a better idea of who was involved."

Tara's head moved, one jerky nod, as if she couldn't complete the full movement. She grasped the packet with shaky fingers, and tipped the contents onto her palm for the second time this evening.

Outside, the streetlights shone and cars chugged by. A bird cried a twilight farewell. Nobody knew how grief bound two girls together at this table. Two strands of mourning, vengeance and guilt entwined into one dark skein.

So far removed from school rooms and homework and summer holidays. My thoughts flicked to Anjelo and his absent self, to Lily and her anger toward me. To the hot young agent who haunted my steps and my thoughts. Would he long to be home, shooting hoops with his dad, rather than doing serious work for his supposedly non-existent agency? What was wrong here that we traded our youth for deadly misadventure?

Tara sighed, resigned. Closed her hand around the pieces, careful not to break the flimsy shards as she opened her mind to accept any message the metal held.

Eyes clamped shut, Tara thrust her other hand to me and I grabbed it. Offering a lifeline, support, forgiveness maybe. Her lids moved, grotesque in their wild rolling.

"Talk to me," I urged her. I wanted to make the process easier for her and if talking helped I wasn't going anywhere. It didn't matter what she said either. She was my friend. For a moment I was torn between the desperate need to end her misery, and the urge to pry open her clenched fist and end its contact with her skin. But at the last moment I stopped. For one selfish reason —Clancy.

"It's a hospital, I think? It's cold, green tiles. So cold." Tara sucked in her breath. "He's a doctor, I think."

Suddenly I knew what she was seeing. The Morgue during the autopsy.

"Can you go further?" I wasn't sure how her talent worked when accessing the memories of the metal she held. "In the past? Or deeper." I knew I probably sounded idiotic and may interfere with Tara's connection in some way if I said or did something wrong.

Silence again.

"She's dead. And then he's cutting her. Slashing her with the claws. But she's dead. No, no..."

"Can you see his face?" My heart knocked in my throat. I wondered if her link to the metal allowed Tara to see or feel the location but it seemed to me then that it would be asking too much.

"Not a face...feelings." I hid my disappointed and waited for her to continue. "He's angry. Blood in his thoughts. He wants something. He's desperate and violent. He's...insane. So much anger and hate. And...frustration. They brought him the wrong girl. He's furious. He tells them to leave her at your apartment as a message."

A memory clicked into place, like a puzzle piece finding its way home. My hoodie from Clancy's office. A piece of clothing strong with my scent. How easy to think they'd gotten me when she'd reeked of Alpha Walker. My body hurt, ached for Clancy; it was my fault after all. I sagged, energy flowing out of me. I just wanted to give in and cry. But I couldn't. Not now. Not yet. Not when I could still make him pay.

I watched her expression change as another vision flickered through her mind's eye.

"There's something else from before.... He likes the claws. He's happy, excited. – There's a woman too. She holds it—I feel her anger." Tara paused, a small cry left her lips as tears slid out from under eyelids still scrunched shut. "She's in so much pain. Her body and her mind. And her rage-oh my-no."

I was transfixed. It seemed Tara absorbed every facet of emotion transferred to the metal. I paused to feel sympathy for her. What must it be like to see so deeply into another person's mind? I shook the thought out of my head.

"Do you have any idea what she looks like?"

"I remember her—the woman, she came with Brand to order the claws. She was angry then too."

"Anything that gives you a sense of where they are?"

"Nothing—just feelings. Not locations."

"Okay." I rose to my feet and cleared the table of coffee cups.

Tara just sat there quietly. "I've got to get going. Are you going to be okay? Do you need me to stay?"

"No, you go. I'm fine." I narrowed my eyes. She stood up and walked over to me, placing her hands on my shoulders. "I promise, I'm fine."

I gave her a quick hug and left her there. Left her to the empty house and to her cold dark thoughts. And I hoped she really was fine.

I WAS SOMEWHAT SATISFIED. We had an idea of who helped to get Clancy killed. I wondered again who this hate-filled woman was. This group of Walkers was a rebellious and dangerous lot. Their violence and anger were spilling over into my life and the lives of my friends.

We had Brand identified already, and I would make him pay. I found my fists clenched of their own accord, and my nails cut into my palms deeper than I realized. I opened them when I felt moisture. I stared, shocked, at the four small, deep cuts lining the center of each palm. My feline claws that had slipped past my mental barrier, totally undetected.

I was fuming. Even my ears were hot and that was not a good sign, especially when I was royally pissed off at myself. Until now, I would never have suspected myself as being guilty of naiveté. Not me, an experienced killer no less. I may not be a full blown worldly-wise adult but I knew a thing or two about danger. Yet somehow I seemed to have nurtured this infantile belief that all Walkers were essentially good at heart. Just because we were different from Humans didn't mean we were all good. So easy to believe it was the Humanity in us poisoning our essentially good natures. Excuses. And prejudices.

Evil lurked everywhere. Tempted everyone.

The concept of Walkers being as good or bad as any Human, was a new one. I'd been taught Humanity was particularly unique in their ability to abuse each other. Perhaps it was the Humanity in the innate nature of this SkinWalker that had taken him over.

I made a call to Logan, and we arranged to meet at O'Hagan's, a local bar, busy and noisy with no place to get distracted by tall dark and hot anything. There were too many things he needed to know and I couldn't afford to get distracted.

LOGAN GOT to O'Hagan's within minutes of Kailin and settled into a table by the window.

She quickly ran over what Tara had told her about the metal slivers and the look on Logan's face turned dark. He'd kept back some of the slivers to do the very same thing; sent them on to Omega's metal singer. But at least with Kailin's friend Tara, she knew the name to match the images the metal singers got from metal.

With a sigh he leaned against his backrest. "So we're looking for a Walker—Brand—who is quite likely the killer." He shook his head. "I've never heard of a Walker killing like this before."

"You and me both," she answered, fiddling with her lemonade.

"Now that we have a name, just let me get some backup organized and we can go in."

"Wait? Why do we have to wait? We need to act now," she snapped, frustrated and upset. Logan wondered if she had any intention of waiting. She was feisty, and independent. And he could understand how she felt but it was her safety he was concerned about. "I had Brand's name from Hiro. I should've done something about it then. If we'd caught him then Clancy would still be alive…"

"Look, you don't know that Kailin. Don't be rash about this. Omega has a team, not to mention fire-power. The smartest thing to do is wait. And it won't be for long. I'll get it arranged tonight and give you a ring."

"But if he's there now we'll have missed our opportunity

because we waited for your team to organize itself." She glared at Logan and he knew her frustration.

"I understand how you feel. But wait. Please. Give me a couple of hours and I'll meet you there myself if Omega takes too long."

"Fine," she agreed and sipped her drink. Logan's eyes narrowed. He thought he detected a hint of insincerity in her voice.

CHAPTER 28

A half hour later I huddled behind a rusted truck, scanning the dark entrance to an abandoned warehouse which loomed before me like the black mouth of Hell. Logan had failed to convince me to wait for him. To go in together. It had taken Clancy's murder to get me to wake up. And Tara's revelation had spurred me on.

I wasn't planning on wasting a moment more.

Meeting Brand was a task I relished, but didn't look forward to doing on my own. My killer instinct was driving me wild. I wanted to terminate him the very same way I did my more difficult kills. A scimitar to the neck, and my little beauty was sharper than a samurai sword only because of the beautifully engineered metal.

Thanks to Tara my sword was capable of performing the most difficult kills. Tara had honed it from a blend of metals she said would make my kills swift and clean. I only used it on special people. Mostly I used my bow. Mostly my kills were long-range. But on those rare occasions when I was unable to approach my target from a distance, I packed my trusty sword and got up close and personal.

But now I wished I'd taken Logan's advice and left Brand to him. This need to be my own boss might be the death of me, once and for all. Not having Anjelo around left me feeling helpless. From the start, Anjelo had been in on this investigation. Now Lily was taken, Anjelo was off looking for her. One text to say he was going to find her and then nothing. It was driving me insane with worry. Worst of all, Grandma Ivy was due back any day now. I was desperate for this whole debacle to be over and done with before she returned.

I gritted my teeth, straining my ears for the sound of any oncoming vehicle in the vicinity. He was late. But I had no intention of waiting any longer. Logan would kill me anyway, once he found out how dangerous Brand was.

The minutes ticked by agonizingly slowly. Black clouds blotted out the stars, throwing the building and my hiding place into pitch darkness. I sunk low, and crept into the empty warehouse, sniffing the air lightly. Oil and metal resonated through the large building.

There. Distinct, bold, the odor of grease and darkness. I could scent him from this far, and I was a good thirty yards away. Unfortunately it also meant he may know he had an interloper on his property. I hoped he was otherwise occupied.

My nose twitched. The whole place reeked. Blood, and sweat, and fear. The fear made absolutely no sense at all. I concentrated harder, drawing deeper from my Panther's senses, to identify how many people were in the room. I heard four hearts thudding, thundering away, blood pounding through veins and arteries, but only one heart racing with panic. Only one body had a blood pressure heightened by unadulterated terror.

Fear dripped off the Human, thick and strong. Their Humanity was easily identified by blood pressure and the inner vibrations of the beating heart. So unlike the latent, but audible strength of a Walker's heart.

Brand and his friends had evidently found themselves a

snack. Damn. This put a serious kink in my plan. I'd come to kill the bastard, not give his dinner a second lease on life. I was also outnumbered. No choice. Proceed with caution. My heart knocked so loud in my chest I was sure it echoed around the room.

As soon as I was enveloped by the scent of blood, hovering like a poisonous cloud haloing a disaster zone, I knew Brand was otherwise occupied and my presence went unnoticed.

A quick glance upward revealed ropes of chains hanging from the rafters so high I could barely see the highest points. The rope-chains hung to a few inches above my head, within reach but thankfully not in my way. Somewhere at the back of the building a door or window was open to a draft. The chains swung in the unseen breeze, dancing eerily above me. Chinking softly.

I crept between rusted tanks and drums, edging forward with cautious steps, pausing, listening. Raucous, grating laughter rang out, setting a flock of pigeons a-flutter. The low hum of voices filtered to me, between the masses of old sawing equipment.

A woman screamed out, the sound shrill with pain and terror. A sound which set my blood to boil. That did it. Never mind the kink in my plans, I decided I would feel loads better once the woman was freed and Brand got his just desserts.

I maneuvered through the gauntlet of rusted, hulking machines of unidentifiable purpose. At last I could see the group. In an instant I knew my chances had dwindled. Dwindled to zero. I was heavily outnumbered.

Brand was having a party. Three men, also Walkers by the smell of them, stood with Brand, forming a rough circle around a young girl. They were shoving her between them, grabbing and pushing and spinning her until she was disoriented and barely able to remain standing.

Her clothing was ripped and in tatters, scratches and gouge-marks covered her body, and terror pooled in her eyes, its strength blotted by endless tears. That was when I saw Brand's face.

Brand's transformation was beautiful in a ghastly way. His features were more feline than human, his jaw thinner and longer, and yet he still retained the personality of his Human face. The beauty was in his hair, streaked dull gold and so reminiscent of the leopard he was, it took my breath away for a second.

And his face reminded me of Sully. So much that I would've sworn it was his twin, if not Sully himself.

When he let out the growl that was more of a scream that chilled my blood, I knew I was too late to save her. I'd moved too slowly. All I could do was watch in silent horror as Brand pulled back razor sharp claws which sprouted from hands ending in a gross amalgamation of human hands and leopard paws.

He slashed her open, neck to hip. She was alive long enough to see her innards spill over her fingers, still warm and soft, onto the sandy floor. Then she dropped to the ground and the four SkinWalkers transformed fully and lunged at the body.

I shivered.

Fear, disgust, and panic rooted me to the spot. I held my breath until I almost passed out. I released the breath when nothing happened. They were so busy with their meal, nothing else would matter until their blood rage was sated.

I sank back against the drum behind me, kept them in my sights, all the while wishing I'd waited for Logan to arrive. If Brand was Sully, it meant he had Lily. Tears filled my eyes as I wondered if he'd treated poor Lily the same way he was treating the poor kid out there.

My initial bravado and desire to rid the world of the scum called Brand had come to a grinding halt. I accepted now, that something more had to be done about this. The clans needed to be warned. Walkers weren't known to prey on Humans in this fashion, and from what I'd learned all my life, very few Walkers went rogue to this extent.

It wasn't the way we lived. The SkinWalkers had a code. No matter the clan, no matter the location, the code was law.

And if Brand was Sully, and he didn't care about Clan code, maybe his meal choices extended to Walkers. In which case, with the number of Walker bodies passing through his club, he'd have enough to feed himself and his little band of blood-suckers for years to come.

Here I sat, ringside to the murder and consumption of a Human being. The hungry sounds and smells of their feeding rousing the bile from my stomach. Walkers like these had lost control, had ceased to see reason or to abide by clan law. They would endanger the entire community.

The feeding sounds were fading as they devoured the body.

My stomach lurched, and I knew I wasn't far from spilling my own guts. The thought of what danger it would bring was enough to settle my nausea. Best to get back outside and wait for the team to arrive.

I moved slowly, staying low and heading back the way I came. Rounding large rusting drums and rolls of chains, fallen free from their mountings in the ceiling.

I was almost home free when I was ruthlessly lifted by the collar, and suspended off the ground. I was barely able to turn and look at my captor. I found myself staring Brand in the face.

He must have finished feeding earlier than the others and I hadn't noticed. I was dead meat. Literally. It wasn't likely he'd be squeamish to feed on a Walker.

He didn't say a word. Brand held me by the collar, let me fall to the ground and dragged me behind him as he returned to his horde. My butt landed on the dust, and bumped along as he went, no doubt wrecking my leather pants.

He flung me to the ground. I came to a rolling stop alongside the three Walkers feeding feverishly off the human remains. They took no notice of me. For that, I was thankful.

Brand undoubtedly understood the danger of parting a feeding animal from its food, and grabbed a handful of my hair, forcing me to move back a little way toward the way we'd come. Then he hit me. A blow to the side of my head, so unexpected I bit down on the front of my tongue, almost severing it. I lingered on the edge of unconsciousness until the rattling of heavy chains got my attention and pulled me back to my horrible reality.

He'd wrapped the chains around my hands, the vice-grip of the cold metal biting into my wrist as he pulled hard on his end. Pain flared in my hands as the chains dug deep into my skin as Brand lifted me off the ground until I hung a foot off. Looking straight into Brand's feral, blood streaked eyes. Eyes that seemed strangely familiar. And a scent that set of warning bells in my head.

I'd been so pre-occupied with being flung around the place I'd paid scant attention to his scent. And now I knew just where I'd smelled that particular eau de Walker before.

Club Wylde.

Hiro's boss Brand, was Hiro's boss Sully.

Until now, he hadn't uttered a word. I wasn't sure he could, my knowledge of the quality of a Walker's vocal cords in mid-change was limited.

"What are you doing sniffing around my place?" His words were raspy, rough, confirming my assumption. But he could growl. And growl he did. Revealing his canines and the glistening tissue still stuck there, remnants of his recent meal.

I was not forthcoming with an answer and received a solid punch to the midsection for my reluctance to chat. I coughed and gasped for air to refill my lungs.

Brand shoved me in frustration and I swung in a slow, wide arc away from him, and then back toward him, completing the circle. When I reached him again he punched, this time, connecting with my jaw, hard. My head spun, and I tried to clear it even though it was incredibly difficult with my head caught tight between both upraised arms.

My heart was thudding again, so fast my Panther clawed to get out. Bound as I was it was impossible to change, so I tamped the need down, with another more vicious need. I kicked out at him. Hard.

He hadn't expected it. The force of the kick to his face was deflected by the slippery blood still coating his mouth and chin. In spite of the deflection he reeled slightly. He pawed the spot I'd made contact with, wiping away a streak of blood and gore with it.

"You are trying my patience." He came closer, growling the words into my ear, sniffing at me. He seemed about to say something else, as he looked at my face. If this was really Sully, he would've recognized me, no doubt about that. He took a step back and looked at me. Perhaps it had been the stench of the Human victim's blood lingering around this end of the building that masked my own feline scent. But now he knew.

"Well, look what we found, boys. A little kitty cat come to play with us." Brand stared me down, this time after grabbing a solid hold onto my jacket collar. He smiled, and my heart plummeted. He was playing some kind of game with me.

His clawed fingers scraped lines in my scalp, splitting skin and drawing blood. He ripped my head back, the angle making it hard to swallow. I was still silent and he seemed not to like it.

"Speak, kitty..." He smiled but it was more a grimace. "Or I will be forced to play a little game you may not enjoy so much." He ran those gruesome claws against my cheek and their sharp edges dug slowly into the skin below my ear. More cuts, more blood.

The moment of silence which followed was filled only with the thought I was probably the most foolish female who ever walked this sorry Earth. Now, I hoped Logan had gotten his shit together and was out there right now, waiting for the right moment to spring me. All I could do was buy time, and silence would get me nowhere.

"I heard about you...you're Brand, aren't you?" I looked him straight in the eye and prepared myself to lie my face off. Better than having it ripped off. I decided to play the game. Pretend I didn't recognize him. Pretend I really was into the whole partial transformation, eating Human thing. Let Brand/Sully think I had no idea what I'd gotten myself into.

"I know who I am, kitty."

I heard snickering behind me. The boys were done with their meal and had come to watch the show.

Brand threw them a cold stare over my shoulder and they fell silent.

"I...I wanted to find out if it's true...that you can transform partway through." I tried to inject a dose of admiration into my voice.

I thought of batting my eyelids but it seemed a bit over the top, and besides, he'd pounded one of my eyes, and it was now swollen and un-battable. Not to mention the fact that I'd come on strong at the Club. He'd know I was faking it. "Nobody believed it when we heard it, but I did."

"So you followed me here?" Brand was slightly entranced by the idea of meeting a groupie, though still slightly suspicious.

I wanted him a little closer, wanted so badly to deliver a sound kick to his groin. Make sure there'd never be any little Brand's running around feeding on innocent people. But I doused the urge. Those claws of his reminded me that nothing stopped him from using my bones to sharpen his claws.

"Yes...I want you to teach me..." I let longing drip from my voice, and laced it with admiration again.

Whatever part of him remained a sentient male would natu-rally soak it up. I was disgusted with how authentic I sounded, and the pretense weighed heavily on me. I needed to have him believe I wanted to join their disgusting little band. It meant I had a chance to survive at least for the next few minutes. I refused to even think about the quandary I would be in if my backup did not arrive soon. Anytime soon would be good. Now would be better.

I swallowed the bile rising within me, and gazed into those bloodshot eyes.

"What will you give me for that lesson, kitty?" Brand made a slow circuit around me. His eyes roamed, his heartbeat increased, and the pheromones built up on his skin.

I delayed my answer. I was hung here like a side of meat, surrounded by rogue SkinWalkers. I had no misconception of what I meant to them. And I wasn't about to encourage him to have a bite.

He closed the distance between our faces. So close I could smell the rot of his breath and the stink of his body. Hygiene was not high on his list of priorities. He grabbed hold of my hair again—seemed he had a thing for my hair—tilting my head back, baring my neck and the bloody spot beneath my ear still leaking wet droplets.

He ran his tongue across the spot, and I cringed, fearing the germs that lay sleeping within his filthy mouth. Fearing too the blood rage that could so easily overcome him. I didn't fancy being his second course.

I struggled and it made him angry. So enraged he pulled hard on my head, so hard I began to see the edges of darkness closing in on me. So hard his hand came away with silky black strands.

He held my hair in his hands, well-won spoils, and laughed. A hideous bastardized combination of high pitch leopard shriek and deep male laughter.

I was shaking. Brand mistook my trembling for utter fear. He was wrong. If I was capable of a blood rage, the time to release it would be now.

No fear, I reminded myself. Fear had a scent. And the last

thing I needed now was for Brand to smell my fear. For a Walker he was far from dumb, he was Hiro's boss after all. The Boss who managed the drug-peddling business while hiding his true identity. He would know the fear meant I was hiding something. He'd bought my story about wanting to join his group. I hoped it would stay that way.

I knew my time was running out when he came to me again, extending his clawed finger to my neck and caressed the pounding crest of my jugular. Something in his demeanor had changed. As if he'd quit playing games with me. His eyes glowed, eager to spill the life in my veins.

My heart clenched and I knew my number was up.

LOGAN ARRIVED at the entrance to the warehouse to be met with silence. He'd used his motorcycle which was always a means of quick getaway. At first he wondered if Kailin had actually waited for him as she'd promise despite his gut saying that wasn't going to happen.

Then he heard it. A strange shrieking laughter coming from within the darkened warehouse. Logan entered the building, treading softly, totally aware that he was walking into a place where the occupants could, and probably would, smell him before he saw them.

He made his way through the high-ceilinged warehouse, following the sound of voices and the squeak of swinging chains, avoiding hulking metal masses.

He rounded a pile of junk-metal and stopped in his tracks. His blood ran cold as he stared at Kailin, strung up on a chain hanging from the iron rafters far above. A Walker, most likely Brand, held Kailin by the hair, laughing.

Kailin's body shook so hard she made the chains squeak as they moved back and forth. Logan's eyes narrowed as he watched her. Anyone would've easily mistaken her shaking for fear but Logan knew her better. She shook with fury.

Then Brand asked, "So tell me, Kailin Odel. How stupid did you think I was?" Logan could feel the anger rolling off Brand in waves. Logan tensed, waiting for the right moment to make his move.

"I don't know what you mean," Kailin responded, and this time Logan heard real fear now streaking through her voice.

"You come waltzing in here, throwing off your Alpha female stink, lying to me. Pretending you don't know who I am. And you expect me to play nice?" Logan knew it wouldn't be long before Brand made his move. His ruthless reputation preceded him. Kailin's life was in danger.

Her eyes narrowed. "Get away from me you murdering bastard. I don't really give a damn who you think you are."

Brand lowered his voice and Logan strained to hear his words. "You walk into my club and ask a bunch of questions as if you had every right to. Then you waltz right in here and pretend to be an adoring fan as if I'm stupid. You know what happens to little girls like you? They always get what's coming to them." Brand sneered as he pressed his claw into Kailin's neck and slit the skin, spilling a stream of hot red blood onto her chest.

Logan didn't wait a second longer.

He exploded into the space behind Brand, sending the Walker's thugs flying in many directions. Logan grunted, satisfied as he heard the muffled grunts as bodies hit ground, and metal.

Then Logan stilled, stood perfectly motionless behind Brand, who didn't seem to care that he'd encroached on his den. Logan regulated his breathing, calmed his heart rate and reached deep within himself for the power. His eyes remained open as he channeled the power to his hands. He knew sometimes his eyes held a strange glow within them. Knew too, that Kailin would see the glow. Would be watching as he used his fire power.

Brand had merely been buying time, waiting. He made a move to run and Logan let his fire loose. It streaked through the air, a controlled blast of heat and flame. Brand stiffened and fell to his knees so heavily Logan was sure he heard the crunch of the partially transformed Walker's knee-caps as they connected with the concrete floor. The veins at Logan's temples rose against his skin. And then Brand fell face first to the ground, and lay there unmoving. Logan wasn't taking any chances. He pulled down a length of chain and bound Brand's hands and feet, leaving him trussed up on the floor of the warehouse, like a Thanksgiving turkey.

Logan gazed at Kailin. He knew from her expression she was in shock, that she was processing the inexplicable thing that had just happened.

He'd been so focused on getting Brand incapacitated he hadn't registered that blood was still streaming from Kailin's neck. He raced to her, un-lynching the chains and setting her slowly to the ground. She gave him a tiny smile before she slipped into unconsciousness.

CHAPTER 29

I regained consciousness, to find myself being tended to by a paramedic, not too far from Brand. Once unconscious he'd returned to his normal human form as Sully. Heat coursed through my veins as I vibrated with anger. He'd led us on, entertained our questions and all the while he'd been behind the whole thing.

I shivered at the memory that I'd so recently thought of Sully as slightly charming and even attractive. Ugh. Now it was all I could do to prevent myself from kicking him in the unmentionables. I needed to know what he'd done with Lily. Hoped to Ailuros he'd left her in one piece.

But right now. I was exhausted, aching all over and feeling overwhelmed.

After the paramedic left, a group of Omega agents arrived and after a few minutes with Logan, began processing Brand/Sully. Good thing I wasn't required to interrogate the bastard. I knew I'd be tempted to kill his ass.

At last Logan approached and for the moment we were alone I didn't plan to wait any longer to ask my questions.

"So are you going to tell me what that was all about?"

For a moment he was silent and I thought he was going to try and avoid the topic altogether, but then he said, "I'm a Fire Mage. I used my power to incapacitate Brand."

"Oh." I couldn't manage anything more than the one syllable. Logan had Fire power? "I guess that explains the exploding tire episode?"

Logan chuckled. "Yes, exactly."

"So are you okay?"

"I'm fine. Just a colossal headache, but that's usual when I have to concentrate really hard."

"What was so different this time?"

"You were just a couple of inches away from Brand. I didn't want to incinerate you by accident."

If Logan was trying to make me feel better, he'd succeeded at the exact opposite. I was officially freaked out.

ANJELO'S ABSENCE was an almost physical loss for me. I hadn't realized how much I'd come to rely on him. Not that he was in any way the knight charging in to help me out. Rather he'd be the idiot hanging onto the horse's tail as it galloped off into the night.

Calls to Iain and Storm came up empty. I had no clue where he was. Why didn't he at least text me to keep me in the loop?

Dear Ailuros, please keep him safe.

I sent up the prayer but something told me I'd need more help than prayers.

CHAPTER 30

Despite the craziness of the last few days I wanted to make time for my patients. Especially now, since Clancy was no longer around to keep her eye on them. My work with the recovering addicts was usually slow, gaining progress week to week. But they were as committed as I was. Pitching up week after week in spite of the emotional roller-coaster ride that came with both the chemical withdrawal and their extraction from the drug community.

I understood a little. Removed from their support network they felt abandoned in spite of it having been their own choice to leave. I admired their strength very much, strength few people would have under such circumstances. Because of their commitment I felt like a heel for letting them down.

I'd finished updating my paperwork a couple of hours ago, cross referenced the notes of the substitute counselor Heide would've arranged, got some filing and reports in order, and spent some time checking my ammunition and stock of vials. I made a mental note to ring Tara—the new gas vials were jamming intermittently. So far, it'd only happened during my practice, but I couldn't risk it on the field.

It could wait a while though.

It was late when I walked out of the building. I'd lost track of time. For once in the last week, I had nowhere in particular to be. Now, walking to the curb to cross the street, life filtered to me. Music blared from a stereo across the street. The rev of a souped-up car engine a couple of blocks away. An alley cat screeched its discontent with her suitor.

But here on my street, it was quiet. An ominous quiet. A black pickup sat across the road, and I hesitated. I knew many of the people in this area, knew faces and cars well enough to know this vehicle didn't belong. I paused at the edge of the curb. Hesitated.

My ears perked, somewhere nearby a scratchy, harsh crackling shattered the undercurrent of silence. Sounds only Walkers could pick up. Now I heard the blurred squeaks of a walkie-talkie. Movement within the cab of the pickup heightened my suspicion.

Around the block, I heard the revving of a motorcycle engine, not sure of the cc but something fast at any rate. In spite of the darkness, the motorbike and its rider were clearly visible as they turned onto the road and sped toward me. At the opposite corner, a couple of kids turned to stare at the shiny, roaring machine.

I found his audacity unbelievable. Did he think I'd stand there, a couple hundred pounds of metal bearing down on me, and wait for the impact? I did the only thing I could think of. Watching him carefully as he got closer, I waited for the last second, and then took a quick step sideways and shot my arm out in front of him, stiff as a pillar, pulling deep on my Panther strength.

The streetlights threw two bright orbs onto the slick surface of his black helmet, lighting his eyes behind the visor for precious seconds.

The shocked surprise on his face was comical. He hit my hand full speed. The motorcycle continued on without him, skidding and ending its travels in a screeching spin.

The rider was much worse for wear. The force of the impact with my iron-hand sent him plummeting to the ground, drawn by the impetus of the bike. He landed flat on his back just feet away. He lay there, gasping and spluttering, holding his chest, while his helmet rolled across the ground coming to a halt over a drain. The impact with my arm knocked the stuffing out of him. All I needed was to shake it a little to loosen it up again.

The low hum of the motorbike wheel spun slower and slower.

Pickup-Guy jumped from the vehicle and sprinted across the street, not bothering to close his door. During the mayhem, he'd gunned the engine, ready to take off once they'd finished me. He should know better than to leave a car idling in this neighborhood. It wasn't likely the vehicle would still be there when I finished playing with my two new friends.

His anger reeked, fueled by the stink of his sweat and fear—not to mention the musk of unadulterated human. He spared a brief, disbelieving glance at the biker dude who lay sprawled on the ground, eyes out of focus, as if the very stars spun around his head.

"Fine. You want to play, so let's play." I flicked the hair out of my face and curled my finger at him in a cheeky 'Come on' gesture. It paid off a tad, as a frown of concern slipped across his face at my confidence.

What he didn't know was I wasn't all that prepared to be so cocky. The only weapon on me was a tiny curved blade in my boot. Although it was deadly sharp and had a vicious point, I needed to be close to use it. Dangerously close.

Even so, I didn't want to damage him more than necessary. It wasn't my thing, killing humans for no good reason. Whoever this idiot was, he was working for someone. No point eliminating the hired hands.

He circled me, like a bull, giving me a wide berth, eyes on me.

Those eyes flickered every few seconds in his partner's direction. Was he wondering how long I would take to turn him into a similar pretzel?

I bent forward, flicking my fingers at him, beckoning him with both hands. And smiled.

He lunged.

I spun around, landed a solid punch to his ribs, and heard the soft crunch as two of his ribs caved in under the force of the blow.

Adrenaline masked his pain and he appeared only winded. For now.

He came barreling at me again. I stepped swiftly aside and kicked his feet from under him. I almost felt sorry for him, until he grabbed my leg as I stepped away. Losing my balance, I fell. At the last second, I spun around and landed on both forearms, my eyes still fixed firmly on my opponent.

I was tiring of playing with him. No real challenge with these two lunkheads.

We both rose, staring each other down. I closed the distance, avoiding a right jab and then a left. Landed a blow to his windpipe leaving him gagging, spread-eagled on the pavement, feet away from his partner.

Biker-dude was back on his feet. Anger emanated from him as his gaze slid from me to the winded man on the ground.

"What's wrong? Can't take a beating from a girl?" I smiled.

He closed the distance and threw a punch. It landed short. Amateur.

Frustrated, he jammed his hand into his pocket and my heart sank as I stared straight into the black barrel of a S&W. I was fast, and strong, but not when facing a weapon powerful enough to blast my brains all over the sidewalk. I gritted my teeth and took my chances.

A super-fast swipe with my left hand, an equally quick duck to the left in case the weapon fired, and the gun went spinning off to the edge of the curb, firing twice as it spun. It was a miracle none of us were struck.

As he watched his weapon skitter away, he bent and reached for his boot, grabbing the blade strapped to his ankle. I almost laughed out loud, but squashed the urge, knowing I'd be the only one to appreciate the irony. My little blade was warm against my ankle. She'd taste blood before long.

He ran at me, swiping the knife in short arcs. It was harder to get close to him this time, protected as he was by the deadly teeth of the serrated blade. He lunged with his unarmed hand and I raised my arm to deflect the blow. Too late I knew it was a mistake, as the blade bit deeply into my forearm. Blood gushed from the wound.

Now I was mad. I'd lost far too much blood in the last week to put up with this crap any longer—the humanity of my attacker notwithstanding.

I reached with both hands for his arm, pulled hard to get him moving toward me, then smashed up onto his forearm while my left hand hit down hard on his forearm. The air was filled with the sickening crunch of splitting bone. The action also worked to plunge the blade deep into his thigh. He collapsed to the ground, clearly not sure which would need his attention, the knife in his thigh or the hand now dangling uselessly from his shoulder.

But the fresh hot blood was my distraction.

My attention changed, focusing on mauling the biker, my Panther's need heightening as my claws lengthened just so. Need to slice a vein open and spill his life-blood right here, filled me.

I was taken aback by the viciousness of my thoughts. My Panther pushed and surged from inside, frustrated and hungry. And, in the struggle with my feline bloodlust, the fight against my desire to rip the human apart, I missed Pickup-Guy as he rose and advanced on me, his knife raised, ready to spill my blood.

I felt the cold steel penetrate my flesh, knew then that it was already too late.

Too late to protect myself and too late for him to get away alive. The wound in my back pulled the Panther out, bent on revenge. Out here in the open, I had to control how far I changed, and I managed to rein it in so only my claws and teeth transformed.

It was all I needed. I turned on him, forcing his hand against the hilt of the blade still buried deep in my back. My hands swept around and, in one fluid swipe, I slashed his throat with deadly sharp claws.

He stopped dead. Touched his throat as the ruby seeped through the slashes in his flesh. I knew before his knees touched the ground he would be dead in the next few minutes. Knew before he fell face down on the sidewalk it was a mistake to kill him this way. Too distinctive.

My claws retracted as regret surged stronger, overpowering my Panther's need. A quick scan of the street confirmed it still remained deserted, but I knew someone would've heard the gunshots, would've rung the police, even if they were afraid to check for themselves.

I grabbed the dying man, lifted his bulk into my arms and in a few strides tossed him in the back of the pickup. It was amazing the vehicle was still there. I approached Biker-dude who'd come around in time to see the last deadly blow I'd dealt to his partner. He had tears in his eyes.

I would've felt sorry for him, except the gash in my arm still bled and the knife in my back was killing me. I grabbed him by the scruff and hauled him to the cab of the truck, tossing him into the driver's seat, broken arm and all.

He sat there, looking at me.

"What are you waiting for? Go."

Back at the blood-soiled scene, I picked up my backpack and the gun they left behind. The need to stamp my foot in frustration was so strong. Again, my blood was spilled all over a crime scene. Well, at least this time I had someone on the inside who'd cover for me.

At least I hoped he would.

I hobbled across the street, gasping for breath.

Stupid. So stupid. If I hadn't been thinking of not ending a human life, I wouldn't have a knife in my back right now. So much for your damned compassion, Kai.

The road and the sidewalk spun a little and I stumbled to the nearest streetlight. Leaning against the cool metal, I closed my eyes for a few moments, taking a few steadying breaths. Then, with stiff, blood-coated fingers, I fished my phone out of my pocket and dialed.

"Hey, Kai," Logan answered.

"Logan? I really need your help and this time it's super urgent," I said, gasping a little with the pain shooting up and down my back. "I need you now."

"Where are you?" Logan asked, his tone gravelly with worry. "Are you okay?"

"I'm outside the Rehab Center, but I think I can make it home. I don't want to stick around here any longer."

"Right, I'll meet you at your apartment then," he said, then hesitated a moment. "Are you sure you don't want me to pick you up?"

"No. I'll be fine. I'll meet you at my place." I cut the call and shifted forward. One foot in front of the other, glancing around, ever watchful. I didn't need another attack. I had to keep moving. A part of me berated my decision to meet Logan at my apartment. He could've picked me up right here. But I really didn't want to be standing around waiting for him, with a knife in my back and barely conscious.

I walked on, my head beginning to throb as my heart pumped harder and faster to make up for the blood I was losing.

This is not the time to pass out, Odel.

I rubbed my temples and gritted my teeth and focused on getting home.

I just hoped I wouldn't pass out before I got there.

LOGAN WAS SITTING on the stairs when the bird cage clanged and rattled its way up. It came to a grinding halt and Kailin shoved the gate open. She gave him a weak smile as she hobbled to her door. Logan rose and held his hand out for the keys. He'd expected a little resistance from the usually independent Kailin, but she just released them with a sigh.

A splotch of bright red at one temple caught his eye and he began to worry more, if that was possible. What had happened? He'd never heard her voice sound that way before; afraid, in pain and in need.

But all Logan did was raise one dark eyebrow at the spot while unlocking the door. He stood aside for her to enter and she limped in and slowly turned to face him.

"I need some help," she said, her features schooled as if determined not to make a big deal of whatever she needed.

"What happened?" Logan's words were hard and angry. Anger came more easily than fear, so he went with it.

She didn't answer, just turned around and dropped her backpack. All Logan could manage was to swallow his gasp. Then silence.

"What the—" Logan frowned. He figured she'd slung the bag over her shoulder, close to the hilt of the blade so she didn't walk the streets with a knife sticking out of her back of her jacket for all the world to see. In case he was in any doubt as to what *he* was seeing, he stepped closer.

"Pull it out," she demanded, her voice low, her body tensed, waiting for the pain.

"Are you kidding?" Logan rubbed his fingers through his hair, strangely numb even though he was an experienced agent.

"Stop being a sissy and pull the bloody thing out. It won't heal if you leave it, and I can't reach the damned thing." She growled the words and Logan stilled, the hair on the back of his neck raising. Instinct told him something, a light niggling thought, but he wasn't paying attention right now.

"Nuh-uh. You need a doctor."

She turned and glared at him, her pain-pinched eyes moist and hooded. "Please. I can't see a doctor. Too dangerous."

"Dangerous? What the hell is more dangerous than being stabbed in the back with a knife? Kailin be reasonable. You need to go to the hospital to get that thing out. You could bleed to death if the blade hit an artery or something."

"The hospital is the worst place for me. I would take it out myself, but I can't. That's why I called you." She was still glaring at him and Logan couldn't stand it any longer.

"Fine. Go and lie on the sofa." He spoke as if he were being forced to eat a meal of road-kill.

Kailin walked meekly to the sofa and settled onto the cushions. Logan bent over her and pressed the torn edges of her shirt apart to get a better look. Then he placed a palm on the left of the wound. The muscles in her back tensed as she readied herself. Logan found himself shaking his head. At her strength or her audacity, he wasn't sure. He grasped the handle of the knife, heard Kailin hiss but ignored it. He had to get a good grip on the knife. Satisfied, he tensed and heard Kailin take a deep breath.

Then he pulled.

She screamed, the sound of it cut deep into Logan and he shuddered. Not that pulling the knife out made him feel ill, but the thought of hurting her caused him actual physical pain.

It was over soon enough. She passed out while he pressed his hand against the wound to staunch any blood-flow.

CHAPTER 31

I don't remember what happened after Logan pulled the damned knife out. Passing out does that. Blurs memories and obliterates pain, even if it's only temporary.

I awoke flat on my stomach, the sharp-edged bite of agony in my arm and back now dialed down to a burning ache, the pain rounded, fuller and hot. The healing stage had begun.

We weren't invincible by any means. A good, old, shot to the heart would do the trick nicely, although in the old days the preference was to pull the still-beating heart from the chest cavity and plunge a knife straight through the throbbing organ. I'd take the shot to the heart any day.

My forearm had been neatly bandaged and taped. My back was stiff and icy hot. It crackled with the tape just above the top of my singlet.

Sounds filtered through to me. A pot clinked against a burner. Some liquid bubbled and boiled away. The whir of the old fan oven provided white noise. It didn't take my Panther senses to tell me that a steak was searing and potatoes grilling.

I sat up to a swimming head, but persevered. My only health restriction was the loss of blood, something a good meal would replenish. I padded barefoot to the door, the pile soft and luxurious beneath my feet. I sneaked a look into the kitchen to catch the maestro at work.

His senses must have been fine-tuned because he looked up and smiled.

"Rested?" He smiled, but the shape of his lips held a tightness; worry, concern. And I felt like a heel knowing I was about to justify the worry and concern with the truth. He had to know.

"Yes, feel better now." Not for long.

He wiped his hands on a kitchen towel and moved to inspect my bandaged hand. Satisfied he turned me around to check the wound in my back.

"The bleeding has stopped. That's a good sign." He was trying to reassure me. "We'll have dinner, then I'll take you to the hospital."

"What for?"

He looked at me as if I was a simpleton. "Stitches. Both the cuts are huge, they need stitches to help them heal better." He spoke slowly. He didn't know the wounds wouldn't need to be stitched. My body would fix them just fine.

Although Walkers had the ability to heal, we still scarred like any other creature. They healed faster, but it would be a few weeks before the scars faded.

His finger traced the ridges of the scar the bullet had left.

"Perhaps, someday, you can tell me how this happened to you? But for now, please explain how come I had to pull a friggin' knife out of your body." His voice wavered. Anger. I could smell it on his skin and found the strength of his reaction quite unbalancing.

"I was attacked at the Center. I had some stuff to pick up." I should've listened to him when he warned me I was a target.

"Kailin, why didn't you call me to go with you? I told you already, somebody wants you dead and they certainly seem to be taking every opportunity possible." His voice rose, and I could hear anger and fear in the timbre. Then he sighed, schooling his features. "Did you get a look at your attacker?"

He pulled a chair out for me to sit and passed me a bowl of chili and a spoon. I almost forgot to answer, as I savored the rich spices on my palate. He'd even thought of a starter to go with the steak. He'd be handy to have around. Grandma Ivy cooked like this—wholesome, spicy food that filled the stomach and the heart. Thinking of her, I glanced at her bedroom door which sat ajar. She hadn't returned yet, butterflies twisted in my gut. Should she walk in now, all hell would break loose. A strange man in her house, a grandchild all stabbed and wounded. What would she make of it?

"Kailin?" Logan tilted his head, looking at me, as if wondering if I was about to keel over and breathe my last. "Did you see your attacker?"

"Yeah. Attackers. A guy on a bike and another in a pickup across the street." I nodded.

"Mugging?"

I shrugged. "Definitely not. They were...intent. Like they had a job to do. But they didn't take anything." They may have wanted something but perhaps I never gave them the chance. "Maybe because I kicked the shit out of them?"

He ignored my comment. "Does the gun belong to them? Or you?" He nodded at the pistol sitting at the end of the counter, black and gleaming. Right next to the blade of the hunting knife, placed on a towel, its serrated edges still clogged with tissues and flesh from my body.

"Not mine. One of them dropped it. I think it was the guy in the pickup."

I gave the gun a nasty glare and returned to my chili as the ice in my veins slowly thawed. Logan took the gun in his hands, turned it over. He popped open the chamber and tipped the rounds into his open palm. Not bullets, but tiny metal vials filled with a sickly green liquid. Shaped like bullets with a clear shell and a hollow center. Not unlike the vials I sometimes used to subdue my targets. I knew Tara would soon be getting a visit from me.

"Well, at least we know they weren't trying to kill you?" As if that was any consolation. They had managed to leave two bloody, painful calling cards. "Drug-filled rounds like these can only mean they'd mean to abduct you. It wasn't a robbery. Wasn't a random attack. Someone had tried to kidnap you. It was deliberate. Organized. They know where you work. They would've been watching you," Logan said, his voice icy, emotionless.

I shivered in spite of the warmth of the room. I'd been calm until now.

For a Wraith Hunter, I was turning into a total wuss because I was being stalked. Where did all my courage go? Probably bled out of me along with a few pails of blood.

"Know anyone who would want to kidnap you? Any jilted boyfriends out for revenge?" He meant it as a joke, but I wasn't paying any attention to his words. My mind was turning over the events of the last few days. The chili bowl lay empty before me, and when he took it away I didn't even notice.

I cleared my throat. "The biker-dude had a mask on. Until he lost his helmet." My stomach clenched, and breathing was an effort. "He drove the car the night the body of the Walker was dumped. That night I'd only seen the face of the driver as the car sped off. When I crossed the road, I'd been so intent on checking on the victim I hadn't noticed the car return. Once the bullets started flying the last thing on my mind was getting a visual of my attacker. But now the details of his face are clearly imprinted in my mind. Biker-guy was the one who'd shot at me. I killed him." I felt a twinge of satisfaction that he'd died at my hand, then wondered where this ruthless streak had come from. I had to be hard and a bit ruthless to kill the way I did, so regularly. But not when it came to vanilla humans.

I had a purpose to my killings.

They weren't just random hits. My marks were Wraiths, demons intent on using their Hosts, killing their souls. As yet, I was unsure of what their goal was, but I had been blessed with this strange ability to track these awful creatures. It was a duty.

I finished talking, my voice remaining a monotone the entire time. My stomach clenched as I watched Logan's face. I was finally being upfront with Logan. Finally telling him I'd been the witness. His features had remained expressionless the entire time. Either not surprised or so far beyond fury that he had to hide it.

Logan turned on his heel and went back to the pots, while I stared at his tense, stiff back. I couldn't gauge how angry he was.

"So...you did see them then? Can you identify them?" he asked, avoiding the rest of what I'd told him.

"Please, don't go all 'policeman' on me. It might be better if we didn't involve the police." My heart knocked against my ribs.

"It's Omega. Not the police. And it's my job... I need to report it."

"Report what? A patch of blood on the sidewalk? There were no witnesses. And my attackers aren't going to run to the police and lay a charge against me, are they? One's dead and the other's well on his way to joining him."

The silence was palpable as Logan paled. He swallowed hard and frowned. "So you killed one of them, maybe both of them. And you expect me to just carry on as if nothing happened?"

"What did you want me to do? They were trying to kill me." I snapped. The glare he tossed at me was hot and angry. "Besides, there's no way we can report it."

"Why the hell not?"

"There's more here than you can see." As much as I was tempted to avoid this whole conversation, I had to stick to my decision to tell him. The only problem was I hadn't the faintest idea where to start.

"Cryptic." He was being very patient. Dishes rattled and clanked.

"Not really. I have something I need to tell you."

He eyed me through the steam rising from the open saucepans.

"Are you into something illegal?"

"No, it's something beyond the law. Worse—I think."

"What's so hard about telling me?" True. This shouldn't be hard. But I couldn't trust how he would react. Magic was one thing, but Walkers were a whole other kettle of feline.

"I need your help—"

"You mean apart from pulling knives out of your body?"

"Yeah...that too." My smile was sheepish. "If I tell you, you're likely to toss me out on my behind."

"I already feel like doing that. And this is your apartment, so I can't toss you out. Your point?" Despite the cold anger that edged his voice he was trying to make things easier for me by throwing in a pinch of humor. It wasn't helping.

"The body...from the community garden?" He nodded, not giving me any information. "The autopsy showed the dead man was a Walker?"

"Yeah." His face was a cool mask, unrevealing. "I told you we had our suspicions." He evaded my eyes. Sure, he'd explained them away as police business, but it seemed unfair especially considering how difficult this skeleton was to pull out of my closet.

"And you said you were familiar with the Walkers." More a statement than a question.

He nodded.

"You know Lily and Evan were Walkers." Had he put all the clues together? The mysterious disappearances, how I knew so many Walkers? Had he wondered how I managed to survive my meeting with Brand without becoming his second course?

"And..."

I'd resolved to tell him, even though my heart ached with fear he'd back away, leave me to my freakiness. He'd been my friend. And more. So far. I knew how I would feel. Betrayed, angry, and disbelieving. But it was better he knew now, so I'd know if we had him on our side.

"So am I." I uttered the last two words in a rush, hoping to soften the blow. He had a thoughtful expression on his face. In fact, he was taking it much better than I'd expected. "I'm sorry, Logan, I couldn't risk anybody finding out." It sounded like a litany of excuses. When he didn't say anything, I frowned. "You don't seem surprised or shocked."

"I'm not. It makes perfect sense. So, you came to me for information and help to track down Evan and then Lily. And you wanted info on the Garden victim? Why?"

"I needed to know what the police knew, what they'd guessed. I had no choice. You were the only person within the department who we knew was not corrupt. Most of the cops at the precinct are dirty. And how were we to know you knew our kind even existed?"

"So you used me." The words came out soft, but hollow.

"No. Yes. But you helped us. And for that we were grateful. We're not very trusting. Humans were the ones burning the wood when we were tied to the stakes. Wiping out our families so we had to live in secret. We have a history too, like Humankind. But Humans destroyed us because of their ignorance. We are monsters."

"What did you really have to do with first body dump?" When I looked up, his arms were folded in a tense twist at his chest and he stared at me, almost daring me to speak, as if he knew my words would all be lies. "Well?"

"I was across the street from the garden when I saw them throw the body out the car. Was on the way to the Center to pick up some stuff. They must have seen me as they drove off because they came back and started shooting. Shot me, actually. Hit me in the shoulder. That's the scar."

"But the wound is only days old." I couldn't blame him for finding it difficult to believe me. Humans did, even when the proof stared them in the face. We belonged in nightmares and spooky tales to scare little kids.

I shrugged. "A gift of our DNA I guess. We regenerate faster than Humans."

"So where were you when the police arrived?"

"In Clancy's office at the center." My heart clenched as I stumbled over her name. "I called Anjelo to help me—I was bleeding buckets."

"And the bullet? Is it still inside there, or did you have to dig it out?" His face was pale, the line of his cheekbones rocky.

"No, it's out." I watched his jaw clench. "We heal faster...minutes instead of days."

I ripped off the bandages on my forearm. Logan darted forward to stop me. And came to a dead halt in front of me. His face changed when he got a good look at the wound. The raw flesh was well on its way to being healed, crusted over with dried blood and dead skin.

He moved around to my back and carefully removed the bandage there, wanting to see for himself. I could imagine the wound as he would see it, the skin sliced open, a gory eye socket without the eye. The red raw flesh inside still knitting together.

The wound would be healing well too; I imagined it would still be raw at the edges but clotting and closing healthily. I was used to injuries, even ones as dangerous as the knife wound in my back. Used to the pain during the healing. But Logan hadn't been exposed to such an unnatural, almost Magykal process.

"Crazy...I know this is real, but it's just crazy." The words he uttered were soft, a conversation with himself. But I knew he knew what he saw. He sucked in a breath. "It's not that I don't know anything about Walkers, but seeing something like this with my own eyes… it's quite incredible."

I thought him being a Mage was pretty incredible too, but I said nothing.

"I'm sorry, the last thing I wanted was to burden you with our problems." I rose, throwing a wistful look at the steak in the oven. "I guess I was…selfish. My people were in danger and I expected too much from you." I looked around for my clothing and headed for my room. And Logan followed right behind me.

"Don't be stupid. You need protection. Think about what happened to you today. You could've been killed. And you're going to put yourself in further danger."

"I have Anjelo and Storm if I need help." Okay, maybe just Storm since Anjelo was AWOL.

"No. I mean, sure, you have them, but I'll arrange a guard as well." I was surprised. And curious. What made him change his mind?

"Why would you do that? You're angry because I didn't confide in you earlier—"

"You could've told me."

I turned away, stalked to my room and grabbed a black sweater from the closet not caring as the hanger swung off the rail and hit the floor with a clank. I wanted to cover my body, hide my scars. Maybe it would bring some semblance of order to this night. Maybe.

"I didn't know if I could trust you. It's not easy for me – for any of us—to trust Humans. How do you think I would've felt if someone I told took the information to the papers? We hide because it keeps us safe from Human society." I tugged my hair from the collar and twisted it up on my crown, holding it up with on hand while the other rummaged through my dresser drawer for a clip.

I stabbed a lethal-looking clip into the knot and stared at the mirror before me. At Logan's reflection.

I refused to look at him. Didn't want to see the questions on his face. I stalked past him, straight into the kitchen, still holding on to the pullover. If he wasn't going to eat, then his loss. I wasn't about to waste a perfectly good steak.

When he grabbed my hand and spun me around the furthest thing on my mind was steak. One look at his eyes, the fear, the worry and the deeper darker heaviness of need. My breath hitched in my throat. We moved toward each other, no control, no reason to stop. Just need. The need to feel his breath against mine, his lips against mine. And his body, all muscle and heated flesh pressed so close against mine.

Our lips collided, moist and burning with desire. He slipped his arms around my waist pulling me closer. My hands curled around his head pulling him to me. Hunger drove me, my thundering heartbeat filled my ears. When Logan grabbed me, lifted me up I didn't think, just sighed and reveled in the pleasure of being so much closer.

He moved a step forward, carrying me as if I weighed nothing and set me on the kitchen counter. All this time his lips never left mine. His hands settled on my thighs, his fingers pressing into the soft flesh. His thumb traced circles against the smooth fabric of my pants, lightning flecks of heat tracing the delicate skin above my knees. Then he tugged me closer and I moaned, wrapping my legs around him, pulling him against me.

His hands slipped beneath my singlet, and he ran them slowly up my back, bare flesh against heated bare flesh. He took care to avoid my wounds which made his touch all the more tender. My need rose, my head began to spin. And I blinked. My Panther strained beneath my skin. I couldn't control it.

Logan's lips left mine as he traced heated kisses down the side of my neck. I opened my eyes and froze. Knew in that instant they were no longer human. Knew they glowed a deep green as my Panther rose to the surface. I pulled away slowly, putting my hand on his chest, needing distance but still craving closeness.

He sighed and kissed my cheek and then moved in for another kiss. I didn't stop him. It had a sense of finality to it. Like he knew our interlude was over. I closed my eyes quickly and pushed my Panther back down to where she belonged. I was annoyed with my loss of control but then again, I didn't practice holding on to my Panther while making out on a regular basis.

The mood was broken but the intimacy wasn't.

Logan grabbed me by the waist and set me back down onto solid ground. At the same time, the oven began to beep, and Logan made a beeline for the steak. I sat at the counter, my mind going over the last few minutes, the coil of heat still sitting low in my belly.

I watched Logan as he brought our dinner over and smiled as we settled into a comfortable routine. We ate and cleaned up. Like a normal couple on a normal date.

But nothing was ever normal about my life.

CHAPTER 32

Grandma Ivy's door was shut, the sound of the shower confirming she was home. Ailuros knew how long she'd be around though. The Odel matriarch never stayed for long.

I grinned and headed for the kitchen. With the kettle boiling, I busied myself cutting up coffee cake and setting out plates and cups.

A few minutes passed and then Grandma Ivy emerged, fresh and beautiful, her bright blonde hair moist and frizzed from her shower, looking far too young to be anyone's grandmother.

"Kai, darling," she murmured, and squeezed me into a deathly tight embrace. The woman may look fragile, but the blood of an Alpha ran strong within her veins.

"Grams, you're home." That was all I could offer before my throat closed up. With the week from hell just behind me, all I wanted was to let her hold me, to forget everything and just be a kid for five minutes.

She held me.

And then, she grabbed me by the arms and thrust me away from her, studying my face in scary silence. "How have you been?

Anything interesting happen while I was away?" The hardness in her question gave me the eerie feeling that she knew exactly what had happened while she'd been gone.

Which was probably why I spilled everything. I skimmed the wraith hunts, detailed the dead SkinWalker and the abductions, the Alpha visits and Omega's paranormal investigations, and skimmed my near-death experience with Brand.

Grandma sat in silence until my monologue was over and when I sat back she slapped the top of the table with a flat palm and said, "Well, I think I have just the thing to make you feel better."

Odd thing to say.

Odder still when she scurried away and returned to place a rectangular box before me. Not a box—more like an artifact.

"Hope you like it." Grandma Ivy plonked herself back into her seat and shoved a piece of cake into her mouth. The action didn't hide the strange expression in her eyes. Concern.

I hesitated. What did Grandma Ivy have to be so worried about? When her gaze didn't waver, I turned my attention to the small, bronze chest. Beautiful flower-shaped rivets held the box in shape at each corner, hinges that curved and curled into viper heads, carvings on each side reminiscent of Roman Gymnasts, and great ancient battles.

I opened the lid.

The hinges didn't dare to squeak. Within the box lay a piece of armor, a bronze armband which looked much like a gladiator's trappings. Carved into the inside of the armband was a set of letters, surely something so ancient the likes of me would never understand it. What an odd gift.

"Wow, Grams. This is insanely gorgeous," I whispered. And it certainly was no lie; the light glistened on the carved surfaces and the images seemed to dance. I had to blink as it became too entrancing.

"It's a really special piece, Kai." Grams' voice lowered, a dead seriousness colored her words and a shiver crawled up my spine. She sounded so serious. Too serious for a simple gift giving. "Put it on."

Didn't sound like a request, and yet I felt like once I submitted there was no turning back. My gut twisted as instinct agreed with me.

"Once you accept this, it belongs to you." Grams was getting weird on me. I raised an eyebrow and was about to giggle when she continued, "And you belong to it."

"Grams, what in Ailuros' name does that mean?" My fingers had stilled in their movement toward the armband.

Grams sighed. "Once you place it on your arm the bracelet will sense whether you're right for each other. If you are, then the locks will jam, and you won't be able to remove it."

"Okay, forgive the girlie question, but what about showering?" I looked at the band—its size would dwarf my hand from elbow to wrist. "And how will it ever fit me?"

"I don't know dear. I just know the bracelet chooses its wearer and gives him or her a special strength." Grams leaned toward me and gripped my fingers in hers. "You and I both know you need all the help you can get."

There were too many unsaid words in that one sentence. Grams knew more than she was letting on.

"So, what's this thing supposed to do for me, make me invisible? Give me super-strength?" The whole story was so far-fetched. What was Grams thinking?

"Protection," Grams said, her eyes so sad I felt an answering clench in my heart. "If you were mortally wounded, you would survive."

The silence which followed rang around the room on painful echoes. How could she seriously expect me to accept what she'd just said? I teetered on the verge of hysterical laughter.

"So, definitely no try-before-you-buy?" *This is so crazy.*

"Nope. No returns once purchased either."

Beneath the banter lay a stone-cold seriousness I found disconcerting.

"Anything else it will give me?"

"Each of its wearers has been granted...a different sort of...ability. Some, who already possess power, have had it multiplied beyond their comprehension. Others have acquired a new power altogether."

"Maybe this isn't such a good idea. How do I know it won't hurt me? Maybe I should think about this."

"Kai, this is hardly the time for you to go away and have a good think about it. You have only this one chance."

I raised my eyebrows; I didn't appreciate being pushed into a corner even if it was my Grandma doing the pushing. I stood barely an inch away from the glowing bronze armor, my fingers almost touching the metal.

Almost.

When they made contact, my twinge of fear was lost within the swirl of electrical energy and iridescent light enveloping both Grams and me. From my fingers to my shoulder, aquamarine light sparkled and twirled around my arm and the band, coils of intangible color which wound from elbow to wrist in a magical embrace.

Within the blink of an eye, the band absorbed my arm into it. Or maybe it was the other way around. Perhaps my arm had called to it. Either way, band and arm now seemed as one.

I blinked and breathed deeply, drawing in some of the swirling green light too. It didn't matter. It didn't seem to have any adverse effect on me. I felt the warm weight on my arm and remembered what had just happened. I remembered, too, that I should be royally pissed off at Grams, but something within my soul had erased those negative feelings.

The weight of the band felt permanent. Forever. I felt the fear of what I'd gotten myself into.

"What just happened?"

Grams looked affronted, as if I'd asked why I'd been molested by the heavenly talisman. Grams cleared her throat. "Kai, this bracelet is now yours, forever. Or until the day someone else needs it far more than you do. It has chosen you."

"Why me?"

"I don't know." She raised her hands in defense. "All I know is that you needed help and this was the best way I could help you —to pass the armband on to you. Hopefully you will find a use for it."

"Where did you get it?" I shook my head, trying to figure it out, and hoping Grams had some answers. "Is it yours?"

"No, it wasn't mine. All I can tell you is that you can trust it. It won't harm you. Its job is to protect you and that's what it will do."

I stared at the golden bronze carvings. At that moment, though, all I could understand was some ancient adornment had taken possession of my arm. It felt warm against my skin. Molded comfortably around my arm. My heart jittered as I felt its embrace. This band wasn't going anywhere.

"Okay so what's it meant to do? How does it work?"

"Look Kai, I can't tell you anything more. You will know what you need to know in good time." Grams stood up, her eyes unreadable. "I can't stay, Kai. I've got to be going again."

And then she strode to her room, grabbed her overnight case and headed out the door with a wave.

I blinked.

I swirled in the wake of another Ivy Odel whirlwind visit.

And this time she left behind many more questions than answers.

I had no choice but to trust Grams.

THE WAFTING AROMA of fresh coffee accompanied the light knock on the door.

I'd called Tara early, inviting her over for a quick chat. She promised coffee and bagels and was on her way as soon as we cut the call. Tara loved to baby me. Being Ethereal she was no doubt old enough to be my great-great-great something. But to me she was a big-sister and a friend.

I sprinted to the door, and let her in.

"Smells great," I said, breathing in the aroma. But as much as I couldn't wait for the coffee, I needed answers about the strange bullets we'd found in my attacker's gun. "You can leave the stuff on the kitchen counter. Can I ask you something before we eat?"

"Of course. Fire away," Tara said as she left the bags and drinks on the counter and walked over to me. "What's wrong? Sounds ominous."

"It is, kinda." I dug into my pocket for the one bullet Logan left behind. I'd been desperate to know what Tara knew, and yet so fearful that she'd admit to making the bullets too. I wasn't sure how I would handle it if she said yes, but I said a prayer and hoped for the best. I opened my palm to reveal the hollow brass bullet containing the strange green liquid. "Any idea what this is?"

I'd made sure to keep my voice neutral and non-accusatory, and it seemed to have helped as Tara leaned forward, not in the least bit offended by the inquiry. "Interesting. Where did you get that, Kai? You getting your ammo elsewhere now?" she asked, raising an eyebrow and throwing me a teasing grin. A grin that faded as I related to her the whole attack episode of the previous evening. "Oh, Kai. That's horrible. Are you okay?"

"I'm fine, though I'd be much better if I knew who made these."

"Okay, absolutely. Hand it over." She opened her palm and I dropped the bullet into it. Tara closed her fingers over the bullet and breathed in and out slowly. "It was made by hand. He's proud of his work...." She tilted her head to the right, as if listening to the metal speak. "He's proud of making the drug. Synthe. That's what he calls it…"

I was relieved I actually had a lead. We had a name and confirmation that the drug and the bullet came from the same person, who was most likely the killer. "Thanks for checking it out for me," I said as Tara returned the bullet to me with a grimace.

"He's not a nice guy, that one. He's got evil in his blood," she said with a shudder.

"I'm sorry to put you through that. It must be horrible seeing their thoughts and feelings."

"It's fine. I just hope they find the guy soon. He's dangerous." Tara rubbed her arms where goose-bumps had formed on her pale skin.

"Come. Our coffee is getting cold," I said, hoping to change the topic and the mood.

Minutes later, we sat at the kitchen counter, sipping the coffee in mutual satisfaction. I was eternally grateful for the caffeine. Not to mention the company. After the meal I cleared up, chucking the paper cups and bags in the trash can. I'd just cleared the crumbs when I looked up to see Tara scanning my face, intent on figuring out what was the matter now. I could tell she still felt a trifle guilty about crafting the weapon who killed Clancy.

I stuck my arm out at her. "Please tell me what in Ailuros' name this is."

Her expression as she goggled at the bracelet would've rivaled any self-respecting goldfish. In the next instant, I was jerked forward only my hips catching at the edge stopped me from sliding across the countertop toward Tara.

I strained my neck to get a glimpse of what was happening to my hand and saw the expression on Tara's face. She held the band close to her; wonder, curiosity and admiration flitted across her face as she cupped the band in her palms, teasing the engraved swirls with her thumbs.

Were it possible for her to be any closer to the band, she'd have had to be kissing the thing. She stared and studied, not paying the least attention to me.

I let out the perfect combination of a snort and a giggle.

The sound broke Tara's adoration and she swung her gaze to me. When she saw I was sprawled on my side, right hand held above my head in an impossibly awkward yoga-like stance, she burst into hysterical laughter.

"Did I do that?" she choked out.

"Nope. I thought it would be a good time to shine the table with my butt. Nothing I can't handle." I was a bit miffed at the manhandling I received. But I still saw the funny side and contributed my own set of giggles.

Until I tried to sit up and a spasm of pain ripped through my back. An agonizing reminder there was nothing remotely amusing about my little dance with the two assassins. I swung around and sat next to her, giving her easy access to my arm.

"Do you think you can get anything from it?"

"It's bronze, so it will be difficult. I can't promise anything. But I'll try." Tara's eyes held a sadness I hadn't seen there before. And I felt a twinge of regret. I had put it there, in a round-about fashion. I wished now I hadn't asked her to read the steel pieces.

But another part of me was grateful. Because of her reading, we now had Brand. Scum that he was, he was the key to finding the killer. This bracelet was a key as well. Key to what? I intended to find out.

"It's warm, and incredibly soft." A startling description especially when the armor was made from solid bronze. But somehow, I understood what Tara meant. It explained how the band had shrunk to fit my arm. "There's violence in it, but goodness too. A...strange combination, but it...fits."

A long silence simmered as Tara searched the metal for memories, or any hint of what its purpose was.

"There's a woman, she feels protective of you, like she does not want you to be harmed. She sent this to you. I am pretty certain it's meant to protect you but it's not clear how." Tara paused and scrunched her forehead. "And something else keeps popping into my head. So strange, it's almost ridiculous."

I waggled my eyebrows in question.

"Some Spartacus guy, wearing a toga and armor. People chanting and praising him. And a monster. A huge octopus kind of creature. I must be going mental."

Tara looked tired and I said as much. She leaned back and relaxed. Pulling her fingers away from the metal to break the link.

"So, we got what? A whole lot of nothing?" I was disappointed. Everything she got was vague and insubstantial.

"No, idiot. We got enough to know that someone out there, apart from your Grandma, is looking out for you. And thinks enough of you to give you this." Tara poked at the armor which lay against my skin. "There's a protection on this bracelet, Kailin. Whoever wears it is strong and powerful. And I think you should use it. Wait and see what happens."

"Let me guess. You're a glass-half-full-kinda girl, right?" I smiled. Tara was right. And, for whatever the reason, the band had chosen me.

I was better off if I quit fighting it.

ara's visit had served to give me some distance from my problems. After we said goodbye I left for a trip to my colony. I'd had time to think about everything that had happened in the last week and what my options were. Had I been a normal child, my elders would've been my first port of call, but I was blessed with both an absent mother and grandmother, the former permanently while the latter may turn up anytime soon. My father on the other hand, may as well be absent for all the influence he had in my life. Given the choice between a visitation with Corin and becoming Human forever, I would gladly have sacrificed my feline persona.

But I did not have the luxury of choice. He was the Prime Alpha of my pack, and I needed information from him.

The house was the same, silent and empty, even when we had all lived here. Iain was out, but my father's car was in the driveway, so he had to be in his office. The man did very little but work.

I squared my shoulders and entered the room. The soft click of the lock behind me made him turn toward me. And for one pathetic second, I held my breath while my body and soul hoped beyond all hope that he would open his arms and give me a bear-hug and welcome me home. Only for a second. I swallowed the thick lump of disappointment lodged in my throat as I met his eyes and saw only a mild curiosity. As if he merely wondered what was so important for me to come see him. Not as if he held the slightest bit of joy to see his child return home.

I studied his face, then. The smooth lines, high cheekbones, dark eyes, unfathomable eyes I'd wished so many times I had the power to soften. A gray memory flitted across my mind—a smiling father filled with love and laughter on whose shoulders I'd ridden, and with whom tickles and hugs were the norm. But when my mother left us, she took with her his smile and his softness, leaving us with this dark shell of the man he once was.

I blinked away the memories, along with the slight moisture coating my eyes. He hadn't aged—it had only been two years after all.

"Hello, Kailin. Have you finally come to your senses?" My father leaned forward, settling his elbows on his oak desk and steepling his fingers.

"I'm sorry, I'm not sure what you mean, Father." I knew exactly what he meant, and it made my blood simmer with fury. I had to tamp it down or my Alpha father would know exactly what I felt soon enough.

"What I mean is have you finally realized that home is where you belong and that you should end this silly nonsense of staying in Chicago?" His voice was clipped, cool as always. Not a hint of emotion.

"No, Father. Actually, I'm very happy there. I'm just here to find out if Iain briefed you on our problem. And if you have heard anything yet from Greer."

"Yes. Iain has told me of our problem." He sighed, and I swallowed my shock. I'd expected him to brush it off as my problem, not his. "Why don't you give me your first-hand version of what's happened."

My Father had just done something so completely out of character; he'd refrained from contradicting me. And now he wanted me to tell him my story. Shock didn't even begin to describe my emotions. But I began my story, starting with a description of the corpse and the horrific injuries he had suffered at the hands of his murderer. I'd barely completed my description of the Walkers claw-tipped fingers when he turned away and I knew he meant to hide his reaction. Not fast enough. I'd seen the recognition flare in those black depths. As if he'd been expecting something like this to happen for so long he'd eventually forgotten about it, and I'd caught him by surprise.

The words tripped off my tongue so easily he would be forgiven had he dismissed the entire debacle as a figment of my crazy imagination. Granted I gave him the watered-down version, leaving out my encounter with Logan, while deliberately detailing my shooting and the second attempt on my life yesterday afternoon. I watched him, perversely studying his expression for any indication of shock or fear for my safety. But I needn't have bothered. His stony facade revealed none.

His back was rigid as he stared out the window. The weather was equally troubled. Obese clouds hovering out west had finally pooled directly overhead, bright flashes lit the dark mass from the inside: converging above us as if drawn to the equally dark turmoil in the room.

Had I dared, I would've been tapping my foot on the polished oak floor while I waited. My teeth were beginning to ache again. I concentrated on forcing my jaws to relax, instead of watching the mahogany clock on the mantelpiece kindly ticking away the moments of my life.

I gritted my teeth again. Blast it. I hated waiting for him, hated having to return to him for help. Knowing he would see this as a sign of weakness, as proof I was unable to make it on my own in the big, and Human world.

The ache in my jaw was answered by an ache of equal proportion in my shoulder. Though now fully healed, the knife wound in my back still throbbed, as if a thousand tiny chainsaw-wielding loggers had converged on the flesh around the wound, merrily stabbing away at my body. A brutal reminder of how near I'd come to crossing the next threshold. I rolled my shoulder slowly, wincing as it completed the revolution, trying to ease the tension around the damaged muscles.

Looking up I saw my father watching me, although his eyes were far away, mulling on a thought. It had grown so dark outside; the entire room was now reflected in the shiny panes, a living mosaic catching the flames as they danced, reflecting the two occupants who gave no indication they were blood kin. No affection even flickered in my father's eyes, nor in the set of his shoulders.

"What's going on?" My eyes narrowed on him. I was damned if I hadn't seen a flash of guilt color his eyes. He'd covered it fast but not so fast that I'd missed it.

With a sigh, he sank into his chair, safely on the other side of the huge oak desk. He lifted an antique gold Parker from its case. He never actually used the pens; the refills were impossible to find anymore. Now he snaked it in and out of his fingers, finding something to focus his attention on. Something besides me, that is.

Okay, get a grip. You didn't come here for a family reunion. Not like you expected hugs and kisses and a welcome home party. Suck it up.

When he did answer I was surprised. I'd half expected to be banished to my room for the folly of pushing him for an answer.

"I'd hoped there would never come a time that I would have to tell you this." He swallowed, and it looked to me like he was finding this all too difficult.

I didn't answer, for fear any interruption would cause him to stop and reconsider. Besides, some tiny part of me relished seeing the man reduced to an uncertain and troubled mortal.

He'd always seemed to me so far beyond real. Unattainable, incomprehensible.

"What I regret is…the last thing I expected was for this mess to end up on your doorstep."

My turn to swallow. Irritation felt like a ball of scratchy twine stuck in my throat. I risked my life almost daily, and he had no freaking idea. As if I couldn't take care of myself. I couldn't control my expression of disbelief.

"Did you think I would've let you go, had I not preferred it?" The smile curving his mouth was cool and arrogant.

I clamped my mouth shut, only because I felt the inside of my lip quiver slightly. I'd walked straight into a minefield of pain filled memories that I'd been safely guarded against in the last two years. I would wait only until he was done talking, then I was leaving.

"I see you have learned the wisdom of recognizing when to back down." I refused to rise to the bait, paused to wonder why he wasted time in the baiting. "There is something you should've been told a long time ago. When you left, it seemed moot. But, considering the information you have brought to me, it is time."

He was prolonging the telling—I was sure of it.

"I know who killed this man."

I said nothing, leaving it to him to fill the deep silences in the now darkened room. Along the wall, the fire still crackled bright and merry, at odds with the not-so-merry emotions I was feeling. An old desk lamp cast feeble light onto the desk between us, throwing eerie shadows upon us.

In that instant, my father seemed an old and weary man.

"The man you are looking for is Niko. I'm quite sure of it."

"Niko?" I was a bit slow to catch on, but I got there eventually as the look on my father's face was a mixture of pain and shame. "You mean *Uncle* Niko? Your brother?"

My father leaned back into his chair, and the sigh he released was clearly one of relief.

"Niko is Pariah."

Corin's words assaulted me in both body and mind.

"Why have you never told me this?" Before I could control my tongue, the petulant teenager took a step forward. "Am I the only one who doesn't know?"

Wishing I could take the outburst back, I rose and walked to the window.

"Nobody else knows about Niko, only Iain."

I found no comfort in those words. In fact, I found them harder to believe than if I was really the only one not privy to the knowledge.

The stubborn set of my shoulders must have given Corin some idea how I was feeling. All the issues I had with my father came tumbling back onto those stiff shoulders. I'd left because of it, and here I was, barely back for half an hour and already I was drowning in an abyss of emotional torment.

For once Corin gave me space to calm down.

"So? What do we do? Do you have any idea where he could be holed up? Where he could be stashing his victims until he's done with them?"

"No. I wish I knew." Corin ran a hand over a haggard face, a vain attempt to wipe away the frustration embedded in it. "We've been trying to find him this past year."

"Why is Uncle Niko doing this? What's his motive?"

"I wish I knew. Your uncle has always been unpredictable." He shrugged, but it was far from noncommittal. His worry was clear in the defeated sag of his shoulders.

"Eh? Unpredictable like trying to kill his own niece?" I blurted, still pissed that my own uncle had his henchmen out to get me.

"Kailin, I'm pretty sure Niko wouldn't deliberately harm you."

"But you don't know that for sure, do you?"

He didn't need to answer.

All in all, the visit with my father had been fruitful. Not exactly successful though, since I left with one bit of information I wished I'd never known.

My uncle who was trying to kill me.

Well he ain't gonna get the chance. Not if I have anything to say about it.

My mind was on my father and his tumultuous revelations. I used the fire escape and entered the apartment, both feet landing inside the room.

Something large and heavy, reeking of damp fur, slammed into me, throwing me against the wall, so hard I heard the red bricks crack.

The imprint of rough brick dented the back of my skull. The skin broke beneath two sets of razor-sharp claws. The world tilted, and my vision began to darken as I slid to the floor. I almost passed out.

Almost. The wretched wolf stood over me, grinning. I scented hunger on him as he licked his jaws. The stench of blood enfolded me, and I winced at the sting where his claws had ripped at me.

This business of getting hurt was seriously pissing me off.

My Panther keened within me and I gave in – freed the claws at my fingertips and sideswiped the beast, gouging the side of his face and jaw, ripping the skin with four deep slashes. The force of my blow threw him aside and he skittered across the floor, claws scrabbling for purchase, whimpering.

As he went he pawed at his face, wiping at the skin hanging from his jaw. He wasn't drooling any longer.

From the back of the room a golden blur raced at me, a Lynx Walker in full animal form, skidding on the shiny floors and bouncing off the concrete columns dotting my loft. My claws lengthened, sharpened. I was ready to do more damage.

Seemed, whoever they were, they were not going to allow me the bliss of revenge. While my attention had remained focused on the approaching brown blur of Lynx, another of the intruders approached on a blind side.

A blow to the side of my head had me skimming the edge of unconsciousness. Strong, large hands grabbed my arm, lifted me off the floor. My entire weight rested on the joint of my shoulder and it stung as the ball began to tear itself away from the socket inch by agonizing inch.

I was grateful for the pain—it served to bring me back to my senses. And make me angry. Furious. I turned my head to get a look at my attacker.

The briefest of views gave me an impression of a heavy beard, large jowls and a well-padded abdomen; a vision of a Viking turned logger complete with checkered shirt and workers boots.

Then, knuckle and bone connected with my jaw so hard it sent my neck twisting in the opposite direction. I heard an ominous crack and hoped it came from the bones in his fingers and not my neck.

Staggering backward I hoped there wouldn't be too much of this. I bruised easily, not to mention I'd had my fair share of bloodletting physical damage in the last few days. Besides, my

Panther wanted out. Pain incited the animal inside me to stop the agony and wreak vengeance. Although my Panther side was a part of me, it had a mother's instinct as with most female felines. Her desire to protect and avenge was strong. Copper spiked my tongue as blood leaked into my mouth from little cuts where my teeth had slit the inside of my cheek.

The sharpness of those teeth against my tongue brought me to my senses and I forced my Panther down, I needed to find the right moment to change.

From my new position, flat on my back on the floor with a heavy booted foot placed on my fragile wrist, I saw my attackers for the first time. There were three of them. Five if you counted the two Walkers in animal form, a wolf and the Lynx, who paced this way and that, as if enclosed within an invisible cage.

Both animals were collared, a pure silver band encircling their necks. From my position, I had a clear view of evenly spaced spikes on the inside of the collars. Spikes which, no doubt, dug into their necks preventing them from transforming back into their Human skin. They'd brought out the big guns.

I could smell the dank fur, the heat of their crazed need to kill. Great sticky globs of saliva dribbled from their toothy jaws and fell onto my polished floors. They hungered for a taste of flesh. These creatures were too far gone for me to bargain with. Fear washed over me. Fear for what my attackers intended for me. Fear for the captivity of the two captive Walkers, held in Change by the collars of silver.

The Viking who'd used me as a punching bag loomed before me. He leaned down and grabbed me by the arm—this time the uninjured one. I felt blessed. He'd stayed away from the hair. He lifted me to stand on feet still rubbery from the first blow to my head.

I scanned the room eyeing my unwelcome guests. The Walker on my left was so unlike the Viking as to be amusing. Skinny, nervous and looking like a puff of air would fell him. His dark eyes darted back and forth between his leader and me, as if he wasn't sure who was more unpredictable or dangerous.

The one female stared at me from behind a veil of garish red hair. The light glinted off the piercings in her eyebrows, lips and nose. They were all Cougar Walkers, which meant they were powerful killing machines. Even so, my mind raced to gauge my chances at escaping.

"Don't even think about it, little Panther," he echoed my thoughts. Mind-reader too. "They have your scent. These boys are the best trackers, you know."

"What the hell do you want?" Anger rippled through me again, white hot. This was my home, and they'd invaded a space I'd kept clear of any violence despite this last week's events. I needed some answers; it wasn't clear if they were here to off me or to abduct me.

I guessed the latter. If murder was their aim, I'd be doggy din-din by now.

"Don't worry that head of yours with too many questions. You'll lose it soon enough." The skinny guy snickered. Usually words like those were fighting words. But I was smart enough to acknowledge when I was outnumbered.

And out-strengthened too. These suckers were huge and rabid by the looks of it—even the ones on two feet.

"Fight me and I will be glad to rip you to pieces and feed you to these two." Lumberjack growled, inclining his head at the two animals pawing the floor beside him.

In spite of the warning, I readied myself to run, or at least try. His senses were keen, picking up on the slight tension in my muscles, and he was true to his word as he grabbed me by the throat and lifted me off the ground. His face transformed, canines lengthened, and claws grew, pressing sharp edges into the soft skin, so close to my jugular. I understood the danger he implied.

I was so close to him now. Even as I struggled for my next

breath, his fingers cutting off my air supply, I could smell his scent, his blood as it thrummed through his body. I could see the vein in his neck, thick and full, so near. All it would take was one swipe to rip it open. But now he had the upper hand, literally.

I kicked at him, my booted feet meeting and bouncing off his thick thighs. When he let go, I fell, heavy and numb, to the floor. I got to my feet, disliking the vulnerability of being sprawled on the ground at the feet of these monsters.

They were strong, and I accepted I had no chance of fighting them all off. The female, yes. She watched from beneath blood red hair that matched her jacket and from the scent of the leather I was afraid to think too hard about the color. Its deep red was reminiscent of fresh blood. She watched, assessed me from behind red bangs, her eyes streaked with fine blood vessels.

These were a different breed of Walker. Mean. Not just their blood rimmed eyes, but their scents emitted the furious need for blood. I could smell the rage on them all, so sweet and enticing.

Life-threatening: they were Brand's types and I recognized the scent of hunger in the room. I recognized too, the mysterious Walker-killer now meant business. His first attempt to take me had failed.

But I wasn't taking his game lying down. Vengeance had a sinister strength of its own. This time justice would be served for a crime personal to me. This time it wasn't mere justice, it was a family revenge. "Who sent you?" I was determined to get an answer.

"Shut up." The redhead stepped forward and punched me in the stomach so hard I bent over, hacking on each breath.

So, when I felt the prick of the needle at the side of my neck, it was already too late. I never knew which one of them did it. Not that I was in a position to prevent the drug from being injected into me.

Before I passed out, I ran my eyes over the disheveled state of my loft, hoping the mussed rug, broken picture frames and blood on the floor would alert Iain or Logan or someone that something was amiss.

The drug worked fast, and I went from awake and angry to woozy and happy.... Finally—dark oblivion.

LOGAN DECIDED to check up on Kailin, and to see if she knew anything new. As he approached her apartment door his body tensed; it was slightly ajar. Not a good sign. Apartment was a mess, claw marks scraped the painted walls, and gouged the wood floor in random spots around the living space. Toppled furniture and a broken lamp confirmed the abduction.

What the hell happened here?

He took another step into the room and kicked something, sending it spinning across the floor. Kailin's phone. He bent to grab it, tucking it into his pocket. He'd check the outgoing calls as soon as he had a minute.

Logan turned, racing back outside, intending to get back to base to try to find out where Kailin was.

But then he stopped in his tracks. On the corner across the street sat a black panel van. No windows. The back doors were flung open and two men threw Kai into the back. Logan wanted to run after them, stop them, but they were already closing the door. He was so focused on the van that he almost missed Anjelo trotting toward him up the sidewalk.

Logan flagged Anjelo down, the boy's shocked face showing he'd seen Kailin being thrown into the van. At least he listened and stayed down. One of the guys and a woman went around the van. Raised voices filtered to him. Fine time for a disagreement but gave him the opportunity to take the number plate down and memorize the voices and the people who were taking her.

If they saw him or Anjelo they'd both be dead. Or at least shot at like they did to Kailin when she found the body. So, he stayed on the corner. Kailin's phone buzzed in his pocket. He withdrew it and checked the message. Iain. Her brother wanted her to call him when she had a minute. Logan's heart knocked against his ribs. Guess it meant he'd have to call Iain back himself.

But the call would have to wait. The doors slammed shut and the engine revved angrily to life. He'd barely had time to climb onto his motorcycle before the van squealed off down the street. Logan stayed close on their tail. He glanced over at Anjelo and did a double take. The boy was running alongside him. For a moment Logan had forgotten he was a Walker. A black panther in a human body.

Of course, the boy could run.

I STAYED VERY STILL HOPING to buy time. People, maybe three, moved around the room, two scents were very familiar. One, a man by his size and breathing, stood before me.

The blindfold was scratchy and stank of oil and sweat. Although I expected it to be removed for the confrontation with my abductor, it stayed put.

I feigned unconsciousness, the longer I got away with it, the better the chances were they'd slip up and throw me a bit of vital information.

I was seated upright on a well-padded chair, my hands strapped to the arms, with my spine flush to a soft, high back, held there by a strap across my chest. I got the sense that once my eyes opened I would confirm it as a dentist's chair.

"Ah, at last. No need to pretend my dear. I know you are conscious. I can hear your heart beat just as well as you can hear mine. It's such a pleasure to finally have the illustrious Kailin Odel in our midst. Aren't we lucky." His voice, so familiar, brought tears to my eyes. And not even the nasty edge it held could prevent them.

Of course, I was unable to reply as the twin to my blindfold was wrapped tightly around my mouth, keeping in place a ball of crumpled fabric, wedged so deep in my mouth that every so often I gagged, and whose origins I preferred never to be educated on.

I was trying to keep the hysteria at bay, ignore the real horror I was facing. The voice was one I'd heard so often through my childhood, one which I'd looked forward to hearing because I'd heard it so seldom.

Uncle Niko was my captor. The man who'd sent his goons out to shoot and kill me was my own flesh and blood. The man who'd killed Clancy—who'd done nothing to offend him, other than be my friend.

I hoped the tears which filled my eyes wouldn't betray my grief by leaking out and marking my cheeks.

"So you finally decided to accept my invitation, kid?" His breath was fetid, wafting over my face.

I felt his finger beneath my chin, lifting my face for his inspection, the slight protrusion of his claw digging into the soft flesh, and I hated every second of it. Hated his betrayal, hated, too, the fact that he was my kin.

"I had no idea I was dealing with family. What say we have a little family reunion?"

I hated him with every pore in my body, hated him worse when the image of Clancy flitted through my mind's eye—her lifeless, blood-drenched body lying on the sidewalk like unwanted trash, the violated shell of the wonderful creature she once had been.

Violent anger took control of me and I struggled against my bonds, beginning a transformation which I finally wanted, despite the fact it would be dangerous and stupid. Some part of my brain, the part which contained most of my logic and common sense, over-rode the wave of rage gripping me. Forced me to control the change and stop before I hurt myself.

Niko had other ideas. I felt the prick of a needle in my arm and soon a heavy numbness washed through my body pulling me deep into unconsciousness.

I LAY ON MY BACK, my hands still bound, the disgusting gag gone, thank Ailuros. A small bottle held a familiar looking green liquid, some drug dripped slowly, snaking along the IV tubing, disappearing beneath the tape on my arm and sluicing into my body. The icy bite of the liquid knifed its way into my veins, only to dissipate warm and numbing into my body.

Oil and metal coated the back of my throat, confirming the drug was winning its one-sided battle to control my body. More than anything I hated my helplessness. Hated not being able to bounce off the mattress and go out in search of my captors.

I surveyed my prison; a pair of grilled windows sat high on the wall to my left. Gray light filtered through. To my left, a warped wooden door shut me in. Doorways to freedom, neither of which I could reach. The walls behind and in front of me were bare. Wallpaper once covered the walls in an elegant rose pattern, was now cracked and peeling, torn off here and there in strips to reveal bare boards beneath.

The floor was wood, naked and icy, the cold of it penetrated through the thin cot mattress beneath me and made its way straight into my bones.

This drug was a puzzle. What devil's concoction succeeded where no other drug, Human or otherwise, ever had?

Soon I had no choice but to give in to the endless pull as it lulled me back into oblivion. I would get my chance. For now, I had no choice but to sleep.

I awoke much later. The bare windows were dark. How long since I'd been taken? Was Logan or Iain looking for me yet? I struggled to recall if I'd made any plans to see either of them, and came up blank. My brain was fuzzy from the cocktail which had been fed into my veins all this while.

It struck me as odd though that the drug was no longer as potent as I'd felt in my last foray into consciousness. My body was no longer numb, my legs and hands tingled as nerves fired greetings to my brain. The dispenser was still half filled with the drug, still attached to the IV tube, still sliding along the tube and making its merry way into my body, wreaking what forms of havoc I knew not.

So, either the drug was losing its potency, or my body was building up immunity. Either way, I was grateful to be lucid at last. I lifted myself onto a shivering elbow, waiting until the world ceased undulating around me. Although tempted to tug everything out of my veins, I didn't want to leave a trail of blood behind me wherever I went. My fingers shook as I unscrewed the IV from the catheter in my arm and sat up. I brought my knees up, rested my head on them as the world spun.

I prayed I would stay conscious. The drug no longer numbed my body, but some residual effect of it still maintained control of me. I felt the intermittent pull as a dizzy euphoria possessed me, enticing my eyelids to shut and my body to seek the soft comfort of the mattress.

But I fought the release of the drug, taking one step at a time toward the door – toward freedom. I grasped the doorknob and twisted, expecting resistance and finding none. I wondered at the complacency of my captors. Did they lay their trust in the effects of the drug? It had worked, yes. But it had also worn off. I still wafted in and out of euphoria and some tiny part of me craved the blissful peace I'd experienced. I shoved the longing out of my head and placed my ear against the door.

It may have been unlocked but the last thing I needed was to walk out of my room slap bang into one of my captors to promptly end up flat on my back on the mattress again. Easy and cautious does it.

I let my Panther take partial control. My ears lengthened, the cartilage softened and flattened, and feline ears replaced Human.

Sounds became finer, cleaner. Almost painful in their clarity. Someone breathed, low and regular, in the next room. Another captive? From the rhythm of the sound the breather was asleep. Whether drugged or not, I was unable to tell. Further along the passage, glass clinked, and feet moved on the bare floor in a scraping shuffle.

Drafts of air wailed through unseen cracks somewhere within the building. A pity though, that all the incoming air brought was air. No sounds of the outside world to give me an idea of my prison's location.

Other sounds filtered through. Muffled voices from the floor below. A toilet flushed. Pipes shrieked and groaned their displeasure. And no footsteps in the corridor outside my room to endanger my escape.

I cracked the door open and slipped through the slim space. I dared not open it wider for fear the rusted hinges may announce my departure to all and sundry. Only when I stood in the passage, with my back to the wall, did I realize my feet were bare.

I didn't waste time puzzling over why.

I crept along, keeping my feet on the boards along the wall. Less chance of creaking beneath my weight. The voices below me rose and fell. The pipes had ceased their complaining. At the end of the hall I reached a stairwell. I'd heard no sounds from the upper level of the house, and the voices were downstairs, so down I went. What a joke. Here I was with the door to freedom right in front of me and I choose to venture further into the lion's den.

My ears, still feline, concentrated on the sounds filtering through to me from behind and below. The silence behind me indicated my absence remained undetected. The staircase reached for the ground floor in three flights, edged by a banister that had once seen better days.

I stayed against the wall again, not trusting the quality or age of the wood risers, preferring not to plunge through the rotten wood to an early death. The descent to the ground floor brought on an attack of vertigo accompanied by intense nausea.

The drugs had worn off leaving behind a drought at the back of my throat and a stomach that heaved and rolled uncontrollably.

Swallowing bile, I escaped the stairs and leaned against the wall. The voices still hummed from the back of the house and I followed the trail of sound, around the banister toward the closed door to what I assumed was the kitchen.

CHAPTER 35

The door was ajar. In the sliver of my view a figure paced back and forth before the table. A woman whose voice sent shivers up my spine.

All twelve bells of the Worcester Cathedral sang a cacophony within my head as I registered the identity of my captor. Straight white-blonde tresses framed a pale face and hung to her waist. I had always envied the paleness of her hair. Those bells were now so loud I couldn't think straight. To hear the instant denial, the excuses my mind drew forth for this impossible vision. Or perhaps in reality I held no thoughts within my shocked mind.

Grateful for the silence still enveloping the narrow passage, I continued my voyeuristic activities peering through the small slit of the open door. The occupants of the room who were visible to my scrutiny remained unaware, thanks to the practiced silence of my approach and the steady breeze which filtered through the broken passage window and swept my scent away.

The table ran parallel to me and I had a clear view of Greer and the three men at the table. All four were intent on the paperwork scattered on the tabletop. Greer's face was curtained by the fall of white-blonde hair as she leaned forward and poked a red nail at the paper. The nail was long, sharp and feline. Greer was partly transformed—a second, unbelievable revelation.

Every so often, within a pack, cubs are born without the ability to transform. It was common enough not to be surprising but in the offspring of an Alpha it was an absolute unknown. I remembered that up until I left the colony at age seventeen, Greer, two years older had still not changed. We'd just thought it was unusual but that it would happen with time. Those years had been filled with Greer's anger and self-recrimination. Our mother's absence hadn't helped her struggle any.

I'd left her behind when I'd escaped the clutches of my claustrophobic and controlling youth, never expecting her to develop a taste for the wrong crowd. The sight of her here stabbed daggers to my heart.

Guilt and horror each had a blade.

Greer seemed willing, though, and more frightening was the air of command she maintained. My breath stuck in my throat which was just as well.

A door slammed somewhere in the building. Fear skittered through my veins. What if they found my empty mattress? Were there others looking for me? I'd counted on their complacency, and now wondered if I'd been presumptuous.

Whether it was my thundering heart or the door slamming so suddenly upstairs, the Walkers within the room turned to the door in unison. I stepped back, one soft tread at a time, until I was against the wall behind me. A door scraped within the room.

My heart throbbed in my throat. I moved to dash back out into the hall, anywhere away from the door, when something round and solid stabbed my hip.

I grabbed it—a doorknob. I had no idea where the door would lead. The thought of getting caught without a way out made my knees lock in rebellion. But I had no choice.

Even if there were options, I had no time to weigh them.

I took chance by the throat and twisted. The door opened with a slight hiss, and I stepped into a darkness more gray than the black emptiness of the hallway, even after I shut it behind me. I pasted myself against the wall behind the door, hoping and praying to Ailuros for her protection.

I dared not go further into the gray darkness. Whatever was down in the basement, I preferred to discover at a more suitable time.

The door to the kitchen creaked open, and footsteps fell in the hall. Then the door opened, behind which I hid, almost fainting as fear swam in my veins thick and fast. Flattened against the wall, I tried even harder to sink into the wooden wall. My heart still beat so loudly I was sure as hell its thunderous sound echoed around me.

Greer and her companions filed into the slim space and descended a flight of rickety wooden stairs. My eyes had begun to adjust to the dull light and I was able to see the stairs ahead of me. One step too far and I would've tumbled to my death and solved all my problems in one flight.

A door opened, and white light filled the stairwell. I caught a brief view of Greer's profile as she entered the brightly lit room. Tears filled my eyes as I grieved for a sister I was sure I'd lost.

I watched as their figures receded into the room and the door closed behind them. I waited only long enough to ensure the hall outside was empty, before I slipped out into the passage and made my way to the front door. I studied the wood paneling of the entrance to my prison and walked to the door.

The iron handle was cold to touch, copper tarnished to an almost unrecognizable golden brown. It was slow to absorb the warmth from my hands, but when it was totally warm, I still held it in a deathly grip.

A grip which was making no move to depress the handle and

open the doorway to my freedom—I had no intention of leaving. Not when I could find out so much more by staying. Even the thought of bringing back reinforcements and possibly arresting the whole gang did not incite an act of embracing my freedom.

I turned my head and looked to where the stairway to the upper floor sat. In the darkness, I had to guess where the risers began and where the landing was. Even so, I knew they were my more immediate destination.

I would find a way out.

Only now, the heartbeat of the captive in the room next to mine called me like a siren. Greer's icy eyes called me equally wildly. Above all, vengeance called the loudest. Clancy's face swam before me in the darkness. I had to find out more.

My heart thundered in my chest. Even while I retraced my steps, I questioned the intelligence of my decision. Although I'd thought about escape, here I was, returning to my cell, back to captivity.

I should leave, find help and bring them back here.

But I needed to find out more. I told myself it was to ensure I had my story straight, so I would have the full proof of the situation. But deep down I had to admit my search here was entirely based on finding out how much Greer had to do with the murderous bastard who had already left a trail of dead bodies, not to mention a trail of wounds upon my own skin.

The upper floor was still deserted as I toed the last riser and crept back to my room.

A sound.

I paused at the door to the room before mine.

Again. A muffled sob.

The door was ajar and through it I could make out the dark outline of a woman, lying in much the same position as I was not so long ago. Oily, unwashed hair curtained her face. And she was sobbing uncontrollably.

I was unsure if the crying fit was the result of the drug or brought upon by some hidden demon she fought, but I stayed in case she was conscious and could talk to me.

A quick glance up and down the corridor confirmed I had no company yet. I tapped a fingernail on the door and the sound echoed around the bare room. I winced, convinced the conspirators could hear the noise downstairs. The captive heard the sound and she looked up, startled.

It was certainly a day for surprises.

Lily.

We exchanged a look that held a thousand conversations. I wanted to free her but knew the decision I'd made to return to my bed was born of a need to find out what these people intended to do, what their intentions were for my people and for the Humans. Most desperately I needed to know what involvement my sibling had in this heinous affair.

I'd discover nothing if I went around, freeing hostages willy-nilly. I needed Lily as well. She was still alive—it stood to reason they had a purpose for her. I had to assume she'd stay that way if I did nothing.

It seemed she didn't expect my help. Her eyes rounded when fell on the line still inserted into my vein—she knew I was a hostage too. Her mouth moved, and she spoke a word which chilled the blood to a standstill within my veins.

"Anjelo?" When I shook my head Lily's face twisted with fear. And regret. She continued in a whisper. "I'm so sorry Kailin. I led them right to you. I was only trying to save Anjelo. I promise. I'm so, so sorry." Tears fell from her eyes, dripping down the side of her face into her hairline.

I dared not respond or ask any questions. I had no way to answer her. I hadn't seen Anjelo for days, since he'd left to search for her. How could I tell her he was missing too? And her confession was no surprise.

As much as Lily and I had never hit it off, I knew enough to be realistic. Torture could make even the strongest of captives talk. Poor Lily. She was skin laid lightly over bone. Starvation, or the drugs, were taking their toll.

I pressed a finger to my lips—hoping she would remain quiet. I had to get back to my room, before someone decided to check on me.

I scanned the corridor, hearing for the first time the dreaded hollow tap of heels on the lower flight of stairs. Two sets of feet rose, stair for stair.

Damn. Someone was coming.

I scurried to my room on anxious tiptoes, closing the door and diving for the mattress. I lay back, screwing the IV back into the catheter still taped to my hand, opening the tap to continue the drip of the drug back into my vein.

I clamped down on teeth I was sure I had already loosened over the last week. I felt the warmth of the drug again, as it swam through me, riding the wave of my blood, seeking synapses to adulterate, nerves to abuse. Thankfully, all the drug imparted was relaxing warmth.

I no longer felt the incapacitating intoxication of the drug as in my first experience, but I had to fake it. The footfalls were getting louder. The door to Lily's room opened. Both captors remained at the threshold.

"She's still no use."

"We should get rid of her then...if she's not g—"

The woman stopped in mid-sentence, as if the man she spoke with had shut her up with a mere look.

"Greer, you are far too eager to put an end to her life."

The door closed, and the footsteps grew closer, the voices louder.

"This one I'm more interested in."

"Because?"

I could imagine Greer's eyebrows as they raised to emphasize her question. Pure venom laced those words. The door opened, a cool draft pushed into the room.

"Because I get to play, to see how the drug affects the precious Alpha bloodline. Not like I would use you for my experiments, my dear."

"You wanted the males. Why did you need *her?*"

"She's...useful. And she's bait."

I would've given anything to be able to see their faces, but I had to pretend to be deep in the arms of a euphoric slumber. I knew how it felt, tried to re-enact my bodily reactions.

I felt fingers on my arm, checking my pulse. Heard someone at the IV stand. Felt cool fingers at my temple. Heard Greer's heartbeat quicken. Fear or trepidation? Could she still harbor some good feelings for me?

I wasn't sure enough to bet on it.

I LAY on the lumpy mattress, only my thoughts for company. Thoughts currently centered on Anjelo. Somewhere, where my heart lived, I felt a harsh twinge.

None of it had registered until the moment Lily had uttered his name. Uttered it with grief and pain and longing strong in her eyes, as if those emotions had lain steeping within wells tapping her soul.

It had been days since I'd spoken to Anjelo. He'd contacted me at last, just before I'd seen my father; a message saying he'd made contact with a shop assistant who claimed to have seen Lily. Anjelo had been religiously walking the streets armed with photographs of her, posting them on notice-boards, using them to find anyone who may have seen her.

So far, he had gotten nowhere.

The police had made no progress either—not even with

Murdoch's network of snitches. I prayed they'd keep drawing blanks. The last thing I wanted was for him to find Lily and put himself right smack in the middle of deadly danger. Niko possessed a ruthless streak that curdled my blood. And I knew one thing for sure.

Anjelo was better off as far away from Lily and me as possible.

CHAPTER 36

*L*ogan lifted the scope to his eyes and watched as Anjelo climbed the trellis and swung onto a rusty upstairs balcony. Logan gritted his teeth. How did the foolish boy know the window he jimmied open hadn't been rigged, wasn't setting off alarms somewhere inside the house? He would've had a better idea if he'd paid attention to Logan's advice and waited before entering the house.

Logan growled his frustration. Anjelo had moved too fast for Logan to stop him. Now he watched as the young Walker turn around and shut the window, concentrating on edging it down without making a sound.

"Don't turn your back," Logan muttered. But even if Anjelo could have heard it, it was too late. He was in no position to see the oversized thug who crept up behind him. All Logan could do was watch as the guy hit Anjelo square on the back of his head with the butt of his pistol.

Logan examined the darkened building for what seemed the hundredth time, hoping the boy would manage to wake up and get the hell out of there. He sighed and let the scope fall onto his chest with a small thud.

"You have got to keep the volume down on those sighs, Logan. The bad-guys will certainly hear us with the racket you are making." Logan glanced at Jess who'd broken through his silent moment of self-recrimination. Anjelo had refused to listen and had paid the price by getting himself caught. There was nothing he could do about him right now.

Logan muffled a groan. "The stupid boy. He just got himself caught."

Jess stared off at the house, her face washing over with concentration. "I can barely sense him now," she spoke quietly, still trying to get a psychic bead on the kid. "He is unconscious, but alive."

"Stupid, impatient, idiotic—"

"No point in cursing at the child. He meant well." Jess and her wisdom again. "Backup has arrived – about a dozen operatives. Everyone is ready to move on your order."

"I just want to get the whole thing over with." Logan wasn't afraid to admit it. He glanced at his watch. "I'm only waiting until Kailin's brother gets here."

Hard to believe only a few hours had passed since he'd watched Kailin being abducted. Anjelo had run all the way to the house, not far behind Logan's bike. Logan's first instinct was to tell Anjelo to stay back. But his search for Lily had drawn a blank. And Logan had seen the condition of Kailin's loft.

Logan was seriously pissed off at himself. How could he have left her alone when he knew she was in some sort of danger?

"That girl's been a walking bullseye for the last couple of weeks. I'm amazed she stayed breathing this long." Logan shook his head. "I should've been more careful. More observant."

Being a Walker certainly seemed to have helped her stay alive. No Human could've withstood the amount of injury Kailin had been subjected to without needing some serious therapy.

The distant throb of a motorcycle announced Iain's arrival. A few minutes later he loped into the bushes and sank down beside

Logan. Calling Iain hadn't been easy. He'd made the call only when he'd arrived at the house and hidden himself in the bushes. Kai's brother had taken the news that his sister had been abducted with a dangerous calm. And all he'd said was he wouldn't be long.

"Which one of you is Logan?"

Logan turned to Iain; it was high time they were introduced. "That would be me." He nodded and offered his hand.

What he faced was a bristling, highly charged Walker, and for the first time in a long while he felt his life may very well be in danger.

And, he looked straight into the face of a man whose image dragged memories out from his past and brought to his nose the scents of smoke and blood and death and anger. The anger his own.

Iain in turn watched him with unadulterated suspicion mapping his craggy features. The Walker's shoulders tightened as he scanned Logan's face.

Logan, on the other hand was thrown back into his past. Into memories of one horrible day in his life which would forever be a day of mourning. Because it was the day his power had gotten free. When he had lost control completely. Irrevocably. He could never bring back the people he killed.

Again, he smelled the burning, the acrid smoke. Heard the screams of terror and pain and of grief.

He remembered the man who now stood before him. Younger, less lined. Happy.

Logan remembered the day he killed Iain's wife.

Now, Kailin's brother sat next to him, waiting for an explanation he had no intention of giving. None of this situation was his fault so why the hell was he feeling so guilty?

"What's happening?" Iain's voice was low, strained.

"Anjelo's done a runner—straight into the lion's den. Idiot kid." Logan shook his head and passed the scope to Kailin's brother. "There was some movement earlier, but nothing in the last thirty minutes."

Iain waved the scope away. "Thanks, I'll pass. My eyes are good for the dark. Unless this thing can see through walls?" Logan eyed him, but all he could see was a faint yellow glow. Nothing distinct to highlight Iain's now feline eyes.

Jess's recon had revealed a large basement beneath the building. The house had been built on a slope, and the basement had one brick wall facing the backyard. This was the team's way in. Logan flicked the strap of the night-scope, officially concerned for Anjelo's safety. They needed to move now; it may mean saving the stupid kid's life, not to mention Kailin's.

$\mathscr{N}$iko's guards shoved and pushed us from the room. Niko followed in silence. The trip down the rickety wooden stairs to the basement, with its dark stairwell, had proved more hazardous to Lily than I.

Her feet worked against each other and she'd fallen halfway down. The guards cared nothing for her well-being and dragged her the rest of the way, her feet bumping each riser as they went. I, on the other hand, had let through my Panther sight.

Greer had followed the horde to the basement lab, lagging behind the troupe of captors and captives, as if unwilling to get too close. She seemed more interested, than concerned, for my welfare. I refused to allow myself to cry—changed the course of my thoughts and concentrated on examining every nook and cranny of the lab, in case I was able to identify an escape route.

Four glassed in cells lined the left-hand wall. The guards threw us into separate cells, slamming the glass doors shut behind us. Niko walked to us, the dull tap of his heels echoing in the clinical room. He stopped a hands-breadth in front of Lily's cubicle and smiled.

I watched his self-congratulatory smirk while locked behind a fat layer of glass.... Helpless. Fuming.

Lily lay on the floor, right where she had been thrown. Her cell was so tiny her outstretched feet brushed the door, while her right arm flung before her, was bent at the elbow and crammed against the rear stone wall. It was little more than the size of a coffin and just as terrifying.

The lab, a sterile, clinical floor-to-ceiling white gave me the creeps. One usually associated white with cleanliness and professional care. But in this particular instance, white represented calculated cruelty.

Niko called over one of the guards, he of the fetid jerky-chewing breath. The guard disappeared, soon reappearing with a dead-weight bundle slung over his meaty shoulder. Anjelo.

The guard bent forward and Anjelo flopped onto the ground, and was dragged and tossed into the cell, where he landed on top of Lily. Niko was one manipulative bastard. He knew Lily and Anjelo were in a relationship, knew she cared deeply for Anjelo. It seemed he intended to toy with their emotions, like a cruel puppet master forcing them to play a scene against their will. Just for kicks.

I recalled how truly sorry Lily had been, begging me to forgive her, for giving him vital information; information leading him directly to me. So many reasons why I should truly hate her. But the ball of tears swimming in my throat was all for her, because I knew how it felt to be alone, how it felt to ache for something I would never get. I knew Niko was about to rip her heart to shreds.

I remained in the corner of my cell, feigning unconsciousness, and getting mighty fed up of lying low to protect myself. I felt naked without my bow, but thankfully the bracelet was still on my arm. Niko and his goons had been unable to pry it off.

Its weight was solid and warm along my arm, and I wondered again what reason Grams had for giving me the talisman. Its runic carvings and heavy gold-like metal both strange and comforting at the same time.

The expression on Tara's face, when she'd run the tips of her fingers along its smooth glowing surface, had been enough to satisfy me. I wouldn't look a gift horse in the mouth. It was protection. But what was it supposed to protect me from?

It could hardly free me from a cell.

A grunt of pain. Anjelo was regaining his faculties next door. Cracking an eye open, I watched as he dropped his weight onto an arm, while massaging his skull with the other. The next second his body stiffened. He recognized Lily's prone form beneath his legs.

Anjelo looked around. His eyes paused briefly over me and the slow deliberate blink he performed confirmed to me at least one person in the room knew I was fully conscious and faking it. He turned Lily over in his arms, as gently as if he were handling a newborn. Brushing hair from her face he placed his next to hers and whispered into her ear.

Sniggers and low laughter drifted to me and I could only assume Niko and his team found the tender sight amusing.

"Anjelo?" I heard the whisper she returned. She uttered his name again, her voice was so filled with remorse and regret that I found it supremely difficult to maintain my charade. Her eyes filled with tears as she gazed into his eyes, droplets spilling as fast as they gathered.

I felt guilty, to be able to hear this private exchange. But since Niko and Greer and all their awful henchmen were also privy to the lover's conversation, it somehow felt right for me to be their positive support.

"I'm so s-sorry." She stumbled on the words, so hasty was she to voice them. "I shouldn't have fought with you. I was being so selfish."

"Shhhh. You don't have to say anything right now, Lil." Anjelo, wanting to spare her from baring her soul in full view of their evil captor, tried to silence her.

"All I wanted was a score. I couldn't think about anything else until I got my next fix." Tears fell from her eyes and ran down the side of her face, disappearing into the hair above her ears, as she lay in his arms. "I lied to you, Anjelo. And I'm so sorry."

Anjelo shook his head, and was about to speak when she cut him off. Now she had the chance she was going to say her peace. "I hid my addiction from you. Because I was ashamed. Of needing the drugs. Of being what I am."

Lily had been forced to keep the deepest nastiness of her life bottled up inside for so long, that now the opportunity was here, the words began to tumble out in a torrent, an avalanche of confessions and apologies which stunned her audience.

I could tell from the way Anjelo's jaw moved—up and down—like a jackhammer, only slowed down to one-tenth speed. The news hit him hard, and I knew he was deeply hurt by all the lies.

"Anjelo, I'm...I'm Pariah."

He looked at her, confusion clouding the thousand emotions warring in his eyes.

"I can't change. Never been able to."

"I thought you didn't change because you disliked your creature?"

"I lied to you. I'm a freak, and I was so afraid you would turn me away." Lily met his eyes, fearless in the face of a final rejection. She must have felt like she had nothing to lose.

The silence that followed was pain filled, gut-wrenching. Had I not still been feigning unconsciousness I would certainly have been biting my fingernails like a chipmunk with a peanut.

But Anjelo had always had his heart in the right place. It was the reason he had followed my trail right out of our colony, the reason he'd banded with Storm to form a protective group for people like him needing a home away from home. The reason he trailed both Lily and myself through the school halls making sure we were safe and unharmed.

"You don't need to say anymore. I understand. You did what you had to do to protect yourself." He began to rock the crying girl, which only seemed to wring greater sobs from her. I knew she hadn't expected understanding and consideration from him. And I wondered then, about her family and how they had dealt with her defect. Did they hide it like my father had hidden Greer's and Niko's condition, even from family? Did they manipulate her, use her, abuse her?

Whatever they'd done had made her leave her home and everything she knew. Probably, in her case, she was better off with the Devil she didn't know.

Finally, she quieted. Lily looked up at Anjelo and smiled through a curtain of sleek tears. At least they were together.

Niko sneered as he watched the young couple. The muscles in his arms tensed, and he gripped them in a macabre hug. He seemed unable to control his aggravation as he stormed to the cell, keying in the code to open the door. Lily and Anjelo, startled by the sudden interruption, stared at him. Lily began to quiver again, and grabbed for Anjelo, sensing as I did, that she would be parted from him again. All I could do was watch from my glass prison, helpless. Useless.

Niko stepped into the cell and hit Anjelo at the back of his head, knocking him out. Niko caught him by the arm before he slid to the ground, lifting him with a superhuman strength. He ripped the young Walker from Lily, who tried to grab at Anjelo's arm, before stepping out of the cell. Niko sneered as he locked the glass door.

"No. No." Lily slammed her palm on the glass over and over again. "What are you doing with him?" She screamed at him so loud that she began to cough.

I rose and followed suit, shouting at my uncle, needing to know he wouldn't harm my friend. Niko spared me a glance. For the briefest moment I saw regret in those dark eyes. Then they iced over, cold and remote again. He tossed Anjelo's battered body at the halitosis-plagued guard, who stepped back to allow the unconscious boy to fall at his feet. The guard lifted Anjelo and dumped him onto the nearest gurney.

Niko chose the gurney deliberately. Lily and I had the best view in the house. I never pegged my uncle for a sadistic bastard, but it looked like he'd become one. Soon Niko had the drip set up and was feeding a clear drug into Anjelo's veins. My heart hammered in my throat and I banged on the glass again, but he paid me no mind at all.

Niko readied the defibrillator, absently massaging the handles of the paddles with his thumbs while the machine beeped its way to readiness.

Niko placed the paddles onto the young Panther's bared chest. Anjelo's body bucked with the force of the electricity which charged through him. Niko waited, watching Anjelo's vitals on a monitor at his side.

I watched, tears blurring my vision and moistening my cheeks. Anjelo's eyes rolled erratically, as if deep in REM sleep, but the force of the drug seemed to have total control over him. When his body ceased its intermittent shivering, Niko repeated the shock treatment. I felt the energy surge through my own body as I watched the poor boy tortured by a man who would've been an elder in our clan.

Someone who should've been the protector and not the persecutor.

The second charge of power triggered Anjelo's change. His skin rippled, darkened. His limbs thinned and lengthened. The garish light bared Anjelo's profile, and I watched as the ridge of his forehead rose, his nostrils widened and flattened, and his jaw lengthened. I'd seen Anjelo change only a handful of times but never in such crude clarity.

It was infinitely painful to watch this abuse of my friend and not be able to put an end to his suffering. Then Anjelo lay on his side, tremors coursed through his feline body and he gazed at me through wide, black, liquid eyes. It must have been fate that ensured the boy now faced Lily and myself.

Cruel fate, to allow him to watch the agony and grief splayed across our faces.

Lily lay on the floor, her tears still not spent, as she shared in his agony. Anjelo's paw twitched, pulled against the leather straps which held him down. Inevitably they were much looser on his feline limbs.

But he was within the thrall of the drug; it did not occur to him to try to escape, that the bindings were loose enough and all he had to do was shift his body and he would be free.

Niko laughed.

The harsh bark echoed around the tiled room, although the glass walls of my prison served to dull the sound. It did not detract from the stab of pain I felt.

The sound was ominous in its freedom from conscience. As if now that Anjelo was in animal form, Niko had no reason to care what he subjected the boy to. Anjelo was not as meek as Niko assumed.

Life flickered in his eyes as the drug wore off. Niko couldn't have given him a strong enough dose. Anjelo tilted his head to get a better look at his captors' placement and as my uncle moved to the side of the gurney, filled with an arrogant surety his plan was going his way, Anjelo took the opportunity afforded him.

He flew at Niko, snarling and growling and snapping at his persecutor's face and hands. Anjelo meant business, teeth meeting over and over again. Blood dripped from Niko's wounds as he tried in vain to defend himself. In a blink, Anjelo had Niko flat on his back, staring up at bare and hungry teeth.

Niko lay on the floor, quivers of fear running through him. He stared up at the furious Panther, with beseeching eyes. Anjelo sniffed at Niko. If I were free from my glass cage I would've smelled the odor of raw fear mixed with feral anger. Hatred pooled in the saliva dripping from Anjelo's jaw.

I watched as Anjelo fought his innermost desire to sink his teeth into this man and wreak his vengeance. Being so close to Niko's blood would stir the fire inside him. I glanced over at Lily, worried what this might do to her if she survived this ordeal. How would she deal with the memory of her lover killing another in front of her eyes? He swiped a heavy paw at Niko's head and knocked him unconscious.

Anjelo's teeth closed over Niko's neck, he seemed driven, controlled by his fury. Greer screamed something at the guards and they both rushed forward, grabbing Anjelo by the head and body, pulling him off Niko. Anjelo struggled but one guard had his head in a vice grip.

They threw him off Niko. In an instant, Anjelo changed again, lying on the cold white tiles, naked, skin moist and glistening.

The loud shout of the gun broke our concentration and my shocked gaze flew to Anjelo. And the dart sticking out of his neck, swaying in an invisible wind.

ogan rose from the screen of bushes and readied himself, while Jess waited behind him, ready to attack. He focused the energy within his core, strengthened it, tighter and tighter, until the point where he was unable to hold onto it any longer.

Then he let go.

Holding the burgeoning force in check worked very much like a sling, the energy so tightly coiled that when released it flew like a missile. Logan hadn't taken long to perfect his talent. It was only his guilt and grief which hampered the progress in the very beginning.

But that was a long time ago and he refused to consider the possibility that he would lose Kailin like he lost his mother.

The orb of energy didn't glow or shimmer.

A good thing considering the darkened backyard. The brick wall simply exploded. The parts of the wall which did not disintegrate were shaken so much as to loosen the bricks from the mortar so all that was needed was a slight shove to topple what was left.

The lab was still lit brightly by the overhead fluorescent

tubing, but Iain, Logan and the rest of the operatives slipped in under cover of the raised dust and the disorganized mayhem.

THE EXPLOSION ROCKED the room and spurred us straight to our feet, faces pressed against the glass, eager to see some progress to our escape. We had instinctively drawn closer to each other in spite of being sealed in our respective cells.

Lily looked at me. Her eyes, rimmed with red from the tears she'd shed for Anjelo, now held a faint glow of hope. My heart ached for her. Her behavior of the past was forgotten. How could I hold onto snippy comments made by an angry teenager toward a sister she was jealous of and didn't understand?

I watched the mayhem outside. Saw figures slip into the room. Watched the dust settle slowly, Niko's goons batting it away, hoping to see what caused the commotion. It only stirred the concrete and mortar powder more.

My full attention was on the mayhem outside my cell, and I barely registered the lack of air within the cell. Only when I keeled over, did I feel the pressure of lack of oxygen pulling me down. I fell to my knees, hitting the windows with my palms.

A vain attempt; I was sure nobody would hear me.

I keened for breath, rasping, wheezing. My lungs compressed and hurt like the blazes. When I raised heavy eyelids hoping to see someone on their way to help, I caught Niko watching me. My uncle gazed at me the way a kid would watch an insect die.

Morbid fascination and not a shadow of pity or regret.

Next to him, Greer watched in horror. Torn between her allegiance to my uncle and the shock of watching her sibling die. At least I knew that some form of affection existed for me.

I slumped, my head propped against the glass between the cells as I slid to the ground. I must have slipped into the first stages of unconsciousness. The bright blinking spots of light in my eyes faded into blackness. Just as suddenly, my lungs filled with oxygen again.

Oxygen and dust, which sent me into a fit of uncontrollable coughing.

The side of my face and my arm stung like crazy. I tried to rub the irritation away, and my fingers came away bloody. A glance around me revealed I sat in a puddle of shattered glass. Someone had destroyed the walls of the cells, allowing Lily and myself to breathe again, giving us back our lives.

"There, by the wall. Kill them." Niko's voice broke on the hysterical shriek, slurred on the spittle which flew from his bruised lips as he aimed a shattered claw at the intruders.

He was nearly apoplectic when he watched his two goons simply crumple to the ground.

While Niko had his attention and anger focused on his unconscious employees, I rolled onto my knees and stood on shaky legs, dusting myself off, heedless of the glass shards slicing little jags into my skin. I'd seen a gun spin and slide under one of the lab tables near. And I needed a weapon.

Whatever happened to the guards, it seemed couldn't be duplicated on Niko or Greer, as both were still standing. I looked around for my insane uncle and for a second had no idea where he was.

Until his fingers grabbed onto my hair and pulled me against him.

"Put your weapons down."

It seemed a strange thing to yell just because he had me caught. That was what I thought until I felt the prick of a needle on the soft flesh of my neck. Damn. The needle he held to my neck was attached to a rather large syringe filled with an ominous green liquid. I assumed it was not Happiness Serum. I felt a sickening fear embed its claws in my gut. Niko was crazy, liable to do anything.

He could kill me to get off on it.

"If you want the girl alive, put your weapons down. Now."

I stared at the three figures in front of me. None of them were armed.

"If you co-operate with us, things will look much better for you in court," Logan's voice rang out.

Finally. He'd certainly taken his time. But what in Ailuros' name was he up to? Buying time?

Niko must have thought Logan's offer was as hilarious as it sounded to me. He laughed so hard that the point of the needle pierced my skin just enough for a trickle of blood to slide slowly down my neck.

Logan, taking stock of the blood edging its way along my neck, stepped forward.

"Stop. You're hurting her."

My uncle sniggered as he pressed the syringe deeper into the soft skin of my neck. Pain arced at the point where insidiously sharp metal speared sensitive flesh. For all the pain it was still only a threat. The point had only broken skin so far.

"You had better keep your distance boy. I don't care who she is—I will kill her if you don't listen."

Logan scowled, not certain how to make sense of Niko's comment. Until Iain stepped into the light.

I was so relieved to see my brother that my knees sagged, and I fell against Niko for a moment. Only until I felt the needle poke against my skin again, my movement pressing the sharp point against my neck. I stood up straight immediately, almost uncaring of the needle as I stared at Iain.

Tears filled my eyes.

"Iain? Now what is my all-important nephew doing mixing with the common people?" Niko's voice was harsh, his words ice.

"What are you trying to do, Niko?"

Logan's expression went from scowl to confusion and then astonished realization when he processed the nephew tidbit. He met my eyes and I gave the tiniest of nods still very much aware of the deadly sharp needle pressed against my neck.

While Niko's attention was focused on my brother, I sagged lower in my uncle's arms, until his grip loosened somewhat. It helped that Iain decided to step closer to us. I dropped lower as soon as I was sure the sharper edge of the needle pointed away from me.

Niko, surprised by the sudden loss of control over his captive, over-compensated and swung his arms around me to grab better hold. I side-stepped the grab and swung my fist straight up, into his throat.

I rolled away, keeping an eye on Greer as I went. Her face bloomed scarlet.

What in Ailuros' name was her friggin' problem?

First, she was upset when she thought I was about to keel over and die, and now she's pissed because I got away from Niko. Perhaps it was the reminder that I could fight, way better than she could.

I couldn't think further on it. The air in the room grew dense and metallic. Almost suffocating but filled with a bright white light. I scanned for the source of the light and found a shining white pillar spanning the room from floor to ceiling.

Logan and half his backup team charged. He went straight for Niko, while Iain and the rest attacked Niko's guards. Jess rounded the room and helped Lily to her feet. A sigh of relief escaped me. At least she was safe. She had a lot to do before accepting who she was; trying to convince herself she was not responsible for Anjelo's death would be the hardest part.

The room, now filled with the grunting sounds of contacting blows and groans of pain, blurred around me. The pressure of the air bore down on me. I turned to check how Jess was doing getting Lily away.

Greer slammed into me, dropping me to the ground. We both

fell hard, Greer on top, squishing me with all the force she could muster.

She was as slight as I was, as Alpha strong too.

I fell with my armored hand beneath me, the round edges cutting into my ribs without mercy. Stunned both by the fall and Greer's audacity, it took me precious seconds to plan my attack.

Greer shifted her weight, and I shoved my knee between our bodies. A thrust and I pushed her away. She was not the only one partially transformed, and I concentrated on shifting a tad bit more to give me the edge. I should've felt guilty that I had the ability at my disposal, but I couldn't find one ounce of sorry within me.

She flew at me again, rage controlling her more than common sense. Greer raised her hand, aimed it at my head, and ran at me. Although she didn't have skill on her side, she possessed a viciousness I'd never developed, even in all my experience with killing Wraiths.

I grabbed her hand, pressed down and twisted hard. She gasped. When she dropped to her knees I knew I had her. The thin bones of her wrist strained under the pressure of my fingers.

But I wouldn't hurt her. Couldn't bring myself to break anything in my sister's body.

In a fluid move, I lifted the twisted arm and held it at her back. Any attempt to free herself and she would cause more pain. Greer growled in frustration, the Human sound of sheer anger and not the feline sound at all.

"Unhand him."

The voice ringing out from the center of the mayhem was strong, booming and a touch arrogant. As if the speaker knew that though the room was unaware of his presence, all he needed to do was speak and all occupants would bow to his command.

He was infinitely correct in his particular wisdom. Though not about the bowing part.

Everyone paused or slowed their attacks, searching for the

commanding voice within the throng of writhing, attacking bodies, while still keeping a solid eye on their opponent. The voice emanated from the middle of the lab, from the same point where the sharp white light rose to touch the ceiling.

My eyes told me nothing was there.

My bracelet, on the other hand, was vibrating a song against my arm, so much so that my forearm was numbed. I searched through the dust and the light and at last the form of a man took shape.

He took form from nothing, in the spot from which the voice had rung moments previously. It wasn't often I was privy to the sight of someone materializing out of thin air, and my shock at the sight loosened my lock-hold on Greer's arm and tipped the scales in her favor.

She struggled against me, trying to twist free, while most of my attention was focused on the strange addition to the chaos of this room.

I waited, along with everyone else, for the new arrival to speak. But, we were giving the opposition the upper-hand, in exactly the same way the stranger's interruptive entrance had allowed Greer to loosen my hold.

He stepped out of the light and my heart pounded in my throat. Anjelo. The hooded cloak he wore shielded his face from the rest of the room, but he looked up and met my eyes. My first thought was for Lily, and I breathed a second sigh of relief on her behalf. At least she was not here to witness this macabre picture.

How could it be Anjelo?

My confusion was short-lived. His cloak glowed, easily mistaken as a reflection from the pulsing white light behind him. But, although it glowed with the same brightness the color was different. A coral tinge to it that sent shivers through my body.

A Wraith.

Right here among Walkers. That was a first. A walking Human corpse was easy to kill.

Anjelo would be much harder.

Logan had Niko in a stranglehold, halfway on his knees. Niko was using his dead-weight to pull Logan down to the ground in the hope of getting free.

The Wraith pointed at Niko and said, "Release him. He is mine." His voice boomed again, sending a dull tingle into my eardrums.

Where did he think he was? The Wraith's lordly attitude wasn't going to get him anywhere today. Who in Ailuros' name was he, and what did he want with my uncle?

A medallion swung around his neck, and bland fluorescent light reflected against the runic symbols carved into the bronzed medallion so similar to the band on my arm. It seemed both pieces were charged by the presence of the other.

The initial denseness in the air which I'd felt on arrival of the Wraith had dissipated, but now it returned with a vengeance. The bracelet throbbed mercilessly on my arm.

A warning?

The lab seemed to shrink and expand at the same time. The breath struggled in my lungs, as if some invisible heavy hand was trying to deflate it, press all the air out of me.

Strangely too, the walls of the room seemed further away than they looked. I had the feeling if I walked to the wall behind me, I would walk forever without reaching it even though it was less than ten feet away.

I stared at the Wraith, confused and a little afraid. He was unlike every other soul-sucker I'd ever come across. He had power and he even had Magyk.

But worst of all, he had Anjelo.

CHAPTER 39

Fury heated my head and dulled my grief, so I held onto it as strongly as I could. I stared at Anjelo's face, my blood running cold for the first time being confronted with a Wraith. How could Niko kill Anjelo and then turn him over to the Wraith?

I drew in a shuddering breath and I glanced at Logan and the rest of the team. Their faces mirrored the shock and dismay I knew was clear on my own. None of them knew what I intended, and I hoped they would stay well away. Choking back hot tears I ran full tilt into the Wraith, trying to forget it was Anjelo I was knocking over.

My hands made full contact with his when we impacted. Repulsion rippled through me at his reptilian coldness. My reaction pushed me off high alert as I quivered and stalled the urge to shiver in disgust. The Wraith knocked me back, away and onto my ass. He scrambled to his feet and I followed suit, mirroring his fluid movement.

From beneath the folds of his gray cloak he produced a sword, the beauty of which captivated my attention. The blade gleamed in the bland fluorescent light, its bulk carved from some unrecognizable ebony glass, obsidian or black diamond. It glittered and glinted, totally overcoming its deadly purpose with its sheer beauty.

Perhaps he used some form of Magyk to produce the weapon. I was sure it hadn't pressed against my body when I fell on him. He lunged toward me with the obsidian beauty. I swung aside, clearing the vicious arc of the swipe with a mere hairs-breadth to spare.

I heard the rest of Logan's team resume their offense against Niko's little army. They'd soon try to get at the Wraith, come to help me. Minutes went by and I was still dancing around the Wraith, avoiding the vicious point of his sword and trying to figure out how I could possibly defend myself.

Help would be great.

I glanced around in frustration and had to tear my eyes away from the strange scene I glimpsed in one quick sweep across the room.

The rest of the Omega team had encircled us, trying unsuccessfully to break through an invisible barrier surrounding both myself and the Wraith. Our little battle—one I was successfully losing—was taking place within a Magykal ball of protection created by the demon I fought. Jess was a study in concentration, trying to destroy the barrier.

I was tired, weak and without a weapon. Soon the Wraith had me breathless, with knees almost giving up, ready to cry uncle. The next blow struck me hard.

Thank Ailuros, my instinctive reaction was to lift and block with my armored hand. The sword struck the armband with a clanging shout, spitting a shower of blue and white sparks. I keeled over again from the force, while my arm ached with the vibrations of the impact. I was certain the bones in my arm were shattered beyond repair, but as the pain faded I tested the hand and found the limb pretty much in good working order.

I was down, but not out.

The Wraith moved in on me. He knelt and leaned over my face. He was intent and arrogant, knowing he'd won this battle. His foul black mouth came closer to mine, and as bad as mine might have reeked what with not coming in contact with a toothbrush for over twenty-four hours, I was pretty confident it smelled a helluva lot better than the fetid stink which permeated the hole in his face.

"Now you are mine, Hunter." He laughed, the sound echoing sharp and flat like the crunch of gravel. "I have been searching for the one who has been destroying my people in the last few years."

Then, before I could ask him anything further, he began to breathe in. Air from deep within my lungs deserted me, following the Wraith's pulling breath. My chest was empty, lungs deflated. Darkness edged my vision. As much as I wished I could claim my actions to be the result of considerable forethought, it was only desperation controlling my next moves.

I kicked him full in the groin. Right before I wondered whether Wraiths were constructed like Humans and Walkers with similar super-sensitive male parts. Even if he did, would the kick have a similar effect on a Wraith anyway? Fortunately, for me he reeled from the impact. Plenty of time to get back onto my feet. I didn't spare any precious seconds to wonder if he would recover quickly.

What I did wonder, though, was how he knew I was a hunter. It's not as if I had my moonlighting job tattooed on my forehead.

The Wraith recovered quickly and came back with a certain vengeance. "You will not escape me, Hunter." He raised his sword and swung it at me with all the force of his body behind the swipe. "I have been tracking you. But as elusive as you have been, you could not escape me, could you? Imagine my surprise when the thoughts and memories of this body revealed to me who you are."

Puzzled by his strange comment, I watched in slow-motion as his sword closed the distance between us. Because I lacked a weapon, or any protection whatsoever, I raised my armored hand again to deflect the strike. I hoped the little metal bracelet could withstand a second powerful impact. Hoped my hand would withstand the force of a second blow. I would never have admitted it, even though I knew Logan and his team were watching, but I shut my eyes before the blow hit. I didn't want to watch in case the bracelet disintegrated and I ended up losing my arm.

Again, the impact almost loosed my arm within its socket, rippling through the bones of my hand. Pins and needles tingled into my fingertips. It was the repercussion of the impact though, nothing more. My arm was still intact, I was not bleeding, and no bones were shattered beyond repair.

Thank Ailuros. The metal of the bracelet had done its job really well—protected my arm from the black sword.

This time the impact also reverberated back to my attacker, sending the sword spinning from his hand and onto the floor in an ominous crack. The Wraith howled his fury and bent to retrieve his weapon. Fed up with the battle he was losing against me, he charged at Niko, and Greer who had sought a dubious refuge beside our uncle. I wondered how wise it had been as I wasn't at all confident in Niko's family fidelity.

"You will not escape me, Hunter. And don't worry about your Walker friend. I'll keep him safe with me. I am sure he will prove very useful, for a very long time. His mind is filled with bits of information about you Kailin Odel, Hunter of Wraiths." A column of shimmering blue light grew behind the Wraith, and he stepped backward into the brightness.

Niko screamed, "No, don't leave me here." He grabbed onto the Wraith's arm and was pulled through the light, with Greer hanging on, her face twisted in horror. The outlines of their bodies flickered in the gleaming pale light and then disappeared from view. In the next moment, the blue pillar simply vanished, and with it the Magykal protection around me.

Logan and Iain were beside me in a flash. Thankfully, I was

conscious long enough to provide them with a smile of relief before I succumbed to the pain and the welcoming blackness.

PEOPLE BUSTLED AROUND ME, voices filtering through my hazy sleep. But it was not the constant bustle of people which woke me. Waves of excruciating, agonizing pain lapped at my arm. Like vicious waves on a treacherous shore, they kept coming, each time deeper and more unbearable than the next. I lifted my body to sit up, resting my weight on the arm that didn't hurt like the fires of Hell.

The world tilted precariously. Vertigo gripped me as I noted the ground below the stretcher. I scrunched my eyes up. Perhaps ending my view of the ground would stop the hurly-burly in my head. But it did nothing. I grunted, disgusted with myself. I needed to be on my feet. Not flat on my back.

The Wraith had confirmed Anjelo was still alive, and that meant I had to find a way to save him. Anyone close to a Wraith was in some sort of danger. Niko and Greer were in danger too. I found it hard to give a damn about them right now, but my heart ached that Anjelo could be in mortal danger while I lay here, wasting time.

I shivered, a deep roiling movement which made me whimper when my quaking arm quivered too.

"No, Kai, you need to stay down." Iain spoke close to my ear. "You shouldn't be trying to move around."

I shook my head and swallowed as I felt his supportive hand at my back. My throat was lined with sandpaper.

"Something's wrong..." I breathed the words as speaking hurt too much.

"What? Are you in pain?"

I managed a feeble nod, my eyes leaking hot tears. Iain stared at me in disbelief. It wasn't often I admitted to being in any sort of pain.

"Where?" Already, he was running a keen eye over my body, searching for wounds and not finding any.

"My arm...under the bracelet." I felt like a little kid again. The urged to give vent to a wracking sob was uncontrollable, but all I did was moan.

"We need to get the damned thing off," Iain said. He fiddled with the heavy buckles, then huffed with impatience as the armor refused to budge. At last he stopped, acknowledged his attempts were futile. Logan stood a foot behind Iain, watching, a scowl pulling his perfect brows into a not-so-pretty mess. He made no effort to try his hand at removing the bracelet.

I lay back, morbidly sorry for myself. Even I had no idea how to remove the friggin' armor. As much as I appreciated it had saved my sorry life a few minutes ago, all I wanted now was to get it off. I lifted my throbbing arm and inspected the bracelet closely. I'd thought the armor had gotten through the fight undamaged. I could've been wrong, though.

The indentation in the metal was obvious to even a cursory inspection. What wasn't so clear was the thin line of broken armor running alongside a parallel pattern between a bunch of engraved runes. So easy to miss. I'd done just that.

Something, perhaps a part of the bracelet, now dug deep into my arm sending shards of agony through it. Neither Logan nor Iain had any idea how to help. At the moment, even a little bit of Niko's drug was a welcome thought. I closed my eyes and slipped into a pained, fitful sleep.

THIS TIME I was roused from my pain-free bliss by the comforting voice of Grandma Ivy.

"Kailin, wake up." Her hand was warm on my shoulder.

My eyes opened a slit. What did she want now? The pain was incredibly unbearable. Easy to endure while unconscious. Now, awake, it was enough to make me want to pass out willingly. Grams lifted the arm encased in the damaged armor.

"It's taken a pretty good beating, hasn't it?"

"Eh, in case you haven't noticed, so have I." Utter pain brought out the bitchiness in me. Reduced me to a sullen, petulant mess.

She ran her finger along the dent, laying no pressure and ensuring she didn't inflict any further pain. With a slight jerk, she drew her finger away to reveal a thin cut already welling with blood.

"Something's in there...very sharp. By the pain you're in I'm assuming it's quite deep." Grams inspected the cut on her finger, a scowl crossing her face. Then, turning to me she asked, "Do you still believe the bracelet is unnecessary? That it still has nothing to do with you?"

I didn't have to think about my answer.

"No. Not anymore. I think I have it for a reason. And until I find out what the reason is, I'm keeping it." I released a long breath and stole another. "So hands off, go get your own bling, Grams."

"Good." That was all she said before she turned my arm over gently, as if she tended a newborn lamb. She undid the metal couplings on my inner arm, calm as you please. I was flabbergasted. Ever since I'd received the armor, the thing had stuck to my arm like it had suckers from Hell. A pity I'd had no idea all I had to say was 'I believed'. But even as I thought those thoughts, somewhere inside me I knew it would never have been so easy. Until today, I'd still borne my doubts about the bracelet.

Not anymore.

A cold breeze hit my arm as Grams removed the bracelet from skin which hadn't seen air or light in days. My skin looked wrinkled and on the thin side but pretty good for its extended incarceration.

Except for the three-inch gash and the sliver of black glass lodged within it.

Iain and Logan leaned in for a better look, and Grams stepped back and out of the way. The agonizing pain was exceeded by my intense curiosity as Iain stood back and prepared to remove the sliver.

A flurry of movement brought medical supplies to my stretcher. Iain pulled on a pair of latex gloves and grabbed a set of gleaming tweezers. He knelt beside the stretcher getting nose-to-hand with my wound. I gritted my teeth and clenched against the pain I knew would come.

And immediately regretted the movement. The flexing of the muscle caused me pain beyond anything I'd felt until this point. I shut my eyes against the tilting of my world, but it didn't stop.

I chomped on my teeth and opened my eyes again, gasping for breath. Iain was inches from me, holding the tweezer between steady fingers. His eyes rounded, eyebrows curved in question. 'Are you ready for it?' I knew I wasn't ready at all. In fact, I would've preferred to run as far away as possible.

But I couldn't escape.

I looked at my brother's face, lined with worry. Why had I assumed it would be tough to get him to pay attention to me? Only because when the crap hit the fan he turned up to help. But I'd rather have him only when I needed him than not have him at all.

I gave him a short jerky bounce of my head which passed for a nod. He bent over my arm and gripped the paper-thin piece of the obsidian sword. Over his head I saw Logan a few paces away, his face gray and gaunt. His entire demeanor was strange, drained, and bordering on emotionless. He caught my eye and tossed me a small smile. A mere trinket compared to the great big ones I was used to, but times like these a girl had to take what she got. I returned the smile and turned to watch Iain.

He gripped the shard with the teeth of the tweezer and I waited for it to move. Waited for the agony. But it wasn't agony filling me. It was a disconcerting surprise as the fine edge of the shard Iain gripped within the tweezer shattered into three vicious slivers. I gasped, as Iain swore.

"This thing is so fragile. It might splinter more if I try to remove it." Iain's brow was furrowed with worry and sweat.

"No. Keep going. It has to come out." Grams' voice again. "We have no idea what it is. What if it poisons her blood if you leave it in? She will die."

"Then it has to come out." Iain bent back to my arm and the tweezer hovered over the ominous black sliver. This time he gripped it in a thicker part of the sliver and gently, slowly pulled it from the depths of the wound. I stared at the size of the largest piece. It didn't seem to want to end as it was pulled from my flesh.

But finally, it was out. A quarter of an inch wide and glistening with my blood, the cause of my agony also happened to be at least two inches deep.

I had to remind myself the piece had split into three and the original shard would've been easily three times wider. It explained the pain I'd been in. As illogical as it sounded, I felt nothing as the sliver was slowly extracted from the deep wound. Blood seeped from the angry red lips of the wound as soon as the vicious obstruction was removed.

Iain looked up at me, waiting for the go-ahead to try for the next piece. I clenched my teeth and nodded. Twice more I was gripped within the teeth of pure agony, until all the pieces were out and Iain was satisfied the wound was clear.

Logan came over and said, "I have a message for you, Kailin." I looked up. "A Byron Teague said to say thank you."

I gasped. "They found Evan?"

Logan nodded. "Yes, a bit weak but he will recover in time," he said as he bagged the pieces of black glass to send off to the lab, while Iain cleaned and bandaged the gaping gash. The pain was still there, but at a level I could endure without embarrassing myself. I lay back, trying to relax, a haze of exhaustion blanketing me.

The news that Evan was safe made me feel so much better.

I had a moment of quiet when Iain and Logan were both off on their phones, bosses and fathers in no particular order. Grams cleared her throat next to me and I smiled and turned in the stretcher, dropping my feet over the edge and making space for her to sit next to me. She wasn't a very large woman and the stretcher could handle us both in a pinch.

"How did you know to come?" I knew I'd been unconscious for a while, so I hoped she'd fill me in.

"I came home for a day and saw the apartment in a mess. Called Iain..." she shrugged. "And he told me you were here."

"Thanks for coming Grams. I'd never have figured out how to take the band off without you. And now that those shards are out I'm feeling a whole lot better." I nodded, turning on the stretcher and sitting up. "Now I have to find a way to get to Anjelo and Greer. And Uncle Niko. I'll try and bring them all back."

Grams' face darkened and her eyes glistened. "We lost Niko a long time ago, Kailin. There is a madness in him that's changed him so much. I don't see my son in the killer he has become."

I hugged Grams then, certain no words could make her feel better about Niko and what he'd become. "I'll try to bring him back. Maybe there are doctors who can help him." But Grams just nodded, a sad faraway look in her eyes.

"Bring who back?" Iain scowled. "I hope you don't mean you are going after them?"

"That's exactly what I mean."

"Kai, are you insane? You don't even know what you are getting yourself into. Stop being ridiculous."

"Iain's right, Kai. Omega can put a team together and we can go look for them." I stared from Iain to Logan and knew then that neither man would let me go. So, I just nodded, "Fine. But someone better come up with a plan soon or else I promise I will go alone." They both frowned and nodded too. And seemed to believe me.

Grams didn't.

She turned to the guys. A moment passed, then they shared an odd glance before walking off and giving us some privacy. When she turned to me she smiled. "Didn't know you'd mastered the art of the perfect lie." I blushed and said nothing. "Never mind them for now. I came to give you this."

She held her hand out until I opened my palm. She dropped a bronze disc into my upturned hand. Grams looked around at the mayhem. Omega had cleared out Niko's thugs leaving behind their forensic team.

"What's this?" I studied the disc, turned it over in my hand. Shaped like a donut, the bronze disc was covered in tiny symbols. A quick scan confirmed a combination of various ancient languages, Gaelic and Egyptian being the ones I did recognize.

She lowered a voice to a whisper. "It's a key." She looked at me, hesitating. She quickly resolved whatever inner conflict it was that gave her reason to pause and continued. "You need it now. Although I will probably have some explaining to do once a certain person finds out what I've done."

She smiled.

I appreciated she had gotten herself in trouble for me, but it was all very strange. Grams had been keeping a bigger bunch of secrets than I'd ever known.

"So what exactly does this 'key' do?"

"It opens a portal...a pathway to the Wraith's dimension. So you can save your m—your sister and uncle." She rose, dusting off her clothes even though there was nothing to dust. Her dark jeans and jacket were immaculate. "You need to be near dark water."

I frowned. "Dark water?"

"Yes. Water that goes deeper than other standing pools. I suggest the docks. The water at the edge of the piers goes deep.

The disc will open the Gate to the Wraith-World. You will see a bright light. You need to jump into the portal while it is open. Don't waste any time. The space of the portal is dark, but it is safe."

I nodded. I understood that the elements held a power beyond our simple comprehension. Grams had given me the means to save Anjelo, Niko and Greer. But although I did want to save my uncle and sister, I wasn't sure either of them deserved it.

CHAPTER 40

I held the bronze disc in my hand, testing its weight. It was heavy as if gravity worked twice as hard on it, in punishment for opening the Veil. Lights from the dockside buildings caught the ridges of the yellowed metal inscriptions as I tilted the donut shaped key. Intricate runes curved around the entire surface of the relic.

Ancient scripts were not my forte. I hadn't had time to think about finding a rune translator. Perhaps it would've helped to know what the darned thing said. Now I was putting my life in the balance and trusting that Grams knew what she was talking about.

But I could trust her. With my life.

I'd be in deep trouble with Iain and Logan when they found out I'd gone despite my promise. But how could I not go? I was the one who could fight the Wraiths. As far as I knew neither Iain or Logan or even Omega had much experience with them. I had to go and save Anjelo. And just pray it was the right decision.

I walked to the edge of the pier, shifting my messenger bag to the side. It was more convenient for pulling weapons out quickly; I'd brought my crossbow, and my trusty dagger just in case. I touched the bronze band on my arm. I'd put it back on, felt almost naked without it. Despite the little cut in the metal I felt safer with it on.

I'd take my luck wherever I could get it.

Dark waves rolled and slapped against the wooden supports beneath me, while angry gusts of wind ripped at my clothes and threw hair around my face. Neither were very reassuring signs. I held the disc over the water; Grams had said to keep it horizontal.

So I did.

Later, I couldn't recall what I'd thought would happen. The last thing I'd expected to herald the opening of the Veil to the Dark-World was a pillar of light. Bright and white, it struck the empty center of the key and passed through into the murky black waters. It took on a force of its own and was pulled from my hand to hover before me, over the water.

Looking up was of no help. The light did not originate from the Heavens. Another sign that was not so good. Some powerful energy began to pull me closer to the edge of the pier.

Damn. I was *not* looking forward to a swim in the bay.

Cats hate water and while I wasn't averse to getting wet, I was *not* keen on a night-time swim in murky waters of questionable cleanliness. Sure, I loved my showers and baths like the next girl. But a cold dunking fully clothed was enough to turn a purr into a snarl anytime.

In the end, I didn't swim. I flew.

I was lifted off my feet and tossed right into the center of the light and right into the middle of the key. My mind was telling me it was not possible. But, my body was proving me wrong. I passed through the hole in the center of the key and lost all feeling in my body.

A good thing since I was sure being squeezed bodily through a hole the size of a golf ball wouldn't be a painless or enjoyable experience at all. It was over as suddenly as it began, and I found myself teetering on rubber legs. My equally rubber feet were grateful for the feel of solid ground beneath them.

Blinded by the icy brightness of the Gate's light I was terrified of what might be lurking in the darkness surrounding me. One out-flung hand connected with the solid rock surface next to me.

My eyes were slow to adjust in this utterly lightless place. As my breathing normalized I found I was able to see the light reflected against the rock wall next to me. I squinted, running my fingers across it and found it was composed of a quartz-like substance with edges alternating between brutally sharp and baby-bottom smooth.

Although no light shone from anywhere around me, the rock-face glowed in places, reflecting this unseen light and sparkling cheerily in the awful darkness.

A sound echoed toward me. I was in a tunnel. A tunnel carved out of solid black rock. The shuffling sound drew closer and then something slammed into me, tossing me on my stomach, a sharp instrument piercing my neck. I was so getting tired of people sticking things into my neck all the time. My sight was now fully restored and, in the dimness, I could make out the dirty black soil right in front of my face.

I was now royally pissed off. Whoever they were, they had three seconds to get off me. I lifted my arm and was about to hit backward with my armored arm when I heard a sharp gasp. My strike went amiss, my attacker shifted their weight and I was hauled up by the collar of my jacket.

In a move so quick and easy to miss, my attacker pulled the high neck of my polo down and in the same motion pulled me back and slammed me against the wall. It was impossible to move. I could see the hooded figure in front of me. A glimpse of a pale cheek—a woman. Only her strength defied her female curves.

"What the hell are you doing here?" The words were hushed yet filled with a ferocity I was unprepared for.

I was so stunned I was unable to respond with much more than a gulp.

"What are you doing here? How did you get here?" She paused, then grabbed my arm and lifted it to the dim light scowling at the key. "And how did you get this?"

"Grams gave it to me," I said, pulling my hand away and tucking the key into my bag.

"Ivy. I'm going to kill her." Strange; those words were uttered in anger and yet a tinge of affection simmered within the dire threat. "You had better get out of here. You've gotten yourself in enough trouble already."

She turned to leave, and almost disappeared into the shadows before I came to my senses. Although she attacked me she'd left me very much alive. She was the only 'ally' I had here. I caught her sleeve with my fingers, intent on halting her departure. What my action did was to pull the cloak open as she continued to walk away. She turned to me, to pull the fabric out of my fingers.

A movement which tipped the hood of her cloak back and revealed her face.

The pale cheeks and ebony hair were still as perfect as I remembered. Even those granite eyes glittered with the same intensity from my long-faded memories.

"Mom?" I heard my voice quiver, on the edge of tears.

My mother tried to keep her features hard and controlled. But the slight sheen to her eyes was my real undoing and I would've burst into tears—if it hadn't been for the memory of all the hurt and pain I felt since she'd left me.

All the long years of loneliness and silent tears shed into pillows, for a mother who hadn't loved me enough to stay by my side. The memories staunched my tears and dried my eyes.

The rush of footsteps on hard ground reverberating up the passage, pulled me out of memory lane. The sound echoed, and I was both afraid and unbalanced again. Two figures approached;

most likely guards. Unless we had the ability to blend into the rock surrounding us, we had absolutely nowhere to go.

I centered my weight and tugged my sleeve. This time I was prepared for a fight. Tara had honed hollow needles as fine as threads, which she'd filled with the poison. She'd refused to tell me what the liquid was. Just that it was fatal to a Wraith. I'd thought of gift horses and asked no more questions. I'd slipped the hair-thin needles along the seams and cuffs of my clothing.

Anywhere I was sure I wouldn't be pricked myself. Although Tara had reassured me the poison was not deadly to Walkers, I preferred not to take the chance.

Now I slipped a needle into each hand and waited as two Wraiths approached. Their faces were shadowed by their cloaks and I'd rather not see what would be revealed beneath those dark hoods. I moved slightly ahead of my mother, sure of my weapon's power to take the two suckers down. They advanced fast.

Some part of my mind had always expected these Wraiths to be made up of bits of smoke. From what I'd seen in my experiences of killing them, they turned quickly into black smoke and disappeared through the Veil. It had never occurred to me they would be corporeal.

Even when I'd been constructing the tools to kill them, I must have unconsciously expected them to be spirits. Probably why when they attacked I was, for a brief moment, disoriented when I was body-slammed by the one nearest me and I ended up on my butt in black dirt. He came at me with one booted foot and his cloak shifted to reveal some sort of protective armor beneath.

Above the foot now digging into the soft flesh of my upper arm, was a muscled thigh and calf covered in a black, scale-like armor which moved as he did, and molded to his body. Some technology. Beneath the pain I made a note to take some of the armor back with me. Perhaps Tara could learn from it to create armor for me.

I swung my protected forearm across my body and connected

with the side of his knee. Enough power injected into the strike to disable him temporarily, if not break bones. If he had bones in his knee. He stumbled forward. I grabbed him by his upper arms and pulled him toward me. Using the momentum of his fall I tossed him over my head. He landed in a crumpled, grunting heap.

Then, slowly, he got to his feet.

Damn. He was almost invincible. With the Panther power in each move, any normal man would've been out like a light by now—Human or Walker. But this soul-sucking parasite kept on getting back on his feet. He was covered in armor. Until I found a vulnerable place to get the dart through.

It was time to bring out the big guns.

I had to resort to getting down and dirty. I curved my torso and jumped back up onto my feet. The constant hum of energy which lived beneath my skin rose to the surface. I let my claws, ears, eyes and teeth transform. Let my Panther nature fill me up. Then I gave it control. I dropped to a knee, the rest of my body still in Human form but now filled to the brim with raw, bristling feline energy.

I could smell his fear. See his movements before he even made them.

Talk about the upper hand. He never knew what hit him. I pounced from my low position. A stance which gave him the impression he would have plenty of time to avoid me. I let out a snarl as I flew through the air, claws spread, nostrils flared. My Panther nature hungered for blood and I hoped desperately that I wouldn't give in.

Especially not while my mother watched; my mother who had never seen her children in their feline forms.

The sound of scuffling and a muffled, male grunt confirmed my Mom was holding her own against the other soul-sucker. A second whoosh of breath confirmed she had a mean left hook. I hit my attacker again, focusing the energy of the blow in the claws. I aimed at the neck, and I hit my mark.

An oily, glistening black substance spilled onto the Wraith's cloak, and onto the dark floor. He looked at me, confused and surprised.

My claws came away soaked in the icky blackness. It took me a few seconds to accept it was blood.

Dang. Wraiths bled black blood.

I thought it was sort of cool, and quite appropriate. Black souls, black hearts, black blood. I turned and studied my handiwork. The Wraith lay spread-eagled on the ground, arms out flung.

The passage was silent, and I felt a quiver of fear in the pit of my stomach. Mom. But when I turned she was fine. Staring at me, but physically uninjured. Her face was awash with emotion. Perhaps it was the sight of my partially transformed body which repulsed her. So, I began to transform back to my full Human form.

"No." She took a step toward me, hand outstretched to halt my actions. "Don't change back. Not yet."

My surprise at her request had instinctively stopped the Change so I stood there, listening for the next round of footsteps sure to come. My mother stepped close and laid her hand on my cheek. I wanted to jerk back, away from her warmth. I had craved her touch for so many years that the simple warmth of her skin called tears from my eyes. She cradled my face, marveling at the change my jaw and eyes took on when partly transformed. My eyes were deeper, larger, greener. My jaw was longer. She could see the feline in me.

"Was it hard, baby?" I knew she meant the Change.

"I guess, but everyone goes through the same thing." Her question reminded me she hadn't been around for me through those years, and they rekindled my anger.

"Not everyone. The Change is worse for Alphas and you know it."

I couldn't deny it. Iain had warned me it would hurt but I'd been so blasé about it. When it struck with its omnipotent agony, I was still taken by surprise. Never made a joke about it again.

My mother's eyes filled with tears, but I didn't want to get emotional. I had questions. "What are you doing here?

"I'm doing my job." I raised an eyebrow and waited. "I'm a hunter, just like you. And right now, I'm on a delicate mission."

"How long have you been here?"

"A few hours."

"Have you seen Greer?" I asked, glad I could change the subject, although the new subject was no less emotionally taxing.

"What? No. Why?" All tenderness was now obliterated and replaced with pure suspicion. "What happened?"

"A Wraith brought her here with Niko."

"Dear God." The fear running through her face was a tangible thing. I felt it pulse right through my gut. She knew something I didn't, something horrible enough to freeze her in her tracks in spite of the imminent danger. My eyes thinned in suspicion.

What was she keeping from me?

"What do the Wraiths want? Why are they doing this?" I asked.

"The Wraiths have been possessing Humans for decades even though it's been forbidden for centuries." Mom paused. "Can you describe him?"

"Er ... he was using my friend Anjelo's body. And he had a bronze medallion around his neck."

"That's Widd'en."

"Freaky name. So, *he's* the reason there have been more possessions recently?"

"Yes. Widd'en is a rebel. He led a small fanatical group who believed Humans are just soul-fodder for the Wraiths. He's been spearheading a revolution in Wrythiin and some of that has overflowed into the Human world." She nodded. "Come, we shouldn't waste any more time. I think I know where we might find them." She paused, stared at my face, then headed off down the passage with me keeping pace.

There was something about the way she looked at me, or perhaps the tears in her eyes. And the fact we stood in another dimension, fighting the same evil blood-suckers.

I'd been a toddler when she abandoned us, I knew her more from photographs and videos than memory. The subject of Mom had been treated as if she had died all those years ago. And her departure had hurt my father so deeply. So much that he had completely withdrawn from his children.

"I should be saying I'm sorry I left you. But I'm not." She shook her head, as if a thought had come to her and she was refusing to listen. I relished a brief burst of pure anger and hurt before I digested the words and its meaning, "At least you were safe. Until now."

Her face tightened with anger as we hurried through the tunnels. Seemed she now remembered exactly where we were and what we were doing, and she was back to being angry again.

"What are you so angry about?" I'd disappointed her somehow and it hurt to see the anger so bright on her beautiful face. Besides, she had no right being angry with me. No right at all. "What did I do wrong?"

"I tried to protect you from this." Her gesture encompassed more than the gleaming black tunnel. "He was supposed to protect you."

"Who? Dad?"

"Iain."

Hurt, anger, confusion. I wasn't sure which emotion was strongest, but at this point anger won. "Iain knows? He knew why you left us? That you were back and alive and well?" My voice raised to a feverish heat. Blood pounded in my veins and I fisted my hands, as if the simple action would staunch the tears which filled my eyes.

"Not for a long time." Her eyes were somewhere else as she delved in her memories. "About a year ago, I contacted him. To see how you were doing...you and Greer."

"Why?" A year was exactly how long I'd been hunting the Wraiths.

"Someone was hunting in the city. And I needed to make sure it wasn't either of you girls. Iain was pretty sure you were busy with your counseling." She stopped and faced me, her eyes narrowed as she studied me. "Obviously he was mistaken."

"Nobody knows. Not even Dad." I tacked that on and was satisfied with the pain I saw in her gray eyes. What she'd done to him was unforgivable. Gone sixteen years without so much as a goodbye. She'd ruined his life and only when I watched her grief did I realize she'd gone through the very same agony she'd put us through. "Why did you do it? Why did you leave us? Was it something we did? Someone else in your life besides Dad?"

She drew away from the barrage of questions. But, with the stone wall at her back, she had nowhere to go. The passage was still silent for a moment before she started to walk again.

"You owe me an explanation," I said. She nodded, and it surprised me. I'd been prepared for resistance or denial and her agreement was unbalancing.

"You do need to know. Now more than ever."

I waited for her to continue, still amazed the woman whom I'd dreamed and imagined and wished for was standing right in front of me. I was torn between the desire for my Mom to hold me close, and the infinitely more powerful need to hurt her right back, for all the pain she'd caused me over these years.

What a baby I was.

"Then tell me what do *you* have to do with all of this?"

"My Mage-power is the ability to kill Wraiths. Something almost unknown for normal people. Or Walkers. But recently,

Widd'en found out there was another Hunter just as powerful as I am."

I stared at her, understanding dawning on me. "And *I'm* that Hunter."

"It's passed down through the women in my family. I'm powerful, but I think you are far more powerful than any one of us." She shook her head again, as if unable to believe her own words. "I tried to protect you. Knew it was probable either you or Greer would inherit it. I thought if you both stayed in the colony then you wouldn't ever have to find out. Seems you did. Is it only you?"

"If Greer has it, she has never said so. Besides, she doesn't speak to me much. There's something really wrong with her."

"What? Is she sick?" Mom's forehead creased with worry.

"Not exactly. She's Pariah."

The shock on my mother's face was worse than what I'd seen when she'd first laid eyes on me. "What? No. Oh, poor Greer. When—"

"Her Change time came late. Or that's what I'd assumed. I've been gone two years now, Mom. After my own Change. Greer's time hadn't come when I left. Still, nineteen is not too old so I never knew what happened."

"Your father...he would've been angry and upset when you left." She turned away. The gleaming black of the stone wall was suddenly more interesting than the painful revelation about her daughter. "Seems I did a terrible job of protecting you girls."

"I could've used my mother during my Change-Time." I was still angry she hadn't been there to support me through the confusion and pain, like all the other kids' moms.

"I wouldn't have been able to be with you, Kai. It wouldn't have been allowed."

"For Ailuros' sake, why not? All the other kids had their Moms." Until that moment I'd thought I was above the immature whining of a teenager. Apparently not.

"I am not a SkinWalker, so why would you ever have expected that." Her eyes narrowed again, and I stepped closer and sniffed her. I had to give her credit for submitting to such a personal investigation, even if it was her own daughter doing the sniffing.

I breathed in the scent of my mother.

The sweet odor of perspiration hung over her. Nobody fought with such tenacity without breaking a sweat. As odors went it wasn't at all repulsive. The spice of her blood was a soft frankincense, calming and not at all like the spice of a Walker's blood. My ears caught the pounding of her heart, so unlike mine that it was the final confirmation of what my mother really was.

Human.

What had she been up to all these years? The knowledge she was a powerful hunter in her own right was as much a revelation as her species. Why did my father keep this bit of information from me? Did Greer and Iain know what she was? Confusion riddled my brain.

My turn to take a step back. This whole thing was too much to absorb. When I saw my mother's expression I paused. Hurt warred with disappointment in her body and the set of her face.

It was too late. My action may have seemed like a rejection. But it wasn't, and it was too late to convince her she was wrong.

CHAPTER 41

From the sound of the crunching boot steps coming toward us, I knew we had to leave. I wondered what would've happened to me had I arrived in this dimension a mere foot to the right. I'd have been permanently solidified within the dull black rock. I only had a second to shiver at the horrifying thought.

Then they arrived. We fought valiantly. Now I knew their weak point I used my needles to incapacitate as many guards as I could. Mom, too, managed to take down a good number herself. But they were relentless. They kept coming and it soon seemed like it was an entire army we fought. Two to one odds quickly became four and just as quickly progressed to six, which was when the fight was over for Mom and me.

Pretty much man-handled, wrists held tightly behind our backs, we were marched along dank darkness broken by the flickering blue-white flames of torch-light. None of the guards had pulled any of their punches and we were both sore in dozens of places. Mom was going to have a shiner tomorrow morning.

If we saw tomorrow morning, that was.

More torchlight, and then the black dirt gave way to well-swept ground, the jagged rock facings to smoothly planed surfaces. Someone had decided to do a little bit of interior decorating. I swallowed and choked on the thought. It became much easier to cease with the hysteria when I was viciously jabbed in the ribs by the nearest guard.

We were pushed through a carved archway leading to an open circular room. Pillars of black rock held up a ceiling as smoothly planed as my cheek. Taking pride of place in the center of the room was a perfectly round pool of dark and oily liquid. The pool was bordered by blue flames, similar to those of the torches' light.

Blue flames danced at random on the surface of the pool. It was actually quite pretty, and had I been unshackled I would've jabbed myself in the ribs as punishment for such blasphemous admiration of these evil creatures.

The tour ended at the edge of the pool. I craned my neck to see over the six-foot creatures who formed our guard. Mom did the same. A shuffle of movement and they parted like a sea and melted into the shadows to reveal one lone hooded figure. I was so over these pretentious hoods.

What in Ailuros' name were they hiding beneath those cowls? Nothing worse than the corpse of the Cougar Walker I'd found, surely.

Silence blanketed the room and only the tiny fluttering of the blue flames dared to disturb it. Each of the guards seemed frozen in place. I looked over at Mom and she raised her eyebrows. Perhaps some kind of hive mentality. I hadn't heard any instruction given to them, but their simultaneous shut-down implied they obeyed a command only they heard.

My heart clenched when he turned. The gleaming medallion which hung on his neck confirmed it was the Wraith who'd possessed Anjelo's body. Then I was awash with relief. If I could find where he was keeping Anjelo, I could save my friend.

The Wraith's face was lit by the blue pool-lights, the face

beneath the cowl nothing even *my* imagination could've created. It was the visage of a specter or a ghost; skeletal, white skin clinging to fleshless bones, in a face framed by a fall of white hair. His sunken eyes were black and shining like the viscous pool which we surrounded. His mouth was a round, dark orifice and my nightmares filled in the blanks with rows of hideously sharp, yellowed teeth. The medallion glinted again on his chest, and I was reminded that he had my sister and uncle hostage.

The Wraith turned his head slightly to address my mother. His almond shaped onyx eyes studied her while his awful mouth curved in a terrible smile. "I cannot believe it." His voice was low and rumbling and totally out of place because of its essentially Human quality. If I shut my eyes, I could imagine any regular human enunciating those words. "Finally, we have captured the elusive Celeste."

I did a tiny double take—I'd almost forgotten my mother's name. She'd been 'Mom' for so long it was hard to imagine her as having another identity, despite her absence.

"And you came right to us. How helpful." His voice echoed around the bare rock walls. "To what do we owe the privilege of this visit from the mighty Celeste?"

Hatred poured off him in waves. Mom must have done some really bad things to him for that level of animosity. Then he looked at me.

"And the offspring of the great Hunter. You came. Just as I expected you would." He smiled that smile again, this time wider. This time I saw the teeth of my nightmares. Fewer teeth but still sharp and ugh. "Earth-Worlders are so predictable. So, driven by sentimentality."

"What have you done with Anjelo? Where are Niko and Greer?" I wasn't sure I'd voiced my thoughts until I heard my voice echo around the cave.

"What have you done with them?" Mom questioned him again. This time with a little more strength. I was still quaking in my boots, hellishly afraid to challenge this horrible creature. "Widd'en, I swear if you've hurt even a hair on my daughter's head I will kill you."

"Oh, my dear Celeste. Do not tell me I have the pleasure of the presence of both your daughters, now?" Widd'en laughed the sound grating on my ears.

Mom's face fell as she realized her mistake. He hadn't known that Greer was her daughter, but she'd just handed him more power.

He flicked his wrist and the guard beside me disappeared through a nearby arch. Mom's guard took a few short steps back, the better to keep an eye on both his captives. Seconds passed before my guard returned, dragging a bound and disheveled Greer.

Trailing him was another guard carrying Niko over his shoulder like a sack of potatoes. My heart moved to my throat as I took in Greer's swollen face, and the look of surprise, then confusion and shock she threw Mom from across the hall.

The guard bearing Niko tossed his burden to the ground and took a step back. Widd'en nodded at the pair who bowed and left in silence. A movement of air behind us revealed Mom's guard was also making a quick and silent exit.

What was he up to and why get rid of the guards?

Niko landed at the edge of the pool, so close to the flames that pale blue shadows flickered on his arm. Widd'en kicked him in the ribs. Hard. Mom and I gasped, shocked, flinching on behalf of my uncle.

"He wasn't much help." Widd'en's shrug was noncommittal. "Not much help at all."

With those words, he gave Niko a second, more powerful kick. The blow was enough to shift Niko nearer to the edge of the pool. So much that his torso tipped over the edge into the black murkiness. The weight of his upper body dragged the rest of him into the pool.

We watched the scene as if in slow-motion.

As his body disappeared below the surface, Mom cried out and ran to the edge of the pool, peering over the flames. She stayed well away from the water. The black, oily liquid gave no sign of my uncle's body floating to its depths.

I hoped he had been dead before his fall. How was I going to tell my father he no longer had a brother? That I'd been unable to save him? Mom's despair was somewhat comforting; at least she felt the same way. Poor Greer—she'd been much closer to Niko than I had.

Greer's face was a study in anger, but I saw no grief. I saw an angry, hardened woman where my sister should've been.

"Widd'en. You bastard," Mom cried in anger.

"Oh, my dear, why? What was so special about him?" He looked straight at me, gleaming black eyes piercing straight into my soul. "Ah. The most powerful Wraith Hunter to ever grace the dimensions." He sketched a bow, though a look of abhorrence swallowed his face. I got the feeling he didn't like me very much.

Mom rose quickly and took a stance in front of me. "Leave her alone."

"I have a proposition you may be interested in, Celeste." Mom waited in silence. I did not like the sound of this proposal of his. Didn't trust him at all. "Since I have both of your lovely daughters, how about you decide which one of them will stay with me and which one gets to return home." He grinned and licked his lips with a tongue as black as night and forked like that of a snake. Yikes.

Mom's face lost at least three shades of color. What a nightmare of a choice. One I didn't intend for her to have to make.

"I don't trust you," Mom said as she shook her head.

"As a show of good faith, I shall open the portal. You choose the daughter and she may leave any time she wishes."

Mom glanced at me. It was plain she did not believe him. In

that second, I knew she meant for us to use the portal and leave as soon as we got the chance.

But it meant she would remain behind, in the captivity of Widd'en. Every bone in my body rebelled against this idea. I was still fuming at her defection, fuming at the revelation she'd contacted Iain but not me. I was so angry at all the lies, it didn't matter much her reasons. She'd hurt so many people with her stupid choices.

I looked at Greer who, in spite of the cloud of hate enveloping her, understood Mom's intention. Greer gave a slow, long blink, letting Mom know she understood and would do as she asked. Traitorous bitch.

How could she be so calm about abandoning her mother when we'd so recently gotten her back? Unless she suspected Widd'en wouldn't keep his promise and she intended to get out while she could.

Obviously, the most important person to Greer was herself. Whatever she said and did, I had always known that deep within, she was numero Uno. Lie upon lie was wound around her at every chance. And now she had the ultimate opportunity to give me what she considered my just desserts.

I was the Alpha child.

She was Pariah.

That was no fault of mine; it seemed I bore the blame anyway.

Greer had sided with Niko, her need to find a way to fully transform overriding all else. No point asking her now why she had so effectively betrayed her people. I knew she would leave the moment she got the chance, but I refused to let the hurt control my actions.

Unless I did something fast, Mom would end up trapped here in Wrythiin.

Widd'en smiled that horrible smile of his; well pleased with himself. He grabbed the medallion from around his neck and flung it forward where it hovered over the center of the glistening pool. Soon an expanse of blue light shot through the hole in the center of the rune-inscribed key.

Neither Mom nor I were the least bit impressed by this light-show. Greer on the other hand had been pulled from the lab back to Wrythiin through an already open portal.

I had to get Mom out of the Hall and figure a way to get Greer out too. It would be more difficult with Greer on the opposite side of the pool. With the portal open, Widd'en now beckoned Mom forward.

"I don't have all day, Celeste. Have you made your decision? Daughter number one," he waved a hand at Greer. "Or daughter number two."

I was certain he had no plans to keep his promise. Which meant I had to save Mom right now.

So, I took my chances and ran around the edge of the pool and straight at him. On the way, I gave Mom a shove. She fell heavily on her side. From the gasp of pain she uttered, I knew she'd been hurt. But she was a big girl. And I was trying to save her life.

It took Widd'en a moment to process the fact he was under attack.

Time enough for me to get close to him. My fingers had been busy assessing the number of needles remaining. After the battle in the tunnels I was left with two. Had to use them sparingly.

Before I ran at him, I'd gripped a needle between my fingers, hoping to get a chance to plunge it into his armpit. I had to get close if I were to succeed.

His solid black eyes widened as he saw me close the distance. I slammed into him before he could react, the impact throwing him onto his back. I lay on his chest for the briefest of seconds. I rolled off, skin writhing in disgust at such close contact.

I was fast.

He was faster.

Moved like a blur and was on his feet in seconds. I'd gotten the needle deep in his armpit though he hadn't given any indication he'd felt it penetrate.

We circled each other, mimicking the other's movements until we reached a stalemate.

Light flashed from his hands and I recognized the black sword he'd held to me in the lab. A beautiful thing in its own right, but in the hand of this foul creature it became an ugly weapon of destruction.

No art. Just murder.

He held it in at his shoulder, like a baseball bat. Clearly the master of the Wraith hadn't perfected the art of sword fighting. He swung it in an ebony flash and missed me by a hairsbreadth. He came back at me again and I curved my torso backward to avoid the swipe.

Rule number one—never underestimate your opponent's ability to wield a sword.

It became a dizzying dance. The next swipe caught me on the arm, and thankfully it was the armored one. I prayed it would hold its form as it had in our last encounter. The blow stunned me, sending rippling vibrations through my bones.

Widd'en took the opportunity to swipe again, this time lower. Even though I sprung backward, the swipe cleaved the flesh of my thigh open, and I felt the gush of heated blood flow through the wound.

Damn. I hadn't planned on getting hurt.

Swooning with pain, I almost missed the Wraith-Master as he reached for the medallion to close the portal. Greer didn't see him and jumped. I heard Mom's scream echo through the Hall and knew the reason for the pure agony it contained.

Widd'en had moved the medallion, thus moving the portal.

Even the slightest movement would mean the portal would send Greer somewhere else. But it also meant she would remain there for as long as it took us to find a way to get her out. My eyes filled with tears and none were for my damaged limb. My sister was now gone, who knew where. But Greer was no weakling.

She'd find a way to stay safe and besides, her hatred would give her the energy to survive...

My hand was sopping with blood as I tried to stem the flow. Blood and anger were a temptation to my Panther that couldn't be stopped.

I had no intention of even trying.

Heat sluiced through me, flesh and bone simmered hotter than the pain which still fired my thigh. My limbs lengthened, thinned. My eyes deepened, cheeks heightened, skin furred. With a final, sickening rip, my clothes fell to the ground and I stood in all my SkinWalker glory, canines bared, pelt glistening as dark as the sword Widd'en carried.

As elements of surprise went, I would certainly have won first prize. At least it caught the sucker off guard. Enough for me to pounce. Out of the corner of my eye I saw Mom rise to her feet and run toward us, favoring one leg.

I liked the two-to-one odds better.

As I sprang at him, he lifted his sword and held its point straight at my chest. Mom came at him from the side and hit his arm full force, throwing him off balance. The sword clattered to the stone floor and I suffered a mental wince.

Such a beautiful weapon. I hoped it wouldn't be damaged.

Distracted by Mom's side-swipe, Widd'en didn't see me land on him. My weight threw him to the ground, and I sank my teeth into his neck. A death grip from which even I was unable to release him until my adrenaline slowed. Black goo spurted from the wounds and filled my mouth, coating my tongue with a bitter, oiliness.

Ugh.

He bucked and kicked—violent, angry movements, but my jaw gripped tight. At last the fight drained from him along with most of his blood. He was dead. While I remained locked onto his neck, Mom rose and threw the medallion back over the pool to open the portal. She came to my side, stroking my back like she would a cat.

"Come now, release him, Kailin." Her voice was soft and comforting, washing over me in calming waves. I growled at her, somewhere between don't-touch-me and please-help-me. "Shhhh. Come, Kai. Leave him."

My jaws unlocked, and I released the dead Wraith's throat. Took a few steps back and sat heavily on my haunches. My thin legs quivered like a newborn's as the last of the adrenaline faded. Heat filtered through my blood again as the Panther retreated and I returned to my Human form.

Weak and naked at my mother's feet.

She knelt and held me in her arms as I desperately swiped the dark slick blood from my chin and cheeks. I was desperate to get it off.

"Honey, it's alright. You did good, Kai." I felt a rush of air and something large covered my naked skin. "Time to go home."

Mom supported me as I rose on shivering legs and we walked to the edge of the pool. I stared longingly at the sword, as I passed inches from it. I had no energy to bend down and grab it. The blood loss had continued through my transformation, only stopping once I'd fully transformed into my Panther form.

Thankfully, the transformation back hadn't ripped the wound open again but the loss of blood meant I had very little energy left.

I held onto my Mom's hand and squeezed. Ready to go home.

"Now." She whispered the words and shoved me, adding to my momentum as I made a weak effort to jump to the brightly shining light. I turned to see her step back and pick up the sword. She'd known I'd wanted it.

She stepped back a few paces more, gaining distance for her jump when two Guards came hurtling into to Hall, running straight at her.

I flailed in mid-air, screaming, "Mom. Run."

She ran but, hampered by her limp, not fast enough. Tackled by the Guards she tumbled to the ground. Before she hit the stone floor she twisted her torso and flung the sword at me.

As the black sword spun, reflecting a thousand pinpoints of colored light, and as I stared straight at my mother, I lost consciousness. My last thought was of her mother's eyes. They were filled with a message.

She was strong. The encouraging nod she'd given me was an instruction.

I will wait for you to come for me.

CHAPTER 42

I was so deep in grief I barely registered my arrival back in Chicago. Thankfully, I landed on the pier and not in the murky water. The sword followed me through the light and landed next to me with a solid thunk. I only had a few seconds to wonder how near the slice would have been had it landed two inches closer to my good leg.

Then I passed out cold.

Voices filtered through a gray haze. I heard the rushing of heels on the wood of the pier. The plank's vibrations rippled against my cheekbone. My lids fluttered open.

The three men in my life halted before me just as my head ceased spinning.

My father. Furious.

Iain. Furious.

Logan. Furious.

Just looking at them, I'd had enough. Macho over-protectiveness across all species.

What in Ailuros' name were they doing here? How did they find out where I was?

My head pounded while my leg throbbed as if my heart had

decided my rib-cage was no longer suitable lodgings. I sat up. Had the presence of mind to grasp for the cloak. Nudity was not appropriate when all three men were so angry.

Especially when my father and brother were two of those men.

Logan rushed to me, crouching beside me. "Kailin, are you okay?" Then he swore, lifting his hand, now red with my blood. "Are you hurt? What happened?"

I moved the cloak aside just enough for him to see the slowly knitting gash in my thigh. Relief would've smoothed his features had he not been furious as well. "I'm fine. It's already healing." I felt Iain and my father hovering but neither commented on my injury.

My eyes scuttled around, in search of the sword.

"You looking for this?" Iain asked, twirling the obsidian weapon in his hand, one finger teasing the fine tip.

"Be careful with that."

"Well, well, the Panther can still strike even while bleeding all over the place." He smirked.

"Shut up, Iain." I'd had about enough for one evening. Iain wouldn't find all of this so funny once he knew where I'd been. And who I'd left behind.

"I need that sword, so you'd better be careful with it." I glared at him.

"Where'd you get it?" The glint in his eye managed to be both amused and angry at the same time. Sure, I understood they were all upset about my disappearance, and probably my damaged state as well. Perhaps they felt superfluous.

When men felt superfluous it was a situation much better avoided.

"It belonged to Widd'en, Wraith-Lord of Wrythiin." That got their attention.

"Belonged?" Iain asked.

"To the victor go the spoils." I waggled my eyebrows at my brother. Beside him my father was very quiet.

I eyed the sword warily. Hoping Iain hadn't drawn blood with the vicious weapon. I found him frowning at my words. I continued patiently, "In most battles to the death the victor has the privilege of taking with her the weapons of her opponent." I turned my head and met Logan's eyes and fire rippled along my veins, a not-too-gentle reminder of where my heart lay. I longed to be enveloped in his strong arms, longed for him to tell me everything would be okay. Logan managed a weak smile, "You think you could help me to my feet without giving those two an eyeful?"

He grinned and nodded, looping his arm around my shoulders. He supported most of my weight while I gripped the cloak to my body. At last I was standing, still leaning on Logan for support.

"Let's get you to your apartment. You need to get some rest, and have your wounds seen to." Logan said briskly. "Then we can all talk."

I limped to Iain, and muttered, "Take care of my sword, dear brother. I may be needing it in the very near future." To his credit he remained silent. My brother may infuriate me, but he knew when I was hurting.

And that's why I couldn't understand how he could've kept Mom's presence from me.

I paused as we passed my father. "Father, we need to speak in private. I have something to tell you." When he looked like he was going to resist, refuse to speak to me, I said, "It's a message from Mom."

My last words were spoken so softly only my father heard them. He searched my face, eyes moist, and offered a short quick nod.

Logan urged me on, leaving my father to his thoughts.

"You have things to sort out with your family. I'll drop you off at your apartment and I'll come see you in the morning—when you're feeling better." At last Logan had found his voice and he'd just closed himself off from me. Was he intimidated by the two Alpha males in my family? He wasn't meeting my eye.

I grabbed his shoulder as he began to walk away. "What's wrong?"

He was pulling away from me and I was desperate for him to stay. The last thing I wanted was for him to leave me too.

My eyes blurred with tears, and though I would've liked to believe they were a culmination of this horrible evening, I knew deep down they were real tears about to be shed for the guy I was crazy about.

I was about to cry like a girl in front of my father and brother —enough proof I needed rest.

"No, you won't. You're taking me home." I looked over my shoulder at Iain and said, "Can you bring Father over to my place? There're a few things I need to discuss with Logan."

Once inside the car, Logan turned the heat up and made quick work of the distance to my house. His silence unnerved me. Made me want to grab his arm and beg him to stay.

"Pull over." I steeled my voice from any emotion.

He looked at me, startled.

"Pull over. We need to talk."

Indecision clouded his eyes and just when I thought he would ignore me, he indicated and turned into a quiet side street.

"Something's wrong, and I have too many things to worry about to have this bugging me too." It sounded selfish, but it seemed the best tack.

Silence filled the car. I waited. He'd talk when he was ready. Although I would prefer sooner rather than later given my state of undress.

"It's something I did a long time ago." When he met my gaze, his eyes were filled with pain. His expression was so similar to the look in my mother's eyes as she watched me disappear into the portal. My lip quivered, then hot tears spiked my lids.

Biting back the tears, I waited.

"Something I did to Iain...although at the time I guess...I was too young to know what I'd done. Or...maybe...too young to understand the consequences of what I'd done." He looked at his hands, as if he held the answers within those twisted fingers. "My powers were becoming uncontrollable. Especially when I was upset. My father had left us and my mother...bless her kind heart...she thought a nice lunch at the restaurant where she worked would do the trick. We didn't know he'd be there looking for her. He'd run out of money, came back for some more. I saw him and...something inside me...went off."

Logan looked out the window, shaking his head as if he wanted to shake the memory right out of his mind. "Everything around me got hotter and hotter until...it just exploded. My mother was holding my hand when we saw him. I never let go of it. She died where she stood next to me...took the brunt of the explosion. I killed 26 people that day including my mother, my father...and Sonia Lake."

All the air went right out of my lungs in a whoosh, and I had to take a few moments to breathe. At last, I turned in my seat, glad the darkness hid the somewhat pained expression I knew was plastered on my shocked face.

"Oh, Logan. It wasn't your fault." I grasped his arm and spoke softly. "How could you have known that would happen? It was an accident, Logan. You need to accept that." I rubbed his arm, wanting to hold him close and comfort the grieving little boy I saw in his eyes.

"How could Iain forgive me for taking his wife away?" He attacked me with the question, but I refused to flinch in the face of his grief.

"He will, Logan. Iain is not an unreasonable man. I know my brother. He has a good heart. He will understand."

I knew deep down I was right, but my words were small comfort Logan. He regarded me, a stricken expression marring his beautiful face. My heart hurt for him. I wanted to touch his face, to hold him, to make it all better, but I didn't.

He needed resolution, not comfort.

"You have to speak to him. It's closure for both of you." Logan looked up at me, startled. He hadn't even thought of the option. But he still resisted.

Shaking his head, "That's a really bad idea, Kailin."

"No. It's a good idea. He will understand. Trust me. Maybe he'll be angry, and he has a right to be. But he'll understand. And you will feel better."

Logan stared out the windshield, lost in thought. Although only ten minutes had passed, it had felt like a lifetime. At last, he started the car and took me home.

DAD AND IAIN arrived a few minutes after I'd had a quick shower and a change of clothes. I'd tried to wipe out the taste of Wraith blood from my tongue.

Brushed my teeth twice to get the fetid flavor out of my mouth but I still felt the bitterness every time I swallowed. My arm hurt like the blazes, but I was impatient to speak to my father.

Ignoring it for now seemed the smartest choice.

They came bearing food and although I grieved for my sister and my mother and for poor Logan, I was incredibly hungry. Iain had remembered my love of Cantonese. I ate with gusto while my guests picked at their food. I hoped the food would help erase the foul Wraith-blood taste.

I looked up and met my father's worried eyes. "You killed the Wraith-Lord?" Finally saw fit to speak. I sighed. Was I teaching a cub class?

"Yes, father. And Mom sends her regards." Until that second, I hadn't realized how angry I was. Even when the color drained from his face, I had no sympathy for him.

Iain's shocked "What?" went almost unnoticed. I turned to him. "And this is where you can be quiet. Don't even bother to deny you knew she was still alive." Fury blurred my vision, clearly exacerbated by the lack of blood in my damaged body.

I rose and beckoned my father into the living room.

Looking over my shoulder I sent Logan a look bearing specific instruction to talk. Leaving Iain alone with Logan was the perfect opportunity. I paused in my step. Logan needed a way to broach this difficult topic, otherwise he'd be flailing about in the dark until I'd finished speaking to my father. The big Omega Agent had no idea how to broach a sensitive subject.

"Iain?" I said. He looked up from murdering his noodles. "Logan has something important to tell you."

Hopefully it would get things started.

My father sat and looked uncomfortable, folding and unfolding his arms. It was hard to look stern and uncompromising while slouched on my couch. I was grateful he relented to my request to talk.

My father usually never did anything unless he wanted to.

"You had something to discuss. Something about your mother?" He was eager for news of his wife, and it occurred to me he still cared for her. I immediately felt guilty. Had I been so blind and selfish not to realize he'd been steeped in grief all these years?

No. Even if he'd been grieving, I'd deserved even the tiniest bit of affection.

I had no idea where to start. So, jumping right in seemed a good enough option. "Care to explain why you never mentioned Mom was Human?"

"But—"

I held up my hand. "Well, Father? Is that the reason you always warned us against getting too close to Humans?" I was desperate to know why he kept it from me. "Who else knew she was Human? Did you tell Iain and Greer?"

"No. I didn't tell any of your siblings. You didn't need to know."

"What about the Clan? Th Council? Who else knew?" I pushed, still infuriated, still hurt beyond belief.

"The elders and most of the adult Walkers."

"And nobody, not even a single person, ever mentioned it to any one of us?" I shook my head, disbelief robbing me of any further words.

"Out of respect to the Alpha. When she left, the subject of your mother was taboo." He was still deeply hurt by her defection, and I had it in my power to relieve him of some of his pain. But not here, in front of Iain and Logan.

Despite my anger I held my tongue. This was a truth between two people and I couldn't speak of it until we were alone.

The silence stretched between us, almost palpable. At last he sighed and asked, "Where is she?" he asked, his voice barely a whisper.

"In Wrythiin."

"What?" He leaned forward intent on my response, wanting to hear me say it was a joke.

"It's where I went, to find Greer and Niko."

"And, did you find them?"

"Yes, only..." I rose and paced. How was I supposed to tell him his brother was killed by the Wraith-Lord? "Mom said she'd left for only one reason—to protect us from him...the Wraiths."

"Why? Why would he be after you?" My father had no idea of my mother's talent for delivering eternal justice to the soul-suckers.

"Because she's a Wraith-Hunter and she knew I had the same....ability." My voice was flat, because I still wasn't sure I believed it. She left me. That was that. No reason why a mother should abandon her children.

He rested his forehead in his hand and said nothing.

"She thought if she left I'd never find out I had the ability." I continued my mother's tale.

"She didn't count on your stubborn streak, did she?"

"Neither did she count on how you would treat us after she left." I had to say my piece. No matter that I was about to bombard him with a triple layer of loss. "I don't think she realized she'd take your heart with her."

My father stared at me, shocked, and perplexed.

"Is that what you think?" His brow twisted in confusion.

"Of course. You avoided me. You're always in your own world. Always preoccupied, we never used to talk or spend time with each other."

I fell into the whine of complaints, but I was still a lonely child. Even though my mother had her reasons for leaving, and my father's coldness had never been deliberate, I still hated the fact that, in the end, I was the one left hurt and lonely.

"I hadn't realized." The silence drew out longer than I expected. "I assume that's why you left?"

I nodded. "Greer didn't stay too long either, did she?"

Corin shook his head. "Greer's inability to change…. That was a shock, especially after Niko."

"Is that why you kept it from me?"

He nodded. "Greer was angry. So very upset. That's why she was so easily seduced by Niko's theories."

"You knew about that?"

"I suspected but there was no proof. I knew he was up to something, even went searching for him when Greer disappeared but I lost his trail."

I recalled my father's absence when I came to tell Iain about the first body.

"He was being influenced by Widd'en."

"What do you mean?" My father hadn't been exposed to any

of the Wraith possession, didn't know much about how the whole possession thing worked.

"Mom told me that Widd'en is the leader of a faction who have been coming through the Veil to prey on Humans. She'd managed to fight many of them off but when I started Hunting, it must have tipped them off that another Hunter was around. So, he *was* trying to find me."

My father's head jerked up and he looked at me in consternation. "He was after *you*?"

"Imagine that?" I said, dryly.

Dad frowned. "What did he want with Niko?"

"I'm still not entirely sure what the Wraith was doing with Niko. But, Widd'en killed him, Father." I watched the grief on his face.

Men show grief so differently from women. We were free to cry, such girls. Men, no matter the species, keep it inside.

True to nature, my father clasped his hand in front of his face and closed his eyes. He looked a lot like a man deep in prayer, but I knew he wasn't.

"How?" he asked, his head still bowed. When I didn't reply he looked up at my face.

I shook my head, hoping he'd take it as a sign that I didn't know the method of the killing.

"Did you see him?"

"He was already dead by then."

"And Greer?"

"She tried to escape through the portal but Widd'en had moved the key, so the destination changed. She made a run for it and went through. Now we have no idea which dimension she is in." I was still not in the least impressed by my sibling's betrayal. Father was shaking his head again.

"Ah, Greer. She's been lost for a while now." It seemed somehow fitting she would end up in the land of neither living nor dead.

"Well, she's lost good and proper now," I said, irony dripping thickly from my words.

"Can we find her?"

"I think so. We will have to get help from a few people, but I think we can, though it may take some time." No prizes for guessing who would be the one trying to find a sister who was willing to watch you die.

"And where's your mother?" He voiced the question with such dread I was afraid to answer.

"The Guard caught her before she made the jump. She'd shoved me through because I was so weak after my fight with Widd'en. But she wasn't fast enough. They caught her just before the portal closed."

I couldn't say anything to make him feel better. What can you say to a man who loses three members of his family in one night, one of them for the second time? I rose to leave the room, leave him to think and pray and grieve and do whatever he needed to make himself feel better.

"Can we save her?" My father's eyes were shadowed as he spoke.

"I'm pretty sure I can. I have Iain and the Omega team." He nodded.

Then my father held me in his arms for the first time in sixteen long years. And I held back the tears of joy and grief and regret that pooled hotly behind my eyes.

"Let me know what you need." His voice emanated from somewhere above my left ear. "Anything and anyone. Iain will help, I'm sure." I didn't pay much attention to his words.

It was the feel of his arms around me I reveled in.

CHAPTER 43

Outside, splotches of bloody ocher etched the sky, which grew brighter as the night receded. I stood at my window for a long time, soaking up the silence of the house. Everyone had cleared out except for Logan. He'd insisted on sleeping on the couch in case I needed him. My heart warmed at the thought.

I didn't like the distance between us, and I would soon rectify that.

The sun was rising.

Burnt orange flames bled into an inky night sky, bright yellow fingers of light followed eagerly. The new day was coming. Clean and bright.

A chance to put things right.

My arm throbbed, but I ignored it to count my blessings. I hugged so many little gifts close to my heart. Held the hurts close too. My sister's hatred hurt me deeply, but I had to find her before she lost her soul forever. My uncle was dead, no redemption allowed to him at all.

And nothing I could do would change his fate.

Perhaps it was time he had some peace. At least Greer could try to make things better if we ever managed to bring her home.

The love that shone from my mother's eyes was a treasure I held closer. The woman I'd grown up thinking had abandoned me, who I'd half-missed and half-hated over the last sixteen years, who had proved to me that she possessed a love for her children that was self-sacrificing and altogether incomparable. My mother.

And this whole disaster had brought my father closer to me than I'd ever dared to hope. It's not as if I suddenly stopped being angry with them. But I allowed myself to understand a little more why they did what they did.

I sighed.

A pair of strapping arms enfolded me within the warmest of embraces. I'd let Logan sleep. Now he was here, toasty warm. I turned in his arms and stared into his eyes. Tiny flames flickered within their depths and I knew it wasn't just my imagination.

His kiss was warm, and comforting. I'd held him at armslength for so long, and now, it felt wonderful to be able to relax with him. The one person I could trust implicitly.

I snuggled closer, hoping to feel those flames again. I moved my arm around him, careful not to jar it. I would never be sure what gave me away. Logan's fingers closed around my wrist.

"What's wrong with your arm?" He lifted my hand, staring at the bracelet as if it had come alive.

"Nothing. It's just a bit sore." I tried to pull it from his grasp, but he held firm and I winced. Any pressure I used on the muscle would hurt like hell, so I tried to keep still. I'd put the armor back on after showering, afraid to even contemplate what the blue-green stain beneath my skin meant. It looked menacing, spreading out like a thousand veins.

Before I knew what he was doing, Logan turned my arm over and began to unbuckle the bracelet. It seemed odd to see him make such quick work of removing it when I'd struggled for days to simply open one buckle.

The bracelet clanked as it landed unceremoniously on the floor. Logan was horrified at the sight.

"What is this?" his face was like a marble statue, drained of every drop of blood. Only a few hours ago the blue-green veins had covered my forearm, conveniently remaining beneath the bronze metal.

Now I stared at what had gotten Logan's full attention. My entire arm was covered with a network of tiny blue-green veins. My heart clenched, and my tongue stuck to the roof of my mouth.

"What in God's name is going on?"

"I'm not sure." I stared at the spindly patterns, perplexed. The web of dark lines had spread so fast, I was now very, very afraid.

"Why didn't you say something?" Logan had gone from tender and loving to bristling and angry in the blink of an eye. "God, you are the most frustrating person I have ever met."

I wanted to say something smart or funny, but the pain had worsened. I could no longer ignore it. I'd assumed I was tired from my portal travel, not to mention the emotional and physical roller-coaster ride I'd been through over the last week or so.

But now, the frightening state of my arm robbed me of anything smart or witty I might have said.

"Let go of me." Suddenly I wanted him to stop touching me. I was stricken with fear this may be contagious and Logan may become infected too. But he held on. The tug-of-war for my arm tired me out, and made it ache more. Logan was going to make his point even if I got hurt in the process. My arm began to blaze with warmth. It went from lukewarm to sizzling and I looked at Logan sharply.

I gave my hand one last painful tug and he let go.

Logan blinked at me, as if coming out of a trance. I rubbed my arm, tracing the warmth as it wrapped around my wrist. I looked at it, expecting to see a purple bruise layered over the poisonous blue, and gasped with shock and restrained delight.

Where Logan had held me within his heated grasp, was now a band of clean, unblemished skin in the shape and pattern of his fingers.

"What did you do?" I breathed, staring at my hand in fascination.

"I have no idea." He ruffled his hair, scratching at his scalp as he thought hard. "I was concentrating, trying to imagine how the lines were moving around your arm and why. I was a bit pissed off too. And then I must have blanked out for a bit."

Logan lifted my hand in his, studying the cured area in silence.

"Did you use your powers to heal my hand?" I went still, waiting for him to confirm my suspicion.

"It's possible the Fire-magic killed the poison. It's not all gone, though." He turned my hand over as he spoke.

"Try again." I stuck my hand out in front of his face.

"I don't think it works like that. The last thing I want to do now is fry your arm to a crisp." Logan let go of my hand slowly, and it grew cool from the loss. "I need to learn what to do, Kailin. I have to learn how to control this."

I understood. Pain etched his face. To force the issue would be selfish. He had an incredible power within him. A deadly power. I wasn't about to push him into using it to cure the sword's poison before he was ready. I wanted to be free from the noxious blackness seeping through my veins, but not at the expense of Logan's confidence and self-respect.

I would wait. Logan would learn as fast as he could.

"Trust me okay? It will work. I just need to know how to use the Fire." I nodded. I was worried, about my mother. About Greer. "Look, you are not alone. You have me, and your father and brother and the whole Omega team to support you. Once your arm is fixed you can go back to Wrythiin with your own army and bring your mother back."

His arms curled around me, comforting, caring, supportive. I liked those words – I was not alone.

Not anymore.

~ To Be Continued ~
Thank you for reading. The SkinWalker Series continues with Lost Soul.

ACKNOWLEDGMENTS

To my favorite girls the Inklings- thank you for your constant support and inspiration.

Thank you to my editor Cassie Hart and my proofreader Karen Mead- for all your hard work in polishing SKIN DEEP for publication. Special love to Cassie for saving my butt at the last moment.

To Sel & the girls- nothing ever gets done in my book world without your support.
And to my readers. Don't stop reading....

FREE STARTER LIBRARY - JOIN MY NEWSLETTER

Get the following titles FREE when you subscribe to my newsletter.

Tee's Newsletter

http://smarturl.it/TeesMailingList

ABOUT THE AUTHOR

I have been a writer from the time I was old enough to recognize that reading was a doorway into my imagination. Poetry was my first foray into the art of the written word. Books were my best friends, my escape, my haven. I am essentially a recluse but this part of my personality is impossible to practice given I have two teenage daughters, who are actually my friends, my tea-makers, my confidantes... I am blessed with a husband who has left me for golf. It's a fair trade as I have left him for writing. We are both passionate supporters of each other's loves – it works wonderfully...

My heart is currently broken in two. One half resides in South Africa where my old roots still remain, and my heart still longs for the endless beaches and the smell of moist soil after a summer downpour. My love for Ma Afrika will never fade. The other half of me has been transplanted to the Land of the Long White Cloud. The land of the Taniwha, beautiful Maraes, and volcanoes. The land of green, pure beauty that truly inspires. And because I am so torn between these two lands – I shall forever remain cross-eyed.

Stalk Tee here:
www.tgayer.com
tee@tgayer.com

facebook.com/TGAyerAuthor

twitter.com/TGAyerAuthor

bookbub.com/profile/t-g-ayer